SOUTH POLE STATION

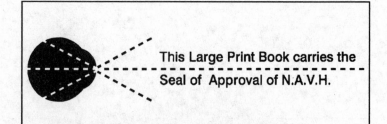

This Large Print Book carries the
Seal of Approval of N.A.V.H.

SOUTH POLE STATION

ASHLEY SHELBY

WHEELER PUBLISHING
A part of Gale, a Cengage Company

GALE
A Cengage Company

Farmington Hills, Mich • San Francisco • New York • Waterville, Maine
Meriden, Conn • Mason, Ohio • Chicago

GALE
A Cengage Company

LIBRARY OF CONGRESS CIP DATA ON FILE.
CATALOGUING IN PUBLICATION FOR THIS BOOK
IS AVAILABLE FROM THE LIBRARY OF CONGRESS

ISBN-13: 978-1-4328-4512-4 (hardcover)
ISBN-10: 1-4328-4512-8 (hardcover)

Published in 2017 by arrangement with Picador

Printed in the United States of America
1 2 3 4 5 6 7 21 20 19 18 17

For Hudson and Josephine, always.

For Manny, without whom
this book would not exist —
and who once advised me
to relax my shoulders.

And for Mom: this one's for you.

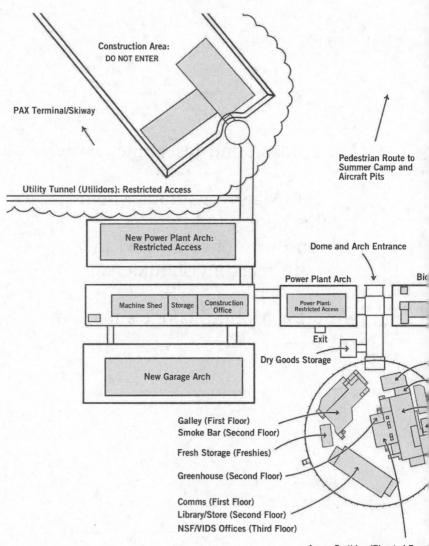

Construction Area:
DO NOT ENTER

PAX Terminal/Skiway

Pedestrian Route to
Summer Camp and
Aircraft Pits

Utility Tunnel (Utilidors): Restricted Access

New Power Plant Arch:
Restricted Access

Dome and Arch Entrance

Power Plant Arch

Bi

Machine Shed | Storage | Construction Office

Power Plant:
Restricted Access

Exit

New Garage Arch

Dry Goods Storage

Galley (First Floor)
Smoke Bar (Second Floor)

Fresh Storage (Freshies)

Greenhouse (Second Floor)

Comms (First Floor)
Library/Store (Second Floor)
NSF/VIDS Offices (Third Floor)

Annex-Berthing (Elevated Dorm

South Pole Station Dome Layout
Fiscal Year 2004
(Not to Scale)

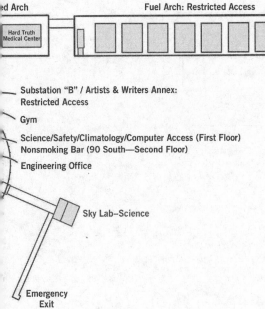

Dark Sector

ed Arch   Fuel Arch: Restricted Access

Hard Truth
Medical Center

Substation "B" / Artists & Writers Annex:
Restricted Access

Gym

Science/Safety/Climatology/Computer Access (First Floor)
Nonsmoking Bar (90 South—Second Floor)

Engineering Office

Sky Lab–Science

Emergency
Exit

AMUNDSEN-SCOTT SOUTH POLE STATION GUIDE
2003–2004
FY04

The National Science Foundation welcomes you to the Amundsen-Scott South Pole Station. This handbook describes facilities, procedures, and safety reminders that will help you during your stay at South Pole.

This year's science, construction, and airlift schedules are the most ambitious in our history, and we have a talented group of people to make it all happen. Our success will depend on our commitment to safety and community involvement.

Located at 90 degrees South latitude, Amundsen-Scott Station has an average annual temperature of −56.7 degrees F, with a record low temperature of −117 degrees F. It rarely snows at South Pole; however, a relatively constant wind speed of 5–15 knots compounds the accumulation.

Most station buildings are located beneath an aluminum geodesic dome, which provides a windbreak for the living, dining, communications, recreation, and laboratory facilities. The main station can accommodate twenty-seven people under the Dome. Additional personnel are housed in modular hypertats and in Summer Camp — a collection of canvas Jamesways, a short walk from the main station.

A series of steel arches houses the power plant, biomed facility, garages, artists' & writers' studios, and main fuel storage. The Dark Sector is located grid west of the station and houses facilities for astronomy and astrophysics research. The Atmospheric Research Observatory lies 300 feet upwind of the station, but the majority of climate change research takes place at the West Antarctic Ice Shelf (WAIS), also known as The Divide.

Please read this handbook thoroughly and don't forget to visit the Geographic South Pole during your stay!

Welcome Aboard,
Tucker Bollinger
South Pole Area Director

POLIE

Do you ever have pain in your chest
    unrelated to indigestion?
Are you often sad?
Do you have digestion problems due to
    stress?
Do you have problems with authority?
How many alcoholic drinks do you
    consume a week? A day?
Would you rather be a florist or a truck
    driver?
True or false: I like to read about science.
True or false: Sometimes I just feel like
    killing myself.
True or false: I prefer flowers to trucks.
True or false: Voices tell me to hurt people.
True or false: I am an important person.

Five months before this pelvic exam of the
mind, Cooper Gosling had received a letter
on embossed government stationery assessing her application to the National Science

11

Foundation's Antarctic Artists & Writers Program. From it, Cooper learned that her portfolio of paintings featured "interesting juxtapositions that suggest an eye particularly attuned to the complexities of human habitation in Antarctica" and "superior technical skill that still leaves room for interpretation," as well as "a frenetic color palette within mainly controlled compositions." There was, the letter had noted tartly, "potential for improvement over the course of the fellowship."

She had been accepted, pending successful completion of physical and dental exams, fire training, and a psychological assessment at the Denver headquarters of Veritas Integrated Defense Systems, the contractor currently running the show in Afghanistan, and also in charge of basic operations at South Pole. The acceptance letter had come with an airline voucher — they expected her in Denver in three weeks. She was advised to travel light and to pay special attention to hygiene.

The night she received the letter, Cooper had driven directly to her father's house to apprise him of these developments. She imagined him falling to pieces, his joy resplendent. Bill Gosling was into this stuff: polar exploration was his deal. Sure, he preferred the heroics of the North Pole explorers, the drama of the Northwest Passage, the cannibalism of Franklin's lost expedition. But his "polar library" included memoirs from the South Pole boys, too: Shackleton, Amundsen, Scott, all first editions. Now that he'd retired from 3M, where he'd been part of the second-string Post-it team, he'd begun work on a memoir of being a polar enthusiast. It would, Cooper could only assume, include many scenes set in armchairs. They'd connect on this South Pole thing, Cooper was sure. He'd offer more than the smile her older sister, Billie, had always described as "faint." He'd confess that she now possessed the skeleton key to his soul.

Instead, he offered her another book: Apsley Cherry-Garrard's *The Worst Journey in the World.*

"The definitive account of the Scott expedition, written by a survivor," Bill said as he placed the book in Cooper's hands. "Make this a priority." (It was in this manner, incidentally, that Cooper had managed to slog her way through Everyman's Library of the World's Most Boring Books.) Cooper searched her father's face, but his expression remained as mild as always. Was it possible he'd forgotten? Or was he trying to tell her not to forget why she was going? Cooper had, of course, already read *The Worst Journey in the World,* had long ago committed entire paragraphs to memory. In fact, the book had been, throughout 1981, Cooper and her twin brother David's deranged bedtime reading. They were eight when Bill shelved Nancy Drew and opened *Worst Journey.* Night after night, he sat on the edge of the bed Cooper still shared with David, and narrated the adventures of what sounded like a rejected Marvel superhero team — Cherry, Birdie, Titus, Uncle Bill, and Captain Scott — as they slogged their way across Antarctica. The saga was the kind of monomyth Cooper would later read about in her comparative mythology electives but would never encounter in real life — Trials! Atonement! Apotheosis! Birdie, Cherry, and Uncle Bill (the fine doctor Edward Wilson), who had set out on the Winter Journey to retrieve an emperor penguin egg, became a holy triumvirate.

Cooper treated each reading as if it were a poetry slam, leaping out of bed during the exciting parts, and falling asleep on David's shoulder during the boring "Spring" chapters, which featured light polar housekeeping and a broken George Robey record spinning on the gramophone. David, on the other hand, listened quietly but intently to everything. It wasn't Cherry's myopia or Edward Wilson's rendering of penguin fat that captured his imagination. It was Titus Oates, the one who walked into the blizzard, his frostbitten foot black and grotesquely swollen. Titus had asked to be left behind; he knew he was slowing them down. Scott and the others refused to leave him so he begged, like a child, and they put him to bed in his sleeping bag. He prayed, loudly, to die before morning, and when he awoke to discover he was still alive, he decided to do it himself. He didn't bother to put his boots on. This time no one stopped him.

The idea of philanthropic suicide was too abstract for Cooper to understand (their mother, Dasha, who felt explorer lit documented "man's endless quest to enlarge his penis," claimed the idea itself was impossible, not to mention inappropriate for elementary-age children). But David was gripped by the notion. Titus's honorable death figured into their play on winter days, David devising scenarios where he'd walk into the woods that ringed their suburban home in order to disappear, leaving Cooper to await his return. When Cooper played Cherry to David's Scott or his Titus, she did little more than hang around expectantly, just as Cherry had. Hoping for months to see the Scott party emerge from the Beardmore Glacier valley, Cherry was always certain the men were just over the rise. As a result, Cooper came to identify with him, this aristocrat who'd bought his way onto the *Terra Nova,* the Scottish whaling ship that carried the Scott party to Antarctica. Twee and myopic, Cherry was a hothouse flower; Cooper was sure everyone must have doubted him. Over the course of the journey, however, he'd become indispensable, and, eventually, its most eloquent witness.

But that was years ago now, and neither Cooper nor Bill had so much as glanced at *The Worst Journey in the World* in a decade. In fact, after the divorce, Bill had begun selling off his rare book collection volume by volume, and Cooper had always assumed that *Worst Journey* had been the first to go. It was burdened by memories that had never made the promised transition from unbearable to bittersweet. The only other copy in the house, David's own heavily annotated mass-market edition, had disappeared.

Cooper took the book from her father and chose to say nothing. Bill gazed out the window at the lightly falling snow. The flakes were fat and hairy, and they descended at an angle. Bill apprised the snow cover. He signaled his approval with a curt nod, and told Cooper to get her coat. Five minutes later, they were outside. It was after ten, but the freshly fallen snow illuminated the backyard as cleanly as moonlight. "Snow is one of the best insulating materials, if used properly," Bill said as he assessed its moisture content by rubbing the soft flakes between his fingers. "The quickest way to die is to stop paying attention."

Winter survival training dictated that you did not travel in a blizzard, he told her. You stop and dig a snow trench or make a snow cave with a hand shovel. *What hand shovel?* You travel with a hand shovel. If you are an amateur and don't carry a hand shovel on your person, you can use your snowshoes. *What if you aren't using snowshoes?* If you are sans snowshoes, you are a dipshit with no business traveling overland in winter. But if you are a dipshit traveling overland in winter with no snowshoes, you use your hands.

Bill and Cooper spent the next hour digging out a trench, a coffin-shaped cavity carved out of the snow. Cooper marveled at her father's efficiency, the certainty of his movements. How well he seemed to know how to do this.

When the specifications were just right, Bill slipped under the lip of the roof by sliding down the snow ramp they'd built to facilitate entry. Cooper peered into the darkness and saw her father supine, his hands behind his head, smiling at nothing.

"What's so funny?" she asked. Bill shook his head, but the smile remained.

"This is how I'd like to die."

"In a snow trench in your backyard?"

"In nature, in winter. Climb in the trench, kick out the roof, and go to sleep. It's like Cherry said. If Death comes for you in the snow, he comes disguised as sleep. 'You greet him rather as a welcome friend than a gruesome foe.' " Bill peered up at Cooper. "Doesn't get any easier."

It didn't occur to Cooper then to ask her father if death was supposed to be easy.

The suburban campus of Veritas Integrated Defense Systems looked like a centerfold from *Maximum Security Prisons Quarterly.* Its cinder-block buildings were divided into quadrants and separated by LiftMaster Mega Arm security gates. A shuttle bus deposited Cooper, along with eight other Pole candidates, at Quadrant 9, where they were photographed and fingerprinted. They followed a Veritas employee down intersecting beige hallways in a disaffected clump. As they waited for an elevator, Cooper saw two men in royal-blue company polos in a break room staring up at a suspended television, watching a recap of Bush's State of the Union speech from the night before. "The British government has learned that Saddam Hussein recently sought significant quantities of uranium from Africa," Bush was saying.

"Holy shit," one of the Veritas guys laughed. "I mean, at this point, you have to go loco on Hussein, right? You have to bomb the shit out of Baghdad." He looked over at his companion. "He's gonna, right?"

The man clutching a vending-machine latte replied carelessly, "Relax, we already submitted a bid."

Cooper and the other applicants were led to a large conference room with a view of Parking Ramp Alpha (parking ramps Beta, Charlie, and Delta were a short shuttle ride from the main complex). Cooper took a seat at the table and looked around at her fellow Pole candidates: all men, all self-consciously hirsute, and all engaged in silent contests over who could fit more carabiners on their stainless-steel water bottles. They avoided making eye contact with Cooper, so she turned her attention to the stack of paperwork in front of her: hundreds and hundreds of questions that had no good answers.

Two hours and five hundred questions later, Cooper and the eight men were allowed to grab a coffee before returning to watch a mandatory video from the Veritas Integrated Defense Systems president. The video commenced with a synthesizer version of "My Country 'Tis of Thee" playing behind scenes of waving flags and purple mountains majesty. The fruited plains dissolved into a shot of a man in a company polo of slightly better quality than the ones Cooper had encountered in the break room. He wore an American flag pin on his lapel, and was looking just off camera.

"I'm Daniel Atcheson Johnson, president of Veritas Integrated Defense Systems, or VIDS. For over seventy-five years we have worked to develop advanced technologies that help planes navigate, reduce traffic congestion, even land astronauts on the moon. With such diverse capabilities, VIDS is much more than a defense contractor. We are a global citizen invested in our collective future. Defense technologies with civilian applications, and the building of bridges between the defense industry and the people we protect. That is our commitment to you.

The guidance chip in a medium-range ballistic missile shares the same technology found in your car's airbag. Think about that for a moment, and you'll realize that the future is VIDS." After a brief pause, during which someone behind the camera seemed to be instructing him to continue, Johnson added, "VIDS — the first line of defense and your trusted partner for a better tomorrow."

The door rattled open, and Cooper turned to see one of the psychologists beckoning her toward the door. Together, the women walked down the hall and into a windowless room. Inside were a desk, two chairs, and a limp spider plant with no hope of achieving photosynthesis.

Once they were seated, the psychologist offered Cooper a sympathetic smile. "Glad that's over, right? I mean, what a drag, all those questions."

"You have to ask them, I guess," Cooper replied, cautious.

"Why do you think we have to ask those questions, Cooper?"

"Why do you ask those questions?" *Christ, why was she repeating the questions back?* "My guess would be to weed out people who may not be mentally fit for polar service," she said.

"Do you consider yourself fit for South Pole?"

"If I didn't, I wouldn't be here," Cooper said, even though she had no idea what made a person "fit for South Pole." But she realized that to a psychologist looking for a problem, she sounded impatient. "I can clarify, if that's allowed."

"Relax" — the psychologist consulted her papers — "Cooper. This isn't a test. It's a conversation."

"I guess what I was trying to say is that I'm going down on an artist fellowship. It's not like I'm an astrophysicist or someone really important on the support side."

"You don't consider yourself important?"

"I just mean that it will probably be easier for me. It's not like people's lives depend on whether I complete a painting or not." *Just mine,* she thought.

The psychologist pulled a piece of paper out of a file, read it, then looked up at Cooper. "Are there any emotional or psychological traumas you feel could impact your potential for success at Pole?" Cooper was irritated by the psychologist's work-around of the obvious trauma — the emotional liability — that she had disclosed on her paperwork. It was as if the woman were trying to extract a confession. Cooper tried to rearrange her face in a way that conveyed both sadness and stability. That it was bad, yes, but that the jagged-glass edges of it had been smoothed over by the last nine months, even if they hadn't. Cooper had never known a jagged edge to become smooth, not unless it was broken off completely.

"You're talking about my brother, right? I mean, if that's what you mean by emotional 'trauma.' " Cooper made quote hooks around the word *trauma,* and the psychologist frowned. "Sorry," Cooper said, and added, "Trauma," this time without the quote hooks.

"Suicide is a major emotional trauma." The psychologist paused, waiting. "Would you like to talk about it?"

Cooper stared into the woman's face, a Glamour Shots advertisement come to life. Did she want to "talk about it"? Did she have a pressing need to unburden herself to a woman wearing faux leather knee-high boots in a building on the campus of the world's second-largest defense contractor? How could she explain that this was the only way you could talk about it, by disclosing it in paperwork, by putting air quotes around it, by gliding along the surface? Cooper knew that explaining this would make her unfit for polar service. That, and telling the truth about David, because if there was a gene for what he had, for the schizophrenic madness that boldly announced itself one day like a Mary Kay saleswoman, then maybe it was somewhere in Cooper, too. Unexpressed, perhaps, or merely waiting for a trigger.

She braced herself for more probing, more note-taking, but suddenly the psychologist shifted gears and told Cooper they could come back to the David question. Cooper knew from months of sliding-scale therapy that the sudden shift away from what her therapist called Cooper's "dominant story" did not bode well for her chances of landing at Pole. She was overwhelmed by the feeling of having been summarily dismissed. She wanted to go to Pole. She had to go to Pole. Cooper had no idea where the sudden desperation was coming from, but she knew she'd rather lie down in a snow trench and kick in the roof than not go to Pole.

The psychologist handed Cooper a sheaf of papers.

"Here are the results of those tests, by the way."

"Already?"

"We have a machine."

Cooper folded the papers in half without

24

looking at them. This caught the psychologist's attention.

"You don't want to see your results? It's actually very interesting. It takes your answers and graphs your responses, showing where you fall in several categories of human neuroses." She turned her copy of Cooper's test toward her. "Take 'tendency toward delusional thinking,' for example."

It seemed to Cooper as if the earth had tilted slightly, by degrees. She gripped the arms of the chair in a way that didn't suggest panic.

"Here is the center line," the psychologist continued, "which represents a statistically 'normal' person. This *x* here shows us where your answers indicate you'd fall. No one falls right on the line." Cooper did not look up from her hands to see where the *x* was.

"Cooper?"

"I'm sorry," Cooper replied. "I'm not much into explanations." The psychologist stared at Cooper for a moment, the tests limp in her hand. *Look her in the eyes.* "I just want to paint at the bottom of the earth," Cooper heard herself say.

The psychologist surveyed Cooper as if she were a thrift store evening gown.

Finally, she said, "Just sit tight for a minute, would you?"

Once the door clicked shut, Cooper pulled at the fabric of her shirt from beneath her armpits, trying to get some ventilation. She fished a compact out of her bag and began studying the swollen zit under her nose. A moment later, she heard the door open.

"People will pity a person with rosacea or shingles," a voice said, "but there is no sympathy in the world for a person with acne. I'm living proof of this." Cooper twisted around in her seat to see a man wearing a tight thermal shirt tucked into what looked like very expensive jeans. "I'm being sympathetic," he added, "not judg-mental."

Cooper had never seen a human enter a room in this way, like an android whose design hadn't included joint flexion. After his confident pronouncement on acne, the man shuffled in, head down, and offered her a painful-looking smile. "Miss Gosling," he said in a faint Southern accent, "I'm Tucker Bollinger, your friendly South Pole area director."

He was a black man with eyes a color she'd never seen before, a mix of yellow and green — Golden Beryl, if you were going by a paint box. He had three piercings in his left ear, all of them empty. His cheeks were hollow and acne-scarred, and Cooper saw there was a kind of beauty about him; yet it was a beauty that had been coaxed into existence. He seemed as guilty as if he'd stolen it, as unconvinced of its authenticity as someone who'd witnessed its creation and knew it to be false.

"They brought in the big gun," Cooper said, snapping the compact closed.

"Am I a big gun?" he replied. "I've been told I have a big gun."

"You just told me you run South Pole," Cooper said. "In terms of guns, that qualifies as an assault weapon."

Tucker moved toward the chair next to Cooper, and seemed to consider sitting for a moment, before placing his hand on the back of it, as if posing for a Matthew Brady portrait. "I'm more of a matchlock musket," he said thoughtfully. "In fact, the parallels are nearly complete."

"So, you're here because I wouldn't look at my test results."

"Sometimes the contract psychologists get responses that aren't on their protocols, so they call somebody from the Program in to double-check. One person's tendency to hole up in her room with Proust is another person's schizoid isolation. Not that I speak from experience." He glanced over at the paperwork on the desk, his hands now thrust into his pockets. "You're in the Artists and Writers Program." He looked up from the pages. "Says here that you've been a live-event artist."

"My first job out of art school."

"Bat mitzvahs?"

"Weddings, mostly. The brides carried kale."

"Better than a caricaturist-for-hire," Tucker replied.

"Barely."

"Well, we don't get a lot of traditional visual artists anymore," he said.

"Conceptual?"

"No, they stopped coming in the early nineties. Now it's mixed-media artists, collagists, and found art. Last season, they had a guy doing paper clips. He made a uterus. He called it a feminist conduit to tactile interaction. There was one sexual harassment complaint."

Cooper felt her limbs relax, and her muscles immediately ached from the tension they'd been holding for the past three hours. Clearly the bar for artistic achievement was low at South Pole.

"Do you have any talent?" Tucker asked.

"Maybe," Cooper said.

"Maybe?"

"It's kind of like psychological exams, I

guess. Subject to protocols." When Tucker didn't reply, Cooper added: "I've been told I have talent."

"If you don't agree, then why are you here?"

"I don't know why I'm here. But I'm here."

Cooper could see this wasn't enough. "What if I promise to just be your typical aimless thirty-year-old looking to delay the inevitable slide into mediocrity?"

"That rolls off your tongue easily."

"Yeah, well, I've said it before."

Cooper thought she detected a slight smile somewhere on Tucker's face, but he didn't let it crack open.

"Then you will fit in very well," he said. "But can you, just for paperwork's sake, give me one line that I can write down on this form? One line about why you want to go to South Pole?"

"I put that on my application."

"That thing about 'new horizons' and 'fresh perspectives'?"

Cooper sighed. "How about to further my creative journey?"

"Insincere."

"For adventure's sake?"

"There is no adventure, only a grind."

"I like cold climates?"

"Stay in Minnesota."

"I want to be somewhere else."

"You're getting closer."

"But if I say that, you'll think I'm running from something," Cooper said.

"It's not 'running from something.' It's turning aside." Tucker thought for a moment. "Or looking askance. Looking askance at civilization. If you apply to go to Pole because it seems 'cool' or because you're looking for 'adventure,' then you'll crack up when you realize it's not a frat party. If you don't fit in anywhere else, you will work your ass off for us. This has been proven time and time again."

He clicked the pen attached to his clipboard and scribbled something. Then he stood up and indicated that Cooper should, too.

"I'll have to meet with the program directors this afternoon to go over the borderline cases."

"I'm borderline?"

"Sorry."

"What about my one-liner?"

"What about it?"

"You're going to use that thing about the personal journey?"

"Unless you have something better. The paper-clip guy said something about a personal journey, and he scraped in." Tucker waited a moment, rubbing his left earlobe between his fingers, but Cooper could think of nothing to add. As she gathered her things, Tucker said, "Listen, shrinks worry about fresh death. Especially a suicide. Unresolved grief does sometimes lead to breakdowns, especially in extreme environments. But then so do delays in booze shipments. I'm sorry for saying 'fresh death.' "

"I don't mind. I guess it is."

"You'll know by tonight," Tucker said. Cooper smiled weakly and watched as he left the room. She could hear his footfalls in the hallway. It sounded like South Pole itself was receding. As she closed her eyes to deny tears an exit point, she realized that she had underplayed the importance of this whole thing. For the first time, she understood it wasn't the lark she'd been telling herself it was; Cooper knew that the jagged edges would continue to lacerate her unless she did something drastic. She didn't quite know why she believed this, but she did. In fact, it was one of the only things she believed in now.

As she stared at the pale, sickly leaves of the office plant, Cooper understood that her chance was slipping away. She was on the verge of being rejected, as Scott had rejected Cherry.

Cherry.

She leapt to her feet. "I've got one," she called down the hallway, where Tucker was talking to a VIDS employee. "A reason to go."

Tucker dismissed the man, and waited as Cooper jogged toward him. "It's a quote, but it's why I want to go down."

"Quoting others suggests avoidance," Tucker replied when she arrived.

Cooper shook her head. "No, it only means that someone more articulate than me has been in my shoes. It only means" — Cooper could hear the hitch in her voice — "that someone else said it better than I could. But it's why I want to go."

Down the hall, someone began brewing a vending-machine latte, and Cooper realized she was holding her breath. Tucker finally clicked the pen again and held it poised above the clipboard. As she spoke, Cooper tried to keep her voice steady.

That night, after a "trust-building" exercise at Applebee's involving Tabasco sauce and 7UP, Cooper returned to her hotel room to find the red cube on the phone blinking. It was Tucker calling to confirm that the shuttle for "fire school" would arrive at the hotel promptly at seven a.m., and that she was expected. Cooper listened to the message twice. She wanted to assume that an invitation to fire training meant she was in, but earlier at the restaurant, over double-crunch bone-in wings, some guy from Spokane told her a story about a woman who'd done the tests, completed fire school, flown to Christchurch, New Zealand, and been allowed to pick out all her extreme cold weather (ECW) gear, before being denied a berth on the flight to Pole because of a "clerical error." It was best to assume nothing.

The next morning, Cooper boarded a shuttle bus with twenty other sleepy people and three highly caffeinated officials from VIDS. She chose a seat next to a pale, heavy-lidded man of about forty. He had poorly maintained ginger mutton chops, a high-and-tight, and the face of a hamster. He was examining a chain wallet with his name, Floyd, spelled out in tiny strips of duct tape. She imagined him straining over this project, fat pink tongue sticking out, Lit'l Smokies–esque fingers arranging the strips in the letters that formed his name. He glanced over at Cooper, so she said, "Hi." He turned away, or possibly askance.

"I've done this three times," he said to the

window. He drew a penis with a cartoonish scrotum in the fog his breath had made on the glass.

"You've done fire training three times or you've been to South Pole three times?" Cooper asked, to be polite.

"Was I talking to you?"

"I'm pretty sure you were."

"It's a mistake to be 'pretty sure' of anything," he said, using quote hooks. Cooper remembered her earlier use of quote hooks and burned with shame.

"Excuse Floyd. He's saying, in his typical incoherent way, that he's been to Pole three times."

Before Cooper could turn to get an eye on the man seated behind her, a VIDS official wearing Ray-Bans atop his salt-and-pepper crew cut whistled to get everyone's attention. "Get ready, folks. This is team-building time," he shouted as the bus pulled into the Centennial State Fire Academy, which was located a few miles from the VIDS corporate campus.

Once everyone had shuffled down the aisle and off the bus, the prospective "Polies" lined up against a chain-link fence. Cooper noticed the guy next to her was stretching, linking his fingers and reaching for the sky. After two days of mingling with the marginally attractive, Cooper was startled to encounter someone whose looks were above average. He was built like a basketball player, at least six-four, with lean limbs and fierce hazel eyes in an otherwise relaxed and confident face. She wondered about his Pole occupation — carpenter, engineer, forklift driver? Cooper decided he was a carpenter, because he had that rangy look that she associated with woodworkers.

He glanced over at her. "You a Fingy?" Cooper recognized his voice as the one that had asked her to excuse Floyd earlier.

"A what?"

He laughed. "You've answered the question. Fingy — stands for 'fucking new guy.'"

"Is that an official term?"

"Official enough. I'm Sal," he said, sticking out his hand.

"Cooper."

"Science or support?"

"Uh, I'm not sure — I'm down on the A-and-W grant."

"Ah, you're an *artiste.*"

"I detect sarcasm."

Sal grinned. "Never."

Cooper turned to watch as a squat two-story building disgorged smoke while people dressed in fire gear ducked in and out, rescuing dummies and laying them on the

35

grass about ten yards away.

"After these cadets finish, we'll start suiting up," the VIDS official said.

"What's this guy's name again?" Cooper whispered to Sal.

"Just call him VIDS. That's what we call all the Denver-based admins. They're interchangeable. It's easier that way."

"VIDS sounds like a venereal disease you'd catch at Blockbuster."

"Good one."

The VIDS official clapped his hands to get the Polies' attention. "While we wait, I'd like to take this opportunity to welcome you to the United States Antarctic Program, also known as the Program. You may be going down there as a cook, a geologist, a custodial engineer, an admin —"

"Astrophysicist!" Sal coughed into his hand. Cooper snuck another look at Sal. It strained her credulity to believe that an astrophysicist could be both physically attractive and supremely self-assured — not that she'd ever met an astrophysicist, which had always sounded to Cooper like a made-up job title.

"In whatever capacity you come down here," the VIDS official continued, "whether you're on the science side or the support side, you hold your colleagues' lives in your hands."

A small woman wearing a pink bandanna raised her hand. "Excuse me but I have a thing with fire masks. For example, I wasn't a good scuba diver because the mouthpiece freaked me out. I could see myself being someone who would take it out underwater, against my better judgment, you know, just because it's a foreign object in my mouth. So I'm just wondering how this, um, tendency, I guess, is going to impact fire training." Scornful chuckles all around. The woman looked at the group. "What, is that a dumb question?"

"All questions are good, all questions are good," the VIDS official said, rubbing his hands together nervously. "What's your name, honey?" Cooper noticed her stiffen at this. Apparently so did the VIDS guy. "I mean, your name?" he stammered.

"Pearl."

"Pearl, I think because the fire mask doesn't actually go into your mouth like a scuba regulator does, you'll be pleasantly surprised by how nonintrusive it is."

Pearl nodded. "Good. Nonintrusive is always welcome."

Over the next four hours, the Pole candidates donned helmets, fire jackets, overalls, boots, and face masks, and endured every worst-case scenario known to man. Forced entry using a halligan and an ax. Extinguishing vehicle fires with dry chemical powder. Crawling through an eighty-foot plastic tunnel called the Gerbil Tube in order to "get used to tight spaces." Some of the applicants folded under the pressure and were hastily wrapped in shock blankets. Pearl did, in fact, find the face mask obtrusive, to the tune of a panic attack in the Gerbil Tube, and so was officially reassigned to the Trauma Team, which, at Pole, would muster to provide CPR or splints in case of catastrophic injury. Some of the Polies, Cooper noted, were studs. Sal had been the only one to locate the "infant reported to be in the building" and drag the miniature dummy out by the scruff of its neck, only to pretend to breastfeed it as the others scrambled to safety.

The last exercise of the day was in the Maze, a smoke-filled, two-story house. Cooper was expected to perform a sweep-search and rescue her victim — a scientist who had joined the group late. She had already seen several other veteran Polies, at fire school for recertification, complete this exercise; they'd exited the synthetic fires laughing and slapping one another on the back. It wasn't easy, Cooper reasoned, but it was probably doable. She awaited the fire chief's whistle, and when she heard it, sprinted into the building.

As soon as she stepped into the Maze, though, she realized she was fucked. The place was a carnival funhouse of stairs, dead ends, and walls of fire. It turned out synthetic smoke wasn't all that different from real smoke — and it obscured everything, so Cooper began crawling. Room by room, she searched for the scientist. Sweat began to dribble down her forehead and into her eyes, steaming up the glass of her fire mask.

"Where are you?" Cooper cried. It sounded as if she were shouting into a pillow. She climbed up the stairs on all fours, and turned into the first room she came to. The ceiling was on fire. Cooper thought she could make out something lying motionless halfway across the room. She got to her feet and scuttled over to the body. It was one of the CPR dummies. Cooper began kicking it mercilessly, her fear and frustration mounting to panic. What if this was a trick? Some kind of test? Maybe there was no one in the Maze awaiting rescue. Maybe the scientist had entered the building and then slipped out the back door, and Cooper's score was based on how long it would take her to realize this.

But then, through the groans of the generator that was powering the smoke machine, she thought she heard something. Someone was humming. Cooper crawled down the hall and pushed open the second door. There, next to the window, was a man in fire gear, on his haunches, cowering. For a moment they stared at each other through the smudged Plexiglas of their masks. Then Cooper kicked his boot with hers and he slowly got to his feet. She took hold of his arm and forced him down the stairs like Lennie Briscoe on an episode of *Law & Order.*

By the time they burst through the front door, a crowd had gathered around the Maze, and it exploded into applause. Cooper pushed the man away from her so hard that he fell to the ground. She tore off her fire mask and tried to get a good breath.

"You were never in danger," the fire chief said, marking something on his clipboard.

As the crowd dispersed, Cooper watched while a medic attended to the scientist, who was now draped in a shock blanket. When he turned his enormous china-doll eyes toward her, she couldn't stop the scowl that formed on her lips.

"Congratulations," Sal said, handing Cooper a bottle of water.

"Thanks," she said. "You think I'll pass?"

"You'll pass."

She looked up into Sal's face, surprised. "Really?"

He nodded, then tilted his head toward the scientist. "So will he."

"Isn't he the one who abandoned the CPR lady-dummy in the bathtub on his first Maze run?"

Sal shrugged. "This is a formality for him. His ticket was punched a long time ago."

"Who the hell is he?" Cooper asked.

Sal glanced at the man. "He answers to 'The End of Science.' See you at Ninety South."

Four months later, Cooper was standing on a slice of sea ice just outside of McMurdo, the American polar station set on the hairy fringes of Antarctica. To the north, the bare volcanic rock of Hut Point Peninsula sloped toward McMurdo Sound in glossy black sheets. Short-stacked dorms, repair barns, and warehouses seemed locked on the basalt as if petrified midslide. Diesel fumes burned her nostrils.

The sun hung low in the sky, an ornament that swung from east to west, never disappearing, until the day it did. On the C-17 that had ferried them from Christchurch, an electrician had told Cooper that when the month-long sunset ended in March and the sun finally hooked around the Earth, leaving South Pole in total darkness for months, she'd forget what it looked like almost at once. "You'll live for civil twilight," he said mysteriously.

As she waited for the National Science Foundation rep to finish gossiping with the pilot, Cooper looked around at the raggedy group of artists loitering a few hundred yards from the humorously big-wheeled bus that was waiting to take them into town. Which one, Cooper wondered, was Harold? Back in Denver, the NSF had assigned each grantee a buddy — a "fellow Fellow" — and instructed them to exchange regular e-mails up until the date of their departure. It was important, the grant administrator had impressed upon the artists, to be supplied with an existing friend at Pole. Cooper had been paired with a biographer named Harold. When she'd asked him about the subject of his book, he had been evasive. After four months of correspondence, all Cooper knew about him was that he was a British ex-pat from Sacramento who fancied peach melba and foxhounds, and who suffered from mild eczema. Harold's knowledge of Cooper was limited to two facts:

that she felt hotdish had never received its gastronomic due and that the fake Minnesota accents in *Fargo* were the blackface of regional phonology. Pictures had not been exchanged, so Cooper had no way of picking Harold out from the collection of fur-lined hoods and balaclavas arrayed before her.

Finally, the NSF administrator, wearing UV goggles and an impossibly large parka, walked toward the group, looking as buoyant as the Stay Puft Marshmallow Man. "Seventy-seven degrees, fifty-one minutes south," he boomed, each word accompanied by a steam blossom. "One hundred sixty-six degrees, forty minutes east." The historical novelist, who'd vomited into his hands on the plane, sighed in recognition, letting everyone know he'd done his homework. "Welcome to McMurdo, everybody," Stay Puft said. "Welcome to Antarctica." The sound of heavy mittens clapping followed this pronouncement, and someone attempted a whistle, then quit halfway through, winded. The high altitude and thin air did not offer enough oxygen for carefree whistling.

"All right, guys," Stay Puft continued, "I know you're moving on to South Pole Station tomorrow morning, but I think there's still time for you to enjoy what Mactown has to offer. We always treat the artists to a game of bowling before they head for Pole, mostly because we put a little money on the game and because you guys are notoriously bad bowlers." *Ha-ha-ha,* the group laughed. *We're bad bowlers.*

"Oh, hey," Stay Puft said to a tall, stone-faced man who was briskly passing the group on his way to the Terra Bus. "Goggles really aren't optional down here, brother. I mean, unless you want to light your corneas on fire."

"Noted," the man said, his consonants tinged with unmistakable Russian frication. "But I'm not Fingy, and McMurdo is not cold."

"What's a Fingy?" someone asked. Cooper felt no need to provide this person with the secret knowledge she'd been given at fire school — she suspected any advantage, no matter how small, could be helpful to her. Stay Puft turned to everyone else and clapped his mittens together: "Terra Bus time! Grab your bags and let the festivities begin!"

Cooper dragged her bag past the other artists, and caught up with the tall Russian, who was carrying his enormous duffel as if it were a lunch box. He'd been seated across from Cooper on the flight from Christchurch, and was imperious and massively bearded. Once or twice during the six-hour flight he had consulted a notebook, but had otherwise barely moved. When he noticed Cooper was keeping pace with him, he looked down at her.

"Hello," he said.

"Hey," Cooper said. "Are you a writer or a painter?" When he didn't immediately reply, Cooper added: "Muralist?"

"You mistake me for artist," he finally said. "I am not here to paint pretty pictures of penguins."

"Carpenter?"

"Now you confuse me with construction personnel. Those are assholes. Science is only reason for people to come here." He looked down at Cooper again. "You are one of these artists?" Cooper nodded. "I do not understand why you are here."

Cooper saw herself reflected in the man's mirrored aviators, which he'd donned in place of the goggles everyone had been issued back in Christchurch. Reflected in his sunglasses, Cooper's head was bulbous, her body a tube. She was ridiculous.

That night, the artists crowded into the bowling alley at McMurdo, Mactown Lanes, which was located in a Seabee Quonset hut that also housed a ceramics studio, and was a gathering point for exactly the kind of people one might expect to find in bowling alleys and ceramics studios. The bowling alley consisted of two lanes and the last existing Brunswick manual pinsetter system in the world. A woman in a bikini top and board shorts was the designated "pin monkey."

As she waited for her turn to bowl, Cooper learned she'd be heading to Pole with an interpretive dancer who hoped to choreograph a show based on the mating rituals of the hydrocarbon seep tubeworm; two novelists, traversing the same ground as the novelists who came before them (*The Catcher in the Crevasse, Fahrenheit-98, The Sun Never Rises, Love in the Time of Snow Blindness*); and Cooper's pen pal, the biographer named Harold.

Cooper watched as the interpretive dancer threw a gutter ball and danced back to her seat under the pink and green strobe lights pulsing to the beat of "Heart of Glass."

"It's rather quaint, isn't it," the man sitting next to Cooper said as they watched the heavily tatted pin monkey get up from her folding chair at the end of the lane and reset the pins. Cooper took in the man's pink jowls-in-training and his friendly, constantly blinking eyes. A portrait would focus on the broad, Truman Capote forehead abandoned by the hairline. These features, and the British accent, could only mean that this was Harold.

"Actually, I'm surprised how ugly this place is," Cooper said. "You think Antarctica is going to be the purest place in the world — like the last pure place on earth — and you get here and it's like Akron." She offered him her hand. "I'm Cooper."

The man's face flushed, and he offered a gap-toothed smile. When he took her hand, his was predictably moist. "I'm Harold, your pen pal!" He giggled. "Now, is there a ghost of a chance that you'd allow me to perform my best Minnesota accent, or would that just send you into a rage? I've been working on it for weeks."

"I'll try to control myself," Cooper replied. "Go ahead."

Harold squared his shoulders and straightened his posture, affecting the standard Minnesotan-at-the-wheel-during-rush-hour position. "Oh geeeee, yoooooo betcha!"

"Not bad, but if you're going for cinéma vérité, you might want to try the phrase 'I'm headed over to Lindy's for the meat raffle.' " Harold positively glowered. "Anyway, nice

47

to finally meet you, Harold." Cooper wasn't sure she'd ever spoken the name Harold out loud before; it came out sounding a little sarcastic.

Harold winced. "As I've been told incessantly since we landed at Christchurch, Harold is a perfectly awful name." He paused, thoughtful. "I don't believe they're naming children Harold anymore. I've settled on Birdie for the duration."

"Birdie?"

"It's the nickname of the bloke I'm writing a book about. I've simply co-opted it."

"Birdie Bowers?" Cooper said.

Birdie went pinker. "You know Birdie? Americans never know him."

Cooper shrugged. "My father's a frustrated explorer, so I'm on a first-name basis with a lot of dead men."

"Yes, there's a whole generation of those kinds of fathers, isn't there? Men cut out for Shackleton's adventures but forced to work as accountants or teachers." He ran a hand across his pate. "It's a bloody shame, actually. There's nothing left for them."

The overheads suddenly dimmed and were replaced by the swirling colored lights found in Cosmic Bowling systems across the globe — Antarctica, apparently, included. Birdie made his way to the bowling lane, and as Cooper watched him test the weight of several bowling balls, she put her hand in her parka and touched the vial she'd carried with her from Minneapolis. As she did so, she imagined Cherry in his bunk on the *Terra Nova* as it neared this continent, and a jubilant Birdie Bowers hauling him out to give him a celebratory dig in the ribs.

The next morning, as Cooper stood on the McMurdo ice runway waiting to board the plane to South Pole, the sun hovered on the horizon, looking as runny as an under-cooked egg. A few weeks earlier, in mid-September, it had risen for the first time in six months. According to the breathless reports Cooper had overheard in the dining room, penguins had gone into hysterics, which had promptly sent a National Geo-graphic cruise tour group into hysterics.

The sea-ice runway was busier than O'Hare, crowded with C-17s and a gaggle of LC-130s from the New York Air National Guard. All of the planes had been outfitted with skis instead of wheels, as well as jet fuel that wouldn't turn to Smuckers in sixty-below temps. It was into one of these LC-130s — everyone called them Hercs — that Cooper climbed, along with the rest of the artists, scientists, and support staff heading to Amundsen-Scott South Pole Station.

The interior of the plane looked like the digestive tract of a cyborg: the floor was littered with various cables, tie-down straps, and metal bars. There were no windows. Cooper strapped herself into a jump seat and, since there was nothing to look at besides red cargo netting and beards, she closed her eyes and tried to sleep.

Three hours later, the sound of the pilot's voice broke through the howl of the plane's engines. "McMurdo was Fiji compared to what you're about to experience," he shouted over the speaker. "And goggles are required, folks. We'll be on the ground shortly. Might want to grab on to something. Could get a little bumpy on the way down."

As if on cue, the plane fell a few hundred feet, before floating up again, and then dropping another hundred. It went on like this for ten minutes. The scientists and construction workers in the jump seats across from Cooper seemed unfazed, while next to her, the historical novelist yelped pathetically. Halfway down the row, Birdie had dropped his head between his knees.

The landing, however, went smoothly, and

as the plane coasted along the ice, Cooper had the strange feeling of being on a seventy-seven-ton toboggan. Relieved cheers filled the cabin as they coasted to the end of the skiway. Almost before the plane had come to a complete stop, the doors were opened and everyone began filing out, but Cooper couldn't move. McMurdo had been the last exit, a place with bowling alleys and an ATM. This was the end. This was South Pole.

When she finally made her way to the exit, she stopped short, holding up the rest of the line as she stared into infinity — sheer white of a character she'd never seen in life or art. She felt light-headed.

"Your goggles," Birdie shouted over the din of the roaring engine. He pressed them into her hands. She pulled them over her head and onto her face, and began walking down the stairs, but on the last step she stumbled. As if in slow motion, she landed face-first on her bag, which had been thrown out of the cargo hold. Immediately, a mouthful of polar air seized her lungs, and she started to choke. It was as if her throat had instantly crystallized. Birdie hauled Cooper to her feet.

"Thanks," she croaked.

All around her was a landscape of snow

without end; there was no horizon. She felt seaborne, bodiless. There was no edge, no crust to hold it all in. Crowded around the runway were groups of people wearing the green parkas that distinguished the Polies from the McMurdo-ites, who wore cherry-red. Again, the tall Russian scientist disembarked and carried his oversize duffel with ease, his aviators glinting in the sun. Cooper watched as other hoodless men in aviators surrounded him, clearly excited to see him. Beyond them was a large silver geodesic dome: South Pole Station.

"How was McMurdo?"

Cooper peered into yet another fur-lined hood and saw Tucker's face. Relief washed over her.

"We bowled," she said, her body beginning to shake from the cold. "Two games."

"Put on your hood," Tucker said, and Cooper complied. "I'm glad you're here. You were missed." The passivity of the sentence only underscored its weirdness. "Come on, let's go inside."

The entrance to South Pole Station had nearly been swallowed by drifting snow. The ramp leading into the dome sloped down into the frozen earth like a long, swollen throat. Cooper stopped to watch a group of people shoveling out a trench that encircled the dome like a moat. On seeing the artists pass into the tunnel, one of the workers stopped and leaned on his shovel. He pointed toward a wooden sign speared into the ice. In handwritten letters, it spelled *Caution! Crevasse of Death.*

"Live it. Learn it. Love it," he said.

As the Fingys inched farther down the tunnel, a town the color of a safety-hazard cone materialized beneath the frozen Spaceship Earth dome. A collection of ugly, two-story prefab buildings sprouted from the dirty ice. One of the novelists began hacking uncontrollably as a tractor and forklift rumbled past them coughing exhaust that wreathed the buildings in smog. Cooper glanced at an enormous digital thermometer hanging over the entrance to one of the trailers. Inside the dome it was thirty-five degrees below zero. Outside it was negative fifty. This, Cooper knew from the station guide, was a balmy summer's day.

Tucker led the artists into the galley, located on the first floor of the largest trailer. As they shuffled in, a pair of guys playing chess looked up at them, then looked at each other, and flashed the international sign of cultural superiority — the *Star Trek* finger-split.

Tucker stopped near the soda dispenser.

"This is the galley. This is where you'll come to eat," he said. "Our production cook is Miss Pearl here." The woman in the pink bandana Cooper had seen at fire school now stood in the middle of the kitchen. She was smiling, both hands on her apron-wrapped hips, her ash-blond hair gathered in a short ponytail, the same bandanna wrapped around her head. A small cadre of galley workers buzzed behind her, preparing for lunch.

"Hi, *artistes,* welcome to South Pole! I'll give you a quick rundown of how the eats work around here, and I'm sorry if I'm short on details — we're in the middle of the lunch prep and also, this is my first year so I'm going by what the binders tell me." In the kitchen, soups bubbled in industrial-size pots and a couple of guys in hairnets chopped vegetables. "I'm told food is really the only unequivocally nice thing about institutionalized life down here," Pearl said as she led the group between prep tables. "We really try to make it special, make it nice. Lots of people have told me that they haven't eaten better food than the food they ate here on the ice." Pearl slipped past the meat slicer, where a thin guy was running a ham across the blade. "And this is Kit. He's our rock star DA."

"District attorney?" one of the artists asked, and Cooper caught Tucker rolling his eyes.

"Nope, here DA stands for dining assistant," Pearl said cheerfully. "Everyone say hi to Kit." Everyone murmured a hello, and the group moved through the kitchen. As Cooper passed him, Kit began moving his pelvis in rhythm with the slicer, tongue hanging out, eyes half closed.

"Your zipper's down," Cooper whispered. Kit shrugged and continued slicing.

Pearl was now standing in front of a stack of cabinets, saying that there were three squares a day, six days a week. "If you need to eat at Midrats, let me or Bonnie know," she said, gesturing to a heavyset dark-haired woman working the stove across from the cabinets. "Bonnie's the head cook."

"Excuse me, but what are Midrats?" Birdie asked, smiling stupidly at Pearl. Cooper could see he was already enamored.

"*Midrats* is the term we use for our midnight meal cooked for the workers on the graveyard shift. It's short for 'midnight rations' — Midrats! Does that answer your question?" Birdie signaled his assent with a thumbs-up. "Anyway, leftovers are stored in the white fridge over there, and you can warm up whatever you want in the microwave. But if you're seriously unmotivated, you can check out the cabinets." She turned around and pulled open the door to a large cupboard. A pile of ramen noodles and plastic-wrapped Melba toast tumbled out. Cooper picked up one of the ramen soup packages from the floor.

"This expired in 1996," she said.

Pearl shrugged. "We're at the end of a long supply chain."

Across an expanse of snow a quarter mile from the Dome, the Jamesways lay atop the ice like giant prehistoric grubs. This tent city, called Summer Camp, was where most of the Polies slept. The rest bunked in the Hypertats, closer to the station, while a select few had rooms in the elevated dorm under the Dome. Cooper was halfway to camp with her bag — bag-drag was an individual sport and a rite of passage for Fingys — when she heard the sound of footsteps, which, on dry Antarctic snow, sounded like boots crushing Saltines.

"Hey," a familiar voice called. Cooper turned to find Sal walking toward her, his rose-red parka a Pollock drip against the starched sky. He grinned at her, and Cooper noticed for the first time a deep dimple in his right cheek. "Technically, I'm not supposed to help you bag-drag," he said. "It's a time-honored tradition to force the Fingys to haul their luggage out to camp." He reached for Cooper's duffel. "But I'm feeling charitable today."

"Except I'm too proud to take handouts," Cooper replied, moving the bag out of his reach with her boot. She hauled the strap back over her shoulder, hoping to give the impression that she found the duffel featherlight.

"Do you even know where you're going?"

"E6."

"Ah, E6. That's where they found the body last season." He grinned again and gestured to the Jamesway farthest from the station. "Last one on the left there." It looked miles away. Cooper groaned, and let the duffel strap slip from her shoulder. Sal slung the bag over his shoulder easily, and together they walked toward Summer Camp in silence.

When they arrived at E6, it suddenly occurred to Cooper that the only things that would be standing between her and minus-56-degree temperatures were plywood and vinyl-coated cotton duck. "I can get it from here," Cooper said, taking the bag from Sal. "Thanks for the good deed." Sal tipped an imaginary hat. As Cooper watched him walk away, she considered how much she hated guys who tipped imaginary hats.

She pulled the Jamesway door open and kicked her bag into the darkened interior. The door sucked shut behind her, and the walls breathed in and out with the Antarctic summer winds. Canvas curtains separated the sleeping quarters, leaving a narrow hallway running down the middle of the Jamesway. Light snoring came from all directions, along with the faint sound of death metal leaking from someone's headphones. All at once, the heater — a massive metal monster set at the back of the tent — kicked on with a congested roar.

Using a flashlight she'd been given back at the station along with two towels and a set of bedclothes, Cooper scanned the doors until she found her room at the end of E6. It was the size of a closet, nothing more than a single bed, a dorm-style desk, and a chair. Cooper clambered onto her bed to peer out the plastic-paned window cut high in the wall. More white without end. She craned her neck and saw that a huge snowdrift hugged the other side of the Jamesway wall. She glanced down at the floor and saw the foot of the drift ended under her bed.

Kicking her snow-crusted bag closer to the dresser, Cooper pulled off her fur-backed mittens before removing layer after layer of clothing until she reached her thermal vest. This she unzipped, before removing her money belt, where she'd been keeping her oil paints since landing in Christchurch three days earlier. The visual arts coordinator at the NSF's Artists & Writers Program had suggested she transport her paints this way if she "insisted" on using oils instead of the obviously more practical tempera; the warmth of her body would keep them from freezing and losing integrity. Titanium white. Yellow ochre, burnt umber. And the workhorse of polar artists, cerulean blue. Cooper rarely opened new tubes — the firmness and fullness of the paints felt as strange as the first time she had held an erect penis in her hand. She was more comfortable using the twisted, deformed soldiers, often capless, found in high school art rooms. So when her sister, Billie, had handed her the bag from Utrecht Art Supplies, Cooper had been shocked. Inside was a set of Winsor and Newton oil paints, and two small containers of turpentine.

"The guy said these were the best," Billie had said. "Something about pigment load. I assume this is a painting term and not a porn sequence."

"I'm not worth these paints," Cooper said, and Billie had grown impatient.

"Stop cringing. Just take them. As we both know, the clock on talent runs faster than regular clocks. Tick-tock."

As with most things, Billie was, of course, right: in art, as in life, your innate talent was valued in inverse proportion to your age. For Cooper, the clock had ticked off almost fifteen years. She'd been plucked from obscurity while in high school by the "Holy Order of the Precocious Child," as Billie called it, when a curator for MoMA, in town for a lecture at the Minneapolis Institute of Arts, had deigned to look at the lobby display where the winners of the Minnesota High School Visual Arts Competition had their pieces set up. Having discovered in junior high that she had the technical skills of a hyperrealist, Cooper had gone all Charles Bell and produced a series of paintings depicting vending-machine charms. The curator was particularly taken with Cooper's absurdly detailed study of a tiny roller skate on a lead chain. "You've brought a sense of allegorical wonder to the obviously tawdry," she'd said.

Within two months, Cooper and her vending-machine series had been featured in *The New York Times Magazine,* alongside the work of three other visual arts prodigies (the title of the article had been "Could These Young Artists Save the American Art World?"). Cooper was bewildered to read that her "preoccupation" as an artist was not just on "gifted creations of likenesses, but also the instigation of psychological states in the observer," when all she'd been trying to do was not look too closely at the things around her that actually mattered. Like what was happening to her brother.

It was around that time that David had gotten worse — though by that point, using the word *worse* was like gilding one of Monet's water lilies. The "Weisman Incident" had made the ten o'clock news on all three local stations (in Minnesota at that time a teenager flailing incoherently on the roof of a modern art museum was sweepsworthy). That was when the painting stopped. Cooper wasn't sure why she'd stopped, only that nothing seemed worth painting. She knew even then that to adults this sounded truculent, but representation suddenly seemed a cheap way to comment on ideas. Interpretation seemed hubristic. Better, Cooper thought, as she watched her parents grapple with David, to leave life in its native language. So the planning had stopped, too. Everything did. And Cooper was glad. She was relieved to once again be unexceptional — but of course said nothing to her family and concerned mentors about this relief and instead stockpiled their pity like she was building up treasures.

But then, some months after one of David's institutionalizations, when it seemed that David, back in high school again, was doing better, Cooper did start to paint again. Small things, mostly for friends, and mostly staying in the well-worn ruts: a butterfly, a still life, a tree. Nothing that had any real meaning to her. Such things were still too dangerous. Eventually, though, she set the crutches aside, and tried to pick up where she'd left off when David had first gotten sick, quietly enrolling at the Minneapolis College of Art and Design after graduation.

She had showings at small local galleries, where people who didn't know her name sipped white Zin and praised the kind of art they could afford while denigrating the kind they couldn't. She sold a few canvases at art fairs, had a couple pieces hanging at the Uptown Caribou Coffee ("Man Staring into Latte" and "Untitled Meditation on Shade-Grown Beans"), and had even been commissioned to paint the skyline of St. Paul for a professor from Hamline University (although she'd blown it after she asked: "What skyline?").

Armed with a BFA and a spotty résumé, Cooper worked as a substitute art teacher, but had been laid off when the Minnesota legislature cut all "nonessential curriculum" funding. She turned to community ed and began teaching "Adventures in Acrylics" to retirees far more motivated than her. Then she turned thirty, and saw that the years behind her were littered with part-time jobs, newsboy hats, half-finished canvases, and visits to the psych ward at Hennepin County Medical Center to see David. She quickly ran out of money, and began work at the same Caribou Coffee where her canvases were still hanging, unsold. She started dating a fellow barista, a twenty-three-year-old emo named Forrest, to whom she lied about her age.

Then one day, the professor from Hamline who'd canceled her commission called to tell her about the National Science Foundation's Antarctic Artists & Writers Program at South Pole. "It's a unique opportunity to experience humility and accountability on a visceral level," he said. "When the paperwork crossed my desk, I thought of you immediately." The words — *South Pole* — had pierced her. Cooper thought she had buried those two syllables and everything they signified long ago. When David became sick around their sixteenth birthday, their fondly recalled playtime heroics had given way to hallucinations and obsessions. To David, South Pole was no longer a place where men went to become lions, a landscape that spawned a thousand daydreams. It was instead a viper's nest of secret civilizations. It was a Nazi hideout. It harbored a portal into a hollow earth, where men like Arthur Gordon Pym and friends sailed into a milky wormhole and vanished. David wanted desperately to be there, and sometimes, when things were bad, thought he was. Cooper felt strongly that she would have been able to handle it all better if *it* — this chemical Grendel that had replaced her brother's fine mind — had allowed Titus and Cherry to stay at South Pole. But these paladins had been erased from the continent — and when they disappeared, Cooper did, too.

She looked down at the tubes of paint in her hands. None of them had lost integrity, so she wrapped them up in the bath towels and put them in her battered green canvas Duluth Pack with the rest of her supplies. Next, she set her books on the desk — a polar library in miniature, with Shackleton,

Amundsen, and the ancient copy of *Worst Journey* her father had given her back in Minneapolis (all of which she'd decided to bring after Tucker assured her little polar literature would be found on the continent itself). On top of the books was where she placed the antique pocket compass Bill had snuck into her duffel, and which she'd found while searching for a tampon during the layover at McMurdo.

Finally, she plunged her hand deep into the pocket of her parka and pulled out a Tylenol travel vial, the *Extra Strength* rubbed out by her constantly searching fingers. It was four and a half inches long, point-eight ounces light, though, of course, the packaging data no longer reflected the vial's contents. Cooper set this next to the compass and lay down on her bed. After a few minutes, the heater cycled off, revealing the sounds of a couple having sex on the other side of the Jamesway. A moment later, they stopped. A woman's voice, dripping with sarcasm, said, "I'll guess I'll just finish myself off then." It was the first familiar thing Cooper had encountered since stepping foot on South Pole.

The second familiar thing was South Pole's computer lab, referred to at the station as the Cube Farm. It looked like any second-rate college's computer science department, with a half-descended projection screen dangling against a whiteboard and three rows of candy-colored iMacs. The lab was half full when Cooper walked in to check her e-mail, and aside from rapid keyboard clicking, mostly silent. As she walked down the least-populated row of computers, she saw one of the Polies was scrolling through photos of disgruntled cats dressed up as circus clowns.

The only e-mail in Cooper's in-box was from Billie.

```
2003 October 11
00:13
To:
   cherrywaswaiting@hotmail.com
From:
   Billie.Gosling@janusbooks.com
Subject: Working the Pole?


C.,
How's Pole? Life at the
World's Most Mediocre Pub-
lisher remains mediocre. Mom
just acquired a book on divi-
nation by punctuation and set
me up with the author of said
```

masterpiece. I agreed to the date because of my long-standing fascination with the Oxford comma. Our first date ended with an exchange of punctuation-related insults. He finds commas guilty of crimes against humanity. I told him double spaces after periods or I walk. If you're in the market for some reading material, I can provide. Illuminati conspiracies? The Book of Thoth? Labyrinth literature? Mom's been on a spree. Meanwhile, I sit here and write rejection notes all day. (Yes, Janus Books does sometimes reject things.) Oh, and I'm supposed to say that Mom misses you terribly and sends you her blessing.

Billie, your sister,
The World's Oldest
Editorial Assistant™

2003 October 12
09:50
To:

Billie.Gosling@janusbooks.com
From:
cherrywaswaiting@hotmail.com
Subject: RE: Working the Pole

B.,
I can only e-mail when the heavens and the satellites align, and the sword is in the stone. I've been here for eight hours and have already lost all sense of time. It's strange down here. Like a strip mall at the end of the earth. There are only nine women. When winter starts in March, there will be four. I'm told that while the odds are good, the goods are odd. The guy at the computer next to me is starting to get really excited — like, bordering on sexually excited — by a cat video, so I need to sign off now. More later.

C.

As she sent off the e-mail, Cooper wondered again why her older sister chose to spend her days photocopying new-age manuscripts and preparing their mother's morning yerba mate. Billie claimed nepotism was her only chance at gainful employment after years of failed attempts, and perhaps this was true. Their mother, Dasha, had climbed the ranks at Janus Books after becoming interested in the questions of "The Seeker." The Seeker was on a journey for meaning, and stuffed into her tribal-feather double-fringed medicine-bag purse were books like the *Tao Te Ching, the Tibetan Book of the Dead, Thus Spoke Zarathustra,* and Ernest Holmes's collected works. After several years in middling editorial positions at Janus, Dasha had learned the hand grips, the passwords, the ritual work, whatever it was that launched a former paralegal into a position of Masonic power, and was now executive editor. In the decade she'd been there, Dasha had transformed Janus Books from a quiet publisher of self-help books, a kind of lapdog for the self-actualizing, to a frothing Aquarian beast. It hadn't escaped Cooper's notice that this ascent took place as David succumbed to mental illness. This fact bothered Cooper — she wasn't quite sure why. Clearly selling self-help books was her mother's coping mechanism, and didn't we all need coping mechanisms? Still, as a rule, Cooper avoided Janus's myrrh-scented halls. But she also understood you had to say goodbye to your mother if you were departing for the seventh continent — even if your mother was wearing a dashiki.

It was Billie who met Cooper at Reception. Her older sister was imperious, angled, beautiful, and cool. Bette Davis in army-navy tactical cargo pants and a black tank top. Even though she couldn't snow camp, Billie had been, until recently, the Goslings' Best Hope: the one with the brains, the Algonquin wit, the ability to produce obscure Jack London references at the perfect moment. These were traits that were highly valued by their father, and so Billie honed them until she could wield them like a prison shank to keep Cooper, and her talent, at bay. Of course, Billie had talent to burn. She'd gone to New York on a playwriting fellowship, begun dating an artisanal tobacconist, and after eighteen months found herself in the midst of fleeting success — a run at the Lortel with the play she wrote between waitressing shifts, an Obie nomination, and the inevitable inability to pen a second play.

Soon, Billie was back in Minneapolis, living in the guest bedroom of Dasha's warehouse-district loft, humiliated by her failures and determined to play out that narrative for as long as possible. In the mean-time, she assisted her mother by logging copyedited changes to *The Visigoth Manager: Germanic Paganism in the Workplace,* and pretended nothing hurt.

As Billie walked Cooper down one of the hallways toward Dasha's office, she'd said, "Did you know that when you do book deals with certain lady folk singers from the sixties, you have to put into the contract that her hotel rooms will be outfitted with reiki candles and a synthesizer?" She stopped in front of a door and knocked. "Such wisdom I have gained while working here."

"Come in," Dasha commanded. Billie pushed open the door, and promptly dis-appeared around a corner. Cooper found her mother leaning back in her Herman Miller Aeron chair, feet on desk, glasses atop forehead, Sontag stripe gleaming in the cold glow of energy-efficient lights.

"Hello, dear."

"Hello, Mother."

"Please don't call me 'Mother.'"

Cooper did jazz hands and shouted: "Hello, Mommy!" This, at least, produced a smile.

"Sit down, honey." Cooper sat in the chair next to the door and waited. Dasha only stared at her, smiling, so Cooper said, "I am now seated."

Dasha looked at her searchingly. "Ant-ar-tica?"

"Antarctica. There's a C in it."

"Polar bears."

"Penguins."

"Clearly, I need to brush up on my geography skills."

"It doesn't matter," Cooper replied.

Dasha sighed deeply. "I want you to know that I understand what you're trying to do, and I give this venture my —"

"Mom, please, no blessing, no benedictions, no burning sage. I just came to say goodbye. Can we just do 'goodbye, good luck, I'll miss you'? I don't even need the 'I'll miss you.' "

"You have my blessing."

"Don't need it, Mom," Cooper half-sang.

"Sweetheart, for me, a blessing is not approval."

"Then what is it? Because it sort of sounds like you're giving me the okay. I don't need an okay."

"Well, for me a blessing is a sincere wish that you get what you want out of this experience. When will I see you again?"

"Next September."

Dasha seemed genuinely surprised. "A

year?"

"That's what I signed up for."

Dasha placed her fingertips together and looked up at the ceiling. "Blessing or not, I need to say this before you leave or else I won't have done my job as a parent: you are an exceptional talent, but you are also a thirty-year-old woman who has never held a long-term professional job in her life. You're thirty, Cooper. I need you to hear the starkness in that. At thirty, routes begin to disappear. And at some point you have to answer for what you are — whether that's a success or a failure."

"What if I'm a Seeker?"

"I'd like to be validated by hearing an answer from you," Dasha snapped. The tone of the conversation — the way it resonated like a faint echo of the kinds of conversations Cooper had had with her mother before the Seeker had absconded with her — soothed Cooper's nerves.

"Let's see what it looks like when I return," she said. Dasha's face fell. These words must have been lodged in some capsule in Cooper's brain, ready to be deployed at exactly the wrong time: David's parting words to them on Christmas, when they'd let him drive himself back to the group home because he'd been so good about his medication, so lucid, that it was almost like he was restored. ("Louie De-Palma is back!" Billie had shouted after two glasses of Shiraz.) He'd asked about Cooper's painting, about Billie's writing. He'd been funny, brilliant — beautiful. Cooper had felt guilty tailing him in her Tempo until he got to the intersection of Forty-sixth and Blaisdell, a couple of blocks from the Damiano House, the group home where he'd been living since his last 5150. When David's counselor had called Bill and Dasha to let them know he hadn't come home that night, and later, when the police put out the "Missing Vulnerable Adult" flyer, Cooper realized she'd failed him a million different ways.

"I know you and Billie choose not to talk about him with me," Dasha said, her voice brittle. "I know you blame me for not being more in tune with what was happening, and I think —"

Cooper felt her stomach begin to churn. "Mom — please."

"Honey, at least let me say this —"

But Cooper couldn't. She couldn't hear this, just as she couldn't forgive her mother for telling mourners at his funeral service that David had been a "bleeding tree." Cooper stood up and walked out of Dasha's office, and it was only when she was in the lobby and saw Billie's face that she realized she had her hands over her ears.

"Gimme a minute," the station doctor called out to Cooper from behind a dirty white vinyl curtain. "Okay, so — that sound fair?" she said to a patient.

"Yeah, that works," the man said. "I can't, like, get lice or anything, can I?"

"Friend, if we had a lice problem on station, I'd be the first to hear about it. Wash the pillowcase if you're nervous."

"I don't want to use up my water ration."

"Then go, live on hope."

The curtain slid back to reveal a man clutching a pillow. The doctor emerged from behind the curtain with a half-empty bottle of Robitussin. This, Cooper knew, had to be Doc Carla, a weathered, lean woman in her late fifties, with thick brown hair pulled into pigtails, a wind-chapped face, and lips that glistened with Vaseline.

"Bartering for the return of unused medication is the work of saints," she said to no one. Then she glanced at Cooper, and cringed. "Well, you look like hell. Come on in, lady."

When Cooper had awoken in her cell-like room in Summer Camp that morning, she'd discovered her right eye was Super-Glued shut and her eyelashes had become a petrified forest of dried pus. She felt like shit. One of her nostrils was stuffed up; the other was flowing freely. Her bones ached and her skin felt clammy. Her South Pole handbook indicated that she should visit the station doctor at the clinic — a place Cooper now knew went by the name Hard Truth Medical Center.

Doc Carla pointed to a metal exam table that looked like it had come down on the *Terra Nova*. "Take a seat." As Cooper shimmied her way onto the table, she surveyed the room: two ward beds, a red standing Snap-on "Intimidator" toolbox, two green oxygen canisters, and an enormous gawking army-issue exam light.

"You probably got the Crud."

"The Crud?" Cooper asked, squinting like a deranged pirate.

"An illness found at the outposts of civilization," Doc Carla replied. She opened an industrial-size tackle box and began digging through piles of medication. "It's like the flu. Most Fingys get it when they arrive." She shook her head in disbelief. "You'd think they'd tell you guys this stuff. Until the doors close for the winter, those human petri dishes from McMurdo are going to keep me in business." All sickness, it seemed, came from McMurdo. This was one reason Polies hated McMurdo-ites, but only one.

Doc Carla tossed a box of medicine on a small metal tray on wheels, then came at Cooper with a penlight. "Probably a bacterial infection of the soft tissues," she said as she peered into Cooper's right eye. "I'm going to give you a course of antibiotics and some drops for the eye." She turned around to fish the drops out of the dorm fridge. "Don't feel nauseated, do you?"

"No."

"Stiff neck?"

"I don't think so," Cooper said, rubbing her neck, which suddenly seemed a little sore. Doc Carla handed Cooper the eyedrops and the box of pills. "Take these so it doesn't turn into meningitis. And lay low for a few days. No sex until the eye gets better. And if you start puking or you can't move your neck, get yourself over here *tout suite.* I might not be able to save you but at least your family can't sue me."

After leaving Hard Truth, Cooper started to meander up the tunnel toward the main station when she was almost run over by a forklift. "Open your eyes, dumbass," someone shouted at her in passing. Cooper watched as the forklift careened up the tunnel, stopped suddenly, and unceremoniously dropped its cargo of crates onto the snow with a crash. Immediately, a crowd of people materialized around the boxes. By the time Cooper arrived, a scuffle had broken out between the forklift driver and the attendant crowd. Several Polies stared sadly into one of the crates.

"You just pulverized an entire case of Cabernet, dickweed," one of them snapped. Cooper recognized the angry Polie as Kit, the DA from the galley. By this time, the driver's insouciance had been replaced by unmistakable fear. He stammered an apology, but it went unheard. Cooper had the feeling that punishment would be meted out later. For now, the group had moved on to more important matters, like getting the crates of booze into the station store before it froze.

"You," Kit shouted at Cooper. Cooper hastily slipped her goggles over her eyes in order to disguise her disfigurement. "Be a pal. Take this Coors Light to the store."

The South Pole Station store was located on the second floor of the comms pod. At McMurdo, the station store offered souvenirs, scented soaps, and *New York Times* best-sellers. Here at Pole, nearly the entire inventory was 90-proof. Besides tampons, chocolate bars, and toothpaste, the stock was comprised of Jägermeister, Crown Royal, and Jack Daniel's available for purchase — and below cost — along with Apple Pucker and Stoli vanilla vodka. Cases of Budweiser were stacked atop cases of Red Stripe. Rows of pale Chardonnay and scarlet Merlots lined the walls, while silver kegs haunted the corners.

Cooper maneuvered her way around the frantic cargo handlers, who were desperate to keep the new shipment from freezing, and deposited the Coors Light next to a crate of sambuca. A Polie elbowed past her and fussily set three vials of angostura bitters on the shelf above her. When he noticed Cooper looking at them, he shrugged. "For the fancy drinks," he said.

Cooper was relieved to discover that wearing snow goggles inside the galley was the kind of eccentricity that could go uncommented upon. She pushed her tray through the cafeteria line, regarding the steaming metal tubs of gelatinous Salisbury steak suspiciously. She recalled Pearl's assertion that many Polies claimed the eats at Amundsen-Scott were second to none.

As she stood at the exit point of the lunch

line, a reedy man in glasses and a T-shirt that read "Denialism: Science for Morons" dropped a note onto her tray. "Could you give this to that guy over there, the one in the Confederate-flag bandanna?" Before Cooper could ask him why so many Polies wore bandannas, he'd slipped away and rejoined a group of other bespectacled men wearing the same shirt. She glanced down at the folded note on her tray, then back at the men, two of whom now clasped their hands and shook them in supplication. She sighed. The possibility that anything other than sexual disappointment and second-rate computer labs might become familiar to her seemed remote.

"What's this?" the man donning the Stars and Bars growled when Cooper handed him the note.

"They asked me to give it to you," Cooper said, trying to make out his face through her goggles. "Those guys over there." The man leaned back in his chair and looked behind Cooper at the knot of scientists. After a beat, he smiled and, without reading it, handed the note back to Cooper. "I know what this is about. Tell them to fold it up lengthwise, roll it into a tiny tube, and shove it deep into their asses. Tell them to pass it like an ass-joint."

As Cooper walked away, she pushed her goggles onto her forehead and read the note. It was a plea to join a pool tournament, addressed to someone named Bozer — presumably the proud son of the South with whom she'd just spoken. She shrugged at the scientists, who looked crushed.

Across the galley, the scientist she'd rescued back in fire school during the partner exercises sat alone at a table, studying a book without turning the pages. Around him, guys in Carhartts and feather boas wolfed down mac-and-cheese casserole and talked about how the load of grade beams that had arrived on a flight the day before had maxed out the vertical cargo space.

"Can I sit here?" Cooper asked the scientist. He looked up, startled, then gathered in his utensils as if they were taking up too much room.

"Yes," he said.

"What're you reading?" Cooper said as she attempted to cut into the rubbery Salisbury steak. The man gently closed the book and placed his hand over it, but Cooper had spotted the title: *Alarmism and the Climate Change Hoax.*

"I find reading as I eat relaxing." He slid the book off the table and dropped it into the bag at his feet. "One has to eat, right?" he continued. "It's inconvenient, this need to eat." He finished off his juice in a long gulp. "You look familiar."

"Yeah, I saved you from the burning synthetic fires of hell, remember?" He looked at her for a moment, as if he were translating her words into his native language. Cooper marveled at the utter strangeness of his face: too long to be comprehended at a glance, and too finely cut to be traditionally handsome. Red patches marred the pale skin of his cheeks.

"Yes, that's it," he finally said. "I failed fire training."

"I thought they DQ'ed everyone who didn't pass."

"Not everyone, apparently," he replied. "And you — you're an artist Fellow, correct?"

Cooper was surprised. "Yes. Though it's been implied that we're parasites that contribute net zero to the station."

"Scientists say that because they can only quantify the value of a Monet by giving you a rough estimate of how many quarks might be in it." Before Cooper could process this, the man gathered his dishes onto his tray and then departed with an awkward wave. Cooper turned to call after him, but realized she didn't know his name. It was as if they'd both silently agreed not to bother with them.

When she turned back to her tray, Cooper found a flyer lying atop her mac and cheese. She looked up to find Sal staring down at her.

"Pick a side, Fingy," he said. Cooper lifted the flyer off her food, and shook toasted bread crumbs from it.

SCIENCE	DENIALISM
– COLLECT DATA	– START WITH CONCLUSION
– DRAW CONCLUSION	– PRETEND YOU HAVE DATA

I, THE UNDERSIGNED, DO DECLARE THAT I SUPPORT THE SPREAD OF:

———— SCIENCE

———— FAIRY TALES

(CHECK ONE)

SIGNATURE: _____

Sal hovered over her, one hand gripping the back of her chair, the other palming the table. Cooper returned the flyer to him.

"Yeah, I'm not signing this."

"Why not?"

"There's no box for Sasquatch Studies," she replied, shoving a forkful of meat into her mouth. She looked up and met his eyes, which had widened in disbelief. Luminescent hazel, with depth. Not like Forrest's, whose mud-brown eyes seemed affixed to his face only because they were required to be there. "Seriously, this is dumb," Cooper said. "You scientists really put too fine a point on things." Sal looked amazed for a moment, and then he laughed. It was a nice laugh, Cooper thought, and the dimple sweetened the pot. Still, he was a little too pleased with himself. Cooper piled her tray with her dirty silverware and headed for the dish pit.

"You are strange," Sal called after her. Everyone turned and looked at her. Pearl took Cooper's plates with a pitying smile, and whispered, "Everyone here's strange."

Armed with her South Pole Station handbook and map, and her painting supplies, Cooper made her way to Substation B, the trailer near the elevated dorm, where the artist and writer studios were located. At the top of the metal stairs leading to the door was a large sign that read *Off Limits/*

Restricted Access. She pulled the door open anyway and nearly ran into Tucker. He seemed unsurprised to see her, and peered into her face.

"I heard it was the Crud," he said. "How bad is it?" Cooper slid the goggles onto her forehead. Tucker recoiled and began laughing behind his closed fist.

"I'm overwhelmed by your compassion," Cooper said, sliding the goggles back down.

"I have nothing but compassion for you, having been afflicted by acne and facial tics for most of my life."

"Well, I'm already on antibiotics, so don't worry yourself sick over me," Cooper said.

"Antibiotics. Well, you are now officially a Fingy."

"God! If I hear that term one more time I am going to rub my infected eye all over you — sorry, that was bitchy."

"It's okay. I like bitches. I seek them out. You have a ways to go, though."

"I'll do better next time," Cooper said, thinking that would make for a very accurate tattoo.

"Come on, I'll show you to your studio," he said, ushering her down a short hallway. "By the way, I hear you've already become enmeshed."

"Enmeshed?"

"You ferried a note between Beaker and Nailhead at lunch."

"What the hell are Beakers and — you know what, never mind."

"Beakers are scientists. Nailheads are construction. But if anyone asks, the Beakers are the prophets and the Nailheads are the patriots."

Cooper growled at Tucker.

They stopped at a door. Someone had taped a postcard portrait of Foucault's cheerful face just above the doorknob. "I'm so glad Denise is back," Tucker said. "You'll like her!"

"Who's Denise?"

Tucker began whistling ominously and sauntered back the way they had come.

When Cooper unlocked the door to her studio, she found it was a small, square room with no window, just a desk, a couple of chairs, and an old easel lying on its side. Someone had carved *Don't eat the yellow snow* into one of the legs. A web of frost grew on the south wall of the room, and in the corners, clear ice collected like tiny frozen waterfalls. The lighting, Cooper noted with disappointment, was abysmal — *On the Waterfront* without the symbolism. On the desk, someone — Denise? — had left a green canvas bag and a pile of books

(*The Sociology of Isolation, Sociological Materialism in Remote Communities, Achieved Status in Areas of Limited Resource*). Cooper let her roll of canvas fall at her feet and began unpacking her supplies.

As she was examining her palette knife, the door opened and a dark-haired woman walked in. "Hi," she said. "Just popped in to say hello. You must be Cooper."

"Yep, that's me," Cooper said. The woman's eyebrows arched questioningly over her cat's-eye glasses.

"Interesting name for a woman." She paused, and turned her eyes to the ceiling. "Cooper. Barrel maker. Lunar crater. D. B. Cooper." She glanced at Cooper. "I'm making associations. Not a mnemonic device, exactly, but I lay these associations down in my memory palace, which should lead me to your name, Cooper, if I become toasty over the course of the winter. I'm Denise. We'll be sharing a studio for the duration."

"Toasty?"

"It's a slang term that covers a whole range of psychological disturbances brought on by the extreme environment here." Seeing Cooper was confused, she added, "I'm a sociologist by trade."

"I thought this was the Artists and Writers' Annex."

Denise shrugged. "Well, this is where I was assigned. I'm not offended by being housed with the artists, if you're wondering — though it does suggest that my field of study is viewed as one with less precision than, perhaps, cosmology. But then that idea would be offensive to artists, wouldn't it? As if they are not precise in motivation. But is art about motivation?"

Cooper wanted to roll her eyes. Of course it was about motivation. But she only said, "I don't really think about those things." Denise, Cooper learned, was on sabbatical from Columbia and was supposed to be in a favela in Rio, living among transitioning transgendered men who injected industrial-grade silicone into their bodies to give themselves hips and breasts. She'd received institutional encouragement to delve deeper into this point on the gender matrix, but here she was, at Pole, four thousand miles away from her research subjects.

"I take it there are one or two transitioning men here to study in isolation?" Cooper asked.

"I like that you're confident enough to joke with a new acquaintance about a sensitive topic. No, after traveling here a couple years ago, I simply lost my passion for my work in Brazil. I felt it best to hand off the research to my younger colleagues. I'm now studying the population here."

"I guess anybody who'd voluntarily come to South Pole is probably worth studying."

"Yes, it's fertile ground," Denise said. "The station population is most analogous to a penal institution — I mean, on a macro level. For a social scientist, it's a dream. I have it all here — defended neighborhoods, degradation ceremonies, a chance to test the contact hypothesis."

"Examples?"

Denise had allowed her glasses to slip, but she pushed them back up now, her face flushed with excitement. "Let's see — defended neighborhoods, that's easy: Beakers are not allowed in the fuel shed or power plant, except for one or two exceptions, while the Nailheads are only allowed near the scientific equipment when occupying narrowly prescribed roles, such as repair and logistical support. Degradation ceremonies would be something like the bag-drag for the Fingys, where they are forced to transport their own luggage to Summer Camp. It's like a perp walk. Something to introduce the novitiate to a total institution and prepare them for external control."

"Christ," Cooper said.

"I know, intense stuff, right?" Denise said. "But I'm most interested in how the scientific community here is going to cope with the arrival of a climate change denialist." She used her pen to scratch a spot on her scalp hidden by her prodigious brown curls. "Hmmm. I keep adopting the terminology of the dominant group. The more appropriate term here would be *skeptic* — climate change skeptic." She pulled on one of her curls until it was perfectly straight, then released it. "Although that, too, is problematic. The scientists here would object to that term. I'm still trying to parse this one out. Anyway, let me know when I lapse into group jargon. It has the potential to affect my neutrality if I'm not careful, and I don't want to go all Margaret Mead."

After Denise left, Cooper realized she'd worn her goggles the entire time they'd been talking, and Denise hadn't batted an eye. She decided she liked Denise very much, and turned to her sketchpad with some optimism. She put on an Etta James CD to drown out the roar of the machines rumbling through the fuel arches downwind from her studio and picked up her pencil.

2003 October 28
20:40

To:
  Billie.Gosling@janusbooks.com
From:
  cherrywaswaiting@hotmail.com
Subject: Changing the subject
  line

B.,
What are you and the High
Priest of Divination by Punctuation doing for Halloween?
It's apparently a big deal
here. You are expected to wear
a costume. Some people bring
their costumes to Pole. Others just cobble something
together. In other news, I got
an eye infection and experienced the finest in frontier
medicine. Drinking is an en-
durance sport, scientists
included, who, by the way, are
currently pitching a collective tantrum about a climate
change denialist doing research here. The overall literary aesthetic can be summarized as Tom Robbins Rox.
Haven't heard from Mom or Dad
yet. Write back. I'm told that

after about three months down here, the letters and e-mails stop because loved ones forget you exist.

C.

p.s. Don't ask me if/what I'm painting.

2003 October 29
00:43
To:
   cherrywaswaiting@hotmail.com
From:
   Billie.Gosling@janusbooks.com
Re: Changing the subject line

C.,
The High Priest of Divination by Punctuation and I have agreed to disagree about the semicolon and have moved on to dry humping on my loveseat. Afterwards he consented to letting me call him Phil. When I asked him what his plans were for Halloween, he indicated that he'd be honoring the ancient roots of the holiday with cocktails at the

Minnesota NeoPaganist Society. Apparently, Minnesota is a hotbed for paganism — Phil referred to it as Paganistan, which I thought was in poor taste, considering our current military commitments. I had dinner with Dad on Sunday. He says he'll write you a letter. He doesn't "do" e-mail, which he believes is written E+MAIL, and which is also how he pronounces it. I choose not to correct him for obvious reasons.

B.

p.s. See, I didn't ask you what/if you're painting.

"And so she comes up to me — now keep in mind, I'm in a hostel in Cheech and I'm in boxers with one of those half-staff morning boners. Anyway, she asks me if I've heard of Larry McMurtry."

It had escaped Cooper's notice that day on the bus in Denver that Floyd looked positively Minnesotan, with the kind of round, ruddy face you'd find in Sauk Centre or Fergus Falls. However, he had made it clear, loudly and often, that he was a proud Floridian, and this, it seemed to Cooper, explained a lot. As she took a seat at the far end of Floyd's table with her lunch tray, she noticed his muttonchops looked even more unkempt than they had in Denver. His sleeve was pulled back just so, revealing a forearm tat of a woman straddling a power pole. Sparks emanating from her bare boobs suggested she was being electrocuted, but in a sexy way.

The group of men sitting with Floyd didn't seem overly interested in his soliloquy.

"McMurtry, right? So, yeah, I cringe," he continued, "but I say, sure, I've heard of him, but I've also heard of Zsa Zsa Gabor. What's your point? Well, she says she's reading one of his books. I say, 'So?' and she goes, 'I think he won the Nobel prize for cowboy writing.' "

Floyd let loose a huge belly laugh, but his friends continued eating in silence. "The Nobel prize for cowboy writing?" Floyd tried again.

Finally, a skinny guy in a stained University of Oregon sweatshirt said, "I thought there was, like, only one big Nobel for writers. I didn't know they had one for Westerns."

"Shut up, man," Floyd said bitterly.

"What did I say?"

"Just stop talking."

Tucker quietly took a seat on the bench next to Floyd and waved Cooper over to join him. As she scooted her way down the bench, her plastic cup of Dr Pepper wobbled, then spilled the length of the table. Everyone burst into applause. Sheepishly, Cooper mopped up the spill with her napkin. Tucker watched but offered no help.

Because everyone was still staring at her, Cooper decided to throw in her two cents about McMurtry. "I think *Lonesome Dove* actually won the Pulitzer," she said, as she balled up the sodden napkin. She glanced over at the skinny guy, who now seemed unwilling to make eye contact with her. Tucker, too, avoided her eyes. She'd done something wrong, but she wasn't sure what. She thought of Denise. Had she just trespassed into a "defended neighborhood"? Quietly, she added: "I'm just saying that'd kind of be like winning the Nobel prize for cowboy writing."

After an excruciating silence, Floyd extended his fish-white hand toward her. Cooper took it lightly — as she had anticipated, it was clammy and damp. "Hi, remember me? I'm Floyd. I'm important."

He dropped her hand. "First of all, nice of you to invite yourself into this conversation and offer a pearl necklace of wisdom. We're always looking for fresh Fingy insight."

"Be nice, Floyd," Tucker said, pushing his salad greens around his plate, but also, Cooper was annoyed to discover, stifling a smile.

"This *is* me being nice," Floyd replied stonily, turning away from Cooper.

"And second?" she said.

"Huh?"

"You said, first, it was nice of me to insert myself into your conversation. I was just wondering what part two was."

"Part two is fuck off."

Floyd picked up his tray, followed by his friends, who quickly swallowed what was left of their food. At the dish pit, they dumped their plates into the sink simultaneously, sending waves of soapy water all over Pearl's apron.

"Come on, Floyd," Pearl shouted, "be a person!"

"Interesting," Tucker murmured, when the men had departed.

"What's interesting?" Cooper replied.

"Just that people tend to treat the power plant manager with kid gloves," Tucker said. "You know, because he's in charge of keeping the heaters going and stuff."

"I had no idea *Lonesome Dove* was such a lightning rod."

"There are hidden sensitivities everywhere. They're like land mines," Tucker said. "Floyd's basically a good guy. *Basically* being the operative word here. He's under a lot of pressure with the construction of the new station, and sometimes he relieves his stress with poorly informed but weirdly elitist literary critiques of popular authors. Best to think of him as our resident Kim Jong-il: wildly unpredictable, with the power to annihilate his neighbors. Helps that Floyd looks a little like him." He glanced over at Cooper and seemed relieved to find her grinning. "The eye looks better."

"Doc Carla told me even if antibiotics are past their expiration date, they can still work. But five years? I was doubtful."

"How's the work going? Has inspiration struck yet?"

Cooper quickly spooned a lump of the potato gratin into her mouth in order to avoid answering the question. Despite her hopeful start in the studio after meeting Denise, she had ended up with nothing. Nothing except a hasty sketch of the *Terra Nova,* which she'd begun out of desperation. Drawn from memory, it was a mess of flying jibs and mizzen sail, and it hadn't been born of inspiration. It had been a product of a stubborn but useless memory.

Sal sauntered over from the caf line and dropped his tray onto the table across from Cooper. "I miss tots, Tucker," he said. "I want tater tots. Fancy potatoes aren't my speed." Then he looked over at Cooper as if he'd just now noticed her. "Oh, hey, it's the strange person who won't sign the petition. You're the dancer, right?"

"Painter," Cooper replied.

"I want to meet the dancer. Is she hot?" Cooper examined Sal the way she had examined the endless still lifes she'd had to paint in art school. He seemed haphazardly arranged, but there was some underlying cohesive structure that she had to tease out. His unwashed, dark auburn hair was boyish-looking, but she could tell he kept his hair longer than he might otherwise so that it would fall over his forehead and hide his slightly receding hairline. He had a nose that, as he aged, would widen and grow almost bulbous and become more visually interesting. His conversation, however, left much to be desired. It seemed as if he were only playing the role of the bro-dude, not living the life. Still, Cooper thought, there was no law that said an astrophysicist couldn't have the personality of a bro-dude.

"You don't look like a Sal," she said.

"What do I look like?"

"Brock? Josh? Colton?"

"Keep it coming," Sal replied.

"Edison. Keegan. Chase."

"So what you're saying," Sal said, swallowing down a mouthful of gratin, "is that I look like the rush chair for Sigma Chi."

Decently handled, Cooper thought. The table next to them erupted in laughter, and a group of smart-looking guys, including the tall Russian scientist Cooper had met at McMurdo, got up and left en masse.

"There's gonna be a Beaker-Nailhead cage match before the winter's over," Sal said, watching the men file out.

"No, cooler heads will prevail," Tucker said soothingly.

"I doubt it," Sal replied. "Alek has the capacity to go Unabomber on people. It's all that Marxist scientific determinism bullshit." Cooper looked at the next table over; it was occupied by a crew of brawny men in various stages of male-pattern baldness. Seated at the head of the table was the Confederate-bandanna-wearing man — Bozer — who'd coined the "ass-joint" phrase that had already found its way into Pole's lexicon. ("Stop being such an ass-joint, Chuck!") Cooper longed to ask Tucker whether Bozer's bandanna bothered him, but something told her to keep the question to herself.

"It seems like the Nailheads rule the roost. I wonder if it's the beards," Cooper said.

"Do the Nailheads draw their power from the beards or do their beards grow lush because the Nailhead is powerful?" Tucker mused.

"Those beards are the result of several years of ice-time," Sal said. "Nick over there — the guy in the Fleshgod Apocalypse T-shirt — this'll be his fourth winter-over. His beard's as old as that. Tuck, remember last year when he let that girl build a hanging fairy garden in it?"

"Four seasons?" Cooper said, disbelieving.

"No — four winter-overs. There's a difference. If you winter-over, you're here for the entire year, including the polar night. Six months of total isolation. No flights in, no flights out."

"Why would anyone do that four times?" Cooper asked.

"You will know the answer to that question before you leave here," Sal said. He stretched his arms over his head and interlaced his fingers, just as he'd done at fire school. "I need coffee." He stood up and looked down at Cooper. "Want some?" Cooper shook her head no. Tucker headed over to the coffee tureens with Sal, and, as if on cue, Denise slid into his seat.

"I'm having a ball watching Tucker claw his way from ascribed status to achieved status," she half-whispered. "Speaking of him as the only man of color at Pole."

"What about all those guys from Hydera-bad?"

"They don't count. There's nothing like observing an American black man in an environment in which he'd not be ex-pected."

Cooper thought it wise to change the subject. "What's the word on this guy Sal?"

Denise thought for a moment. "Sal Brennan. Scientist. Cosmology, I think. He's a veteran — been here a few times before. I have heard he's in the final year of a rather important experiment, though I don't know the details." Denise unfolded her napkin and carefully arranged it on her lap. "I'll have to check my notes. The scientific staff seems to avoid me, so my knowledge of his background is meager. Oh, now this is inter-esting."

Cooper turned to follow Denise's gaze, and saw two gaunt men walking through the galley toward the chow line. Both were draped in Swedish national flags, with cross-country skis on their shoulders, and the Polies they passed were slapping them on the backs and smiling. A VIDS staffer jogged after the skiers.

"See," Denise said, pulling out her notebook. "This is the kind of scenario I find fascinating. What benefit is VIDS protecting by denying visitors food?" As Denise scribbled, Cooper watched the Swedes carefully return the trays and listen politely as the admin explained to them why they couldn't eat in the galley.

"Who are they?"

"They arrived at the station last night — Bozer said they're skiing across the continent. They came straight from Vostok. The Russians apparently treated them like kings. VIDS is only letting them pitch their tent outside the Dome." Cooper knew VIDS tried to keep tourists and adventurers away from the station — people were always trying to cross the continent by ski, by snowshoe, by fat-tire bike. One summer an ultramarathoner made an attempt but went hypoxic three miles outside of McMurdo and had to be carried back on a snowmobile. People still talked shit about ultramarathoners as a result.

Denise and Cooper watched as the Swedes walked out of the galley with their gear. Out of the corner of her eye, Cooper saw Bozer approaching their table. When he arrived, he put his hands on Denise's shoulders and began rubbing them.

"Hey, chicklet," he said.

"Bozer," Denise said warningly. "Don't cross the boundary." Cooper felt he'd already done that with the Confederate bandanna, but said nothing.

"I'm Bozer," he said to Cooper. "I'm sleeping with her." For the first time, Cooper saw an expression of displeasure pass over Denise's face.

"Your lack of discretion is becoming a problem," Denise said. Bozer discreetly laid his fat, crooked middle finger on the table between them, and wiggled it. Cooper tried not to laugh. "There is an unspoken code of conduct here regarding relationships on the ice," Denise said. "At least before winter starts." She turned to address Bozer directly. "You don't formally acknowledge the person in public. You don't sit next to them at meals, and when a transgression takes place, you say 'you've crossed a boundary.' When you say that" — she peeled off Bozer's left hand, which had migrated from the table back to her thin shoulder — "they're sup-

103

posed to stop touching you immediately."

"Okay, honey, but you know I don't subscribe to that kind of bullshit," Bozer said. "We all have an ice-wife, fuck buddy, whatever. What's to hide? Other people get weird about that, but I'm an open book."

"Is *ice-wife* just another term for a hook-up?" Cooper asked.

"So-called ice marriages aren't necessarily commitments down here," Denise said. "But the perceived permanency provides much-needed emotional support, particularly as the season grinds on." She lowered her voice. "Some people in ice relationships even have spouses and families off the ice."

"You're making it complicated, darling," Bozer said. "Alls you gots to do is figure out who's a dyke, who's married, who's open-married, who claims to have a boyfriend, and who wants continual action. Go from there."

"Typically these courtship rituals are kept offstage, à la Goffman," Denise said. "In this social environment, and at this particular time in the institutional cycle, it's important that this basic need be broadcast. You will see this change over the course of the season."

"So that's how you guys got together?"

"Repeat offender program," Bozer said,

gazing over Cooper's head.

"Bozer's been on the ice nine times before this," Denise said.

"Nine times?"

"There's a quaint saying down here," Denise said. "The person who coined it has been lost to history: 'The first time is for the adventure, the second time is for the money, and the third time is because you don't fit in anywhere else.' "

"What's the ninth time for?" Cooper asked, looking at Bozer. He returned her gaze, a scowl on his lips but amusement in his eyes; however, Tucker's voice rang through the galley before he could answer her. "Hello, attention!" Tucker shouted between cupped hands. Everyone quieted down. "Fellow Polies, I regret that it's come to this point so early in the season, but I need to make an announcement. Our fearless communications and logistics director, Dwight, has informed me that our GOES satellite link, which has been overburdened for a week, has just had an irreparable failure. Too much usage. His investigation leads him to believe that a few individuals are using up most of the bandwidth that is shared by the entire station." Some people giggled. "I appreciate the fact that some of you need contact with the outside world in order to have contact with yourself, but it's overloading the system. So, bottom line, get your porn on, but just not over GOES."

Cooper took this opportunity to say good-bye to Denise and Bozer, and approached the galley kitchen with her tray. Pearl was piling a stack of them onto a cart. "Excuse me," Cooper said. Pearl brushed a stray lock of blond hair out of her face with the back of her wrist and looked at her. "What about those skiers?"

"What about them?" Pearl replied.

"They're camped outside. VIDS won't let them eat in the cafeteria." Pearl frowned, uncertainty darkening her normally sunny face. "They have to eat," Cooper pressed.

"I know, but I could get in trouble," Pearl said.

"What about the expired ramen? The Melba toast?"

Pearl leaned back and glanced over her shoulder. "Let me ask Bonnie first."

As Cooper waited for Pearl to get the head cook's okay on the mission, she noticed the VIDS staffer watching her from the coffee tureens. Pearl returned and gave Cooper the high sign, before noticing the admin's owl-like glare. She cleared her throat conspicuously and said somewhat robotically, "Oh, you want to eat at your studio? Let me give you a to-go container." Together, the women shoveled gratin, slices of meat-loaf, canned fruit salad, and carrot sticks into to-go boxes, and eventually the admin turned his attention to a commotion at the tureens: a Fingy cryogenics tech had just learned that neither tureen contained decaf, which had annoyed him, and was then told there was no decaf at the station at all, which destroyed him. While this was happening, Pearl placed the containers into a small cardboard box for Cooper and passed it across the counter. Cooper slipped out the door without being noticed.

Outside, about a hundred yards from the station, Cooper saw a ski planted in the snow with a Swedish flag tossed over it. The flag hung limply, looking hungry.

Cooper kicked at the bottom of the tent with her boot — the winter camper's doorbell. One of the men unzipped the flap. His windburned face took Cooper aback: his skin looked like upholstery.

Inside, it was quickly established that the Swedes' English was perfect, but they seemed unsure of Cooper's, so initially they thanked her effusively with much hand-steepling and half-bows. She took a seat on a pack while they devoured the cold food. The younger one wiped his mouth on his sleeve, then apologized for his bad manners. "Will you get in trouble for this?" he asked.

"Maybe," Cooper said.

"You are a very kind person," he replied.

"Not really," Cooper said.

"No, Americans are very friendly," the older Swede said with conviction, "except for your bureaucrats. But that's true everywhere." He rummaged through his pack and pulled out a package of biscuits. He offered it to Cooper; after months of eating these Swedish cookies, his taste for them was lost forever.

"So, why are you guys skiing across Antarctica?" Cooper asked.

The older one gazed back at her. "Why are you here?"

"I'm an artist. I'm here to paint." Cooper didn't mention the fact that she'd painted exactly nothing since arriving.

"You must come to South Pole to paint?" the other Swede asked, grinning. Cooper was about to reply when she heard footsteps. She cursed softly, and the Swedes quickly boxed the food back up and slid it under their sleeping bags. When Cooper moved to unzip the tent, the younger Swede motioned her toward the rear. He lifted up a sleeping bag and indicated that she should hide under it. Cooper crawled beneath the bag, nose-first into a rucksack containing their dirty laundry. She tried not to gag.

"Excuse me, fellas," she heard VIDS admin say. "I'm just looking for a station member." There was a pause, and Cooper realized the Swedes were pretending not to know English. She envied this ability to disappear from a conversation. "Look, guys, I know she's here."

Cooper pushed the sleeping bag off her head and struggled to her feet. The admin rolled his eyes. The Swedes moved closer to Cooper, like protective older brothers, and she nodded at them, letting them know that it was okay. As she inched her way toward the opening, the older one, noticing Cooper had left behind her Swedish biscuits, slipped them into her parka pocket.

The VIDS admin — Cooper saw from the stitching on the front of his parka that his name was Simon — helped her out of the tent, then took her arm, as if they were going for a stroll across the English countryside. "It's hard to know which end is up when you're down here for the first time," he said. Cooper peered into his parka hood, but his face was deep in shadow now that they were outside in the relentless sun. She could only see his pale lips moving as he spoke.

"I'm figuring things out," Cooper said.

"Yes, I see that. But it's my job to ensure that you're figuring them out right. Taking food out of a federal research facility, for example, is against protocol."

"The Beakers take lunch out to their labs all the time."

"Please don't call them Beakers. It's disrespectful. And the scientists are eating their own lunches, not stealing from our limited food supply and giving it to every foreigner who happens to be passing by." Cooper looked at him uncomprehendingly. Simon sighed. "Look, I know you were try-ing to do the right thing, but the protocols are in place to protect life and government property. What if we get into a fix where our food supply flights are delayed and we're facing a shortage? That food you just gave away could have fed a couple of our support staff. Would you be able to look them in the eye if they had to go hungry?"

By now they had reached the Dome. "Did you receive help from anyone in the kitchen?" Simon asked.

"It was all me," Cooper said quickly.

"Are you sure?"

"Yes."

"And the to-go containers?"

Cooper hesitated. "I — I took them from

the kitchen."

"You mean you stole them," Simon said, with the exhaustion of a put-upon parent.

"I guess."

Simon released her arm. "Cooper, you're an NSF grantee, so I can't write you up — I only oversee the support staff, not the feds — but I will have to send a memo to your grant coordinator about this. I'm sorry."

"What does that mean?"

"It just means that there will be a flag on your file, and if you violate any more policies, they may revisit your grant status." He stared at Cooper for a long minute, and she realized he wanted her to plead with him not to do this, that the only reason he'd brought up the memo was so he could hear her beg him not to send it. She'd given up begging after David died, so she summoned her inner Bartleby and remained silent as the wind picked up around them. Finally, Simon shrugged his shoulders and walked up the entrance tunnel.

Cooper waited until he had disappeared, and then walked across the ice in the opposite direction. She passed the ceremonial South Pole marker — a line of international flags snapping in the breeze, representing the twelve signatories to the Antarctic Treaty, and a mirrored gazing ball set atop

111

a barber's pole. This tourist stop wasn't her destination, though. No, she wanted ninety degrees south — the geographical South Pole, the Pole of her imagination, of David's.

She could see it in the near distance, a polished copper star set atop a stake rooted to an ice sheet. From orientation, Cooper knew that on New Year's Day, this marker would be ceremoniously repositioned to account for its annual drift, as the entire station population looked on. The copper star installed the year before would be replaced by another symbolic work of art wrought by one of the Polies. This year, Cooper had learned via the *Antarctic Sun,* the honor would go to Sal.

But Cooper didn't care about polar tchotchkes. Back in Denver, Tucker had told Cooper that here she could find some of Robert Falcon Scott's words printed on a sign speared into the ice. She gazed at the large square sign now. On the left were Roald Amundsen's bland platitudes, the kind of banalities uttered by those who won races. On the right was a quote from Scott, the words of a man who had given everything, including his life, in his attempt to reach the Pole, only to come in second place to Amundsen: *The Pole. Yes, but under very different circumstances from those expected.*

Son,

I hope your decision to send me the book was not an attempt to gain my acceptance for your lifestyle choice. You won't get it. We've shared some good times in the past — you always did know how to make me laugh. But that's all behind us now. You've made your choice and now I've made mine. Our conversation tonight was our last. There will be no more of them. No communications at all. I will not come to visit, and I don't want you in my house. Have a good Christmas and a good life.

Goodbye.
Leon (Dad)

BORDERLINE-BORDERLINE

When the contract psychologist told Tucker there was a "borderline" applicant waiting in the office, he took her literally. After all, the job site was almost custom-made to attract people with personality disorders: narcissists, anti-socials, avoidants, dependents. Borderlines. The well-adapted chose McMurdo, the Hampton Inn of Antarctica. The slightly less normal picked Palmer Station. Only the margin-dwellers looked farther inland, toward Amundsen-Scott. It was the most remote research station on the planet, a place you went to become unreachable. This, of course, diminished the pool of applicants, so only those with a documented history of psychiatric disorders were rejected out of hand.

There were three widely accepted behavioral predictors that distinguished a successful polar applicant: emotional stability, industriousness, and sociability. But these traits had to be finely balanced against the necessary component of "crazy" required of a person who would choose to spend months upon months in Antarctica. Furthermore, that person had to be interesting enough for others to want to spend large amounts of time with, but not too "interesting." Over the years, Tucker had learned that some social skills were more highly valued at Pole than others: intimate familiarity with Settlers of Catan, detailed knowledge of nonconformist zombie-apocalypse scenarios, and the willingness to grow facial hair competitively, to name a few.

As he looked through the applicant files each season, Tucker would wonder how he had slipped by. Not only slipped by, but climbed the ranks quickly, going from site manager to area director in a single season without the relevant experience typically required for a promotion. He knew nothing about carpentry. Less about logistics. Zero about the allocation of limited resources. The Pole veterans assigned to positions under him knew far more than he did about how the station was run, but they had showed no bitterness at his appointment. This worried Tucker, until he realized that he hadn't been hired for his technical skills. When Karl Martin had offered him a job five years earlier, he'd mentioned Tucker's "cool gaze" and his powers of observation — both key attributes, apparently, for a successful South Pole station manager. It struck Tucker as bizarre that he had not had to submit to a psychological exam himself.

"Not borderline-borderline," the psychologist said to Tucker now. "Borderline, as in she's right on the cut-off."

"Reason?"

"Fairly recent death in the family."

"Cancer?"

"Suicide."

"That's an automatic DQ."

The psychologist wrinkled her nose and grimaced. "Yeah, but she's one of the Artist and Writers Fellows. You know the parameters are a little wider on those applicants. Also, she wouldn't look at the results. Technically a red flag."

"That's a red flag?"

"I know, I actually had to look that up in the manual. No one's ever not wanted to look before."

"What did the manual say?"

"That it suggests avoidance."

Tucker pinched the bridge of his nose. "Naturally. I'll go see her."

"Room two twenty-one."

Tucker walked down a hallway in the

Systems and Solutions wing, which was lined with framed photographs of VIDS's various work sites — the U.S. military's "enduring bases," like Kosovo's Camp Bondsteel, Bosnia's Eagle Base, and Bagram Airfield outside of Kabul. South Pole Station was considered by VIDS to be part of its "Hostile and Developing Regions" branch, but Tucker was far removed from the military ops. Still, it was not uncommon to see military types — mostly black-ops CIA agents — going into the VIDS offices with the contract psychologists for their own exams. Tucker admired the agents' taut bodies, their set jaws, their bristle-brush hair.

When Tucker walked into Room 221, he found the borderline case hunched over a compact, attempting to dispatch a zit. It was an image so devastatingly familiar that Tucker felt as if he'd just walked into his childhood bedroom. Her name was Cooper — the kind of unexpected gender flip he found endearing. Tucker looked at her face, the intact blemish, the right eyebrow ever so slightly shorter than the left, her lips pink and full, her rich, dark eyes full of fear. Even with the pimple, she was pretty, but in a took-you-a-minute kind of way.

Before she spoke a word, he knew this

would be a close call. But that's why they'd hired him. He knew how to make close calls. All but one had been successful. There was the metalworker with Asperger's — VIDS psychologists had argued his eccentricities and wooden personality would cause problems. Instead, the guy had been the most productive metalworker on the team, and was so popular that he'd been voted Equinox King. Then there was the highly skilled maintenance specialist who was a diagnosed bibliomaniac — Tucker had assigned him librarian duties, and filled out thirteen forms, some in triplicate, so the man could sleep in the library. The guy had alphabetized the library within the first week. Bozer, their veteran construction chief, who had been red-flagged one year because of several complaints about his Confederate flag bandanna — both VIDS and the NSF had decided to make Tucker the final arbiter on the matter, because (and of course this was only implied) he was the Only Black Person at South Pole. In interviewing Bozer, Tucker knew he had on his hands a red-blooded clay-eater from the poorest part of South Carolina. But he also knew Bozer was smart and steadfast, a man whose long years of experience in war and on the ice made everyone at Pole safer.

119

Tucker knew that if he gave Bozer an ultimatum — the bandanna or his job — the man would've come to Pole with a naked pate, but angry as an adder. He didn't do that. Instead, he approved Bozer, and his bandanna, and let the admins wonder.

But while VIDS trusted Tucker to make the close calls, even they were worried about Doc Carla. They had not been keen on her. She was considered a "high-risk investment" despite the fact that finding candidates for this particular posting was so notoriously difficult that Karl Martin had called it "a janitor at the porno theater kind of a gig." The type of board-certified physician who was willing to sojourn in Antarctica for six months, preferably a year, for paltry pay and under extremely difficult work conditions was one whose personality might not be described as "charming." Tucker assumed this was a known fact, but thanks to the complicated tenure of Jerri Nielsen, the Pole doc who'd diagnosed her own breast cancer and who was widely considered a personable "normal," the threshold for minimal sociability had been raised (along with the number of release-of-liability forms).

It had not helped Doc Carla's case that

the majority of her practice had, in the years leading up to her posting at South Pole, been focused on drug-addicted prostitutes. It was through this work that Tucker had gotten to know her almost twenty years earlier, and it was how he'd known she'd be the right person for the job. He had been working as a production assistant for a famous documentary filmmaker in New York when he read a short article in the *Times* about a woman doctor who drove a van around the city, handing out condoms and McDonald's vouchers to girls who worked the worst strolls. "Check it out for me," his boss said when Tucker showed him the article. "See if there's anything there."

But when Tucker cold-called Doc Carla's office and mentioned the word *documentary,* she hung up on him. He called back the next day and, disguising his voice, made an appointment for a hepatitis test. A week later, he arrived at her office, which was located in a brownstone in Alphabet City. Sitting in the window was an orange cat, its tail whipping this way and that, its face impassive. When the cat opened its mouth to meow, no sound came out. For some reason, Tucker had always remembered that.

"How old are you, Tucker?" the doctor had asked as Tucker took a seat on her exam table. She tied a piece of rubber hose around his left arm.

"Twenty-five, Dr. Nicks," he said, keeping his eyes on his veins.

"Call me Doc Carla." As she tapped the underside of his forearm, she examined his face. The Bell's palsy, which would render half his face slack and droopy from time to time, had gone away for now, but the acne had not. Tucker averted his eyes from his ugly blue veins.

"Do you engage in high-risk behavior?" she asked.

"What do you mean?"

"Do you have anal sex with men, do you share needles, do you sleep with hookers?"

"No! I mean, no, I haven't done that before."

"Which one?"

"All of them, I guess. Any of them."

The doctor ran her fingers over the inside of his forearms, looking for good veins. The feel of hands on his body was almost arousing, and Tucker felt ashamed.

"But you're gay, right?" she said, in a tone Tucker would come to realize was her version of gentle.

"I guess so." He hated when people could tell at a glance.

"Don't guess so — know so!" she replied.

"Yes, I'm gay."

"But you don't engage in homosexual behavior?"

"Sometimes. Just not that thing you mentioned — not that way. Yet, I guess." He wanted to disappear into one of those magician's dry-ice plumes.

"A gay black man," Doc Carla said. "You sure got it easy, kid." Suddenly, she exhaled — it was almost ecstatic — and said: "Look at these veins. Oh, my. They are just pristine. And look, I don't even need to really coax."

The time seemed right, so Tucker cleared his throat. "I read about your work with prostitutes. In the *Times.*"

She rubbed his skin with iodine. "They check in with me every couple years. I almost didn't talk to them this time."

"Why?"

"Every time they write about me, the do-gooders come out of the walls. I've gotta peel 'em off. They're useless. I can't take their checks because I'm not a charity and if they volunteer one night, they never come back. Their tender sensibilities and all. I just lost my van driver."

"Yes, I read about that in the article."

Tucker closed his eyes as Doc Carla slid the needle into his vein; the initial prick gave way to a dull ache. After a moment, he opened his eyes and saw her attach a small vial to the tubing. Tucker watched as his blackish blood rushed through the needle. He felt dizzy. Doc Carla noticed.

"Jesus, stop looking, honey! Focus on Lulu," she commanded, pointing to the cat, who was still sitting in the window. "It'll help. She's one of the stations of Brahma. What do you do for work, Tucker?"

He hesitated. "I work in film."

She withdrew the needle and prepared a second one. "I've heard that before."

"It's not like that. Legitimate film. I'm just a production assistant."

"Gotta get that foot in the door. I better give you an AIDS test, too, even though you tell me you're a monk."

She removed the second needle from Tucker's vein and held a piece of cotton over the tiny wound.

"Could I go with you once?" Tucker asked.

"On one of my runs?" Doc Carla asked. She studied his face again, the way she had when he first sat down on the exam table. "Do you drive?"

"I've driven before."

She snapped off her plastic gloves. "You ever been around hookers?"

"No," Tucker said.

"You squeamish?"

"No," Tucker lied.

"Then meet me here tomorrow night. And wear old clothes, not this million-dollar shit," she said, flicking the wide lapel of Tucker's Goodwill jackpot find, a purple paisley Calvin Klein dress shirt.

When Tucker met Doc Carla the next night, she'd braided her thick, almost mangy hair and rolled it into a bun at the nape of her neck. The van was parked out front. "You know how to drive shift?" she asked.

"Yes, ma'am."

"Don't call me ma'am. Makes me feel old. And I'm not old. I'm not even forty. Jesus H. Christ."

"I'm sorry."

Doc Carla handed him the keys. "Eleventh, Twelfth, and Thirteenth, mostly between Second and Third. Full of IV-drug users."

"That's where I live," Tucker said.

"Bad blocks," she said. "How'd you end up there?"

"It's where I ended up," Tucker said.

"You know any of the girls there?"

"No."

"They all seem alike when you first meet them — bad makeup, bad skin, neon green or pink high heels, black stretch pants, usually got a hole in 'em. But they've all got their own attitudes. They say finding a specific hooker in New York is like finding a needle in a hay factory, but it's not true. I can find anyone. I've got to. Somebody's got to start keeping track of how many girls this thing kills. They need condoms and doctors and they need food."

The van was outfitted with a little kitchen and a miniature examining room, separated from the rest of the van by a *Peanuts* bedsheet tacked to the ceiling. There were venipuncture and butterfly needles, plastic cc vials, stacks of McDonald's vouchers for free meals, sanitary wipes, tampons, and condoms. Boxes and boxes of condoms.

They pulled up in front of a tenement building on East Eleventh, and within minutes a tiny woman with black hair, half of it in her face, walked up to the side of the van.

"Hey, Doc, you got some tissue or something? I want to get this fuckin' cum off me." Tucker almost retched, but Doc Carla didn't even blink.

"You need to start carrying hygienic supplies, Renata," Doc Carla said, handing the woman a handful of tissues. Renata ran the tissue down her pant leg, then shoved it into her pocket. "Got any free McDonald's,

Doc?"

"If you got time for a test," Doc Carla said. Renata sighed, but walked back toward the sliding door and waited for Doc Carla to unlock it. "I give 'em these vouchers and ten bucks if they take an AIDS test. It's about twice as much as they get for a blow job down here." She walked to the back of the van and opened the door for Renata. "When was the last time I saw you, beautiful?"

"I don't know, Doc," Renata said as she climbed into the van. "The nights all get sort of smushed together. Don't know what's a month anymore."

After Doc Carla drew Renata's blood, other women began materializing like specters out of darkened doorways. An hour later, Doc Carla had Tucker drive into Brooklyn, to an empty lot near the waterfront, in the industrial badlands around the corner from Bush Terminal. The lot was surrounded by a tall metal fence, with a van-size hole in it.

"I made that hole a year ago," Doc Carla said. "There's another one on the other side, but it's girl-size; that's how they get in here." It had recently rained, and the mud was a cesspool of candy wrappers, gloves, scraps of paper, used condoms, and the amber shards of broken beer bottles. Tucker tried to ignore the pins-and-needles feeling taking over the right side of his face.

"See that clump of ailanthus trees?" Doc Carla said. "Pull the van up under those ugly things, by the Dumpsters."

"The Tree of Heaven," Tucker said, easing the car forward.

Doc Carla laughed darkly. "Can't polish a turd, Tucker."

As they approached the Dumpsters, women began appearing from behind them. A few even came out of the Dumpsters themselves, some of which had been turned on their sides and made into rude shelters. Tucker wanted to put the van into reverse and speed away before he saw any more. Instead, Doc Carla opened the passenger-side door.

"There's Sandy," she said. "God, I've wanted to test her again for three months. Sandy!" The woman wandered over. "Did you know what I meant last time when I said you tested positive for HIV?"

"I don't know which one that is," Sandy said.

"It's one of the newish ones," Doc Carla said. She reached into the glove compartment and handed Sandy the same brochure she had given Tucker the day before when she'd sent him home. "You know I never tell you girls to get off the streets. That's not my call. But Sandy — sweetheart — you gotta stop working, honey, because you're going to start killing people. And please come see me. I can help you."

"But I'm feeling good, Doc. I'm getting fat. I don't think I'm sick anymore."

"Who's watching the baby tonight?"

"Oh, the state took her already," she said.

"What'd you call her?"

"Daphne." When she saw Doc Carla writing this down in her notebook, she added, "But they probably already changed it, Doc."

Later, after they finished their rounds, Tucker stole a glance at Doc Carla as he turned the van onto Houston Street. Her bun had come undone, and the braid now lay across her right shoulder.

"Do you do this every night?" Tucker asked.

"Every night." She looked at him sleepily and reached over to touch his face, half of which now hung slack. "Bell's palsy. Have you had it before?"

"Yeah," Tucker choked out. "But not for a long time. Tonight's the first time in a long time."

They drove down Houston for a while. As

they waited for the light at Avenue A, Doc Carla said, "It's stress that brings it on, the palsy. It won't last long. But you probably know that." She sighed. "This may be too much for your tender sensibilities, honey. It's almost too much for mine, and mine are damn blunt instruments."

A sob swelled in Tucker's throat. All he could manage was a thick, "Please."

He could see her studying him, and tried to hold it together, but his need at that moment was depthless. "Your parents," Doc Carla said. "Do they both hate the gay thing, or is it just your dad?" Tucker tightened his grip on the steering wheel, and she noticed. "I'm sorry, honey. I have a bad habit of letting my mouth run."

Two stoplights later, Doc Carla was asleep, her chin on her chest, and her braid falling over the seat belt and across her shoulders. Having her hand on his face had made Tucker feel less alone. Her question, though he'd left it unanswered, had made him feel human. He felt seen. And now he wanted nothing more than to remain forever in this metal beast loaded with condoms and coupons hurtling down Houston on a string of green lights.

Over the next six months, Tucker worked for Doc Carla after work, driving her van and getting to know the girls on the strolls. He never mentioned the doctor to his boss, and his boss forgot about her. When the film crew began work on a documentary about a cadre of squatters in a Lower East Side tenement, Tucker was tasked with locating archival footage at the Museum of Reclaimed Urban Space. That was when he began writing, in the five-minute stretches it took for the museum's archivists to locate the requested VHS tapes. It had started as a diary, but soon became a story, then a novel.

Little in Tucker's life had come easily, but the novel did: he wrote a complete draft in eight weeks. The filmmaker hooked him up with a literary agent, and the agent sold the book. A year later, it was published as *Unfortunate.* The summer after it came out, Tucker had been named the third tine on a trident of "promising" young male writers, christened thusly by *New York.* But Tucker always knew it was Doc Carla they were interested in, not him — the story, not the writer. He tried to forget this. He found that he couldn't.

Tucker waited to tell Doc Carla about the book until he had a copy to give her; he had dedicated it to her. She was not happy. "You lack imagination and integrity. You mined me for material. You took from these women the last things they had — their dignity and their anonymity. This is real life, Tucker, not art. I thought you cared. You're not an artist. You're a voyeur." She took the keys to the van and stopped answering his phone calls.

At first, Tucker ached for her presence as if she'd been a lover. He couldn't sleep. He barely ate. It faded, over time, but there hung about him always a heaviness. For a while, he lived off his advance, but soon he had to beg the filmmaker for his job back. He spent the next few years logging archival footage, applying for licensing rights, and, later, proving his genius for administrative work, as a unit production manager on several well-received documentaries. He found he was unable to write. Doc Carla was right. He was not an artist.

In 1997, after managing a documentary about the birth of the National Science Foundation, Tucker was offered a job as a speechwriter with the NSF's Office of Legislative and Public Affairs. He'd become friendly with a number of admins during filming, including the head of the NSF, Alexandra Scaletta. Tucker moved to Washington, D.C., where he was told to write pithy, diplomatic, "accessible" speeches for her. After the midterm elections, when the speechwriter position was eliminated due to congressional budget cuts, Scaletta decided to take Tucker with her on a trip to Antarctica. She wanted him to suss out the federal research stations, get status updates from the Program's support contractor, and to meet Karl Martin, VIDS's head of Hostile and Developing Regions.

It was during that first jaunt, a visit that took them to all three U.S. research stations in a single weekend, that Tucker had an hour-long tryst with a welder in the comestibles storeroom at Palmer Station. It was his first physical encounter in three years, and he had tried to pass off his inability to work his way through the man's layers of ECW gear as a seductive burlesque. But eventually the welder grew anxious and wrenched off his overalls, his jeans, and his long underwear, and pulled out his well-insulated dick himself.

Although Tucker knew full well the unexpected rendezvous was a fluke, it colored his perception of Antarctica, infusing it with hope. He applied for the assistant manager position at South Pole Station as soon as he got back to Washington. Despite Scaletta's letter of recommendation, Tucker was turned down the first time, due to a "lack of relevant experience," but after his third try, he received an invitation to VIDS's Denver campus, where he was deemed "exceptionally well-suited" for polar service.

One day, several years later and between Pole assignments, Tucker picked up *The New York Times* and read that the city had shut down Doc Carla at the urging of the American Medical Association and sex worker activists, who found her work with prostitutes greatly concerning. The doctors abhorred the McDonald's coupon swap. The activists didn't like the implications of the tests — they infringed on the sex workers' human dignity. And so, after citing her for numerous violations, the Department of Health had confiscated Doc Carla's van. When she refused to turn over the medical records she kept on the women she tested, they suspended her license and took her to court. No one came to her defense because no one she had cared for had a voice.

To Tucker's relief, there was no awkwardness when he got ahold of her. She acted as if there had never been a break between them. He encouraged her to begin seeing private patients again, but she told him she was done. "This was the only thing that kept my work meaningful, Tucker. They've taken it from me now, and I'm done."

"Well, I need a doctor," Tucker said.

"I told you —"

"It's a tough assignment, though."

There was a pause on the end of the line. "Go on."

"It's a clinic that sees injuries and illness not typically encountered in regular medical practice."

"Go on."

"It's a lonely outpost. Populated by difficult patients. Impossible environment. Far from civilization. Lots of drunks. Lots of red tape. Poorly supplied. Plus, you'll be responsible for any dental emergencies."

"Is it in hell?"

"It's at South Pole."

The woman in Room 221 — Cooper — was lying to him because she hadn't prepared. The other artists and writers knew the game. They'd applied for enough grants and fellowships to have become adept at crafting the bloated prose required of artists in search of funding. But Tucker had been at the game long enough himself to know that the less slick the self-presentation, the better the artist. And then there were the eyes — anxious but penetrating. Tucker wasn't concerned about the brother's suicide, even though the contract psychologist was. She was paid to be. He was paid to be intuitive, and he sensed that Cooper was coming from a place of strength. She wanted to go to Pole for the reason he had gone: to avoid becoming a tragic figure.

Still, she was officially borderline, and Tucker would be expected to present some evidence at the final psych meeting that night which counterindicated the initial red flag. One thing that typically smoothed the way in these cases was a coherent, thoughtful reason for wanting to go to South Pole — one that didn't include heroics or escape fantasies. But so far she had nothing for him and, by the time he was halfway down the hall, he had almost given up on her. Still, he wasn't entirely surprised when he heard her calling his name from the doorway of room 221.

"I've got one," she panted when she reached him. She told him it was a quote. History, Tucker thought. No good, and he told her so. But she insisted, and so he acted as if he was going to write it down.

" 'If you are a brave man, you will do nothing; if you are fearful you may do much, for none but cowards have need to prove their bravery.' Apsley Cherry-Garrard. Of the Scott party." There was no imploring gaze, no clasped hands, no more fear in her eyes — just her frank, open face. "I'm a coward. Let me prove I'm brave."

For some reason, Tucker thought of Doc Carla asking him if he knew how to drive, all those years ago. She seemed to be saying then, as Cooper seemed to be saying now, that if you were a coward and knew you were a coward, you would do fine in this life. Maybe that, along with regular chemical peels, was why Tucker had made it this far.

Doc Carla was sitting on one of the metal steps leading to the clinic, smoking a cigarette through her filthy balaclava. Only her tired face was visible. Tucker kicked some snow over a frozen mound of vomit, and took the seat next to her. Doc Carla glanced down at the puke and took a long drag off her cigarette. "Poor guy almost made it to the can."

Tucker watched a grader grind down the entrance tunnel on its way to the work site and noticed Cooper walking across the long expanse under the Dome, alone, hood off but goggles on. She didn't see him, and he restrained the impulse to call to her, to check on her. She had made herself scarce since getting lost a few days ago in the Utilidors — the underground utility tunnels through which Floyd had been leading

Fingys on a tour. Her humiliation touched something deep in his being.

"The Crud's rampant, Tucker," Doc Carla said. "Got four of 'em beating down my door this morning." She took one last drag off the cigarette, then dropped it in the snow. "But the Crud I can handle." Tucker looked over at the doctor; they were not even to Halloween yet and she already seemed preoccupied. Tucker wanted Doc Carla to remain content, but he still wasn't sure if diagnosing hematomas and treating cracked hands with Super Glue was going to keep her happy.

Doc Carla coughed. "So, you think she must've come here knocked up."

"Maybe. But if she was, she didn't know. She wouldn't have come if she'd known."

"That one would come if her legs and arms were chopped off. And you know it."

Tucker thought back to the incident at the comestibles berms two days earlier that had kicked off this whole drama. He had come into the galley after Pearl had radioed him for help — she and Bonnie were making lamb ragout for dinner later in the week, and they needed two lamb carcasses from the berms, which were located a quarter mile from the station. When he'd arrived in the kitchen, Marcy and Cooper were slouched over the metal prep table, having also been summoned. Cooper had been on house-mouse duty all week, a rotating job each Polie undertook at least twice a season that had him or her at the beck and call of the galley.

"About time," Marcy snapped, peevish.

" 'He who forces time is pushed back by time; he who yields to time finds time on his side,' " Tucker replied. "Talmud."

"I don't care what he said, I just don't like sitting here with my thumb up my ass when I could be out helping Bozer on A3." Marcy was Bozer's right-hand woman, a skilled heavy machine operator with four winters under her belt, more than any woman in polar history. She wore stained Carhartts, her dishwater-blond hair tucked into a rainbow-colored knit cap, and she could replace the suspension system on a thirty-year-old tractor with her eyes closed.

"You're in a sweetheart of a mood, Marce," Tucker said.

"I just want to get this show on the road," she growled.

Ten minutes later, Tucker was straddling a snowmobile, his arms around Marcy's waist, with Cooper seated behind him. The engine roared as they sped out to the comestibles berms, rounded mounds of snow that stretched like dikes along the plowed paths. There were berms for many things: wooden spools, obsolete scientific equipment, construction debris. Tucker remembered seeing the berms from the air on his first plane ride in, laid out like Morse code in the snow.

Marcy suddenly gunned the engines and pulled the snowmobile sharply into a doughnut, sending up a sheet of ice crystals. Tucker felt Cooper tugging desperately on his parka in an effort to stay on. When Marcy pulled up to the berm, she braked hard, and Cooper was thrown off the snowmobile before it had come to a stop. To Tucker's great relief, she got to her feet, brushed the snow from her parka, and headed to the berms without even glancing back, barely limping.

Tucker looked at Marcy. "That wasn't very nice."

"Just wanted to give the Fingy a thrill," Marcy replied.

"Or a compound fracture."

Suddenly, Marcy's shoulders convulsed, and a great wave seemed to roll up her back. She listed to the right and vomited onto the ice. Tucker saw Cooper turn at the sound of Marcy's retching. Veterans seemed immune to the Crud, and Tucker had never known

Marcy to be sick. He had a bad feeling about this, but knew it was better to wait on Marcy than to press her. He waved Cooper back toward the berms. A few minutes later, he joined her, and together they chopped away at the snow and ice surrounding the lamb carcasses. "She okay?" Cooper asked. Tucker nodded, but said nothing.

After a few minutes, Marcy finally got herself upright and motored over to the berm. Tucker and Cooper dragged the two lamb carcasses to the cargo hauler attached to Marcy's snowmobile. Without a word, Marcy revved the engine, and as Tucker and Cooper climbed onto the back, she casually vomited again.

By the time they were all walking through the galley, though, Marcy had regained some strength, and even joked with some of the Nailheads on her way to the bathroom. Both Tucker and Cooper followed Marcy into the restroom, however.

"Get this parka off me," she said. Tucker clawed at the Escher landscape of zippers on the heavy coat and yanked it off, just in time for Marcy to launch herself toward the toilet. He backed up against the wall until he was almost a part of it, but Cooper headed straight for the stall and gently pulled Marcy's hair out of her face. This was good, Tucker thought. First, she'd done a tuck-and-roll after being thrown from the snowmobile and hadn't blinked. Now she was helping Marcy puke with dignity. She could be useful. It was good to be useful, especially for a Fingy. Especially for an artist Fellow. Good, good, good! As his thoughts devolved into one-word declaratives, a bigger thought wormed its way through the cracks: Marcy didn't have the Crud. Marcy was knocked up.

As she retched, he kept his eyes fixed on a Robert Crumb Tommy the Toilet poster taped on the wall above the sink. *Tommy Toilet sez: Don't forget to wipe your ass, folks.*

Tommy the Toilet was who Tucker thought of now as he listened to Doc Carla tell him that she'd have to send Marcy home. "NPQ," she added. He winced. No acronym in the polar lexicon was more feared than this — Not Physically Qualified. He knew sending Marcy off the ice was their only course of action, but he also knew that an NPQ on her record would make it very hard for her to return to the ice. If the cause was recorded as pregnancy, she'd never be back.

"Who have you told?" Tucker asked Doc Carla.

"Who have I told? I'm a vault. I've told

no one. But she has to go."

Doc Carla waited for Tucker to reply. When he didn't, she said, "I'm glad we agree." She shifted on the metal steps leading to her clinic and craned her neck to look at the frost fronds hanging from the ceiling of the Dome. "Ah."

"What?"

"I'm just thinking how fun it'll be telling her she's going home. The woman has nothing in life except this shithole." Tucker thought but did not say that this was one thing he and Marcy had in common.

After leaving Doc Carla, Tucker took a walk around the outside perimeter of the station to think. He stopped at the construction site for a while to watch Bozer and his team, which included Marcy, assemble the mezzanine stairs to the A3 module. He wondered what it would be like running the new and improved South Pole Station while watching this one sink under the snow. For a moment, he was overcome by sadness.

Just beyond the site, he saw Cooper and Sal talking out on the road to the Dark Sector. He almost smiled; he liked when the young people got together. Back in Denver, Sal had announced that he was planning on celibacy this time around. Everyone knew how much he had at stake this season, even those Polies who had failed science. Tucker had made a point during training to explain to the support staff that this was an unusually important season for the Dark Sector — one cosmology experiment in particular was in the final stages of long-term research that could possibly confirm or destroy the inflationary theory of the universe. It was, Sal had told Tucker, unprecedented that physicists researching two different models would work on the same experiment: Sal and his team from Princeton were working jointly with the Kavli team from Stanford, both looking for something called b-modes.

The Californians, who moved about the station as a unit, were disciples of Sal's father, the great physicist John Brennan. They were Big Bangers. Sal, on the other hand, had thrown his fortunes in with another pioneer scientist who fervently felt that the evidence pointed toward something called the cyclic model, in which there was no Big Bang, but rather a series of collisions between membranes — the universe being one of those "branes" and the other being just a hop, skip, and a jump across an invisible dimension. There was more, of course, but Tucker had forbid further discussion when Sal started talking about "prePlanckian predictions of dust."

The radio squealed. It was Comms. Dwight shouted something — every other word was lost in static. But Tucker had heard enough to get the gist of things: there was a phone call for him in the office, and, as all phone calls to the station manager typically were, it was urgent.

"I've got two unhappy congressmen on my ass," Karl Martin said when Tucker finally picked up the satellite phone in the communications office. "You need to open the kimono and tell me what the hell is going on with this — what's his name?" Tucker could hear Karl searching through some papers.

· "Pavano. Frank. There have been some minor tensions between the scientists, but nothing out of the ordinary," Tucker said. "Standard territorial posturing."

"Well, I don't know what the hell that means, Tucker, but these guys, they floated the term 'hostile working environment' — at which point I brought in Legal. What's going on down there?"

"I've received no complaints. The grantee has been assigned a lab and is taking full advantage of the facilities." Tucker chose not to mention the T-shirts, the petition, and the ruthless ostracism at meals. He heard voices in the background and the moist sound of a sweaty palm squeezing the mouthpiece of the phone. "I've gotta run into this meeting," Karl said, "but get Scaletta on the horn — she's been getting an earful, too, but she's not returning my calls. See if you can put this fire out."

Tucker had tried for months to get Scaletta's input on the situation with Dr. Frank Pavano, but the NSF had remained silent on the matter. Tucker had thought it wise to add diversity workshops to the mandatory training for research techs who supported the major experiments. Turned out it was far easier for white male scientists to accept colleagues with dark skin or vaginas or both than it was for them to accept the presence of a climate denier in their midst. In fact, all the scientists, regardless of ethnicity or gender identity, hated Pavano, even before meeting him. Meeting him personally, it seemed, was beside the point. As a result, resistance to the training sessions tailored to prepare the support staff for Pavano's arrival was intense, and buy-in was non-existent. To make things worse, Pavano had been unable to secure a research tech, which meant he'd be responsible for all aspects of his research project, including operations, repairs, and soul-crushing amounts of paperwork.

Pavano himself had been given extra counseling by one of the senior psychologists, and when Tucker had asked how it'd gone, she'd said, "He's basically autistic."

"That," Tucker had replied, "will work to his benefit."

It was only when the two congressmen who'd sponsored Pavano's efforts to get to Pole held a joint news conference that Tucker received a call from Scaletta.

"I dropped the ball on this one." She sighed. "Bayless and Calhoun promised to keep the grant on the down-low. Now they're on fucking *Fox & Friends* talking about methane isotope variability in deep ice cores — a concept I can assure you they don't understand, much less pronounce correctly."

"I think we have it under control," Tucker said.

"I knew you would. But I do need to say this: it's vitally important to the Program and to the NSF itself that Dr. Pavano's research is unimpeded, and that all previously agreed-upon resources be made available to him." She paused. "I know that's not technically your purview —"

"I understand."

"I'd also like to minimize media interest in his research. I'm hoping this will die down."

After handing the sat phone back to Dwight, Tucker stared at the collection of *Star Wars* figurines that the comms tech had arranged fussily on his desk. He imagined Dwight reverently bubble-wrapping Yoda and Darth Vader before placing them in the corners of his duffel bag for the trip to Pole. The thought cheered him briefly.

"Everything okay?" Dwight asked.

Tucker picked up Darth Vader. "Do you think he was a good manager?"

"He commanded authority naturally," Dwight replied. "He asked penetrating questions and listened to stakeholders." When Tucker raised an eyebrow at this, Dwight conceded that perhaps Darth Vader wasn't all that good at listening to stakeholders.

Instead of heading out of Comms and back to the admin pod, where he had hundreds of e-mails waiting for responses, Tucker decided to head upstairs, to the library. He found it deserted. He flipped on the fluorescents and walked over to the bookshelves. The maintenance specialist's alphabetization efforts had mostly held, although he did see David Baldacci living with Stephen King.

Tucker let his fingers dance over the

wrinkled paperbacks one by one until they reached a glossy, unbroken spine. He knew which book it was by touch alone. Slowly, he pulled it from between Baldwin and Bradbury. It was clear that it still hadn't been read. As he always did, Tucker turned the book over to look at the author photo, a broody Ettlinger. It seemed like a daguerreotype — limpid, light eyes; snug-fitting white undershirt; a subtly flexed bicep; airbrushed skin the color of weak coffee. The man in the photo was unknown to Tucker now.

DEFENDED NEIGHBORHOODS AND DEGRADATION CEREMONIES IN REMOTE POLAR COMMUNITIES

Denise Notebloom
Department of Sociology, Columbia University
New York, NY 10025

Abstract

Utilizing eight months of direct observation of the sociocultural issues inherent in prolonged isolation and confinement in a remote location, this paper examines the process of psychosocial adaption to an outsider whose presence enhances the in-group's mechanical solidarity. In a social environment in which "monopolistic access to particular kinds of knowledge" (Merton, 1972) is a hallmark feature and *Gesellschaft* a guiding principle, the arrival of a scientist whose views are in direct opposition to mainstream scientific opinion presents a unique opportunity to observe in-group/out-group dynamics. Based on observations recorded in the context of the four distinct characteristics of human behavior unique to the "polar sojourner" — seasonal, situational, social, and salutogenic (Palinkas,

2002) — the in-group's foundational *Gesellschaft*, when confronted with an outsider whose presence threatens the social ecology, transforms into mechanical solidarity. This is manifested in a more vigorous defense of "neighborhoods" against the outsider, as well as more frequent degradation ceremonies. I argue that such strategies are strained to the breaking point in reestablishing social equilibrium.

Keywords: *ANTARCTICA, MICROCULTURES, ADAPTATION, COPING*

THE DANCE OF THE ANXIOUS PENGUIN

The Gore-Tex mitten Cooper was trying to sketch was in bad shape — a small rip discharged yellowed insulation material while the tip looked as if it had been dipped in barbecue sauce ten years earlier. Cooper had found it in the skua pile — a repository for random shit abandoned by current and former Polies. Named for the opportunistic brown seabirds that haunted the Antarctic coasts, *skua* functioned at Pole as both a verb and a noun: you could skua something — either by adding it to or removing it from the skua stream — or you could seek out skua. At McMurdo, the skua took up an entire shed. At Pole, it was located in a cardboard box. Cooper had spotted the mitten after breakfast, and, artistic desperation clouding her judgment, had seen in it great potential to create a work that "accurately reflects your time spent at South Pole," per the NSF directive. As she looked at her first attempts, she felt that although it was shitty work, it was at least better than the fourteen sketches of her own mitten she'd done up to this point. When she returned stateside, she'd have to present her output to a joint National Science Foundation/National Endowment for the Arts committee. She suspected that a study of various polar mittens would not suffice, not that she wasn't trying. She'd completed one panel of a planned triptych — of mittens.

She was trying to remember what grass looked like when someone knocked on the door. She found the *Alarmism and Climate Change Hoax*–reading scientist from the galley on the other side. "Hi," she said.

"I realized too late that we did not exchange names the other day. Tucker told me your name and where to find you. I'm Frank Pavano." The name sounded vaguely familiar to Cooper, like the name of an Italian food company based in Weehawken, but she couldn't place it.

She pulled the door open a little. "Well, Frank Pavano, do you want to come in?"

"I don't want to interrupt your work," he said, glancing over her shoulder.

"There's no work going on here, I assure you." Cooper held the door open wider, and Pavano strode past her, directly to her easel.

Cooper was unused to the frankness of his interest in her art — most people looked everywhere but the work. Instead, Pavano leaned closer to her canvas to study the Gore-Tex mitten drawing she'd transferred from the sketchbook. "You seem to have an interest in protest art. Capitalist sublimation specifically."

"You got that from a mitten?"

He shrugged. "I took some art criticism courses in college to break up the biochem curriculum. But I got C's, so you can take my observation for what it's worth."

"It's worth a C," Cooper said, "speaking as someone familiar with C's." She smiled, and to her relief Pavano smiled back. "You're a Beaker, right? Sorry — scientist. What are you doing down here?"

"Broadly, I'm studying methane isotope variability in deep ice cores," Pavano replied, still studying the canvas. "My early career work was in heliophysics, but I've cultivated an interest in climatology over the years. I received some unexpected funding this year to go a bit outside the scope of my previous research." He scratched the side of his nose with delicate precision. "What about *your* objectives while you're down here? What are the parameters? Do you have to deliver a statement of results?"

Before Cooper could answer, someone knocked on the door. She glanced at her watch. "That'll be Denise. My shift is almost up. Do you want to grab lunch?"

Pavano seemed alarmed by the invitation. "No, I have to get back to the lab. I just wanted to formally introduce myself. On reflection, I realized I'd repaid your interest and kindness with a hasty departure, and I thought I'd apologize." He opened the door, and slipped past Denise wordlessly. A moment later, he reappeared. "Thank you for the invitation, though."

Denise raised an eyebrow at Cooper as she walked in. "I'm curious to see how, or if, he is going to integrate into the scientific community," she said, as she pulled out her laptop and set it heavily on the desk.

"He's nerdy enough to fit in," Cooper said.

Denise shook her head. "No, he's a walking example of the Black Sheep Effect. In cultural groups, like the one here, people will upgrade certain group members based on culturally desirable traits or likability. Look at Marcy, the heavy machine operator, for instance. Because years on the ice are culturally valuable, Marcy is a high-status individual. Off the ice, that might not be true." She opened her laptop, and Cooper saw the background photo was set to a photo of Bozer standing on a beach in thermal socks and sandals. "The flip side is that the 'in-group' will keep group members who threaten the group's cohesion on the outside, making them into a separate out-group. A black sheep."

"Why would this guy be a black sheep?"

Denise looked at Cooper, confused. "A climate-change skeptic working at the world's foremost climatology and atmospheric science research site is not likely to be warmly welcomed by the existing group."

So *Alarmism and the Climate Change Hoax* wasn't the opposition research material Cooper had assumed it to be. It was actually research material. *Pavano.* Suddenly all those outraged comments on the "South Pole Pals" message board she'd scanned six months earlier made sense. "Wait, is this the guy who's trying to prove that the ice under the Pole isn't all that old and could totally fall in line with the whole Noah's Flood thing?"

Denise stared back at her blandly. "No, I believe that's the working hypothesis of a biblical climatologist in Australia whose name I don't recall. I don't know much about Pavano's research yet, only that his findings set him in direct opposition to the vast majority of climate researchers around the world. The rumors surrounding the provenance of his funding only add fuel to the fire."

Everything was coming together now, and Cooper was cheered by the fact that some of the weird social interactions she'd witnessed were starting to seem a little less puzzling. At breakfast a week earlier, for example, people had been talking about how one of the head climate researchers, a paleoclimatologist from Madison named Sri, kept "forgetting" to get "the Denier" a username and password for the West Antarctic Ice Sheet data server. When Sri and his team had hopped a plane for the research camp — known as the Divide — they had removed the Denier's name from the manifest. It was treated as a joke, and no one was disciplined. But the Denier — Pavano, Cooper now realized — had contacted his congressional sponsor, a Republican senator Cooper thought she'd heard of named Bayless, who promptly called his contact at the NSF, and Pavano was immediately shuttled out to the camp and given full access to the ice archives, the lab, and, at Bayless's request, Sri's research site.

Cooper dropped her brushes in a can of turpentine. "Well, it sounds complicated," she said as Denise sat down to begin work.

"All social interaction is complicated, of course, but down here it's even more so, which is what makes my job so fun," Denise replied. "I'm waiting to see if metaphorical effects are amplified at a place like Pole. You know, the idea that holding a cup of hot tea makes people feel warmly toward others, or that a person in a high place, like a cherry picker, is seen as being situated farther up the hierarchy. Last year, Lee and Schwartz found that when exposed to a fishy smell, people actually grow suspicious." Denise glanced over at Cooper. "In sociological terms, you might say that Frank Pavano is a just-opened can of tuna."

A very slight smile was the only indication that Denise had made her first joke.

Back at the Jamesways, Cooper found a note under her door from Birdie indicating that there was an artists' meeting in thirty minutes. Cooper groaned, but she knew Birdie was counting on her to be there. Before leaving her room, she saw her *Terra Nova* sketch had fallen from the canvas wall, where she'd pinned it. She set it on her desk and studied it for a moment. Her sketches were often the products of procrastination, but Cooper kept coming back to this one

— so many times, in fact, that she had completed it. Who knew what it meant? All Cooper knew was that looking at it made her feel better. She pulled on her balaclava and parka for the trek back to the station.

As she hurried out, she accidentally nudged her pee can with her boot. She heard sloshing and realized she'd have to empty it. If she waited another day, she could have a biological disaster on her hands. Pee cans were one of the many secrets veterans kept from Fingys, but after Cooper's act of civil disobedience with the Swedes, she'd apparently garnered some social capital; Pearl had left an empty #10 can, once filled with industrial-grade cling peaches, outside the door of Cooper's room, with a note thanking her for not selling her out to Simon. Now Cooper no longer had to venture outside the Jamesway to use the bathroom, which was located in a separate structure a hundred yards east. However, she still had to walk over there to empty the can into the communal pee barrel.

Reluctantly, she picked up the can with her mittens and pushed the door open with her shoulder. She immediately collided with a man dressed in full ECW gear and watched as at least a quarter cup of her urine splashed onto his bunny boots. His woolen face mask and neck gaiter muffled his angry roar, and Cooper hurried past him before he could get a good look at her, grateful for the anonymity provided by the balaclava and the darkness of the hall.

After emptying the can into a barrel and tucking it into a corner to avoid having to return to the Jamesway, she turned to the warped mirror, and cleared a swath through the condensation. It was time to see how she was faring in terms of polar aesthetics. The rule of thumb, she now knew, was that someone who was a "five" off the ice was easily an "Antarctic Ten." Cooper squinted at her reflection: her infected eye, which had looked like a gelatinous bead for a week, was totally healed. Her hair was so oily it had darkened a few shades — two-minute showers twice a week meant thorough shampooing was now a luxury. Her shaggy bangs fell across her eyes. As she stared at her reflection, she felt she embodied the very definition of the word *mediocre.* She noticed a waffle crumb in the corner of her mouth, and as she flicked it free, her brother's face suddenly seemed to inhabit hers, staring back at her through her own eyes. She gripped the sides of the sink to steady her suddenly weak knees and quickly closed her eyes against the image.

"You meditating or something?" Cooper opened her eyes to see Marcy.

Cooper brushed her bangs out of her eyes. "Sort of." It wasn't three days ago that she'd held Marcy's hair off her face as she'd puked into a toilet. Cooper thought she looked better.

"Well, for a second there, I thought you were doing the rosary," Marcy replied. She seemed as if she wanted to say more. Talking to Marcy was helping. Studying her face helped even more — analyzing the angles of another face obscured David's — and Cooper saw that although Marcy was only in her late thirties or early forties, her skin was already worn and craggy from her cold weather adventures. Yet her mouth had a sweet downward droop to it, like a baby's pouchy lips. Her small eyes were almost as dark as Cooper's, and the lines that radiated from them made her look like a happy Buddhist deity. But right now, the eyes were sad.

"Thanks for the other day," Marcy said. "It wasn't my finest moment."

"No worries. I've had my share of not-fine moments, too. You're feeling better?"

"Yep, fit as a fiddle," she said tightly. "You got your costume ready for tonight?"

"Costume?"

"The Halloween party?"

"Is that tonight?"

"Well, it *is* Halloween."

"I lose track of the days."

"Just wait until winter, honey."

"I don't have a costume."

"Scrounge one up from skua, no biggie."

Marcy reached past Cooper and plunged her hand in the plastic bin containing condoms that was replenished daily. "Tonight's the night to land an ice-husband," Marcy said. "If you want one." Cooper thought she saw the sheen of tears in Marcy's eyes, but they were quickly blinked away. She dropped the condoms into Cooper's hand. "Get laid, honey. It takes the edge off."

Like everything else at South Pole Station, the gym was located in a trailer. On the outside door was a handwritten poster announcing the first meeting of the American Society of Polar Philatelists: *The Harvis Collection in Da' House at Our Next Meeting! Be There or Be Filled with Aching Regret.*

Inside, Birdie had arranged the folding chairs in a circle. Cooper took the one directly beneath the net-free basketball hoop, and watched as the historical novelist and the interpretative dancer walked in together, not quite holding hands. The literary novelist entered alone, listening to his Discman.

"Does anyone want to run the meetings?" Birdie asked, brandishing a clipboard. "The Program insists on a group leader." No one replied, and Birdie tried to hide his pleasure at taking the helm.

"Could I say something before we start?" the interpretive dancer asked, and Birdie reluctantly granted her the floor. "I'd like to start off this meeting with a haiku that I believe may put this whole strange adventure in perspective.

"The man pulling radishes
"Pointed the way
"With a radish."

Birdie looked over at Cooper, but she turned her gaze to the climbing wall to avoid his eyes; she understood that laughter would diminish the power of the radish. Still, the dancer grew frosty at the lack of appreciation, and said crisply, "What are we supposed to be doing at these meetings anyway? I'd like to get a handle on what's expected of me. I tend toward anxiety, and anxiety is not conducive to creativity."

"It can be," the literary novelist said, fiddling with his Discman. The dancer looked at him with disdain and flicked her long braid over her shoulder.

"Yes, well, it isn't for me," she said.

"So far as I can tell," Birdie said, "the Program wants us to meet in an official way once a month and to keep minutes, and then submit them to the officers at the end of this adventure. Why don't we go around the circle and talk about what we're working on?"

"My work deals with the cartographic imperative," the literary novelist said. The dancer leaned over her knees to look at him.

"Cartographic imperative? Like, the desire to map things?"

"Yeah, exactly. Like, why do the people who come down here feel like they have to, you know, name it? Or claim it for their country? I'm really interested in what is behind that motivation."

"And what's the title of your book?" Birdie asked.

"I'm calling it *Mapping the Breath.*"

"Profound," the dancer said, punctuating her point with the kind of dreamy sigh she'd expected for the radish haiku.

"Yeah, I was thinking that, like, mapping the breath is pretty much impossible. And cartography in general is such a hubristic endeavor that it's almost as ridiculous."

"But the book itself sounds self-aggrandizing," Cooper said, before she could stop herself. The tenor of the room changed at once, like a writing workshop suddenly infused with candor. "I mean, at least the title does," Cooper added. Birdie shook his head slowly, stifling a smile. The literary novelist, loose-limbed and squinty-eyed, squinted at her harder. "Yeah, no, I want feedback," he said. "I mean, that's good. In many ways the desire to put a cartographic imprint on land that belongs to all humankind finds a parallel in the canine impulse to mark its territory."

The door to the gym opened and Denise walked in, followed by a blast of cold air. Her glasses instantly turned opaque with steam. "Sorry I'm late," she said as she pulled off her hood. "I'm Denise."

"She's a sociologist," Cooper added as Denise wrestled off her parka.

"I was told this would be a closed meeting," the dancer said stiffly. "I have no interest in being studied."

Denise's plain face radiated serenity. "You needn't worry — my research interests lie elsewhere, though I do have a casual interest in the Artists and Writers contingent because they have, historically, been even more isolated due to their low social status at the station."

"Low social status?" the dancer asked.

A sound somewhere between a snort and a cat trying to clear a hairball exploded from the historical novelist. "So we're pariahs," he said acidly, picking at a mole on his neck.

"Perhaps I was a little too general."

"But low social status means no one likes us," the dancer said.

"Well, in layman's terms, I suppose that would be a fair characterization," Denise said. "Though the term *superfluous* would be more accurate."

"This makes me really anxious," the dancer said to the historical novelist.

"Put it in your work," he said soothingly.

Cooper smiled. *Put it in your work.* This had always been her father's standing advice. Maybe this was the standing advice all exasperated relatives or spouses gave to agitated artists. My first date ever stood me up, Dad. *Put it in your work.* I made a really bad decision having to do with a vending-machine salesman/artisanal tobacconist/urban shaman last night. *Put it in your work.* And it was true, Cooper thought. You *could* put it in your work, and you did, but then the work itself became nothing more than a hall of mirrors, reflecting back all the crappy things that had happened, or which you had made happen, in your life. That was why she'd stopped painting when David was sick. Who needed a mirror when the only thing reflected was loss after loss? She dropped her hand into her pocket, her fingers searching for the vial. She found it and ran her thumb over the serrated edges of its childproof cap.

"Cooper?" Birdie said. She withdrew her hand quickly and looked up. The artists were watching her expectantly. Next to her, Denise scribbled something in her notebook. Out of the corner of her eye, Cooper saw *Thousand-yard stare — already?* written in the margin.

"Sorry," she said. "So, I'm a painter, though since I got here, I'm not sure anymore." There were a couple of appreciative chuckles. "Actually, I probably shouldn't even call myself an artist. A professor once told me that you can't be cynical and artistic, that these traits are diametrically opposed. He said I was cynical. And I guess I am." Hard, actually — "hardened by premature success" were her professor's exact words. Artists had to be porous, he'd said, like sponges, capable of soaking things up and releasing them. If you were a stone, you could do nothing but take up space. And while a sponge could become a stone, a stone could never become a sponge. "So

167

I'm finding the polar landscape challenging to capture because I don't want to do dead-explorer stuff or glaciers, and I definitely don't want to go the route of putting incongruous, unexpected man-made stuff on the ice, like I've seen in other polar art. That feels sort of didactic."

"I actually think that sounds interesting," the literary novelist said. "Like painting a Walmart on the polar cap to make a point?"

"Too obvious," Cooper said.

The literary novelist looked at his nails. "I didn't realize visual artists were interested in subtlety."

As the conversation continued around her, Cooper began wishing that someone *would* appear and point the way — with a radish, a compass, a finger, it didn't matter. She just wanted someone to tell her how to move forward.

After the meeting ended, Cooper stepped out of the gym, and saw a commotion near the door of a construction office at the other end of the trailer. A knot of people, including Pearl, were doing a little dance. Cooper noticed Sal standing with them. "I'll come to the recital but I'm not taking the class," she heard him say.

"What's happening?" Cooper called down

to him.

He seemed surprised to see her, but quickly assumed a look of nonchalance. "Hey, it's Frida Kahlo," he said, walking toward her. "Make yourself useful and paint me something I won't want to drop-kick to Vostok."

"Something with tater tots?" Cooper replied.

"Oh, if you got into tot art and you were any good, I'd marry you."

"Why are the girls all excited?"

"Dave's in from McMurdo."

"Dave?"

"Dave's dance class? The most popular rec class in the history of the Program?" He noted Cooper's skepticism. "It's kind of a big deal. Starts Thursday, if you're interested."

"Nothing could induce me to go to Dave's dance class."

"Fingy, when you can't walk your dog, mow your lawn, get a coffee at the place where you know the guy who makes it, you will begin to find dance class with Dave appealing. And if Dave doesn't show up for the dance class, you'll go apeshit. You have the expectation that he will be there and he better well keep his fucking commitments, because Dave's dance class is all you'll have to hold on to down here once those doors close for the winter."

All this bluster, but he was grinning. "And now I have to keep my own commitment to show up at the Smoke Bar and get wasted before the Halloween party. Adios." He turned and began walking away.

"Where's the Smoke Bar?"

"Winter-overs only," Sal called over his shoulder.

"Come on."

He stopped walking. "All right, Fingy. Follow me."

Smoke Bar was located on the second floor of the galley trailer. Cooper had heard about the Smoke Bar, but had never been able to suss out its exact location. All the summer workers and most of the scientists congregated at the other bar, 90 South, which was the Señor Frog's of Antarctica. Smoke Bar was Chumley's — back when you had to be somebody to get in. Gaining entry to the Smoke Bar was, Cooper understood, a privilege.

When they reached the top of the metal stairs, Sal blocked the door and turned to look at Cooper. "You're about to enter a very delicate ecosystem, so when we get in, go sit with Tucker, who will be drinking vodka neat at the table under the dart board. I'll introduce you to the Beakers when it makes sense. They get excited and weird around ladies, seeing as they're in such short supply here. I have to manage their expectations." Cooper knew Sal was bullshitting, but she didn't mind. He pushed the door open with his shoulder and let Cooper enter.

As she walked in, The Smithereens' "A Girl Like You" was playing at max volume. Cooper took in the foosball table, a disco ball, and the stripper pole. Twinkling fairy lights hung from the ceiling, along with at least twenty purple Crown Royal sacks, below which ashy clouds of cigarette smoke created a small weather system. The bar itself was a piece of plywood on crates, behind which a man in a George W. Bush mask was dispensing drinks from a series of mini-fridges lined up against the wall. Everyone bought their own liquor at the station store, or shipped their own booze down to Pole before the season started. Cooper had settled for the cheap New Zealand beer that came in cases on every flight in, but her supply was down at 90 South with the rest of the Fingys'.

Cooper spotted Tucker at a table with some galley workers and assorted Wastees — the people who handled garbage and sewage — and she and Sal silently parted ways.

"I know a guy whose credit card was stolen," a guy without a chair was telling the table. "The thief ordered a really expensive cell phone and also sent him a Lobstergram. Guy cancels the card, and Lobstergram didn't want the lobster back. The guy was allergic to shellfish so he gave it to a friend." This raised no response, and no one offered him a chair.

"Anyway," a tall man with Cher-like hair and a sparse, preadolescent-style mustache said. "As I was saying before I was so rudely interrupted: you play the Antarctica card off the ice, you're laid ninety-nine times out of a hundred."

"Doesn't work for women," a dark-haired woman said, her feet on his lap. Cooper recognized her as Pearl's boss, Bonnie, the head cook.

"Why?" her cloak-wearing companion asked.

"No man sitting at a bar is gonna get his dick hard if a woman tells him she's just back from the ice chip, except maybe another Polie. And in that case, it's just a reflex."

Tucker took Cooper's arm and simultaneously pulled out a chair from another table.

"Congratulations on gaining entry," he whispered. Then to the group, he said: "This is my friend, Cooper." Cooper cringed. The first thing she'd understood when she'd arrived was that introductions were for the desperate; the fewer you required, the stronger you appeared. Pole was a place where people simply became known.

"You tell us you don't have friends, Tucker," Bonnie said, "that you're a lone wolf."

"Well, Bonnie, I'm starting fresh," Tucker said. Cher then introduced himself as Dwight, "the wizard-god of Logistics and Comms." Too late, Cooper realized Tucker had slipped away.

"Judging by your attire," Dwight said, "you are neither Beaker nor manager, neither galley slave nor Wastee. Reasonably attractive, yet with no obvious male companion." He paused and looked over at Bonnie. "Wow, this is exactly like cosplay."

"No, I recognize her. You were in the kitchen the other day," Bonnie said, scrutinizing Cooper's face. "I think you're a VIDS psychologist, trying to blend in with the population."

"I'm a painter," Cooper replied.

"They sent people down to paint the walls?" Dwight asked, incredulous.

"Artist," Cooper clarified. "The NSF sends artists down each year to do . . . whatever."

Bonnie reached across the table and offered Cooper her hand. "Well, let me formally introduce myself — I'm Bonnie, the head cook." Cooper took Bonnie's chapped hand for a shake, but Bonnie grasped Cooper's and pulled it toward her, caressing it. "Dwight, honey, feel her skin." Dwight ran a bored finger over the top of Cooper's hand and withdrew it, nodding.

"So pink and soft," Bonnie cooed.

"That's how we find the Fingys when there's a blackout and we need fresh meat," Dwight said in a monotone. "Their soft, infant-like skin."

Cooper excused herself to beg a beer off George W. Bush. She cursed softly when she noticed, again too late, that the man sitting to her left was Floyd. "Who's more heroic," he asked his companion, brandishing a glass of whiskey, "a woman doc who got a common disease, but who was also trained to deal with it, or the pilot who successfully landed a Herc in the middle of a polar winter to evac her?" He paused here, letting his rage build. "You tell me which demands more bravery. You tell me who risked their life. Do you even know the pilot's name?"

"Dude, I'm just trying to have a drink," the guy said wearily, pushing his fingers in and out of a plastic jack-o'-lantern's mouth.

"Major George R. McAllister," Floyd said. "You remember that name." He glanced over at Cooper. "You, too — George R. McAllister. Oh, hey, I know you. You're the McMurtry apologist. Who the hell let you in?"

Luckily, death metal began blaring through the speakers at that moment and Floyd skipped over to the stripper pole and started gyrating. While everyone guffawed at this, Cooper noticed Sal was watching her, but he quickly looked away. She watched Floyd for a while — he was surprisingly agile — and finished the Canterbury ale Bush had loaned her, but it gave her a headache. She was about to leave when Birdie walked in, his thick glasses reflecting the lights from the revolving disco ball. He carried a bottle of Dewar's bearing his name on a piece of masking tape and two highball glasses pinched between his thumb and fingers. He took a seat next to Cooper.

"Who told you?" she asked.

"Told me what?"

"About this place — who let you in?"

Birdie smiled and opened the bottle. He

poured out two measures, then handed a glass over to Cooper. "She did." He nodded toward Pearl, who was throwing darts with a couple of dining assistants.

"You're kidding me."

"This strains your credulity? I'm not offended. It strains mine. Look at her. She's gorgeous." Cooper looked over at Pearl. For the first time, the pink bandanna was off, and Cooper saw that both sides of her delicately shaped head were shaved to the skin, leaving only a thatch of blond hair, which had been pulled up into a ponytail. She was wearing a black headband with glittery cat ears, and when she laughed, Cooper could see what Birdie meant.

Cooper clinked her glass to Birdie's. "Cheers."

"How's it going, then?" Birdie asked. "The painting, I mean."

"Mittens," Cooper said. "All I've got is mittens. And there's no way to justify that as art." Not that she hadn't tried. *The mitten is a talisman, an image of worship in a place where god is dead. It's a study of both the humility of the simple garment and the hubris of our belief that it protects us from this savage continent.*

"You?" Cooper asked.

"I'm having a hard time pulling things

together myself. Now that I'm here, Bowers grows elusive." Cooper could feel Sal's eyes on her again, but didn't risk a look in his direction this time.

"I can't imagine caring enough about a person I've never met to spend years researching his life and writing about him," she said. "You'd have to be obsessed."

Birdie nodded. "Biography is not a genre for the lukewarm. Bowers was just a sledger, like me, head down, strap over his shoulder, the only one on the Scott expedition without skis. He was optimistic to the point of being demented. Cherry said there was nothing subtle about him. He wasn't complex like Cherry, who was a head case. He's not intrinsically interesting like Scott either, nor a hero like Titus, and thank god he wasn't a narcissistic ass like Teddy Evans. There are no scandals to unearth on this fellow, no dark side. I suppose I'll need to find a dark side. I'm told we all have them."

"Except me," Pearl chirped as she passed. She leaned down between Cooper's and Birdie's chairs and slung an arm around them both. "Dark sides are for moons, not people."

Birdie nearly snapped his neck watching Pearl continue on to the bar top. Cooper told Birdie she had to hit the john. She passed Sal's table on the way to the restroom, and he reached out as she walked by and hooked his fingers through one of the belt loops on her Carhartts. He was leaning back, his chair resting precariously against the wall — sodden, and more attractive for it, a feat Cooper had never seen achieved before. Next to him, his Russian cohort, Alek, looked up at her with bleary eyes.

"Where you going, strange person?" Sal said.

"To the bathroom."

"I come with?" Alek said thickly.

"Sure, that's going to happen."

Alek fist-pumped toward the sky. "She says this will happen."

Sal squeezed Alek's shoulder with his free hand. "Alek's drunk on moonshine."

"Samogon," Alek growled.

"Sorry — samogon. It's a moonshine they make in the Urals. NSF thought it was isopropyl alcohol and let it pass. You met Alek, right? You can call him Rasputin."

Alek frowned. "Always Rasputin. Why not Gorky or Pushkin?"

"Because you're an evil monk, not a literary genius," Sal replied.

Alek extended his middle finger and thrust it skyward. "Why do I allow you?" he bellowed.

"What do you actually do, Alek?" Cooper asked.

"I am here to help Sal win Nobel."

Cooper was intrigued enough to hold her pee. "This is important research season for our team," Alek continued. "For world." He lifted his glass of clear liquid. "I drink to it."

Sal looked embarrassed. "Samogon makes Alek sentimental," he said. "Ignore him." He gestured to a chair. "Sit down. I want to talk to you about something." Cooper took the chair, and Sal leaned over the table. "I hear you're getting cozy with Frank Pavano."

"Cozy? He visited me at my studio the other day." Sal leaned his chair back again, resting his knees against the edge of the table. "Does this have something to do with your petition?" Cooper asked.

"I can't hear of this man anymore," Alek said, and took his samogon to the table where Birdie was sitting with Pearl.

"His work must be legit if the NSF funded his research," Cooper said.

Sal made a guttural sound in the back of his throat. "Look, last year, a couple of Republicans in Congress got letters from their constituents saying that they couldn't get the literature on alternate explanations for climate change in the schools, they

179

couldn't get federal funding, they couldn't 'teach the controversy.' Then one of these morons — guy named Bayless, out of Kansas — realizes that serious science is done at Pole and not one scientist is down here trying to prove climate change is a hoax. He gets constituents to flood the NSF with letters, joins forces with another Bible-thumping congressman, Calhoun, goes on *Fox & Friends,* they do their thing, open inquiry, whatever. Of course, this has absolutely nothing to do with the fact that Bayless and his own personal Lennie Small are up for reelection next fall."

"So the NSF caved to political pressure?"

Sal shook his head. "Officially there was no 'political pressure.' In fact, NSF rejected Pavano's application initially. Then all of a sudden he's funded and NSF releases a statement that says they support the general principle of academic freedom and inquiry and are sending Pavano down here to disprove climate change."

"Is there anything there? What's his science?"

"Let's not use *science* and *Pavano* in the same sentence, okay?" Sal said. "Pavano is collecting ice-core data from the Divide that he'll use to dispute the models that indicate Earth is going to become a giant Bunsen burner. At the same site, I might add, where the real climatologists are extracting and analyzing ice cores that will prove that it is. His presence on the ice means that somewhere a real climate scientist did not get his grant approved." He raised his glass. "And so, my darling painter person, the fact that Frank Pavano is at South Pole Station is officially a sign of the end times."

"You're not a climate scientist. Why do you care so much?"

"If you were a scientist, you wouldn't ask that question."

All around them, people were starting to leave to get dressed for the Halloween party. "You coming?" Sal asked. "Everyone comes. It's a polar spectacle."

Cooper looked over at Birdie — his face was rosy and tears were streaming from his eyes. Pearl rubbed his shoulders as Alek held an empty glass of samogon above his head triumphantly.

"I guess so."

Tucker appeared at their table, his hands clasped in front of his body. "Frosty Boy's back," he said. Sal threw his head back and punched the sky with both fists. Tucker turned to Cooper. "Frosty Boy is a soft-serve machine that delivers flaccid ice cream in a continuous stream."

"He's probably spent more time under the loving, quasi-sexual ministrations of the maintenance specialists than he has actually dispensing soft serve," Sal said.

"Why keep it around if it doesn't work?" Cooper asked.

"You can't just come in here and replace things like Frosty Boy with something that works better. We grow attached to these temperamental pieces of crap. They're rejects, just like us."

A half hour and scavenged costume later, Cooper found herself standing in the darkened gym wearing a Freddy Krueger mask and surgical scrubs while a five-piece band calling themselves Coq au Balls covered an Avril Lavigne song as a joke. No one was laughing. On the booze table beside her, a jack-o'-lantern vomited seeds and pith. Cooper watched as the VIDS and NSF administrative staff jogged onto the dance floor, singing along to "Sk8er Boi." She worked her straw through a slit in the Krueger mask and drained her screwdriver. A ghost-memory flickered in Cooper's mind of Billie, at fourteen, advising her that *liquor before beer, you're in the clear and beer before liquor gets you there quicker.* Or was it *never been sicker?* Whatever. Next to her,

Dwight groomed his Chewbacca mask with a small comb. When he noticed Cooper watching, he trilled at her.

Halfway through her third screwdriver, everything in Cooper's line of vision began to take on the soft edges of a high school senior portrait. She scanned the crowd. There was Bozer, dressed as a hobo, a play on Tucker's widely adopted moniker for him, *hobosexual,* a man who was the opposite of a metrosexual, a man who gave not two shits about his appearance. ("Like Michael Moore," Tucker had said helpfully.) Holding a woman's purse on the end of a stick, and wearing torn culottes, Bozer was showing off a handmade birdhouse to a Fingy meteorology tech, who apparently believed his story about the rare "glacier sparrow" that nested at South Pole. Across the gym, the interpretive dancer was sporting a rainbow clown's wig and enormous novelty sunglasses in the shape of hearts, and Electric Sliding with the historical novelist, who really was just shuffling.

Cooper turned away from the stage in time to see a woman from McMurdo walk purposefully toward Sal and grab his hand, pulling him back toward the dance floor. Through the eyes of Freddy Krueger, Cooper considered the woman: so that's what

Sal liked, she thought. Women who wore oversize football jerseys, hot pants, and slightly off-kilter trucker's hats and called it a costume.

"This is the annual start-of-the-season hook-up," Tucker said, stepping next to Cooper. "Whoever you hook up with becomes your ice-wife or ice-husband for the season." He looked out over the crowd of bearded Britney Spears and wobbly space cowboys. "Choose wisely."

"I'm trapped in a bad remake of *Meatballs,*" she said.

"One wonders if a *Meatballs* remake could be good?"

"What is the sound of one hand clapping?" Cooper replied.

"I know it seems like a frat party, but it won't last. The beginning is always like rutting season on the Great Plains."

"What about you? Do you have an ice . . . person here?" Cooper asked.

"As Calvin Coolidge once said, 'I have found out in the course of a long public life that the things I did not say never hurt me.' " With this, Tucker wandered away, and Cooper finished off her screwdriver. Now she was sufficiently drunk. She pulled off the Krueger mask and threw it high into the air, not bothering to watch it fall in the middle of the makeshift mosh pit by the stage. She spotted her parka hanging on the NordicTrack that had been shoved into a corner of the gym. On her way over, she passed Birdie and Pearl, who were deep in conversation. "And they have these things called 'meat raffles,' " Birdie said, his face still flushed from Alek's samogon. "Meat raffles!"

As Cooper made her way to the door, the lights suddenly dimmed — everywhere she looked, jack-o'-lanterns leered at her, their crooked mouths illuminated by battery-powered votive candles. By the door, she had to force her way through a knot of Beakers dressed as approximations of Christ's apostles (bedsheets and beards). "Finally, the waiter leaves," one of them was saying. "And that's when she leans over and whispers, 'I don't believe in carbon dating.' So I said, 'I don't believe *we'll* be dating.' "

As soon as she stepped outside the gym trailer, the icy air wrapped itself around Cooper's midsection, and she realized she hadn't zipped up her parka. When she tried to join the zipper parts together, the world tilted and she felt certain she could feel the speedy rotation of the earth on its axis. She leaned against the tire of a forklift and steadied herself. Below her boots, though, the ground circulated like a frothy whirlpool. She raised her head and stared in wonder at the sunlight pouring into the long entrance tunnel; she knew it had to be well after midnight, but it was as bright as a Folgers morning. The thought of fresh air pulled her forward.

Halfway down the tunnel, she took a deep breath — the cold air rinsed through her lungs and the world stopped spinning for a moment. Then she saw the row of metal folding chairs blocking the entrance. A large handwritten sign had been taped to a chair. It read: *NO, YOU CANNOT GET SOBER BY GOING OUTSIDE! RETURN TO PARTY YOU DUMBSHIT.*

Cooper remembered her studio — it was technically under the Dome. Maybe she'd be a better painter drunk than sober. They said Hemingway was. Hemingway wasn't a painter, Cooper reminded herself. And who was "they"? *Hemingway wasn't a painter. Hemingway wasn't a painter.* She chanted this line out loud as she circled back to the artists' annex. A couple making out in the cab of a Caterpillar stopped to stare at her.

When she arrived at the door to her studio, she tapped the postcard of Foucault for good luck. Upon walking in, though, Cooper came face-to-face with her *Mitten in*

Winter canvas, and her heart sank. The painting now struck her as revolting. She glanced over at Denise's desk; a large cardboard box had been set atop a stele of textbooks. Cooper knew it was filled with slightly less than twelve gross Blue Razberry Blow Pops; the candy was circulating among the station population as currency. (Someone had already been called into HR for simulating fellatio on one of them during the sexual harassment training video.) But Cooper wasn't looking for candy. She wanted the box cutter Denise had used to open the package. When she found it, she pushed the blade up and watched as its geometry changed the farther it extruded. She lay it flat against her forearm to test its sharpness and discovered that a slight change in angle could draw blood.

She turned to her canvas and thrust the blade into it. It didn't rip cleanly — the canvas resisted and the first cut frayed. It was only when she retracted the blade a few degrees that it became an efficient tool of destruction. Cooper ripped long, jagged lines through the mitten, and the fabric peeled away from the gashes, dropping fiber at her feet. Every sound — the thrumming bass from the party next door, the vibration of the power plant, the creaking of the ice

— faded, save her own thumping heartbeat. Then, slowly, she realized someone was pounding on her door. She froze, hoping whoever it was would walk away, but the knocks continued, taking on a percussive quality.

"Who is it?" Cooper called.

"Herbert Hoover."

Cooper unlocked the door and opened it a crack to find Tucker's pockmarked face. He was holding two steaming cups of black coffee. As he handed her one through the gap in the door, his eyes traveled to Cooper's shredded canvas. "Ah, killing your darlings tonight, I see." Cooper opened the door wide and let him pass through into the room.

She sat down heavily on the stool and sipped the bitter coffee while Tucker took off his parka and hung it on the back of the door. He kicked the ribbons of canvas into a pile and removed the frame from the easel. In its place he put one of the blank canvases Cooper had stretched and prepped the week before in a fit of optimism. As he tidied the room, Cooper could feel the high-octane coffee sobering her up, sip by sip.

Finally, Tucker turned to her, his muscular arms hanging awkwardly at his sides.

"You didn't mention it on the application," he said.

"Mention what?"

"That you were a prodigy. *The New York Times Magazine* thing. Whether you had or had not saved the American Art World at age sixteen. Incidentally, according to my online research, it's still at risk."

Cooper's head swam. "That person no longer exists."

"Don't be dramatic."

She fixed Tucker with a glare. "Would you trade on fleeting success fifteen years after the fact?"

Tucker winced.

"I am not an attractive person but I am an honest one. You can ask me anything. I will tell you I am single and a homo. I relate to you because when I was your age, I was also someone who had hopes and dreams. I find as I grow older that I like to give the young people advice. And my golden rule is this: If you are going to be self-conscious, try to be funny about it or insightful. Otherwise, and I'm guilty of this, it is nothing but self-indulgence. And smile more — easier said than done if you have had Botox and a job like mine."

He picked up her sketchbook and held it out to her.

"What?" Cooper said.

"You're going to paint my portrait."

"I don't do portraits."

"Just pretend you're at a wedding. I can get some kale from the kitchen if it would help."

Cooper looked at Tucker's face, ruthlessly pitted by years of acne, and yet strangely smooth from all the chemical peels. Despite its imperfections, though, his face was a limpid image, perhaps the only truly clear image she'd seen since she'd arrived at this confusing place. She was starting from zero anyway, so she selected the sharpest pencil from her pencil cup and pulled her sketchpad onto her lap.

"Do I seem straight to you?" Tucker asked as Cooper began to work. "I mean — am I queeny?"

"Why are you asking me that?"

"I've been advised several times to 'be a man.' In corporate scenarios, mainly. It's made me question my masculinity."

"Well, whoever said that is an asshole."

"You didn't answer the question."

With the side of her hand, Cooper blended the outline she'd drawn of Tucker's head. "Why are you down here?" she asked. "Give me a one-liner."

"Smartass."

"I want to know."

Tucker looked down at the cup of coffee in his hands. "One day, I decided to embrace a new manifesto, and I say this without being glib or self-deceiving: always look for the positive in all situations. This credo is also self-serving, since in my case, anyway, negativity causes facial afflictions."

As she sketched, Cooper thought the eyes would be most difficult; the eyes always were. But Tucker's were uniquely challenging. The startlingly green irises disappeared beneath his upper and lower lids, but the eyes themselves had a slight downturn at the corners. Sometimes, there was a flatness to them, as if he had checked out. Other times, rarely, they looked almost manic. Still, as she worked, she felt a kind of peace, as if her brain were cooling off. All she had to do right now was draw a picture.

"Here's what I learned, Cooper. If your current environment is not conducive to a satisfying life, then you change your environment. That well-worn advice about your problems following you wherever you go? Patently false. I find I can live well at South Pole, which is good, because I want to live long enough to find out if John Cougar Mellencamp gets buried in a small town."

"Hey."

Cooper looked up from her sketchpad.

"You're working."

Cooper grinned. "I guess all I needed was coffee — and Herbert Hoover."

"I am but a humble servant," Tucker replied.

As she worked, looking from her paper to Tucker's gentle face and back again, Cooper was overcome by a feeling she hadn't touched since David was alive, since she'd stood on the edge of the woods and waited for him to return — the conviction that the world could become known if only you looked hard enough.

2003 November 01
06:23
To:
    cherrywaswaiting@hotmail.com
From:
    Billie.Gosling@janusbooks.com
RE: Changing the subject line

C.,
My Internet research tells me that you have to take another psych eval in a couple months because you're staying through the winter. My guess: you have to fail the psych exam with flying colors in order to stay.

Would crazy people, if collected together, actually form a unit of sanity, their respective psychoses canceling one another out? Dad drove up to Grand Casino Hinckley last week. He and some other 3M retirees got schooled at the poker table by a bunch of elderly Hmong men who literally had no tells. Afterwards, they went to see Styx at the Events Center. OK, I have to go — there's a manuscript by Carlos Castaneda's last lover waiting to be photocopied. Mom acquired it last year and now has "buyer's remorse." Question: Did you ever wonder if Christ wore the cloak of the Illuminati? Me either. But Mom assures me that a huge "sub-sub-segment" of the New Age population wants an answer to this burning question, and I live to serve. Dad tells me the real money is in explorer lit anthologies. I didn't have the heart to tell him the market for explorer lit died with "talking machines" and lineament.

B.

2003 November 03
11:08
To:
 Billie.Gosling@janusbooks.com
From:
 cherrywaswaiting@hotmail.com
Re: Changing the subject line

B.,
The Halloween party was a bust. I got drunk and left early. In other news, I completed a triptych. Mittens. Actually, one is a glove. Which means I can assign it meaning. It was originally supposed to be all mittens, but I destroyed one of the panels in a fit of Artistic Angst. Tucker, the station manager, convinced me to "start fresh or become a tragic figure," so I also started a portrait. In other news, there's a guy. He spoke to me at length about the

dangers of politics intruding on science, but all I could think about when he was talking was how weird it was that an astrophysicist could be extremely physically attractive. That never happens. Why does that never happen?

C.

When Cooper woke the next morning, her left eye was encrusted with dried pus. Cursing, she hauled herself out of bed and felt around for her ECW gear. She was embarrassed to have to go see Doc Carla about her eyes again — it was her fault for not taking the entire course of antibiotics.

She pulled on her parka and, out of habit, thrust her hand into the depths of the pocket to touch the old Tylenol vial. To her horror, she realized the cap was loose — not detached, but nearly. She removed it from her pocket, and after checking to make sure nothing had escaped, pressed the top down firmly. She held it in her hand and stared at it through her good eye for a minute. What the hell was she doing, carrying this around like a talisman? And what was her plan for it anyway? She'd only ever gotten as far as getting it down here. She hadn't considered what she'd do with it once she arrived. She set the vial on her desk, next to the compass. She'd have to deal with it at some point, but not now.

As she walked down the entrance tunnel toward Hard Truth, she passed yet another guy holding a large pillow to his chest. He stopped short and looked hard at her. Suddenly, he began fumbling in his pocket for something. "Hey," he said, shoving another folded note at her. "Will you give this to Bozer?" In a place where Beakers were peering into the beginnings of the universe, how could a pool table be so important? Tucker had so far refused to intervene, hoping the situation would resolve itself with a frenzy of broken test tubes and bent levels that would allow the hostile energy to dissipate without causing bodily harm. Denise, on the other hand, remained convinced that only when one of the groups established dominance would equilibrium be restored. Cooper snatched the note from the pillow-clutcher's hands without a word. *Bozer,* it read, *The cases of Schlitz will arrive on the morning flight from McMurdo. We expect reciprocity.*

When Cooper got to the clinic, the door was locked. She knocked, and heard Doc Carla bark, "Wait!" After a minute, the door opened just slightly and Tucker's face appeared. He took one look at her, then slammed it shut. Cooper could hear people talking on the other side. Suddenly, the door flew open and Tucker pulled her in.

Toward the back of the room, Marcy huddled on a chair, a blanket pulled over her shoulders. "Oh . . . I can come back later," Cooper said.

"Stay," Marcy said. "Learn from my mistake." Tucker had his head in his hands. The feeling in the room was familiar — Doc Carla's rugged bedside manner a little too forced, Tucker's silence, Marcy's resignation. This was the Trinity of the Unfortunate Event. Cooper had been through its rigors before. It had been present during David's third 5150 hold — the day Cooper had run out of her shift at Caribou Coffee when he'd been found on the roof of the Weisman Art Museum, flapping his arms and walking in tight circles, unresponsive to the museum's security officers, and then, later, the police. "That's what happens to everyone who sees the Damien Hirst exhibit," Billie had said at Hennepin County Medical Center, where they had traveled to meet the cops. Bill had laughed at this. Cooper still couldn't forgive him for it. That was the only thing she had left to forgive him for — the laugh. When

Cooper had glimpsed David as the orderlies walked him down the hall to the back ward, he looked like a mannequin, his arms bent at weird angles, his legs stiff. Cooper, still wearing her latte-stained barista's apron, had watched in horror as he'd hobbled down the hall until he and the orderlies stopped before a set of white doors. With a swipe of a key card, the doors opened and swallowed him up.

Cooper was still standing there, frozen, when a nurse shoved something at her. "He was waving this around when the cops got to him. Most of 'em, if they're raving, they got a Bible. Never seen this one before." Cooper took the book without looking at it. She knew which one it was. Only when the nurse was halfway down the hall did Cooper dare to look: the ghostly image of three men — Edward Wilson, Birdie, and Cherry — silhouetted in the mouth of an ice cave.

Every night that week, Cooper stood outside in the backyard with Bill, staring at Hale-Bopp through the telescope. It was March, and for three months the comet had been a smeared fingerprint on the sky, but now, as it approached second magnitude, it grew brighter, it grew tails — one yellow, one blue. It had split at the root. Toward the end of the week, Cooper overheard Bill in the kitchen saying *care facility* and *Cloza-ril* and *menial jobs* and Dasha saying, "In some cultures, schizophrenia is a form of shamanism." Billie, uncharacteristically, remained mute for days. And the book that the orderlies had had to rip from David's hands, with its crenellated spine and its portrait of their men, remained Cooper's secret possession; the *Worst Journey in the World* was now the most important thing in the world.

Doc Carla gripped Cooper's upper arm roughly and propelled her to the sink. "I don't have time for this shit," she snapped. "You should've finished the whole course of antibiotics." She forced Cooper's eye open like it was a clam and squeezed eyedrops into the seam.

"I have such a good pee can," Marcy said thoughtfully. "I mean, it's the best one on the station. Epoxy-lined steel. Substantial volume. It even has a top. Damn. I take that pee can home with me between seasons. I use it when I'm off the ice." She looked over at Tucker. "Sometimes I become immobi-lized on a toilet. I don't know why." She shook her head. "No, you know why, Marce. You know. You know it's because you have no idea how to be outside of this place." She laughed bitterly. "You know what's funny is that about a week in, some guy in the machine shop, some asshole loaner from McMurdo, was telling me how he didn't think women should be on the ice at all. He tells me that in the military there's this 'phenomenon' of female service members getting knocked up so they can be relieved of their duties. Says, 'It's an easy out, like a no-fault divorce.' And you know what? I agreed with him."

Marcy looked worn and tired, her wild hair pointing in all different directions. "Well, it's my own damn fault." She shook her head. "It's dumb to say it out loud, but, Christ, I thought I was too old to make a baby. I haven't bled in a year. I thought it was over for me. I guess I got lazy. If anyone else finds out, especially the guys, my long and storied career here will go down in flames."

"It's happened before, Marcy," Doc Carla said. "And it will happen again. Human nature."

"If it were some other chick, Doc, I'd be standing there with everyone else wishing she was dead. As it is, I'll be the only one wishing I was dead, but at least I'll be off the ice when everybody finds out."

"You're leaving?" Cooper asked.

"This shit's an automatic NPQ," Marcy

replied.

"Couldn't you come back? Afterwards, I mean."

Marcy looked from Cooper to Tucker and Doc Carla and back again. "Afterwards?"

It took a minute, but Cooper's question finally penetrated, and Tucker pushed himself off the wall. "After your R-and-R trip. To Cheech."

"What the hell do I want in Cheech?"

"It'd be tough to find a provider in New Zealand who could help," Doc Carla said casually, "but let me work on that. Only if you're interested of course."

Marcy understood now. She leapt up and looked at Tucker. "You'd take me back? No NPQ?"

Tucker caught Doc Carla's eye. She nodded, and Tucker put his arm around Marcy's shoulder. Tears began leaking from Marcy's eyes, and she wiped them away angrily. "Then put me on the fucking manifest," she croaked. "Next plane out."

"You should still do your seasonal meeting, Marce," Tucker said.

"Yeah?"

"If you don't, there will be talk after you leave. Act like nothing's changed. Meet with the girls, and people will know you're coming back. You'll just have to come up with a reason why you're taking your first-ever R-and-R."

Marcy nodded. "I can come up with something." She turned to Cooper and thrust out her hand awkwardly. Cooper took it uncertainly and let Marcy pump it a few times. "Hey, man," she said. "Thanks."

"For what?"

"I was driving so hard, and so fast, I missed the exit ramp. You didn't. I owe you."

Cooper shrugged. "I guess there's a reason I'd rather be a truck driver than a florist."

A few weeks later, a rumor began circulating about a reporter from the *Miami Herald* on his way to the ice, having been thoroughly vetted and approved by the NSF based on his prior friendly coverage of the Program. NSF thought he was likely to produce a piece that would put a shine on things, and therefore safeguard the Program's budget from conservative freshman congressmen, all elected in the recent midterm elections, and whom Sal described as "Tracy Flicks with dicks."

"God, I hope he's Cuban or something," Bonnie said as a group of Polies, including Cooper, settled in to watch a VHS of the 1987 World Series. "I want to see someone other than Tucker who has skin with melanin, for chrissakes." She looked over at Dwight. "No offense, honey."

"None taken," he replied, arranging the tail of his cloak behind him as he took his place on the sofa. Cooper fell into one of the La-Z-Boys and watched as Tom Brunansky made his way to home plate. Pearl was knitting another pair of leg warmers for a woman in Dave's dance class, and had just frogged her last row of stitches when Sal and Alek stalked in toward the middle of the third inning. Alek was holding another bottle of samogon.

"Turn on game," he said.

"It *is* on, Einstein," Bonnie snapped.

Sal took a seat on the arm of Cooper's recliner and said nothing. Pearl caught Cooper's eye and gave her a quizzical look, but let the awkward silence go.

Finally, after an inning and three glasses of samogon, Alek stretched his mantis-like arms and sighed. "So," he said. "Information. I have some. Pavano agrees to debate."

"Who?" Pearl asked.

"The climate skeptic," Cooper said.

"Please don't call him a skeptic," Sal said. "All scientists are born skeptics. Pavano is not practicing science."

"Debates are against regulations," Dwight said. "If he's going to talk, he has to call it a

203

lecture."

"This would be incorrect term to use," Alek said, as Kirby Puckett adjusted his cup on the edge of the batter's box. "Pavano doing presentation on climate change would be like lecture on baby dolls."

"I did a lecture on quilt making last month," Pearl offered.

"Yes, but you didn't advertise a lecture on quilt making that was really a lecture on Bigfoot," Sal said.

"I'd go to a lecture on Bigfoot in a hot second," Dwight said.

"I'd go to one on baby dolls," Pearl replied.

"Guys, you're not helping," Sal said.

Cooper knew from *Worst Journey* that there was a great tradition of lecturing at South Pole. On the Scott expedition, everyone had been expected to produce a discourse on a topic that could be considered a specialty. In addition to being a fine physician, Edward Wilson was a brilliant artist, and he lectured on sketching. Debenham on volcanoes. Titus on "horse management" — even after all the ponies had died, his ideas on equine caregiving were apparently still worth hearing. Eighty-plus years later, lectures continued to be popular events at Pole, except now the talks were about things like "Subglacial Lake Properties on Polar Plateaus" and "Crafting with Crown Royal Bags."

Alek informed everyone that Sri had approached Pavano at Midrats and asked if he'd consider a lecture on his ongoing research so the rest of the station could understand what was behind the "controversy." Pavano had refused to go into specifics, citing his sponsoring university's confidentiality policy, but had agreed to a big-picture presentation, with time for Q&A. This kind of setup could easily be turned into a debate if the moderator was game.

As Dwight and Pearl were discussing the ethics of this bait-and-switch, Sal suddenly sat up and said, "I have a new rule: if you refuse to accept the central tenets of science and insist on trying to destroy science education in our schools, then you don't get to benefit from it. Turn in your iPod, throw away your computer, and no more vaccines for you. Live by your principles. Also, no synthetic fibers. That's in the Bible."

"Well, I don't even believe in vaccines," Dwight said.

"You had to get them before you came down here," Pearl said.

"I know. I'm just saying I don't *believe* in

them."

On the television, fifty thousand homer hankies waved in unison as Kirby Puckett chugged around the bases.

It wasn't until mid-December that Cooper next saw Frank Pavano, fumbling with his parka in front of the clinic.

"Hey," she said. He looked up at her, startled. "I've been looking for you. You've dropped off the face of the earth."

"I've been out at the Divide for much of the last month," Pavano said. He successfully zippered his parka. "I'm on my way to the shortwave carol sing. Do you want to carol?"

"You like caroling?"

"I find I'm in the Christmas spirit."

Together, they walked to Comms. This trading of carols was another Antarctic tradition, along with the Christmas tree the ironworkers built out of metal scraps, a collection of aluminum glistening in the twenty-four-hour sunlight. When Pavano and Cooper arrived, they found twelve other people in ridiculous hats crowded around a shortwave radio. This motley crew of Polies, named the Singing Skuas, sang mangled hymns into the radio to the McMurdo station choir — the Mactown Madrigals —

who had been rehearsing since September and were therefore tools. Both groups hoped their carols also reached some of the field camps scattered across the continent, including the ice-coring climate camp on the Divide.

A man wearing angel wings and a halo on a wire handed Cooper and Pavano sheet music, and the group began singing. "The Twelve Days of Christmas" to modified lyrics. "Twelve berms a-growing, eleven carps a-siding, ten waste pallets weighing, nine galley slaves cooking, eight smokers lounging, seven loaders loading, six congressional delegations, FIVE FLIGHTS A DAY! Four tourist herds, three expired condoms, two thermal gloves, and a glacier sparrow in an aluminum tree!" Cooper was surprised to learn that Pavano had a beautiful, crystalline singing voice.

"Are you coming to my presentation this weekend?" Pavano asked as they pulled on their parkas.

"I'll be there. Are you going to talk about your research?"

"I'm going to talk about my ice-core analysis and the so-called climate crisis. The scientific staff offered me an opportunity." He halted and analyzed her frowning face. Cooper was reminded of the smoking computer icon her Macintosh would display during an irreparable failure. "You seem skeptical," he continued haltingly. "Don't worry. I'm used to hostile audiences. Perhaps I can change one person's ideas about my work."

But Cooper thought his words came out like a series of deflated balloons. "You don't have to do it, you know."

"I want to," Pavano insisted. He looked at the ceiling and seemed to be searching for a thought. Finally, he said, "I'm clued in. I've seen the T-shirts, I've seen the drawings in the game room. I know what they say."

"So you know they're trying to trap you into a debate," Cooper said.

Pavano nodded. "In fact, I'm glad people care so much. Climate change will become a central policy point in the next few years." He pulled on his reflective snow goggles.

"Come on, let's go look at the Christmas tree."

They walked down the entrance tunnel in silence for a few minutes, the sounds of their breath coming through their face masks almost in sync. Outside, Cooper blinked against the sun, then looked across the ice through her goggles, toward the great invisible boundary that separated the six-month day from the six-month night. She thought about the catalog of polar art she'd studied on the flight from Los Angeles to Auckland — some of the painters had chosen to paint the explorers, but they made certain their work underscored the great hubris of these adventurers, not their heroism. The painter who'd depicted Shackleton's ship listing in the hard-packed blue ice had taken care to emphasize the continent's triumph over the "cartographic imperative," by making the men translucent. But, in fact, the vast majority of the work deemed resonant enough for inclusion in the catalog had been nearly featureless, experiments in light, shade, and variations of blue and white using acrylic and ink. Oil, it appeared, was passé, as was chiaroscuro: the place was too flat, too dead-seeming, for body.

"Let me ask you a question," Cooper said. She pointed at the horizon with her mitten. "What do you see when you look out there?" Pavano gazed at the smoking ice — a light wind had lifted the top layer of snow. "I'm supposed to see something profound," Cooper continued. "I'm supposed to translate this profound thing through art. But to me, it just looks like snow."

Pavano considered the plateau, his arms hanging slack by his sides. In his stillness, his profile seemed to Cooper to take on the aspect of bas-relief. He was Lincoln on the penny.

"Just as I thought. Impossible," she finally said, and began walking again. Pavano didn't walk with her.

"Wild horses," he said.

"Wild horses?"

"Yes, to me, the sastrugi over there looks like a herd of wild horses. Running into the wind, just about to leap into the high prairie grass. Frozen, naturally."

Cooper looked at Pavano, surprised. "I'd give that a B-plus."

"You're a tough grader."

"Should I grade on a curve?"

"Only if it's not the Keeling Curve," Pavano said, and chuckled. Cooper resolved to look up the Keeling Curve later. They walked a little farther in silence. "Have you been out to the ice-coring camp yet?" he asked. "Ah. No, of course you haven't. What I meant to say was that you should come out to the ice-coring camp. It's a slightly different icescape. It might jog something loose, perhaps provide some inspiration."

"That'd be nice, but they're not handing out Airbus rides to tourists like me."

Pavano seemed to think about this for a moment. "Then come as my research assistant." Cooper laughed, but Pavano continued. "I'm entitled to one, though they haven't exactly made it easy for me to find a willing volunteer. Currently, I've been assigned one of Sri's research techs, though she's made it clear that she has no interest in being part of my project."

"I don't think they'd allow me to get anywhere near the site. And anyway, I don't know how to do research."

"Isn't this research?"

"What, taking a walk?"

"Metaphorically, all research is a long walk."

"And all great literature is set in Madison County," Cooper replied.

They reached the Pole marker. Just a few feet downwind was the Christmas tree. At the very top, a snowflake of aluminum nuts sparkled in the sunlight.

"I find myself thinking of that tree as I fall asleep at night," Pavano said. "It's one of the most beautiful things I've ever seen."

Cooper regarded the tree for a moment, then Pavano. "If you can get me on the manifest, then I'll go," she said. Pavano turned his radiant face to Cooper and smiled. His smile plucked something deep inside her, and a feeling — familiar and yet out of reach — washed over her. Her heart began to pound and she silently recited, *The urge to jump reaffirms the urge to live.*

She left Pavano without saying goodbye and hurried toward the machine shop, praying to find it empty. It was deserted, and she slunk between a grader and a bulldozer. Her face was numb and her fingers felt only half there: she could bend them, but even bent they felt as if they were straight. She rubbed her mittens together, but this did little to distract her from the powerful feeling that had overcome her as she stood with Pavano. The urge to jump, she told herself again, affirms the urge to live. This had been drilled into her head by different therapists, who told Cooper the feeling was common, that it even had a name: high-place phenomenon. The desire to throw oneself off a building was the brain's misinterpretation of the instinctual safety signal. But at the time she had first encountered the impulse, it did not feel like a signal. It seemed very much like a voice. Cooper and David had just turned eighteen. He'd been strange for two years, but had not yet been accurately diagnosed. The first diagnoses — attention-deficit disorder, generalized anxiety, bipolar disorder — had initially inspired hope, but had faded like fireworks. This was the twilight time, before things became clear.

They were, all of them, standing atop the Dahl Violin Shop in downtown Minneapolis — Billie, Dasha, and Bill in the background, Cooper and David standing at the edge of the roof. Below them, the Aquatennial parade streamed past. The Queen of Lakes sat perched atop her float like a doll.

The impulse to leap off the edge seized her without warning. It was a drumbeat, a song. Her mouth went dry, and it felt as if her limbs were filled with sand. It was the most powerful feeling she'd ever experienced. She gripped David's hand, and he looked over at her in surprise.

"What's wrong?" he asked.

"I kind of want to jump off," she whispered. "I don't know why."

David turned back to the parade. "Because he's telling you to," he replied coolly. "Don't worry — I hear him, too. There's only one way to make it stop, you know."

Goose bumps rose on her forearms. Here was confirmation. The faceless thief had taken him.

A snowmobile careened through the shed, sending a shower of snow crystals over Cooper's head, and she forced herself to begin walking back toward the station. Nothing about Pavano was like David. Nothing, except their loneliness.

■ ■ ■ ■

Cooper spent the hours leading up to Pavano's presentation trying to realize in oils a sketch she'd made after her walk with him. The colors combined to create too-dark grays and Disney-like blues. Everything was contrasty and obvious. And, again, everything was flat. She turned to the portrait of Tucker she'd begun on Halloween. She'd sketched most of the painting out on the canvas already, and had gotten as far as the right eye with her oils. But now the eye was too big: it dominated the canvas grotesquely. After staring at it for a few moments, Cooper realized that of course it was supposed to be grotesque. She grabbed her eraser and briskly removed the rest of the sketch, including the weak attempt to capture Tucker's sharp facial structure, the unintentionally cubist lips, and the left eye that was not only smaller than the right, but also oddly shaped. In erasing, she felt she'd accomplished enough to soak her brushes in turpentine and head to the galley for Pavano's presentation.

When she got there, the room was packed with Polies — even the artists had shown up. Cooper took an empty seat next to Sal and Sri, whose messy thatch of black hair and tired eyes suggested he had clearly spent too many hours squinting at ice cores. Dwight, who was handling the moderating duties, tapped the microphone twice, then said, "Icebreaker to start." When everyone laughed, he looked around, puzzled.

"Dwight is deaf to puns," Sal whispered to Cooper.

Dwight cleared his throat, and tried again. "Tell us a personal thing about yourself, Pavano. And by the way," he added, looking out at the audience, "each questioner will have to do the same when he asks his question."

"I enjoy Rollerblading," Pavano said.

"What's the worst thing about Rollerblading, Pavano?" Floyd called from the back, where he sat with Marcy. "Telling your mom you're gay!" The room exploded with laughter.

"Careful, Floyd," Simon, the VIDS admin, warned.

Dwight pulled a scrap of paper from a small pile on the table in front of him. "Okay, first question goes to my lovely companion, Bonnie."

Bonnie got to her feet. "My name is Bonnie and a personal thing about myself would be that I am the head cook here and that I hate vegetarians because they make my life difficult. And then my question is: What's up with ice cores, and why is everyone mad?"

The audience tittered.

"I think I understand your question, Bonnie," Pavano said, with a voice that possessed all the treble and pitch of a window air conditioner. "You are interested in the controversy surrounding ice-core analysis."

"Sure," Bonnie said. Next to Cooper, Sri bounced in his chair, and Sal placed a hand on his friend's knee.

"Prevailing scientific opinion states that ice cores will reveal patterns of climate change," Pavano continued, "even evidence of volcanic eruptions. However —"

"Look, most of us understand basic ice-core analytics, right?" Sri burst out, wrenching around in his seat to look at everyone in the audience.

"Here we go," Sal murmured.

"Drill down a million feet, take out an ice core, look at the rings, analyze. Summers get warm, so the ice melts and you get clear layers. Winters, no melt, you get snow layers, a milky layer, and you look at the air bubbles trapped in the layers. People who have dedicated their lives to analyzing these cores know what they are looking at; they know how to interpret the data."

Pavano cleared his throat. "What Dr. Niswathin is saying is that it is widely assumed — and I use the word *assumed* intentionally — that each ring pair, the clear ring and the milky ring taken together, account for a single year: the clear ring accumulates during the summer season and the milky ring appears at the conclusion of a winter season. That's how you get estimates of a hundred thirty-five thousand years of ice data. But on what evidence do we base our assumption that each pair represents a year?"

"It's rather obvious," Sri said.

"That is the fallback position of the researcher with bad data," Pavano replied with a smoothness that Cooper hadn't thought possible. "I'm not here to debate geology, of course, but if the earth is billions of years old," he continued, "why isn't there more ice at the North and South Poles? Is the earth, as you posit, billions of years old, or is there any chance the polar ice cores show us that other models might have some validity? If they do, what does that say about your team's climate-change research?"

One of the climatologists on Sri's team raised her hand. "Before this, you were a vocal proponent of intelligent design. Intelligent design is not a scientifically accepted theory. You don't even believe in the validity of radiometric dating."

"I am often surprised by the parochialism of mainstream science," Pavano replied.

Sal leaned forward in his seat. "And I'm surprised that the oil industry landed a bought scientist at a federal research facility."

"Are you suggesting that I manipulate my conclusions to align with the financial interests of my funding source?"

"I'm saying that you and whoever signs your checks are making a cottage industry out of global warming denial because the money's good."

"If I were willing to alter my views to ingratiate myself with a funding source, I'd be an extremely vocal proponent of so-called global warming, seeing as most of the grant money seems to go to researchers who take man-made causation as fact. As I've argued with you before, there is nothing unscientific about looking for other explanations. But let's step into your line of expertise: the origins of the universe."

For a moment, the men shared a look that betrayed some level of intimacy, and everyone in the galley caught it.

"Sounds like a desperate ploy to distract from your poor science, but go ahead," Sal said.

"Time and time again, scientists like you have failed to provide any meaningful explanation of how the universe began. You can tell us what it looked like; you can tell us how it was done. You can't tell us why."

"Why? This is all about god?" Sri exclaimed. "Of course! It's what you do. I mean, look at your paper on the structural dynamic stability of Noah's ark. I read that." He looked over at Sal. "We all did."

For the first time that evening, Pavano looked flustered. "That was an early publication, and one that I regret. And I've said so in print. I will add, just for interest's sake, that some models of ice cores do suggest significant quantities of snow accumulated immediately after the Flood, that perhaps as much as ninety-five percent of the ice near the Poles could have accrued in the first five hundred years or so after the Flood —"

The room fell quiet, as if Pavano's words had gone beyond the pale and could never be taken back. Cooper and the other nonscientists looked at one another, confused.

"Holy shit," Pearl whispered. "I think he just said Noah's flood is a scientific fact."

"Sri, you're wrong," Sal said. "This isn't about god. This is about money. Frank Luntz is why Pavano is going to become a very rich man."

"Frank Luntz?" Bonnie asked. "Sounds like a hot dog company."

"Frank Luntz advises the Bush administration about various policy decisions. Last year somebody got hold of a memo he'd written about how to handle what he called this 'global warming problem.' Luntz and everyone else in the White House knows global warming is real, that it's man-made. Luntz told them the scientific debate is closing against them, but isn't fully closed — that there's just enough time to keep the public uncertain, to keep it thinking that there's no consensus in the scientific community. No big policy changes need to be made if the public thinks there's widespread disagreement. Pavano enters stage right."

Pavano shuffled behind the podium — his face had drained of color.

"So you're saying, what?" Pearl asked, her brows furrowed. "That he doesn't actually believe what he's saying? That he's gonna make stuff up while he's down here?"

"To believe in climate change —" Pavano tried, but Sal interrupted him.

"See, look at his language. He's talking

about Santa Claus, the Easter Bunny. Scientists don't believe in things. They either know things or they don't."

Cooper could tell that Sal had just walked into a trap, because Pavano suddenly seemed very focused. "Just like those who once promoted the Big Bang as fact — as the gospel of how the universe began — suddenly change their minds? Tell me if this sounds familiar, Dr. Brennan: 'Humanity's deepest desire for knowledge is justification enough for our continuing quest.'"

"Don't take Hawking's words in vain," Sal said.

"So Stephen Hawking's your prophet, and yet you desecrate what many others find sacred."

"And now we've fallen down the nerd-hole," Bonnie groaned behind Cooper. "In like, a minute, they're gonna start talking Elvish."

"He's putting up a good fight, though," Pearl murmured over her shoulder.

"You guys have gone way off the rails," Dwight said, exasperated. "Can we get back to Bonnie's question about ice cores?"

"Yes, tell us what research you're trying to thwart while you're down here," Sal said.

"Unlike other grantees on the ice this season, I'm not trying to thwart anyone's research," Pavano said. "Alarmists are finding it difficult to explain away the fact that Antarctica's sea ice is at record levels. It's not melting. To the contrary, it's quite robust."

"The record amount is only three-point-six percent over the 1981 to 2002 mean," Sri cried. "I mean, this year the edge of the ice extends out only thirty-five kilometers farther than it does in an average year. It's actually getting thinner."

"In climate science, it seems to me, anything is possible," Pavano said.

"Could Antarctica melt?" Pearl asked. Cooper noticed a couple research techs roll their eyes.

Pavano chuckled. "I think the scientists in this room would agree that even if man-made climate change was real, it would take thousands of years for it to grow warm enough for the Antarctic ice shelf to melt. In fact, that kind of catastrophic ice melt would require heat of apocalyptic proportions. But because I dispute the assumption that the earth is warming, it's nothing I worry about."

"So what you're saying," Pearl replied, "is that the earth is not warming up like everyone says, that global warming isn't real?"

"What I'm saying is that very little research has ever been funded to look for natural mechanisms for climate change. It has simply been assumed, by the scientific community, that global warming is man-made."

"I would actually prefer that the earth was not warming," Pearl said.

"It may not be," Pavano said.

"That makes me feel better."

"No, Pearl," Sri shouted, "don't go over to the Dark Side!" This resulted in a chorus of protestation. Amid the shouts, Cooper noticed Sal quietly stand up and walk out of the galley.

That night Pavano pinned to the large bulletin board in the galley an abstract from a just-published paper by Willie Soon from the journal *Climate Research,* which claimed "the twentieth century is probably not the warmest nor a uniquely extreme climatic period of the last millennium." By the next morning, it was gone, and in its place was a hand-drawn flyer: *Breaking News Update: Climate Change Jesus super-excited about new developments, says "you're getting warmer!"* Next to this was a muscle-bound superhero Jesus, with a bubble coming from his mouth containing what one of the Beakers later told Cooper was the Schrödinger equation. Climate Change

Jesus was set upside down, coring ice with his crown of thorns.

PRODUCTION COOK: 5:00am–3:00pm and 4:30pm–10:00pm

PREPARES HOT BREAKFAST: including pastries, fills juice machine and breadbox

PREPARES LUNCH. Soup Daily
Assists with dinner.

Shops for own menu items on regular basis and general kitchen use items every other week on rotating basis with Head Cook (Bonnie)

Menu will be provided. Both cooks are accountable for the food and adhering to the APPROVED menu. Special occasions/holidays are excepted from the menu.

Food is to be used from Berm B first. Call in items from Berm A only after ensuring they are not available from Berm B. Food rotation is very important to its quality.

COOKBOOK KEY
EBF: Enchanted Broccoli Forest
MW: Moosewood
MWC: Moosewood Cooks for a Crowd
SL: Still Life with Menu
SP: South Pole 3-Ring Binder

BASIC ROTATIONS

Pasta 2 × week

Mexican 1 × week

Italian 1 × week

Seafood 1 × week

Alt every other cycle: Italian chicken fingers
   with patty, Tuna

Melt with Seafood Croissant

ENCHANTED BROCCOLI FOREST

There were many ways to make things disappear at South Pole Station. After all, there were twenty-three different categories of waste. "Dormitory biological waste" — bloody bandages, used tampons, snot-soaked Kleenex — was stored in fifty-five-gallon open-top drums. Galley food waste — like onionskins, uneaten oatmeal, and trimmed fat — was packaged in Tri-Walls lined with three layers of polyethylene gusseted bags. But the category that Pearl found most relevant to her purposes was the "domestic combustibles," also known as the "burnables." This category included paper towels, cigarette butts, food wrappers — and cookbooks that had been carefully dismantled, page by page.

Enchanted Broccoli Forest was the first to go.

Still Life with Menu was the second.

Pearl wasn't sure if *Still Life* would be

missed, but she knew *Enchanted Broccoli Forest* would. It was a go-to. Vegetarians sometimes requested *EBF*-specific dishes. But a week had passed, and still Bonnie said nothing about the missing cookbooks. Pearl couldn't have known that Bonnie would lose the kitchen over the inedible Carrot-Mushroom Loaf from *Moosewood Cooks for a Crowd.* She only knew Bonnie would lose the kitchen eventually. It was why Pearl had agreed to take the job in the first place.

No one knew that Pearl had been waiting for a Carrot-Mushroom Loaf moment since she landed at South Pole in late September. She'd been hired as production cook, the junior position to Bonnie's head cook. Pearl had applied for the top position, of course; she hadn't spent ten miserable years in various eateries and ship's galleys to become second fiddle in an institutional kitchen. (Nor did she go to Antarctica to become Alice Waters, but you had to pay the bills and government work paid well, especially when room and board was free).

But Bonnie was a lifer; and after a certain number of years on the ice, lifers received the privilege of turning jobs down rather than having to reapply for them. Bonnie would never turn down a job at Pole, and it took only a couple of days on the ice for

Pearl to understand that the woman would not be easily overthrown. She had allies. Those allies were other lifers, and they'd lost their taste for edible food some years earlier. Calling Bonnie to account for the state of the food at Pole wasn't going to be an effective strategy. The operation would have to be subtler than that, requiring the actions of a person exhibiting the traits of monomania. Not all of the traits, of course — that kind of psychological profile would be peremptorily red-flagged by the VIDS team. Just a few of them.

"Can you focus obsessively on a single thing?" Tucker had asked Pearl back in Denver after the psych exam. "Can you be insane when it comes to this single thing — improving the food — and be rational about everything else?"

"What do my results say?"

"That's why you're in my office."

"Then you already know the answer."

Pearl had arrived at Pole in the midst of an overhaul — a new station was being built just hundreds of yards from the current one. The National Science Foundation had been soliciting and rejecting plans for a new geodesic dome for years. Six months before Pearl came to Pole, they'd finally approved a plan. It was a matter of some irony that the firm that had won the design contract was based in Honolulu.

One of the modules under construction would house the new galley with what Tucker had promised Pearl would be state-of-the-art appliances, stainless-steel prep tables, and more capacity — however, it wouldn't open until next season. The kitchen in which she'd be working this season — the old kitchen — would present challenges. The galley on the Icelandic herring boat she'd crewed the summer after high school had been better equipped.

September 30, 2003

Perhaps the cramped conditions are what killed Bonnie's creativity. Or maybe it's the six-packs she puts away at the Smoke Bar every night. We'll see. There's a galley staff meeting tonight to go over the season's menu. I'll observe and say nothing.

By the time Pearl was aproned up and scrubbing her nails for the first meal of the season, she had only seen Bonnie a couple of times since that trust-building exercise back in Denver. Bonnie had come into training hot. She was pissed. Pissed that she'd had to go through fire school again, and even more pissed that she'd have to deal with a Fingy production cook. Her previous production cook had left for the cruise ship circuit, and Pearl sensed that the parting had not been amicable. The trust-building exercise had done little to improve Bonnie's outlook on the season to come. Granted, the "trust facilitator" contracted by VIDS had made a poor choice when he'd picked the "eye contact with touch" exercise. Pearl and Bonnie stood across from one another in the meadow adjacent to the fire school, eyes locked, hands clasped. But Pearl saw the pride in Bonnie's angry eyes. Pride was easily exploited.

March 12, 2003, at training

Met her today. Big woman — my height but weighing in at about two bills. Wouldn't tell me anything about what to expect, says all "Fingys" have to fend for themselves. Wouldn't tell me what Fingy means either. She hates my undercut, said it was "punk, fifteen years late." I'm trying to be friendly, but she's not having it.

The first days in the galley were like any

of the first days Pearl had spent in a new kitchen, be it on land or at sea — getting used to her surroundings, examining the supply lists, memorizing her duties, and getting to know her co-workers. Kit, a skinny guy with lank brown hair pulled back in a ponytail, was the main DA — the dining assistant who was responsible for everything from cleaning tables and filling the milk machine to stocking the napkin dispensers. As head cook, it was Bonnie's job to write up the menus and manage all kitchen operations.

"Bonnie is a loner by nature," Tucker told Pearl the first week in. "Being at Pole goes against every fiber of her being."

"I thought Pole was like the loner's Disney World."

Tucker shook his head. "You have to at least possess the capacity to enjoy the company of other loners."

"Then why is she there?"

"Dwight, our comms tech. They met at a Sheraton in New Orleans. He was the IT guy, she was buffet cook."

"She followed a guy down here?"

"It's not all that uncommon. Like two negative electrons, two misanthropes can bind together with the force of —"

"Negative electrons repel each other,"

Pearl said.

Tucker paused. "Huh. Well, that explains why Sal Brennan has banned me from the Dark Sector."

Her days began with a 4:30 a.m. alarm. The sun shone as brightly then as it did at noon, which made getting up fairly easy. She'd make her way from her room in the elevated dormitory under the Dome (the galley staff received superior accommodations) to the kitchen, where she'd prepare hot breakfast for 105 people and put her proofed pastry and bread dough in the oven.

At first, Pearl adhered slavishly to Bonnie's menu. Huge warming trays filled with bright yellow scrambled eggs, vats of gluey oatmeal, white and wheat bread. The Polies seemed unperturbed by the monotony, although Pearl did notice that those who took oatmeal loaded their bowls with raisins, brown sugar, and nuts, as if trying to bury it under an avalanche of condiments. One guy even used salsa.

October 15, 2003

Bonnie says it is acceptable to bake in quantity and freeze items after they have been double-wrapped and dated. This is bullshit. She says "acceptable" but she

233

means "required." I don't freeze my pastries. It does a disservice to me, to the pastries, and to anyone who tries to choke them down. Plus, the freezers smell like fish. Trying to figure out a nonconfrontational way to handle this — too early in the season for a fight over breakfast foods. I plan on bringing up the oatmeal issue soon, though. It's pretty low-stakes. A little seasoning, cinnamon and nutmeg, maybe, or even a couple teaspoons of vanilla or almond extract — hell, even a dash of salsa — could go a long way.

Between meals, Pearl had to make the rounds of the storage units, recording temps and noting stock levels. The units outside of the galley trailer, in dark corners of the Dome, were the worst — the air was as cold there as it was outside. The giant freezer where they stored the meat products actually had to be heated. As she scanned the shelves, Pearl marveled at the quantities required for every meal. Thirty pounds of orange roughy for fish and chips. Nothing less than twenty-eight pounds of ground beef for Texas Tamale Pie. Grilled Reuben called for twenty pounds of corned beef, and the veggie Reuben needed five pounds of tempeh. Pearl glanced down at the monthly menus on the clipboard — it was like an endless repetition of the same twelve meals. She knew she could do better than polenta pie and fucking tofu nut balls.

Pearl thought the station greenhouse was a nice touch, though. It was a steaming shoe box set atop the stairs on the annex berthing building. When Pearl opened the door, she had to break about fifty pounds of suction force, but once she did, she was treated to the smell of soil and green things, smells that Pearl had already forgotten — earth, compost, ripe melon.

October 19, 2003

I told Kit I'd take over greenhouse duty and he looked like he wanted to kiss me. The greenhouse will be the key to my success. That and getting rid of the cookbooks.

Personas, not personalities, were important at Pole, so Pearl settled on being a flaxen-haired scrub with a penchant for pink bandannas and self-deprecating jokes. Her requisite edge came from her undercut, which she kept up using a pink Bic twice a week, an operation that required two mirrors and an hour of her precious time. She was a small woman with what Sal had called the "face of a Pilgrim." The scar above her right eyebrow — courtesy of a two-hook herring rig — suggested the correct amount of toughness and allowed her to affect kindness, solicitude, even motherliness, without losing credibility. She took up knitting again, and her wares became quite popular. She knit during Movie Night, she knit at the Smoke Bar, she knit during the station lectures. The station was clearly in need of a Goody Two-Shoes. Pearl could be that Goody Two-Shoes. She could be whatever she wanted.

Meanwhile, she continued her quest to run the kitchen, which included feigning respect for the VIDS bureaucracy. But it wasn't until the two Swedes came through the lunch line that Pearl realized the bureaucracy could help speed Bonnie's exit. As soon as the Swedes showed up in the galley, Simon had had his eye on them.

"I'm sorry, but station rules prohibit us from serving you meals paid for by American taxpayers," Simon told the Swedes. "If you have foodstuffs you'd like to cook in our kitchen, you are by all means welcome to do so after the kitchen has closed."

"It's okay, Simon," Pearl said, "I have no

problem giving them some food."

"That's very kind, Pearl, but that's against protocol."

"I'll give them my meal — they can split it."

"Again, that's kind and selfless, but simply not possible."

The Swedes smiled at her and set their trays down. Pearl had turned away in time to catch Bonnie searching the bookshelves for *Enchanted Broccoli Forest.* She watched as Bonnie's fingers danced from spine to spine and back again.

Soon, lunch drew to a close, which meant it was time to stack the dirty trays on a dolly. Cooper approached Pearl with her tray, and asked about the Swedes. She wanted to ferry some food out to them. It took Pearl a minute to see the possibilities of such an operation — it wasn't until Cooper mentioned the expired ramen that it hit her. Pearl could facilitate this breach of "protocol," but as head of the kitchen, Bonnie would get the blame.

"Let me get the okay from Bonnie on this," Pearl told Cooper. She walked to the back of the galley, past Kit, who was going through boxes, looking for the missing cookbooks, all the way to the back door. She stood there for a respectable amount of time, then returned to the caf line, where Cooper stood waiting.

"She says it's okay," Pearl said.

October 28, 2003

Bonnie got called in by HR yesterday. They said she'd violated protocols by authorizing the delivery of station food to the Swedes camping out on the plateau. She denied it, of course, blamed it all on Cooper. Cooper won't talk, thinks she's protecting me. VIDS can't do anything about her — she's NSF — so they wrote Bonnie up. Bonnie told Kit and me that it was the first violation on her record, ever. Still hasn't mentioned the missing cookbooks to me, though. I plan on dissembling the three-ring binder (SP) tonight. There's nothing of value in it anyway. I volunteered to take the Midrats shift from Bonnie. She seemed surprised and actually thanked me. She told me the swing shift gets harder on her as she gets older.

One day, Bonnie mentioned that Marcy had called an all-women's meeting in the library.

"What's it for?" Pearl asked, as she

prepped for lunch.

"Seasonal Staking of Claims," Bonnie replied, whipping a vat of minestrone into a ruby froth. Her greasy dark hair had escaped from her hairnet and was plastered to her forehead.

"What claims are we staking?" Pearl asked.

"It's how we parse out who's hooked up, who isn't, and who's fair game. It gets hairy when somebody steals someone else's man 'cause she didn't know there was a claim."

Pearl didn't have a man, unless you counted the British ex-pat, Birdie. He'd been making eyes at her since he arrived. There was nothing wrong with the guy — he was a little soppy, but his accent made him rather endearing. In fact, he was almost lovable, in a goofy kind of way. Unfortunately, he wasn't much of a looker — balding, with beady eyes and ruddy cheeks — but that didn't matter. Even if they struck up a friendship, they likely wouldn't be swapping bodily fluids. Pearl had been celibate for five years on purpose. She felt that she'd reached the Bodhi Tree of sexual enlightenment, and this stint at Pole might make her a Buddha. It wasn't that she was asexual — there had just been too many disappointments for it to be a coincidence. She felt misled about sex. *They must not be doing it right,* she'd thought at first. Then, *You must not be doing it right.* Then, *Maybe you're gay.*

She'd given her virginity to a seasonal cannery worker in Cordova, Alaska, the summer between her sophomore and junior years of high school. Without her foster parents' permission, she had followed a school friend from Portland up to Alaska to crew on a herring fishery. The friend hooked up with a deckhand, which, in hindsight, had been a far better bet. Pearl noticed too late in the game that the cannery worker had a womanish nose that quivered, and a tiny, timid mouth. When he brought her back to his rented rooms on the harbor, he told her he was an art student at University of Alaska. Later, she realized that this disclosure should have prompted a hasty exit, but she was sixteen and not well versed in the portents of bad decisions. They stood around in his rooms awkwardly, looking at his canvases. Each was a rendering of SpongeBob SquarePants engaged in lewd acts. "A concept run amok," he told Pearl. When they finally got into bed, he went limp and would not touch her anywhere below her waist.

Back home in Portland a few years later, Pearl ran into a baseball player from high school she'd had a crush on (he was playing for Lewis & Clark College now) and after an hour-long conversation at Starbucks, he brought her back to his off-campus apartment, where they had sex: the first time to get it over with, and the second time because maybe it would be better. The sex felt to Pearl like a battering ram trying to breach a cervix. How funny, she thought as he grunted behind her, that all the electricity between them in high school — the furtive glances, the long stares — translated into this National Geographic special on the mating rituals of bonobos.

When a psychologist at VIDS headquarters had warned Pearl not to get pregnant — "selfish and avoidable," he'd said — Pearl had announced her celibacy with pride.

The psychologist had just laughed at her. "Yeah, I saw that on your questionnaire. There's condoms aplenty down there, but just do me a favor and pack birth control. A pregnancy puts everyone at the station at risk," he said.

When Pearl ventured to ask how a pregnant woman put the station at risk, the guy smiled and leaned forward in his chair, as if recounting the details of an NFL game. "Spontaneous abortion. Massive blood loss. Early labor. Hypertension. You want the menu? 'Cause there's more."

"I don't need the menu," Pearl replied. "I was just curious."

"Well, now you know."

"Do you offer this menu to your male applicants?" Pearl asked.

The psychologist laughed again. "When men develop the ability to get pregnant I'll consider it."

Marcy's meeting took place on the fourth floor of Skylab, an orange tower connected to the Dome by an underground tunnel. It housed laboratories, a music rehearsal space, and Bozer's pool table. When Pearl arrived with Bonnie, most of the other women were already sprawled on the Naugahyde sofa. Pearl was unable to tear her eyes away from the sofa — its very presence meant that a Naugahyde couch had been approved on a cargo list, loaded onto a C-17, and ferried down to South Pole. Surely, such things could not be possible, she thought.

"You okay, Pearlie?" Marcy asked, tapping the chair next to her. Marcy's appearance was even more disturbing than the sofa's — her face was drawn, her eyes sunken into her face, limned by purple shadows. Her unexpected R-and-R had sparked rumors of a cancer diagnosis.

As if reading Pearl's thoughts, Marcy yawned. "Shit, I'm tired. Bozer has us pulling double shifts three times a week." Pearl quietly took a seat.

"Let's lay it all out on the line tonight, girls," Marcy said once everyone was seated. "Time to stake claims."

"Aren't some of you already in relationships?" Cooper asked, rubbing her swollen eye with a ball of Kleenex.

"Honey, I'm not trying to play a game of Clue here," Marcy said. "I don't want to end up fucking Colonel Mustard in the Library, only to find out that Mrs. Peacock blew him in the Ballroom. Look — most of you know I do this every year. There's nine of us and about a million of them. It's easier if we know the score before we get too far into this magical mystery tour."

"Obviously, Dwight's off-limits," Pearl said, glancing over at Bonnie.

"Obviously," Marcy said. "What about Floyd?" When no one replied, Marcy nodded. "Yeah, poor Floyd."

"Sri would be cute with a different chin," Cooper offered.

"Sri is married," his lab tech replied sadly. After a pause, she added: "I like his chin."

Someone knocked on the door.

"Who is it?" Marcy barked.

"Denise."

"Enter."

Denise pushed the door open with her shoulder. "Sorry, everyone. I lost track of time." As Denise struggled out of her parka, Bonnie leaned over to Pearl. "When she's in the room I feel like a lab rat," she whispered.

Denise heard this and held her hands open, as if to show Bonnie she wasn't carrying recording equipment or a gun. "I'm just here as a Pole female. Is that okay?" Bonnie grunted and crossed her arms.

"Back to the matter at hand," Marcy said. "What about the men artists?"

Pearl felt her stomach turn over.

"The historical novelist is hooking up with the interpretive dancer," Cooper said. "And the literary novelist has a thing going with one of the cryo techs. That leaves Birdie."

"That the one with the birthmark on his face?" Marcy asked.

"No, that's the historical novelist. Birdie's the one who's constantly mooning over Pearl," Cooper said.

All of the women turned to look at Pearl, and her face burned with embarrassment. So others had noticed his attentions. She tried to gauge the women's interest in him without asking outright. No one had leapt up at the mention of his name. And he seemed harmless, didn't seem the type to wheedle or plead for sex. Pearl imagined him growing old waiting for her to take his hand — even his name suggested the gentle flutter of wings. And anyway, the Polies had advised her to ally herself with a companion for the duration; as a woman, she would have her pick, so she picked Birdie because he looked like a man who could be strung along. Pearl remained silent, but knew her raging blush made it obvious.

"Okay, Birdie's taken," Marcy said. She nodded at Denise. "Bozer's spoken for. Floyd, nobody wants, and besides, he has that mail-order bride out of Novosibirsk. Sri's got a chin problem — also, married. Everyone else is fair game, right?"

As Marcy looked around at the women, Pearl could see deep sadness etched on her face. She could see the other women saw it, too, but they said nothing. "That's it, right?"

"What about Sal?" Cooper said quietly.

Marcy smiled for the first time since she'd walked into Skylab. "Sal's all yours, honey," she said. Pearl was relieved to see she wasn't the only one whose cheeks were on fire.

Running Midrats gave Pearl a distinct advantage, though it was not without its drawbacks. On the plus side, there were fewer mouths to feed, so Pearl could spend more time on the food. The con was that the Midrats crew was made up of staunch Bonnie allies — grizzled old hands who'd formed an ironclad bond over this midnight meal. It took a few weeks before their irritation over the change in personnel faded.

Pearl hewed close to the set Midrats menu at first — irregularities raised eyebrows at Pole. Routine was vitally important to the operation of the station and to the minds of the people working there, and curveballs were not appreciated. So Pearl started by cooking exactly what was on the menu. *Sloppy Joes on a Bun (Tempeh Joes on a Bun). Honey Dipt Chix with Mashed Potatoes, Gravy (Pilaf). Texas Tamale Pie (Veg. Tamale Pie). Turkey Club Sandwich w/Pasta Salad (Szechuan Rollups w/Tempeh).*

Once the Midrats meal had been served, Pearl would hunch over her notebook, trying to meld flavors in her mind, to imagine what dishes might revive the long-dead taste buds of the veterans without creating resentment. She identified the foodstuffs that were lowest on the totem pole: dates, Melba toast, lentils, capers, tempeh.

Found out Bonnie has hated the plantains we get in bulk ever since she tried a Sweet Potato and Roasted Plantain gratin (*Still Life* p. 123) to bad reviews. She told me she tried to get the plantains off the shipment list but VIDS says they're a cheap source of potassium and don't get mushy as quickly as bananas do. Typically she sautés them in butter and brown sugar once a week and serves them as a breakfast side. I already have three potential dishes in mind, but since I'm charged with the daily soups, I'm going with a plantain *sopa.* Tucker has warned me about the "parochial tastes" of Polies, but I think he's only talking about the repeaters. The fresher Beakers and support staff still have taste-memories of halfway decent food. Won't take much to reawaken that.

When Bonnie had been running Midrats, she lumbered in a half hour before service, pulled the prepped ingredients from the fridge, and started cooking. Pearl rarely left the kitchen after dinner service now. She took her time with the meals, and the meals on the menu not only tasted better, they also looked better. The presentation was nothing out of the ordinary — fussiness would have resulted in ridicule. But it was just different enough to create a sense of beauty that was almost invisible.

She also started pickling vegetables. This activity was an acceptable use of the station's vinegar stores because the supply of fresh produce would run out about a month after the station closed for the winter. Pearl pickled everything from carrots to the tiny gem-like chili peppers grown in the greenhouse. To be festive, she tied ribbons around the jars and displayed them near the condiment tray. One night, she canned an entire shipment of damaged peaches, and set one jar aside for Birdie. When she handed it to him, he was so happy, he kissed her. To Pearl's surprise, it wasn't horrible.

For the first meal swap, Pearl decided to start with the vegetarian meals, since they'd likely arouse less attention and because the vegetarians tended to have a more forgiving palate. The scheduled Lentil-Walnut Surprise (p. 147, *MW*) was bypassed in favor of a black-pepper-glazed tempeh, served with sherry-braised leeks, fried capers, and hoppin' John. The sherry was cooking sherry a year past its expiration date and the hoppin' John was made from a five-year-old bag of dried black-eyed peas that Pearl found in the pantry. Still, Pearl thought it stellar. No one at Midrats said a word.

A week before Thanksgiving, Pearl served her Plantain Sopa — a cream-based soup made from ripe plantains — and her pickled chili peppers. She paired it with a buckwheat flatbread. This time, three people came up for seconds, including a non-veggie maintenance specialist.

November 15, 2003

Bonnie came into the kitchen this morning furious. Someone told her about the plantain soup. I couldn't ask if the review was good or bad because she was like the Tasmanian Devil. She said all menu changes had to be approved by VIDS, and went on and on about the importance of proper authorization. I spoke to Tucker about it this afternoon, and he hemmed and hawed for a while, but then said he'd make some calls. Tonight, right in the middle of dinner prep, he came in and told Bonnie that VIDS had authorized me to make any menu changes I wanted during Midrats. She walked out, leaving Kit and me to deal with the rest of dinner service.

Word quickly spread that Midrats meal was by far the best meal served at Pole. The ranks of midnight diners swelled, and the graveyard crew complained that they couldn't get a table. For them it wasn't about the food; it was about the company. For the new arrivals, it was the opposite. Pearl's changes to the Midrats menu had now extended beyond the vegetarian option and into the main entrées. One night she took the leftover Cornish game hens from the previous year's food stock and broiled individual birds with a glaze made from her own stash of homemade sour cherries. The desserts were beyond anything anyone had seen at Pole before: buttermilk panna cotta (in which Pearl could hide expiring milk — a perpetual problem), lemon chiboust, pumpkin tiramisu. Meringues and soufflés were out of the question due to the elevation, but Pearl could live without them, and the Polies didn't know what they were missing.

Thanksgiving was turkey three ways — smoked, fried, and roasted — with Kit smoking seven birds outside, on the far side of the Crevasse of Death. "Fifty fucking below, ladies," Kit reminded Bonnie and Pearl. "I think that's enough selflessness for a day off."

"Dream on, honey," Bonnie replied, in a decent mood for the first time in weeks. But then Pearl felt a piece of her die as she watched Bonnie spoon jellied cranberries out of aluminum cans; the sound they made as they plopped, can-shaped, into the serving dishes was as gross as an overdubbed movie kiss.

Yet Bonnie surprised Pearl with other culinary efforts. From out of nowhere, she produced a jar of fermenting kombucha. She also delighted everyone with an enormous batch of real mashed potatoes — Bonnie had pulled some strings to get a crate of russets from McMurdo. For the holiday meal, Pearl had been relegated to pastry chef, and she did well: pumpkin and pecan pies, of course, but also a pear galette and 105 servings of pot de crème.

As Pearl looked out at the darkened galley, at the Polies stuffing their faces, at the paper turkeys and Pilgrims hanging from the ceiling and the twinkling fairy lights, she felt something strange. Not peace — the job was still unfinished — but a kind of serenity that she had not experienced in years. The feeling that, if she could make it hers, this kitchen could become a home.

After Thanksgiving, the main meals reverted

to the usual, but now people were talking openly about the superiority of the Midrats meal. Bonnie was only left with the two Moosewood books: *Moosewood* (MW) and *Moosewood Cooks for a Crowd* (MWC). Pearl continued to find it strange that she said nothing about the missing cookbooks. She'd watch the woman sitting on an up-ended crate in her tiny office off the galley, squinting at online recipes. From time to time, she'd shout out, "We got pistachios?" or "Any starfruit from Cheech?" Invariably, they were always a few ingredients short.

One morning, during the lull between breakfast and lunch prep, Pearl was crouched in the freshie shack, tearing up pages from *Moosewood* and shoving them into the pockets of her parka, when the door flew open. She clumsily shoved the cookbook onto one of the produce shelves, but it was too late. Bozer had seen.

"What do you want in here?" Pearl said.

"I gotta measure the shelves for the new freshie shack," he said, a smile playing at the corners of his mouth. He brushed past Pearl and reached up to the shelf where she'd hidden the cookbook. When he pulled it out, several of the torn pages fluttered to the ground. He started laughing. "I knew it. Knew it from the minute Bonnie told me those books was missing." His narrow, unknowable eyes traveled the length of Pearl's body. He scratched the side of his face; the sound of his nails against the wiry hairs of his reddish beard sent a shiver of disgust down her spine.

"You planning on sticking around?" he asked.

"What are you talking about?" she said, trying to sound tough.

Bozer placed *Moosewood* back on the shelf, next to a crate of Spanish onions. "If you're going to run a lifer out of a job, you best be prepared to become a lifer yourself." Pearl's cheeks burned. "Now, I'm not saying the old girl is any great shakes in the kitchen. Maybe she done run her course here. I'm just saying that you oughta plan on making this a multiyear gig if you're gonna go to that kind of trouble. Now, meantime, here's what I need to see from here on out: barbecue once a week, make it ribs."

"Or what, you tell everyone I forced Bonnie out?"

Bozer spun a level in his hands. "And make it come with cornbread and potato salad."

"We don't get cornmeal here."

"Then use back channels."

"And if I refuse?"

"Honey, if the Polies find out you double-crossed Bonnie, things won't go well for you. My requests are small."

Pearl was annoyed, but if this was the price of intrigue, it was cheap. She nodded at Bozer, and stepped aside so he could begin measuring the shelves. On her way to the door, she reached for *Moosewood,* but Bozer casually moved it beyond her reach.

That night, Pearl invited Birdie to her room for the first time. She wanted to show him the notebook — not the pages in which she'd documented her plan to take over the kitchen. Just the recipes. The book had been with her for eight years. It was hardbound, indestructible. Green leather, strong binding — pockets on the inner boards that bulged with scribblings, recipe cards, and other detritus from her various gigs. It was her book of tricks. It had every recipe that had ever worked, including the ones she'd written herself. She didn't know why she was showing it to Birdie. She hadn't shown it to anyone.

With the clean, pink nail of his index finger, Birdie pointed to a handwritten table written in the margins of the first page. " 'Oven, liquid, sugar' — what is this?"

"A chart of high-altitude adjustments.

Baking at elevation." She leaned closer to Birdie and placed her own finger next to his. "Take sugar, for example. Because the elevation is so high at Pole, I have to remove a tablespoon of sugar from every cup I use or else everyone's teeth will fall out. Increased evaporation increases the concentration of sugar. It makes everything taste too sweet, plus it weakens the structure of whatever I'm baking." Gingerly, she picked up Birdie's hand and set it in his lap so she could begin turning the pages. She flipped until she got to the recipe she wanted.

"I made this one up when I was a set-net deckhand on a tender out of Nome."

"Seawater Bread?" Birdie said.

"It's really basic. Dry yeast, a little sugar, four cups of flour, and a cup and a half of warmed seawater. I got it right off the deck. Let it proof overnight, drop it in the oven around five a.m., and voilà, fresh bread in the middle of the Norton Sound."

Birdie took Pearl's hand and placed it on his chest. "You're the most remarkable woman I've ever met," he said.

"Why, because I can make bread from seawater? Anyone can do that."

"No," Birdie said. "Because you did." Pearl didn't know why she felt embarrassed; she tried to pull away, but Birdie held her fast. Maybe it was all the things he didn't know. The things no one knew. She thought back to the day she walked onto that longliner docked at Cordova Boat Harbor on the Orca Inlet, a seventeen-year-old foster-home runaway. She'd just talked to Captain Whitty about crewing on his March halibut trip, and she was halfway down the dock before she remembered she couldn't take no for an answer. Not without fighting for a yes, anyway. It's what she'd been doing her whole life by that point: seventeen years spent fighting for a yes. The ones in Cordova who didn't fight — the former highliners, the ones who collapsed along with the herring fishery after the oil spill in '89 — they walked around town like half-people. Pearl knew she was too young to be a half-person, so she'd turned around and marched back up toward Captain Whitty's boat and pounded on the door with her fist. "Open the door, Captain," she'd shouted. "I gotta say my piece." She heard him curse, but the door eventually opened, and with it came the unmistakable odor of a ruined dinner.

"Well, say it, then," the old man growled.

"I can work on no sleep and still have a smile on my face. I can splice line, I can cook, I got a strong back and a good head on my shoulders. And I make the best damn coffee in the state. And if you don't like how I work, you can throw me overboard. I don't care. But you'll give me a chance."

They'd stood facing each other for a minute, the only sounds the waters of Prince William Sound slapping against the side of the boat. That was when Pearl glanced over Whitty's shoulder and saw the remains of his dinner smoking on the galley stove. "Plus, it doesn't look like you know how to cook," she said.

"I do okay," Whitty grumbled, but he stepped aside to let her pass. She walked into the cramped cabin and glanced at the frying pan. A black lump of something emitted a thread of smoke.

"What was it?" Pearl asked.

"Spam and white bread," Whitty replied, as though he were saying "filet mignon."

Pearl grabbed the pan and tossed its contents out the galley window and into the harbor. "I'll cook for you," she said, "but I also want to fish."

"You're too small," Whitty said quickly. "Not strong enough."

"Try me."

After making the captain a proper dinner — chicken à la king — Pearl had walked home that night in the gathering dusk of evening, gainfully employed and free. The ghostly outline of the Chenega mountains rose up in the gloaming. And up on the hill above the harbor, the lights of Cordova turned on one by one.

Bonnie's final mistake was the Carrot-Mushroom Loaf, a culinary disaster that occurred the third week of December. The thing sat on the serving platter like a hunk of human feces, the warming lights bouncing off its gelatinous exterior, giving it an unnatural sheen. It went untouched. The fact that Bonnie now had only one cookbook excused nothing: that the recipe was buried in the back of the book, as if even the Moosewood Collective knew it was a crime against carrots, only amplified the mistake. The kitchen at South Pole Station was built for desperate circumstances, but Carrot-Mushroom Loaf was an indisputable sign of surrender.

The next morning, Pearl and Bonnie were summoned to Tucker's office. Pearl whistled as they walked across the Dome toward the admin module, but Bonnie remained silent. Her dark hair hung limply around her face and she kept her eyes on her boots. Pearl started in on "Free Bird," just to see if Bonnie would say anything. It took a full minute, but Bonnie finally raised her head. "Shut the fuck up," she said, though it sounded halfhearted.

Inside Tucker's office, Pearl could barely sit still. Her knees bounced at sixteenth-note intervals. Bonnie sat slumped in the other chair, her hands clasped over her belly. Tucker studiously avoided looking at Pearl, and instead focused his gaze on Bonnie.

"I made a mistake," Bonnie said sullenly. "It won't happen again."

"This isn't about the Carrot-Mushroom Loaf, Bonnie," Tucker said. "I imagine that carrots and mushrooms suspended in aspic have an interesting mouthfeel." Pearl noticed the corners of Bonnie's mouth turn slightly upward at this. "This is about scheduling. You know we're constantly tinkering with schedules."

"Not in the galley."

"There's a first time for everything."

"That's why she's here, I guess," Bonnie said. Pearl felt her heart begin to race. Now that the moment was at hand, it was proving excruciating. Tucker kept his eyes fixed on Bonnie. "You need a break from this relentless schedule. You and I both know that with construction of the new station, we've seen an explosion in the transient population. We've got staff coming and going from Palmer and McMurdo, and the fluctuations have had a major impact on kitchen operations."

"So?"

"I think letting Pearl take on the head cook responsibilities for a while will give you a much-needed opportunity to relax, refresh — reflect."

"I think Bonnie's handling the kitchen just fine," Pearl said. "I mean, with the missing cookbooks, anybody would have to get creative."

Bonnie shot a withering look at Pearl. "Funny thing about those missing cookbooks. I never had a problem with them until you came."

"Bonnie, this isn't a demotion," Tucker said. "Your salary remains the same, your contracted job title does not change. It's just a change of pace. It's less work for the money."

Bonnie sat forward in her chair. "I don't come down here to do less work, Tucker. I know this has been the plan from day one. You want me out."

"Bonnie, please —"

"You think I'm an idiot? They tried to DQ me on the physical. Morbidly obese? Borderline hypertension? Never a problem —

for four years, never a problem — and then suddenly Richard Simmons is signing off on the VIDS physicals. The union had to get involved." Bonnie jerked her thumb at Pearl without looking at her. "So you bring her down, have her hide my cookbooks, and deliberately turn the crew against me. Her fake-ass sunshiny bullshit is unmistakable. She's a sociopath." Bonnie hauled herself out of the chair. "You both are."

After Bonnie left, Tucker dropped his head into his hands. Pearl felt immobilized. Her legs had stopped bouncing. The nervous energy now seemed to bind her to the chair.

"Can you handle the winter alone?" Tucker said into his hands.

For a moment, Pearl was tempted to say, "Isn't that why you hired me?" Instead, she nodded. "No problem."

After leaving Tucker's office, Pearl returned to the kitchen, where Kit was peeling radishes and humming along to his Discman. Wordlessly, she walked past him and stepped into what used to be Bonnie's office.

It was a mess of papers, file folders, and dirty dishware. Pearl cleaned off the desk where Bonnie had mapped out so many meals, and took a seat on the wooden crate she'd used as a chair. She picked a food scab off the cover of *Moosewood Cooks for a Crowd*. There were so many colorful Post-its attached to the pages that it looked like a small parade float. Pearl was about to close the book and toss it on the pile of papers on the floor, when something caught her eye. An inscription on the inside of the cover.

Someone once said, "Cooking is like love. It should be entered into with abandon or not at all." We've abandoned our sanity already by going down to Pole. All we've got is each other, and this book. Make 'em drool, honey.

Your man, Dwight

From: Warren Slownik
  (wslownik@nsf.gov)
Date: January 18, 2004
  3:30:58 PM EDT
To: Tucker Bollinger
  (tbollinger@vids.com), Karl
  Martin (kmartin@vids.com),
  Carla Nicks
  (cnicks@vids.com), Simon
  Murphy (smurphy@vids.com)
Cc: Alexandra Scaletta
  (ascaletta@nsf.gov)
Status: URGENT
Subject: CONFIDENTIAL: Injury
  Incident

A quick thank-you to everyone
who provided input during
today's conference call. I've
passed your questions and
concerns on to Alexandra. In
the meantime, I want to reit-
erate the importance of protecting our grantees' privacy
by keeping this incident out
of the media for as long as
possible. An e-mail has been
sent to all VIDS support staff
and NSF grantees regarding the
incident, so please be pre-

pared for questions. I'm certain there will be many from this group. In the meantime, any press inquiries should be directed to Alexandra's office.

I've attached the injury incident report, prepared by Dr. Nicks.

Warren

THE DIVIDE

2003 December 26
03:13
To:
  cherrywaswaiting@hotmail.com
From:
  Billie.Gosling@janusbooks.com
Subject: Beakers

C.,
I am sorry to report that Phil
and I are no longer an item.
He said he needed a partner
with more of a "buy-in." He
said my cynicism is "poison-
ous." Mom promised not to sign
him up for another book. She
launched a jeremiad in editorial board yesterday about
climate change and polar bears
and how ironic it was that
most of the world's research

on global warming is taking place smack-dab in the polar bear's natural habitat. No one besides our new intern chose to remind her that there are no polar bears at the South Pole, but that's only because he doesn't yet know fear.

B.

p.s. What the hell is a Beaker?

2003 December 30
20:34
To:
   Billie.Gosling@janusbooks.com
From:
   cherrywaswaiting@hotmail.com
Subject: RE: Beaker

B.,
A Beaker is the South Pole term for a scientist, even though I've never seen any of them handling beakers. I'm sorry about you and Phil. Put it in your work. The climate change denier did a Q&A and the whole station turned out for it. I didn't really under-

stand what was going on, but the Beakers were frantic by the end. I'm told this Denier — his name is Pavano — is down here because of "Congressional interference." Anyway, the guy invited me to go with him to the ice-coring camp as his "research assistant," probably because I'm the only person who's nice to him. He's definitely not trying to put the moves on. The guy comes across as sort of asexual. I imagine him genitals-free. Anyway, we leave in a couple weeks. I'll report back.

C.

The morning after Frank Pavano's lecture, Cooper met Sal and Sri in the cafeteria line. They both looked hungover. "My brain hurts," Sri said as he spooned Pearl's Orange Walnut Spice Oatmeal onto his tray. "It spent all night looking for those IQ points I lost to Pavano's ravings." Cooper picked up some buckwheat pancakes and poured Pearl's chokecherry syrup over the stack.

At the table, Sal set his tray down heavily

and stared at his food. The early consensus was that while he was clearly a bought man, Pavano had put on a good showing. Several Beakers were convinced he was actually an atheist — overnight they'd dug up speculative Internet posts from 2000, when Pavano had been questioned at some conference-on-a-cruise-ship about irreducible complexity. He'd indicated then that faith in a higher power was not a prerequisite for accepting the theory of Intelligent Design. These atheistic tendencies were noted and puzzled over — was he pandering, trying to play both sides against the middle, or was he the Sasquatch of the Intelligent Design debate, an atheist Creationist?

"Don't be sad, man," Sri said, slapping Sal on the shoulder. "Pavano shall be defeated."

"Maybe in the long run," Sal said. "But by then it might be too late."

"I know why you're upset," Cooper said. "It's Pearl." Sal looked across the table at Cooper, a half smile on his face. He looked tired; Cooper saw for the first time that his auburn hair was tinged with wiry grays.

"Pearl what?" Sri said. "What does Pearl have to do with anything?"

"No, she's right," Sal said, still looking at Cooper. "She is exactly right. Pearl is the test case. She was buying in last night. She was feeling guilty about participating in a consumer economy that is leading to the destruction of the earth. Remember what she said? 'I don't want the earth to be warming.' "

"So? None of us do," Sri said.

"But when Pavano told her it wasn't, she said that made her feel better. She was relieved. Pavano gave her the out she was looking for."

"Pearl is Everywoman," Cooper said, through a mouthful of pancake.

Sri looked from Sal to Cooper and back again, his black unibrow furrowed. Suddenly, his eyes widened. "And it took Pavano two-thousandths of a second to plant doubt in Everywoman's brain." He stared at the wall. "Shit. People are so dumb."

"Pearl's not dumb," Cooper said.

"No, sorry. I didn't mean Pearl literally," Sri said. "Her oatmeal is awesome."

"The problem isn't brain power," Sal said. "It's hope. They're hopeful. Deniers provide hope. We don't. We're doom and gloom, and that's what makes it so easy for Pavano to convert."

"What the hell does hope have to do with science?" Sri asked.

"Nothing. That's the point. Pearl doesn't

269

want to believe that the earth is going to burn to a crisp because human beings are assholes. Pavano can offer a different story, rainbows and lollipops," Sal said.

"And Pavano can also sound science-y," Cooper said. "Or science-y enough."

Under the table, Sal nudged her boot with his.

"I just wish I could get into Pavano's head," Sri said. "I bet the blueprints for world domination are in there."

"Or Exxon's annual report," Sal said.

"Well, maybe I can help," Cooper said. "Pavano invited me to the ice-coring camp. On the Divide." The men stared at her uncomprehendingly. "We were talking about painting and sastrugis and stuff, and I just told him that I was hyper-focused on mittens and not because I want to be." Cooper decided not to tell them about her portrait of Tucker or the one she'd started of Bozer. "So he offered to get me on the manifest for a flight to the Divide when he heads back in a couple weeks. To get some ideas. Different vistas."

"Well, isn't that generous," Sal said.

"But you can't go to the Divide!" Sri exclaimed. "Only approved scientists and techs go." He looked over at Sal. "Hell, I'm the head climatologist and it took me two weeks to get my paperwork processed."

"I'd be going as a 'research assistant.' He says he doesn't have one," Cooper said.

"That's because he shouldn't have one," Sri growled. "However, he's supposed to be borrowing one of mine." He tapped Sal's forearm. "NSF put him on my project budget. Like a leech."

"At least he's just looking at the core archive," Sal said.

"No, man, they're talking about letting him core," Sri said. "And not only that, they want my tech to fire up the Badger-Eclipse drill for him." He sighed. "Well, luckily NSF will never approve a non-grantee as a research tech."

"Actually," Cooper said tentatively. "About that. Apparently I'm already approved. They can't call me a 'research tech' but I'm allowed to go to the site with him as an 'assistant.' Something about a congressional override? I had to sign a bunch of release-of-liability forms."

The men stared absently at their oatmeal, looking sick.

Cooper took her tray to the dish pit before beginning the long walk to Summer Camp — Denise had the studio until noon, so Cooper thought she'd grab a nap. She was zipping up her parka outside the galley trailer when she heard Sal calling her name.

"Wait up," he shouted from the stairs, where he was fumbling with his parka and mittens. He half-jogged to where Cooper was standing. "I almost forgot. I have something for you. Come with me."

Sal had a room in the elevated dorm with the other physicists, who were mostly from Palo Alto or Madison, cities that were apparently hotbeds for astrophysicists who liked ice-time.

"Yo, Sal," a guy in a toolbelt said as they passed him. "What's the word on the new Pole marker? You come up with a design yet?"

"If I did, I wouldn't tell you, sweetcheeks," Sal said.

"Just don't disappoint us. All eyes are on you, my man."

"I thought the Nailheads hated the Beakers," Cooper said after the man had passed them.

"Unlike the vast majority of my Beaker brethren, I respect the Nailheads. We wouldn't be here without them. I let them know that on a regular basis." Sal pushed open a heavy steel door. "Therefore, I am not hated."

An overwhelming stench of body odor hit Cooper full on. "Oh shit," she choked.

"Welcome to the Beaker Box. I should've warned you. Scientists smell worse. No one knows why."

Cooper looked down the narrow hallway at the solid doors, the absence of enormous heaters, and the comparatively luxurious quarters of the Beakers and senior Nail-heads. "Why do you guys get the nice rooms?"

"Because we're important," Sal replied.

As they walked down the hall, men in various states of undress sat hunched over tiny desks, studying papers or working on their laptops. "Skirt alert," Sal called. A few doors slammed shut; others flew open, and were followed by shaggy-haired heads.

Sal's room was much bigger than Cooper's, with a large desk and an Ethernet connection. Their beds were the same size, though, she noted with satisfaction. Against the back wall, a small window looked out onto the runway and, beyond that, the Dark Sector. Sal crouched down and began flipping through books stashed in a bookcase fashioned from an apple crate. Finally, he pulled a hand-bound book from the shelf and handed to her. It was plain, *White Album*–style, and the length of a novella. The cover was torn and the pages had been stapled together. It was titled *The Crud: Or*

How to Deal with All the South Pole Bullshit.

"I have to say, I'm already intimately familiar with the Crud," Cooper said as she flipped through the book.

"This is about the existential Crud. It's full of stuff not found in the *South Pole Station Handbook.* Think of it as a secret resource for coping when things get hard. And they will get harder, trust me. There's a sequel waiting for you when you finish."

"Why are you giving this to me?"

Sal reached for his anorak. "Because I'm invested in your mental health, as it relates to the tot-art you're working on for me," he said. "But be careful with it. VIDS would give up two antiballistic missiles to get a hold of this book. This is the last remaining copy on the ice. The rest of them are in Al Gore's lockbox."

"Right next to my ability to produce decent art," Cooper said, tucking the book under her arm.

"Art's easy," Sal said. He pulled on the anorak. "Just present a subject and make a statement about it." He grinned at her. "Don't get mad. I'm kidding." He picked up a stack of papers from his desk and waved them at her. "By the way, everyone completed the survey, except you, Tucker, and Pavano."

"For someone with such big cosmic questions to deal with, you seem really worried about weirdly inconsequential things."

"Inconsequential? I don't like politics in my science. Do you?"

"I don't have politics or science."

"Well, that's your problem, then. All art is politics." He pointed at *The Crud.* "Do not let this fall into the wrong hands."

"That may have already happened," she said.

"No," Sal said, tapping the book gently, and brushing Cooper's fingers as he did so. "It's definitely in the hands of the person who needs it."

When she finally arrived at her room in Summer Camp, Cooper found a piece of paper attached to the door, flapping in the draft. *To the (wo)man who spilled his/her piss on my boots and then fled (piss-and-run): Identify yourself. Otherwise I'll be forced to spend the rest of the summer looking for you. Signed, Super Angry but Willing to Forgive at the Right Price Electrician in D3.*

She tore the note off the door, grateful once again for the anonymity provided by polarwear, and opened the door. After removing her ECW gear, she got under the covers with *The Crud.* The table of contents included chapters like "The VIDS Cluster-fuck," "How to Score a Shower Curtain and Keep HR from Confiscating It Because for Some Reason They're Illegal," "Surviving DVs: Distinguished Visitors and Other Annoying VIPs," and "Why McMurdo Sucks." The book indicated, for example, that McMurdo-ites were mostly unfit for true polar service. Apparently, the fact that Discovery Hut was within walking distance of McMurdo, and that this historic site was a preferred location for clandestine blow jobs, caused the polar philatelists no end of grief. (It was also why Cooper had not felt moved to visit Discovery Hut during her layover at McMurdo — that, and the fact that it had been mobbed by cruise ship passengers, all of whom were still wearing life jackets.) McMurdo-ites also sucked because of their obsession with penguins; they were not above slithering across the ice on their bellies to get photos of indifferent Adélies.

Cooper's reading was interrupted by a commotion in the hallway — the canvas-duck walls rippled with the constant opening and closing of the Jamesway door. By the time she'd scrambled out of bed and opened her door, a squirming mass of bodies had filled the hall. Everyone was getting into ECW gear. Suddenly All-Call —

the station's public address system — crackled on, and a robotic Speak & Spell voice began chanting: "A fire alarm has been reported. Please stand by for further instructions." Before Cooper could fully process these words, Kit grabbed her arm.

"You're on the fire team, right?" he said. Cooper thought for a moment — yes, back in Denver she had been assigned to the fire team. She scrambled back into her ECW gear and was almost out the door before she thought to grab the vial. She was stuffing it into the deepest part of her parka when Kit yanked open her door and pulled her down the hallway.

Outside, a flock of snowmobiles awaited them, piloted by the heavy machine operators who'd been on shift at the time of the fire call. Kit helped Cooper onto one, then climbed on in front of her, and they zoomed off toward the Dome.

"Do you see anything?" Kit called over his shoulder. Cooper pulled her face out of Kit's parka to look. Nope — just the half-sunk diamond dome and the orange Skylab tower behind it. No plumes of smoke, no sign of fire, besides the insect-like agitation of the Polies Cooper could now see mustering at the station entrance. The snowmobile they were on zipped past the Pole marker and entered the tunnel.

Under the Dome, the fire team was pulling on bunker gear and hauling air tanks off the ground and onto one another's shoulders. Bozer and Floyd were leading a group of Nailheads down the entrance tunnel to Skylab, where Tucker stood wearing a massive amount of firefighting equipment. "I got another one for you," Kit shouted above the din and pushed Cooper into Sal, who was spewing acronyms into his radio, which was promptly spewing them back. Sal pointed urgently, and Cooper wandered off in the general direction where he'd pointed, joining Birdie, who was already outfitted. He slammed an air tank against Cooper's back and pulled the shoulder straps around her arms.

Cooper's heart pounded and she realized she was sweating. She lifted her nose in the air, like a dog scenting the wind. The only smells she could detect were gasoline, exhaust, and, somewhere on the edge, the scent of Pearl and Bonnie's evening meal prep drifting out from the kitchen. "We'd be smelling smoke by now if it was bad, wouldn't we?" Cooper said to Birdie. He only blinked at her.

Suddenly, the activity level slowed down. The chorus of muffled walkie-talkie voices diminished to occasional solos, and the robotic All-Call voice was no longer chanting like a Gregorian monk. One by one, snowmobiles roared down the entrance tunnel. As the din subsided, All-Call came on again, but this time it was Dwight's voice that was chanting: "This has been a false alarm. A false alarm. Please return your equipment to the stations. Repeat: This has been a false alarm. Please return your equipment to the stations. Postmortem at All-Hands Meeting."

Cooper's legs began trembling. She kicked the air in front of her, as if to remind her legs that they were functioning limbs, but this only made things worse. A prickly heat climbed up her torso, up her neck, all the way to the top of her head, causing her face to flush; it felt as if someone had placed a cinder block on her chest. She lowered her body to the ground, trying to maintain some semblance of control. When the tears came, she was only half surprised.

She didn't know how long she'd been sitting there when someone slid their arms under hers and hauled her to her feet. When she pulled off her goggles and wiped her eyes, she saw that it was Pavano. His face was obscured by his balaclava, but his limpid eyes were unmistakable. By the time

Cooper had gathered herself enough to mumble a thank-you, Pavano was already halfway down the entrance tunnel.

"I want to see a bird," Dwight said.

"I want to smell a new book," Pearl replied.

"I want to fondle a fresh bell pepper, and then eat it," Cooper chimed in.

"I want to pet my cat."

"What does cat hair feel like? I forget."

"I want to hear a child laugh."

"I want to go barefoot."

"I want a drink."

Everyone turned at this, like a litter of kittens following a tracking light, to see Marcy standing in the door. Or a weak facsimile of Marcy. She was drunk. Cooper knew this because Marcy was holding herself steady against the door frame leading to the Smoke Bar. Old Marcy never needed anything to steady her gait. She never showed up at the bar already drunk. But now here she was, her normally proud shoulders slumped. It was as if one of the major structural supports holding up the geodesic dome had suddenly sunk ten feet into the ice. Everything still standing, but the building was catawampus.

Cooper and Sal got up from their chairs

at the same moment and helped Marcy to a seat. Floyd threw his head back and laughed. "Oh, this is rich," he said. "She's back. The case study for Why Women Shouldn't Be at Pole."

"Says the shapeless mass of existential impotence," Sal muttered, as he returned to his seat next to Bozer.

Floyd ignored this and focused his piggy eyes on Marcy. "So is it true?"

"Is what true?" Marcy said without raising her eyes from the table. Her voice sounded bruised.

Floyd continued looking at Marcy for a minute. "You stupid slut," he said. Sal stood up from his chair so fast his knees hit the edge of the table and sent the beer bottles wobbling. Cooper saw Bozer grip Sal's arm and hold it firm.

"So who's the daddy?" Floyd said.

"Mechanic at Palmer," Marcy replied.

"Oh, so a one-and-done."

Marcy finally raised her eyes and looked at Floyd. "My specialty." Cooper saw something change in Floyd's face — a minuscule shift in the angle of his eyebrows, a faint tightening of his lips. Before he dropped his eyes, Cooper could see they'd changed, too, had widened, child-like, with pain.

The silence of the room felt alien. Cooper

watched Bozer calmly sip his Schlitz, his hand still gripping Sal's forearm. Finally, Floyd hauled himself out of his chair and walked over to Marcy. No one spoke as he leaned down and whispered something into her ear. She nodded, and Floyd stroked her messy hair before pulling her head toward his.

When Cooper walked in the gym for the second artists' meeting later that week, the interpretive dancer was not sitting next to the historical novelist, and he was clearly pissed off about it. She, on the other hand, was exuberant. "That false alarm last week was just the kick I needed, because I'm swimming in inspiration," she said. She flicked her Joni Mitchell hair over her shoulder. "I actually think I'm on the verge of a breakthrough." She leaned toward Birdie, the only person who appeared to be listening. "I met this Argentinean gentleman online who's doing research on Weddell seals at McMurdo — something about their estrus cycle. I'm thinking about transferring down there. Since it's mating season, there would be a chance for me to observe contact improvisation in the wild."

"But wasn't your project based on the movements of the hydrocarbon tubeworm?"

Birdie asked.

"Yes, but I didn't realize how difficult it would be to interpret its vascular plume. This seal research is brimming with possibilities. I learned from this Latin genius that in order to do the research you have to capture the female Weddells by drawing a canvas hood over their heads, tying it closed, and then taking a vaginal swab."

"You can dance about that?" Birdie asked, incredulous.

"I see it less as a dance than a choreographed crime scene," the dancer replied.

"I hate Argentina," the historical novelist said from across the room, his arms crossed. "Full of Nazis." It occurred to Cooper for the first time that the historical novelist bore a striking resemblance to Karl Rove.

"He's quite spiritual," the dancer said thoughtfully. "Shaman-like, really. I like how he can summon sacred energy. I can actually feel it in my heart."

"You know what I feel in my heart?" the literary novelist said from deep within the hood of his University of Iowa sweatshirt. "I feel nothing. It's contracted like polar ice." He groaned. "Christ, even my similes are stale."

"You feel disconnected from yourself because you have put all that you are into your manuscript," the dancer said. "You do not exist outside of your work."

The literary novelist retreated further into his hood.

Birdie cleared his throat. "This is our second meeting, so I think it would be wise to assess what we've produced since being on the ice as a way of holding ourselves accountable. Seeing as I've been quite unproductive since arriving, I will yield the floor."

The literary novelist raised his hand. "I wonder if we can talk a little about the world-building that goes on here. I mean, we've been here for a few months now, and the novelty of, you know, living at South Pole quote-unquote has worn off, at least for me. Taking this from a literary perspective, I feel as though" — he cast a sidelong glance at the open notebook on his knee — "there's this completely separate reality that people down here have constructed for themselves. I definitely still feel like an outsider, like I haven't been fully embraced. I mean, no one even came and got me during that fire drill. If it had been a real fire, I would have been charcoal."

"They didn't come get you because you're a freak," the historical novelist snapped. "All of you are. I haven't met one normal person yet. Not one." He stood up and began pacing.

"And why exactly are you here?" the interpretive dancer asked him. "Have you figured that out yet?" Cooper heard frost in the dancer's voice for the first time since the unfortunate radish haiku.

The historical novelist snorted. "To keep my head down and write."

"And you couldn't have done that back in Poughkeepsie?"

"As I've explained to you in great detail, it's impossible to situate a speculative World War Two battle set at South Pole without actually being here. Why is that so hard to understand?"

As the dancer and the historical novelist bickered, Cooper realized that the literary novelist was actually on to something: the Pole community was, in fact, a parallel universe in miniature. It was a place you could go where people weren't flying planes into buildings or shooting up schools. They were just bickering about Poughkeepsie and satellite phone calls and pontificating on the hydrocarbon seep tubeworm's vascular plume. Most people off-continent didn't even remember this place existed, except maybe a handful of bored newspaper reporters and the schoolchildren in De Pere,

Wisconsin, with whom Sal corresponded.

Cooper tapped the literary novelist on the knee. "Hey, when you were a kid, did you ever lock yourself in the bathroom and pretend it was a house?" He stared at her uncomprehendingly. "You know, like a cottage in the Black Forest: bathtub for your bed, sink for your cooking needs, the cabinet beneath the sink for your oven?" Nothing. "Look, I guess my point is that for me, South Pole is like my fantasy bathroom-cottage. You can pretend you have everything you need here. People might pull on the doorknob and threaten to kick the door down, but you know they won't do it, and you can be safe here until you're ready to face whatever ends up being on the other side of it. I like it here because this isn't the world. It's somewhere else."

"And it also has a toilet, so the parallel is complete," the historical novelist barked. "Christ. I'm counting down the days until I can get out of here."

"You're just mad that the Argentinean swabbed your girlfriend," Birdie said, and held out his pink hand to Cooper for a high-five.

Cooper finished *The Crud* the second week of December, having learned important things like where all the waste from the toilets went (a "lake" beneath the ice), and was ready to read the sequel, *Skua Birds in Paradise: Wintering Over at SP,* which Sal kept hidden in his room. Knowing Sal always skipped game night, she decided to venture over to El Dorm with *The Crud* to find him and *Skua Birds in Paradise.*

When she approached his door, she could see that it was half open, and that there was a woman in the room. The banter was intimate, the low lilt typical of people who have recently swapped bodily fluids. Cooper tried to turn back silently on her bunny boots, but the right one squeaked on the linoleum and brought the banter to a stop midsentence. The Frosty Boy tech in the hotpants and trucker hat who'd flown in from McMurdo, and who, Cooper thought irritably, might never leave, appeared at the door.

"Who is it?" Sal called out to the tech.

"A girl," she said flatly. This was a rare enough occurrence in El Dorm that Sal came to the door himself. His shirt was off. Cooper tried not to look at his chest, but ended up staring directly at it and quickly took in the details: no hair, some definition, not too much, nipples symmetrical and the color of strawberries. Sal edged past his visitor and closed the door against his shoulder.

"Don't tell me you already lost *The Crud.*"

Cooper handed him the book. "To the contrary. I'm ready for the sequel."

Sal's demeanor immediately shifted. "Meet me in the library in ten." He closed the door in her face.

In the library, Cooper perused the shelves, noting that there were duplicate copies of every Douglas Adams book ever written, as well as the compulsory copy of *Zen and the Art of Motorcycle Maintenance.* She was pleased to find that Tucker was wrong — there was a copy of Shackleton's *South.* It just had never been opened.

"This will generate gossip," Sal said when he walked in. He locked the door behind him. "Now, it goes without saying that you do not read *Skua Birds* openly. Admin has a bounty pool on both books — winner gets an extra R-and-R off-continent, so motivation is high. Now turn around."

"What?"

"I can't let you see where I keep it."

"Fuck off," Cooper laughed, but she turned to face the back wall, on which hung every winter-over group portrait in Pole history. She stopped counting at thirty. As Sal shuffled around behind her, she studied the photos. They went from sepia in the 1950s to black-and-white in the '60s to color in the '70s and beyond, and yet the composition of each was remarkably similar: beards abounded, one person in a cowboy hat, another eschewing his parka for a flannel shirt, someone caught midsentence.

Just below these photographs was a lighted display case filled with brass sculptures — the old geographic Pole markers, which were replaced each year on New Year's Day. The 1999 marker was a gleaming copper bottle cap with the continent etched on top; 2000's depicted the South Pole under a wavy magnetic field, with the words *To Inspire and Explore* running the perimeter; another, its year unmentioned, was a rotating sextant.

"These are beautiful as hell," Cooper said admiringly.

"The Pole markers are works of art," Sal said behind her. "Each year someone gets to design the new one. It's a huge honor."

"Who gets it this year?" Cooper asked, even though she knew. Sal placed his hands on her shoulders and turned her around to face him.

"Yours truly."

"Why you?" Cooper asked. "Oh, right — your super-important experiment."

Sal handed her a paperback with a black

cover. This one didn't even bother with the title.

"Well, this is certainly inconspicuous," Cooper said.

Someone pulled on the door of the library, and after a momentary pause, pulled on it again and again. Cooper wasn't sure why, but she found the length of time that passed before the person's hand told his brain that the door was locked hilarious, and started laughing. The door rattled in its frame as the angry Polie pulled and pulled on the doorknob, as if the door were only playing games with him and would open eventually. Cooper could not stop laughing.

"Open the effing door, you ass-joints!" the man shouted. This sent Cooper into fresh hysterics. Sal rubbed his face vigorously and held his hands over his eyes for a moment, trying not to laugh with Cooper. "After finding us here together in a locked room," he said, "people are gonna think you're my ice-wife."

"But you already have one," Cooper said with a hiccup. "I saw her in your room."

Sal tilted his head. "Beth? She's just an ice-friend. Who is returning to McMurdo tomorrow."

"Finally."

Without warning, he leaned down so that

his face was an inch from Cooper's. "Does that ease your mind, Fingy?"

"I was very upset," Cooper said, hoping the obvious sarcasm obscured the truth of this statement. "When I saw her, I was afraid the Frosty Boy had gone on the fritz again."

Finally, Sal unlocked the door and stepped aside to admit the *Star Trek* finger-split guys Cooper had seen the first day. They stalked past Cooper, muttering imprecations, *Break-out: Normandy* in hand.

When the rumored journalist from Miami finally arrived at the station, he turned out to be a ginger with a germinating goatee. He arrived cheerful, walking the station with an NSF public relations rep who shadowed him like a junior high hall monitor. As Cooper passed the men on her way from the studio to the galley, she smiled to be friendly. Sensing the possibility for a positive encounter that could result in good press for the Program, the PR rep stopped.

"A and W, right?" the rep asked, assessing Cooper's paint-stained overalls. "What discipline?"

"I'm a painter," Cooper replied. The rep scribbled this down, then asked her name, and scribbled that down, too.

"Tim, this is one of our artist Fellows," the rep said. "The NSF sponsors writers and artists every year to come down and —"

"Right," Tim said vaguely, looking down the hall toward the exit. "I profiled that paper-clip artist two years ago, remember?" He glanced at Cooper. "But I guess I should cover my bases."

Tim fished out a reporter's notebook from his parka. "What do you think artists bring to the conversation about what goes on at the Pole?" He asked the question like a Red Lobster waitress about to go on break.

"Is there a conversation about what goes on at Pole?" Cooper asked. The PR rep shifted his weight.

"Apparently," Tim said, "or else I wouldn't be here. What are you painting about while you're down?"

"The imperative of the explorer."

"And how do you interpret that?"

"Mittens."

"Fascinating," Tim said, tucking the pen into the coil of his notebook.

The rep gave Cooper a withering look.

Cooper continued on to the galley for lunch, and found Tucker and Dwight engaged in a heated discussion.

"But wouldn't you time travel if you

could, Tucker?" Dwight said as Cooper set her tray down next to him. Tucker shook his head silently as he separated the carbs from the protein on his plate. Dwight gave a huff of disapproval. "You're telling me that if you could go back two hundred years, you wouldn't?"

"Before or after the Fugitive Slave Act?"

Dwight pounded the table with his fist. "You always make it about slavery!" Cooper watched as Dwight stormed off with his tray.

"Do you want me to slip ex-lax into his coffee?"

"That's just Dwight doing Dwight," Tucker said, pinching his eyebrow. "I'm a little on edge."

"What's going on?"

"That reporter from the *Herald* is working an angle about Pavano and his research."

"I figured. What's the big deal?"

"The Program was hoping to keep Pavano's presence on the ice a nonissue. They don't want it to become political." He looked up at Cooper. "I once thought that all you needed to get by in this life was a pleasant phone manner. Of course, that was when I was a telemarketer."

When the *Miami Herald* published Tim's story a week later, it had nothing to do with mittens or the construction of the new station. Instead, the headline was "In World's Last Bastion of Objective Research, Politics Intrudes." As Tucker had predicted, the article focused on Pavano's work on climate change, and how two conservative U.S. congressmen had gotten him on the ice. Bush's approval rates were plunging, and both men were up for reelection in their home states the next year — they hoped the "global-warming hoax" and the federal government's reluctance to fund "skeptics" would whip their constituents into a lather.

Somehow Tim had lost the PR rep long enough to sit down with Pavano for an interview. Tim portrayed him as the kind of fool who would spend his career trying to make sense of Piltdown Man. There was mention of the remoteness of Pavano's lab space, an ad hoc office in the Dark Sector. It was, Tim noted, on the very edge of the Sector, far from the labs of the other climate scientists at Pole.

The article also revealed personal information about Pavano, which the Beakers seized upon: he had been an Indiana science prodigy as a youth and had been courted by Stanford and MIT. He'd chosen Stanford and received degrees in astronomy and physics, specializing in heliospherics, but had had difficulty placing his research papers due to a plagiarism charge early in his career. He had rehabilitated his reputation enough to land a position at a private Midwestern college, where he worked for nearly ten years before he was, again, accused of plagiarism.

Tim had tried to get Beakers to comment on Pavano, but they had, at the NSF's request, remained silent. The piece ended with a quote from one of the congressmen who'd been responsible for getting him to South Pole:

When reached for comment, Senator Sam Bayless (R-KS) said, "In the real world, outside of the ivory tower, science is a vigorous debate, not a museum piece. Just as there is no scientific agreement about the so-called Big Bang, there is no scientific agreement about the causes of so-called climate change." Rep. Bayless added, "I'm proud of my role in helping the National Science Foundation understand that diversity in science is a good thing."

Cooper found the sidebar accompanying the article more interesting than the political implications of congressmen bickering with the NSF. In coming to South Pole Station for the research season, Tim wrote, Pavano was reuniting with a former college roommate: an astrophysicist named Sal Brennan, the son of a highly respected theoretical physicist from Stanford. Dr. John Brennan had, with Alan Guth, helped introduce the idea of cosmic inflation. He had also plucked Frank Pavano from the cornfields of Indiana and brought him to Stanford, only to have Pavano decline to work on Dr. Brennan's team.

Tim reported that, at the same time Pavano was studying heliophysics across campus, Sal had taken up the mantle of his father's uncompleted work — the search for b-modes, the gravitational waves that would, if found, prove the inflationary theory to be correct. And he'd come close once: in 1999, Sal had been part of a South Pole–based experiment that had discovered that microwave radiation was polarized. (Tim didn't elaborate on the import of this finding, and Cooper assumed that, to minds more subtle than hers, the discovery spoke for itself.) But then something had changed. Sal lost confidence in the inflationary model and decided to leave Stanford in order to do his post-doc work at Princeton with Peter Sokoloff, a theoretical physicist who had developed a rival theory to the Big Bang. This theory suggested that rather than the explosive genesis that Dr. Brennan and others had posited, the universe had come about as the result of the latest collision with a parallel world.

"Sal Brennan now believes what his father calls the Big Bang is nothing more than an echo," Tim wrote. "The two men have not spoken since early 2000, when the younger Brennan left for Princeton." Tim went on to report that others working in cosmology — particularly adherents to cosmic inflation — viewed Sal's model, which was a novel refinement of Sokoloff's, with skepticism. However, Princeton's joint South Pole–based experiment with Stanford's Kavli team was without precedent, and could possibly result in the elimination of one of the models by year's end.

"None of the cosmologists working on the standard model at Pole this season would go on the record about Sal Brennan's research," Tim wrote, "but some indicated that he and Frank Pavano's research interests had more in common that one might think."

Cooper absorbed this information avidly. Her own disagreements with her father ran along the lines of whether oars and paddles really were two different things. In some circles, she now realized, it was possible that a father would disavow his son over a difference of opinion regarding the origins of the universe. Or maybe it was just in Sal's circle that such a thing could happen. Either way, it was now clear to Cooper that Sal was not just a bro-dude with a taste for tater tots. There was a whole universe behind his laughing eyes.

"Journalists never get science right," Sal replied when Cooper found him on the climbing wall in the gym that night.

"What about Pavano? Did he get Pavano right?"

Sal dropped from the wall and rubbed powder off his hands. "Pavano's so awkward he makes even theoretical physicists uncomfortable. He was always too much in his own head, so he could never collaborate with anyone on papers. Then he started plagiarizing — and trust me, you have to work really hard to convincingly plagiarize helioseismology research. He couldn't get tenure and got the boot. With no home institution, he couldn't get funding. Without funding he was fucked."

"But he's here," Cooper said, "so clearly he's not totally fucked."

"Well, lucky for him there are people who make a living looking for failed scientists."

"But what about the plagiarism? Wouldn't that tarnish his rep?"

"You keep forgetting — it's not about the science. Plagiarizing a couple graphs in an obscure research paper? No, that's nothing more than a love bite. It's about the messaging. Did you read the rest of the piece?"

"You mean where they talk about you and your research? I stopped reading after the part about the branes and the parallel universes. It got too science-y and I lost interest."

He rolled his eyes. "Of course that's the part that is going to change the world, but sure, god forbid it get too 'science-y.' " He picked Cooper's parka off the floor and threw it at her. "Come on, I want to show you something."

Minutes later, they were careening across the ice on a snowmobile, flying over sastrugi and hitting every frozen crest so hard Cooper could feel her fillings clattering. The wind was ferociously cold; Cooper thought her face was going to peel off. She looked over her shoulder at the Dome growing smaller and smaller as they sped toward the metal city where so much science was done at South Pole: the Dark Sector.

She pulled her face out of the back of Sal's parka in time to see two enormous funnels, open to the sky and surrounded by scaffolding, and a couple of large, blue prefab buildings embraced by metal staircases. She was amazed at how impermanent the structures of the Dark Sector looked, like a mutated, multilevel trailer park. The place seemed deserted. Once inside, Sal led her into a large room filled with humming supercomputers and servers and endless coils of cables, all feeding into a large enclosed cable tray. He showed her the calibration station, and his face flushed with geek joy when he took out the blueprints for the Arcminute Cosmology Bolometer Array Receiver (ACBAR, he called it) that would be installed on the telescope next year.

Cooper began to lose track of the number of flickering computer screens and exactly what was supposed to be happening, but that was okay. She was almost getting it. This was what the Beakers were always yammering about. This was, in fact, Sal's world, and she was weirdly drawn to it.

Sal brought her to a small, cluttered cubicle. Her brain immediately filled in the gaps of time when she didn't see Sal during the day. He was here, going over readings with Alek and the other research techs. Sal flipped through some papers on his desk

300

and started to say something, then stopped. He flipped through more papers, and Cooper cast about for something to say but came up empty. Finally, Sal cleared his throat. "Yesterday, I was looking over measurements of CMB anisotropies, and I thought — where will she be sitting at dinner tonight? Will she be wearing that ratty Vikings T-shirt again? Will she come to my table or will I have to go to her?"

If not for the description of the Vikings shirt, Cooper wouldn't have known Sal was referring to her. He looked at her expectantly. Here again came that weird seizing feeling in her chest of being on a precipice, and she could not immediately figure out how to respond. Sal laughed, and looked away. "I'm sorry. Usually when I make women uncomfortable, it's on purpose."

"No, I'm sorry. I'm not uncomfortable. I'm — I'm surprised. One minute we're talking about telescopes and words I can't pronounce, and the next minute — you said that. Sorry."

"Okay, now we've both apologized for nothing." He pinched the bridge of his nose like an exhausted teacher. "Look, I'm not used to subtlety in polar courtship. This is me telling you I like you. This is me telling you that sometimes I wonder where you'll be sitting at dinner or if you'll come into the Smoke Bar afterward. And that, after finding out from a Florida newspaper that I'm a total disappointment to a world-class scientific institution, not to mention my own father, if you still want to talk to me, I can usually be found here." As Cooper struggled to take all this in, Sal gestured toward yet another door. "Come on."

"Where are we going?"

"The 'scopes. That's why I brought you out here."

After inching along a metal scaffold bridge, dusted with fine ice particles, they arrived at a wooden frame — not a window, not a door, just a portal. Cooper peered through it and saw yet another incomprehensible scene of metal, wires, and mirrors. But as Cooper looked at it, it seemed to take a shape. "It looks like a metal coffee filter," she said.

Sal blinked at her. "That's actually a completely accurate way of describing what this telescope does. Except instead of coffee grounds, it catches neutrinos and maybe b-modes, if I'm really unlucky."

"Unlucky?"

"The Kavli team from Stanford is looking for b-modes, which, if found, will confirm the inflationary theory — the Big Bang. Lisa

Wu would lay down her life to get a five-sigma on the presence of b-modes worming their way toward us from thirteen billion years ago. Of course, if she does, then my model is eliminated."

"The one where the universe is just a bouncing ball?"

Sal considered the telescope for a moment. "Do you believe in the Big Bang?"

"Believe in it? I thought it was a done deal."

"Not a done deal. Not yet. I don't buy the inflationary theory of the origins of the universe. I like a different model. I like the one that says there wasn't a Big Bang. That the universe is not infinitely expanding. That our universe collides against another universe — a brane — every few trillion years and this spurs something that looks like a 'big bang' but is really a big bounce. The theory is completely compatible with every finding now held up as evidence for the inflationary theory, completely in line with what the WAMP satellite has detected. In fact, our models — the inflationary theory and the cyclic model, which is what my model is called — are like twins. They share 99.99 percent of their DNA. Only their mother can tell them apart. But if Lisa finds b-modes, the cyclic model is smoke."

"What if she doesn't find them?"

"If she doesn't, those waves are too small to measure, and all those temp fluctuations and galaxy seeds were created in a process gentler than the violent expansion the inflationists promote. The cyclic model is like the lover's kiss of cosmology. In my opinion, it's the most compelling scientific theory outside of gravity and evolution."

"Then why does it seem like you're the only one who believes it?" Cooper said. Sal looked discomposed.

"I don't *believe* it," he said. "That's not how science works. But I find it compelling enough to devote my life to it. The inflationary theory has serious conceptual problems. It's extravagant, for one thing — about as fine-tuned as a Beverly Hills housewife. It also dabbles in the anthropic — it takes life into account — and that moves it from physics to metaphysics."

There was an opening here, Cooper thought, one she could slip through by asking a big but simplistic question. She wanted to connect with him in a way that went beyond their moment in the library. She decided to go for it. "How can something come from nothing?"

It was clear at once that Sal was irritated, but Cooper didn't know why. "And there's the metaphysics, right on cue," he said.

"I'm just asking a question," Cooper said, confused.

Sal looked at her for a moment. "Ah, I see now. You're not asking me how it happened. You're asking me who pulled the trigger." He turned away and tinkered with the telescope. "Shit."

"What?"

He looked over at Cooper. "Nothing. It's just — I think you're spending too much time with Pavano. These are his questions, not yours. Dumb questions are not attractive."

Cooper felt humiliated. Blistering heat coursed through her body. "Well, since I live each day in service to what you find attractive, I'm devastated."

Sal stared at her in surprise — Cooper herself was surprised — and both fell silent.

"Why is it so hard to talk to you?" he finally said.

"You brought me out here so I'd ask questions, right? Or did you just want me to *ooh* and *ahh* over your big telescope? I asked a question because I'm interested. In this. In you. You're telling me you and Alek sit out here and talk about the minutia of the beginnings of the universe and it never occurs to you to ask how it started?"

"That's all we do."

"No, I mean how it started before it started."

"And I am answering your question with precision: the universe is cyclic, it is built and destroyed, and then it is rebuilt. It bumps up against another world, from which we are separated by a dimension, and this sets off a bounce, what inflationists call the Big Bang."

"Before that. Before any of it, Sal."

"These are questions every kindergartener asks, Cooper."

"Have they gotten an answer yet?"

Sal started pacing the metal scaffold. "You know what gets old real quick? People trying to ask if there's a god in about a hundred different ways. Do you realize how ridiculous that sounds to someone who knows what the universe actually looks like? Is it my job to pretend like we're all on equal footing here, that we're all smart and all of our answers are equal and we all get certificates just for showing up? That may work in art, Cooper, but that doesn't work in the real world. Science doesn't work that way."

He studied Cooper for a moment, and then seemed to grow remote. "Oh, I see. It's meaningless to you because it doesn't take you into account." He laughed. "I know exactly what you want me to say. That your precious 'Big Bang' was the eye of god opening. When I don't play your game, you ask me if I can prove that it wasn't. Here's a real question for you: Would you even want me to tell you if I could?"

Cooper and Sal stood staring at each other. Cooper could see both certainty and fear looking back at her, until Sal blinked, and only certainty remained.

At the Smoke Bar that night, Cooper sat in silence with Birdie, watching Floyd and a contract plumber grind against a dining assistant to the strains of Electric Hellfire Club.

"Quit hogging the girl," the plumber shouted at Floyd.

"Has anyone seen Sal?" one of his research techs called from the door.

"He's up in El Dorm fucking that cargo handler," Floyd replied.

"No, I just saw him in the library," Denise shouted from the bar.

"You're seeing things, then," Floyd said, "because he's definitely getting his cargo handled right now."

Sal's research tech grinned sheepishly and walked out.

If Cooper hadn't already been completely

soused, the exchange would have stung. Instead, she turned her attention to a half-full beer on the table that did not seem to have an owner. She drained it and set it back down. Next to her, Birdie slowly pushed the bottle away with his index finger.

"Well," he said, "unless I'm much mistaken, I've just witnessed a moment of desperation," he said. "What's wrong, Cherry?"

Cooper responded by pushing back her chair and getting another beer from the bar. She wandered around, pausing at various tables, and after downing a Jägermeister beer bomb with the contract plumber, walked up to Floyd and began an impassioned but incoherent defense of Larry Mc-Murtry.

He merely waved her off. "Go sober up, honey."

She sauntered back to Birdie's table, but he was in deep conversation with Pearl now, so she decided to lay down on the floor and rest her eyes. Some time later, she found Tucker looming above her like a monument — he was wearing sunglasses, and in them, Cooper saw herself, twice. She realized she was using someone's bunny boot — Birdie's? — as a pillow. A new face appeared next to Tucker's — an unfamiliar pink face with a mouth like an earthworm. "Are you okay, love?" The face swam in and out of view, and it wasn't until she noticed the surplice that Cooper realized it was the chaplain in from Palmer Station.

"I'm okay," she slurred. "Just wanna sleep." She dropped her head back against Birdie's bunny boot with a thud. The next thing she knew, Tucker was hauling her to her feet.

"I'll escort her to her room," she heard Tucker say to the chaplain.

"Encourage her to come talk to me tomorrow, will you," he said. "Best to cut these problem drinkers off at the pass, I think."

"Come on," Tucker whispered in Cooper's ear. He dressed her in her ECW, and escorted her down the stairs and across the Dome. As she emerged from the entrance tunnel, the crisp, thin air seemed to slap her halfway sober. Like a riderless horse galloping over a hill, vague but searing shame appeared and overtook her. She summoned every shred of competence she had to put one boot in front of the other.

"I'm sorry," she said.

"Don't be. Public intoxication is an occupational hazard."

"You have my paperwork. You know I'm not a drunk."

"Situational alcoholism is a documented disorder," Tucker replied.

"And it's not even cold," Cooper cried, as she blinked into the sunlight. "I'm at South fucking Pole and I'm not even cold!"

"It's thirty degrees below zero."

Cooper shook off Tucker's grip and skipped across the snow. She stumbled and fell face-first, her reflexes too slow to break her fall. Tucker turned her over and looked down into her hood.

"I'm going insane," Cooper heard herself say.

"You know what Foucault says," Tucker replied. "Madness can be silenced by reason."

This comment hit Cooper like a steel-tipped ice chopper to the head. She scrambled to her feet and pushed Tucker with both hands. "Take that back!" An expression of shock passed over Tucker's face, quickly replaced by sadness. Cooper pushed him again. "It's reason that is silenced by madness, and you know it. Take it back!"

Suddenly, Tucker gathered her into his arms, into a firm, bigger-than-the-sky embrace. "Forgive me, Cooper," he said. Then, just as suddenly, he pushed her away and turned back toward the station.

The Jamesway was deserted. At her door,

Cooper found a small package, wrapped in brown paper. She tucked the package under her arm and shouldered her way into the room. She successfully unzipped her parka on the third try before sitting down to work off her damp long johns and assorted under-clothes.

Once she'd stowed her ECW, she opened the package. It contained a bottle of Scotch. A note was included, which was decorated by an amateurish but endearing drawing of two penguins. The penguins were regarding each other from across an ice crevasse. The note, written in immaculate but minuscule print, read, *In hopes of inspiration. (They say Scotch was the drink of choice at Scott's Hut.) Thank you for your kindness. My invitation to the Divide still stands. You're on the manifest if you want to be. Frank Pavano.*

Placing the note from Pavano on her desk, she picked up the old Tylenol vial. She ran her thumb over the cap, thought about opening it, then decided against it, setting it next to the compass. She lay down on her bed with her boots on to wait for the room to stop spinning, and after about an hour, it did. She staggered over to her desk and laid a blank piece of paper on it. She stared at its brilliant whiteness for so long that iridescent green specks began flying across the page. Finally, she picked up a sharpened pencil and began sketching.

Fifteen minutes later, she had a crude drawing of a vending-machine charm in the shape of Frank Pavano. It was the first drawing she'd completed since the last mitten in the triptych, and it was that fact, rather than any merit inherent in the sketch itself, that calmed Cooper's nerves.

She heard the door to the Jamesway open at the end of the hall. The squeak of bunny boots echoed down the corridor until the footsteps stopped at her door. The sound of heavy mittens being removed was followed by a confident knock.

"You decent?"

"Wait," Cooper said. "Just — hold on." She struggled into her thermals and tucked the sketch she'd done of Pavano between the pages of *Worst Journey.* Finally, she opened the door to find Sal in his green parka and gaiters, frost on his eyebrows and his beard. He pushed his hood off his head with his forearm.

"Tucker told me you got obliterated at the Smoke Bar. He asked me to check on you."

"He's exaggerating. I'm fine. As you can see."

"Well, I told him I'd check on you. So I'm checking on you." He glanced around her room. "Can I come in?"

Cooper stepped aside to let him pass. He spotted the Scotch and picked it up.

"Mackinlay's?" There was reverence in his voice. "Where'd you get this?"

"It was a thank-you gift."

Sal looked over at Cooper. "From who?"

"Pavano."

"Frank Pavano gave you this?"

"There was a note. It's on the desk."

Sal read it, then tossed the sketch back on the desk. "He offers you 'inspiration'?" The ice groaned beneath the Jamesway, shifting.

"I'll take what I can get," Cooper said.

"Why is Pavano sending you gifts?"

"I think this is his way of being human."

"In my line of work, sharing research is like swapping bodily fluids, so I'm sure it's the same with art. Not that this is art." Then he saw Cooper's sketch of the *Terra Nova* taped to the wall. "Now this — this looks like art," he said. He leaned close to it, his eyes roaming from the ship's figurehead to its masts and riggings. "This is fucking intricate, Cooper. You did this?"

Cooper stepped next to him. "It's the *Terra Nova*. The Scottish whaler Scott brought to Pole."

"Holy shit," he said softly. He turned to look at her. "This is good, Cooper."

"You can have it," Cooper said, not quite knowing why she said it. "I mean, if you want it."

"Of course I want it."

Cooper reached across him to remove the sketch from the wall, and as she did so she felt she was toeing the edge, the parade passing by below her. She handed him the sketch and he set it on the desk without taking his eyes off her face. He touched her cheek with his cold hands like she was the most fragile thing on earth. They stood like this for what felt to Cooper like hours, and yet she had no desire to break their silence, or even move. Suddenly, Sal inhaled sharply and shook his head. "I'm just going to say it: I think you're beautiful and I want to be near you. Can that be enough?"

Cooper responded by leaning into him and, hesitatingly, kissing his mouth. She pulled back to see if this had been a welcome gesture, but his eyes were closed.

She sat on the edge of her bed and watched as Sal dropped to a knee in front of her and began unlacing her bunny boots, unthreading the laces through the eyelets unhurriedly. Once he'd pulled off her boots, he held her feet in his hands and looked up at her. "You should be wearing your blue boots," he said mildly. "They don't get your

314

socks wet."

Then he helped her pull her long underwear over her head, and each time his cold hands brushed her skin, it seemed like getting a good deep breath was impossible. A sense of urgency began to rise up and grip Cooper as Sal undressed her. She scooted back on the bed to make room for him, and watched as he pulled his overall straps off his shoulders, like Cooper imagined a lumberjack might.

But as he reached for his belt, something changed in his expression — he looked at her as if seeing her for the first time, and froze. His suspenders hanging off his waist, and his blue thermal stained with old sweat, the cuffs pushed up to his elbows, he pulled away. He shook his head twice, like he was shaking off a blow.

"Oh god, what?" Cooper said. She looked down at her bare arms and curled into herself, drawing her knees up to her chest. Sal's back was now against the canvas door.

"I don't know," he said, his voice strange. "Something's wrong about this. I'm confused."

His eyes searched the room, landing on everything but Cooper's face. Then they found the compass, the antique compass — baroque, incongruous, but necessary. "The compass," he said. "Who brings an antique compass to Pole?"

"Who cares?" Cooper said weakly.

"No, it says something. It means something," Sal said. "It's messing me up." Cooper didn't believe him. Of course it wasn't the compass. They both knew this was a lie. The compass, with its dumb glass face, was itself a lie Bill had told Cooper again and again since the day he'd dropped it in her hands — that it was all you needed to navigate yourself to safety.

As she watched Sal pulling his suspenders back over his shoulders, Cooper realized there was no longer a reason not to reveal that lie — no reason not to step off the precipice, and no one to stop her from doing it. So she told him about Saganaga, how it had been during the trip to the Boundary Waters with Billie and their father two months after David was found that Cooper had gone wandering, gotten lost. She'd stumbled back into camp around ten at night, her panic long since replaced by indifference to her fate. Billie was already in her sleeping bag. Bill had been chopping wood; he hardly looked up. "You had a compass and you had our coordinates," he'd said, as if she'd only been out to use the latrine. "Obviously, you don't know how to use

316

either."

The next morning, Cooper awoke to find he'd designed a compass course outside of camp. There was a log. Then, ten feet away, a stone. About two yards from that was a Nalgene bottle. Past that, the small wooden box containing David's ashes.

"I decided last night," Bill said. "It's up to you to get us to Lake Gray. You have the map and you have the compass. If we're not there in two days, we turn back. He remains in the box." Cooper had no time to absorb her father's anger before he roughly shoved the antique compass into her hands. He then grasped her shoulders and positioned her until she faced the woods. "What does it say now?"

"North."

"Wrong."

"Who cares," Billie said sleepily from the door of the tent. "That's what GPS is for." But something inside Cooper, a half-buried but strong and relentless feeling, took hold of her and said, I *care*.

But they never got to Lake Gray, not that time, and Cooper held the box in her lap the entire drive home.

All this Cooper told Sal not because she wanted him to understand her — it no longer mattered what he thought about her

317

— but because she wanted him to know that, even if the compass was a lie, she was not. She told him about Cherry and Titus, about her imaginary journeys with David, how Edgar Allan Poe had infected his vision of South Pole, and how she'd come here to make sure their first idea of Pole was the right one, to reclaim it from the lies. Sal listened to all this, his chin on his chest, but when she was done, he said nothing. Cooper felt completely alone.

"I'm sorry," he finally said, grabbing his parka from the desk chair. "I know I'm being a dick, but I really don't know what to say. I need to think."

Cooper understood then that she had unloaded her baggage at his feet and he'd kicked it once or twice before deciding it was too much trouble. She continued hugging her knees, head down, and listened to the rustle of his parka, the metallic étude of his zipper going up, catching, going down, then going all the way up to his neck, and, finally, the sound of his boots retreating down the hall.

Cooper got out of bed, moved her desk chair to the back wall, and climbed on it. She pushed aside the towel she'd hung over the small window, the one she'd looked out of that first day. It was nearly three in the morning, but stark sunlight poured into the room. Outside, the sky was a pale and taut canvas. She glanced down at her desk, and saw the *Terra Nova* sketch was gone.

Sal and the lead of Stanford's Kavli Institute experiment, the elusive Lisa Wu, had been persuaded to lecture on their teams' respective effort to determine the origins of the universe. Cooper had only seen Lisa on one other occasion — at Pavano's lecture a month earlier, watching silently with her research techs. She was a tall, plain-looking woman with completely horizontal dark eyebrows. Her wan bearing was relieved only by the aquamarine rhinestone stud she wore in her left nostril.

Once the crowd settled down, and someone had found Lisa a can of mineral water, she began outlining the basic tenets of the inflationary theory: that the universe grew at unimaginably fast rates during the first fraction of a second after the Big Bang, that the expansion has slowed down, but not stopped, and that the theory, as endorsed by Linde, Guth, and Hawking, along with most mainstream physicists, had achieved five of the six "milestones" that would settle the question once and for all. Cooper had zoned out during the exquisitely detailed explanation of these milestones, but she perked up when she heard Lisa acknowledge that the rate of expansion initially exceeded the speed of light.

At this, a meteorologist raised his hand. "I thought the whole point of the speed of light was that nothing can exceed it."

Cooper noticed Lisa glance at Sal, who was sitting in the front row awaiting his turn. She replied that the meteorologist was correct — technically — but that "in physics, we've learned to expect the unexpected."

"That sounds like a slogan for a beer," Pearl whispered to Cooper.

As she started to wrap up, Lisa glanced over at Sal once again. "Before I turn the stage over to Sal, I feel compelled to say something else: Sal's father, Professor John Brennan, is the reason I'm standing here. He's the reason my whole team is here, really. He believed in each and every one of us, and we consider it the biggest privilege of our lives to be part of this experiment that he designed more than twenty-five years ago. It was only recently that the technology advanced to a point where his theory could be tested." Her eyes darted back toward Sal. "Some thought, perhaps continue to think, that this theory was impossible to test and therefore not scientific. Professor Brennan showed that it is, in fact, testable. And it was Professor Brennan who first understood that the matter and heat in our universe are regularly distributed, that this is not chance, but a cosmological principle."

Sal shifted in his seat. "But that might not mean a lot to those of you who don't live and breathe the Cosmic Microwave Background. Inflation created a uniform and stable cosmos; it can happen again," Lisa continued. "Perhaps it already has. This theory offers a view of the universe in which we are not alone, suggests that there are other universes in pockets of space and time. That's the inflationary theory in a nutshell, and though it's a hard nut to crack, I'm confident that by the end of the research season, we'll have the answer to our most pressing cosmological question."

Everyone applauded, and as Lisa walked past Sal to her seat, Cooper saw him whisper something to her. She remembered what it had felt like as Sal held her foot in his hand. She pushed the thought away.

Sal wrenched around in his chair. "Do you guys mind if Alek tells a joke first?" No one objected, so Alek stepped forward. "This joke happens near Munich. Heisenberg goes for drive and police stop him. Police says, 'Sir, do you know how fast you go?' Heisenberg say: 'No, but I know where I am.' "

Approximately one-sixth of the audience burst into peals of laughter, while the other five-sixths remained silent. Once Alek had returned to his seat, Sal approached the podium. "The Beakers are laughing because they got the joke, not because it's funny — trust me. Anyway, I'm not going to get into a rigorous defense of the cyclic theory of the universe or an attack on the Kavli team's work, but I will indulge myself in delivering one brief roundhouse kick.

"Professor Wu said something that I have to correct, and that is the idea that some of you may have about what she means when she says 'regular distribution.' This makes the universe seem like a calm and orderly place. It is not. If the inflationary theory were true, then the majority of space is an uncontrolled, chaotic place undergoing brutally violent inflation, powered by the kind of energy that tells Einstein to fuck off. But they'd also have you believe that hidden in the folds of this cosmic Technicolor Dreamcoat are those 'pocket universes' that Lisa mentioned, where ponies run free, the wind whipping through their manes — or, the flip side, an alternate world where you are living the life that would have unfolded had you decided to run that red light in 1998 and killed your family in a car wreck. To make matters worse, the inflationary theory is the Intelligent Design of cosmology —"

"Sal, that's not fair," Lisa said.

"Let me finish first, and then see if it's not fair. The inflationary theory is the Intelligent Design of cosmology because it is heavily reliant on the anthropic principle, which is the idea that the physical laws that govern the universe must be compatible with the fact that life exists."

Next to Cooper, Pearl raised her hand. "What's wrong with that? That seems logical."

"Yes, it does, but in cosmology, and in Intelligent Design, it is being used to explain features of the observable universe that people like Professor Wu, and like my father, cannot explain. This is the sign of a deeply flawed theory."

"I don't get it," Pearl replied.

"Simply put: instead of physical laws explaining the complexity and diversity of life, they are using the very fact of life to explain the complexity of physical laws. That's not how science works."

The Kavli team began moving about in

their chairs, and one of them seemed about to speak when Pavano rose from his chair in the very back of the room. "Your own mentor has said that just because a prediction is consistent with the evidence does not mean the theory is right," he said.

"Yes, and he also said that a scientist must show that the theory has correctly identified the root cause of the phenomenon. And the inflationists haven't." He hesitated and, for a moment, his eyes met Cooper's. "As I told someone just the other day, it's a question every kindergartener asks: What happened before the Big Bang? The greatest minds in inflationary theory cannot answer that."

"And you can?" Pavano replied.

"Not yet. But I believe my team and I will."

"Then let me quote Susskind," Lisa said, standing up now. " 'The field of physics is littered with the corpses of stubborn old men who didn't know when to give up.' "

"You're right, Lisa — I don't give up easily."

"Then enlighten us, Sal. Tell them about your own personal *Hitchhiker's Guide to the Universe.*"

"It's simple, and there's not a single fine-tune in it: the Big Bang was not the beginning, but was instead the seismic instant marking the separation between our current period of expansion and the cooling from a previous one. What we know as the universe is actually a membrane, or what we call a *brane.* We theorize that our planet exists in a universe that contains at least eight unobservable dimensions. Our brane is separated from another brane by one of these dimensions, and when these two branes collide, it creates what inflationists consider a one-off event — the Big Bang. However, we believe this event actually happens every trillion years. Like a child's sand castle on a beach, it is built and torn down with the regularity of an ocean wave."

The Kavli team snickered.

Cooper raised her hand. "What would that look like?" Without turning around in her seat, Pearl offered Cooper a thumbs-up. Sal walked to the whiteboard and drew an image that looked like two pancakes being used as cymbals. "Like this," he said.

"No. I mean, what would it look like if I were standing right here when it happened. I want an image, not a diagram."

Sal dropped the marker on the table. "You're asking what it would look like if you were there, in the middle of it?" Cooper nodded. "It would be the stuff of day-dreams. The most beautiful thing imaginable. First, the approach: You wouldn't feel it, but something enormous would be moving along a dimension you couldn't see. Then, when you collided with it, space would be infused with a nuclear brightness, an ungodly burst of radiation, and it would become hotter than a billion suns. Everything else in the universe — the galaxies, the planets, the stars — everything would be evaporated in an instant. The quarks and gluons that made up everything in the previous cycle would join the flood of new quarks and gluons created at the moment of the collision." He met Cooper's eyes. "The cycle would be renewed."

"So if I'm made up of quarks and gluons," Dwight said, "and, of course, I am, you're telling me I will live again."

"What I'm saying is that in our model, the universe is not lost in a sea of multiverses, not one of countless and random possibilities. Instead, it's a single, cycling entity."

Pearl set her knitting aside. "So we just bang and crunch over and over again?"

"I'm saying that every trillion or so years, the universe remakes itself as an echo of its previous form. Controlled evolution. Every corner of space makes galaxies, stars, planets, and presumably life, over and over again. Instead of being a product of chaos and unexplainable beginnings, the cyclic model — our model — has an explanation for 'what happened before the Big Bang.' It's fucking elegant as hell that evolution works just as well for the structures of galaxies as it does for opposable thumbs." He looked over at Lisa and the Kavli team. "Now, all that being said, if we find measurable b-mode polarization this season, none of what I just proposed is true."

"And that would be bad," Pearl said.

"No," Sal replied, "that would be science."

Suddenly, the galley door burst open, and an empty Heineken went sailing through the air before shattering against the back wall. Bonnie stood in the doorway, unsteady. Cooper noticed pink blooms on Bonnie's cheeks and a milk-white beauty about her skin that she'd never seen before.

Bonnie brushed her lank hair out of her eyes. "I don't mean to interrupt, but I'm going on record right now that I'm glad this shit is over." As she propelled herself into the galley, knocking over a pair of empty chairs, Dwight sprung to his feet to stop her, but tripped over the hem of his cloak. "Get out of my way, you stupid-ass skill monkey," Bonnie growled. Cooper looked over at Pearl. She had drawn her pink bandanna over her eyes and was slumped in her chair as if trying to dissolve. Next to her Birdie stroked her knee soothingly.

"Bonnie, stop," Dwight pleaded. But Alek stood up and pounded the top of one of the dining tables. "You stand up here," he said. "Let everyone hear." He assisted Bonnie onto the table.

Once Bonnie was steady on her feet, she looked down at everyone. "I just wanna say that I'm outta here tomorrow. Tucker and the powers-that-be have decided to demote me but I refuse to spend an entire winter at South Pole chopping other people's onions." Pearl's face remained obscured behind her bandanna. "So this crazy adventure's over for me, but guess what? I'm glad it's over. I'm glad it's over, and here's why: it means the end of the bullshit I've been dealing with since October." She looked down at Dwight. "You don't come to South Pole to 'strengthen your relationship,' Dwight. You don't come here to push boundaries so you can exchange sex e-mails with a fucking mini-doughnut vendor you met in a cosplay chat room!"

Dwight sank down in his chair.

"Come on, Bonnie," Sal said, laughing. "Stay. We love your hoosh."

"Nah, Sal. My time has passed. It's time

for you guys to eat another woman's hoosh." She soft-shoed her way off the table and walked out of the galley.

Birdie turned around in his chair to look at everyone. "What's hoosh?"

The lectures over, everyone filed out of the galley and into their respective bars and lounges, Cooper hung back and waited for Pavano. "Someone slipped the flight manifest under my door last night," she said.

"Yes, everything's been arranged. They're expecting us." He scuffed the floor with one of his boots. "I take it you are still interested in coming?"

Cooper watched as Sal stalked out the door. "More than ever."

The West Antarctic Divide was one of the most remote locations on the planet, but it was also, Cooper was certain, one of the loudest. The metallic roar of industrial generators made the screams of the 319's engines sound like a kitten's purr. The site was strewn with communication flags of all colors, from lemon-yellow to Achtung-orange; these were attached to one another by lengths of rope, designed to guide anyone caught in a whiteout. A plywood admin building stood sentry at the entrance, with a communications shack attached. Beyond those stood what looked like a dollhouse version of the fuel arches at Pole: these were, Cooper gathered from the hand-drawn map Pavano had made for her during the flight from South Pole, the drilling arch and the core-handling arch. So it was here that the fate of the world, or the global warming hoax, would be decided. This was sacred scientific ground, but to Cooper it looked like any other stretch of Antarctic ice occupied by humans.

Cooper and Pavano stood at the end of a long line leading into the admin shack, manned by an effusive NSF field rep, whose guffaw seemed to echo throughout the entire camp. Cooper and Pavano hadn't exchanged words since leaving Pole; the flight had been uneventful and characteristically deafening. Conversation was out of the question, and Pavano had spent most of the ride staring at the cargo rack just above Cooper's head.

"Pavano, Frank — and research tech," Pavano recited when they reached the front of the line. The rep looked down at his clipboard for a moment too long. Cooper could tell he wasn't reading anything.

"Would you excuse me for a moment," he said, before disappearing into an adjoining room. Cooper could hear whispers and the sound of shuffling papers. The rep returned, looking sheepish. "Your, uh, research tech is not approved," he said, his eyes not quite meeting Pavano's. "She has not undergone basic safety training."

"I was told this requirement had been waived since she is an NSF grantee and underwent safety training in Denver," Pavano replied.

"I'm just telling you what I know," the man said. "You can talk to the site manager if you want, but for now, she can't touch any equipment. You're in Sector 4B." He pointed to a shelf stocked with bright neoprene bundles. "Tents and camp stoves over there."

"What are my access hours to the ice-core archive?" Pavano asked.

The rep looked embarrassed. He consulted the clipboard. "Says here that you will have access to the core-handling room at 0300 hours; you may access the archive freezer at that time." Three a.m., Cooper thought. Jesus.

"And the coordinates for my coring site?" Pavano continued, unperturbed.

"Well, yes, there's a bit of a problem with that, too, I see."

"What's the problem?"

"That request has been denied — it says

331

here that there are some safety concerns." Behind them, the people in line sighed. Denied requests led to long delays and grumpy core techs, who were in the ice archives waiting to be spelled. But to Cooper's surprise, Pavano didn't argue. He thanked the rep, then gathered his bag and stepped over to the shelf where the tents were wrapped in neat, ornament-like balls. Astonished, the NSF rep watched as Pavano scooped two tents from the shelf.

"Sector 4B is this way," Pavano said as he led Cooper out the door.

"Wait, don't you want to —"

"Argue? I knew exactly what would happen when I arrived. People are reassuringly predictable. Which makes my job easier."

"It's your job to get railroaded?"

"In a sense."

Cooper laughed. "You are so weird."

"I find I am just weird enough."

The walk from the central site to sector 4B was comparable to the walk from the station to Summer Camp at Pole, but Cooper wanted to crawl the last twenty yards — the air was so thin it felt as though she were sipping air through a straw. Her whole body hurt. Sector 4B turned out to be a ghost town. Vacant tents dotted the landscape, their nylon flaps dancing in the wind. Pavano dropped the gear. "I'd say they put us all the way out in Antarctica, but we're already here, so I'll say they put us in Siberia instead." He gestured toward the perimeter of camp. "Take a walk," he said. "I'll put up the tents."

Cooper was bent over her knees, huffing. She cocked her head up at Pavano and squinted in the sun. "How are you breathing and talking at the same time?"

"I did some high-altitude cross-training in preparation before the season began."

"Well, goody for you," Cooper gasped. Pavano almost smiled. "I'll help with the tents. I'm pretty good at setting them up. Lots of practice."

Pavano shook his head. "No, go walk. Look around. Maybe you'll get inspired."

"Maybe I'll die of hypoxia."

"Either way, a different perspective."

As Cooper began trudging away, she heard Pavano call after her, "Follow the flags."

"I'm sick of following flags," Cooper muttered.

The sun was merciless — bright with burning hydrogen and helium but offering no heat. That the continent on which she walked was wrapped around the bottom of the planet — that rock and ice could adhere to a curve — suddenly seemed a ridiculous notion. Cooper squinted, trying to conjure an image of Cherry, or even Mawson — the redoubtable Aussie survivor of a different adventure, with his skin peeling off in thick sheets, his tongue swollen, and his gums black as ink. Several of the Program's past artist Fellows had painted images of these men haunting the ice, sometimes literally as ghosts. But when Cooper thought of them, they faded quickly, replaced by other, more familiar ghosts.

As she walked, she kept thinking of what she hadn't told Sal that night in her room, of what had happened after that trip to Saganaga. About how she and Billie had returned to the Boundary Waters a month later without Bill, and without his knowledge, to take matters into their own hands. At their launch point, a group of men had appeared, wearing Duluth Packs on their shoulders and many-pocketed cargo pants. As soon as they saw Billie pulling the canoe off the car rack, the packs had dropped from their shoulders, hitting the hard grassless soil on the edges of the launch point simultaneously.

"We're good, boys," Billie said, grunting as she lifted the canoe on her shoulders. Her curse-soaked stumble confirmed the men's initial impulse. Two of them walked over to where she stood, slipped their shoulders under the eaves of the canoe, and raised it off her shoulders.

"Thanks, guys," Cooper said. Billie turned to her and mouthed an emphatic *fuck you.*

"You two planning to portage?" a scrawny guy in shorts asked. "We-no-nahs are a bitch." Cooper said nothing, chastened by her sister's soundless curse. The big guy looked at Billie, down the length of her body and then back again, assessing her suitability to the task and finding it wanting.

"You guys aren't going in alone, are you?" he asked.

"We're meeting our old man at Saganaga," Cooper said. "It's a test." Billie said nothing to contradict Cooper's easy lie.

"A test?"

"A competence test," Billie said, picking up the lie with ease. "We do this every year. He marks up the map. He goes in two days before us. We find him." These words came out of Billie's mouth without cadence or emotion, and Cooper saw her sister's lively eyes had turned dull and cold. She wanted the men gone.

"Wow, that's hard-core," the scrawny one said.

"You know what's really hard-core," Billie

said, and to Cooper's horror, she dug the baggie out of her pants pocket.

"Billie, don't," Cooper said.

The guy peered at the baggie, and broke into a grin. "Dope? Yeah, that's real hardcore," he said.

Billie walked up to him and dangled the bag in front of his Maui Jims. "Guess again," she said. From where Cooper was standing, the guy looked like the figure in Magritte's *The Son of Man,* except instead of a bowler he was wearing a bad buzz cut and instead of a green apple in front of his face there was a Ziploc containing David's cremated remains.

The guy took a few steps back. "Jesus. You can't do that, you know. It's illegal."

"You gonna tell on me?"

"No," the guy said, even more quietly this time. "I'm just saying."

Billie put the baggie back in her pocket and walked down the ramp, leaving Maui Jim gaping after them. The big guy had set the canoe on the launch point, and held it steady as Cooper stepped in, and when she did she felt like she was stepping off the edge of the earth.

Later, when the men's voices had faded to silence and the only sound was the whisper of the paddles whirlpooling the water,

Cooper remembered how the tangled mass of streams and rivers on the navigation map became a single ribbon of clear water. You took it on faith that on the other side of the granite islands, with their forests of spruce looming over the clearings, another waterway, another lake, another body, lay glinting like steel in sunshine. Maps were promises.

They paddled across the lake in silence, except for Billie's occasional call to switch, or to draw left or right. Billie favored her left stroke, and they were continually listing east. As the sun rose higher in the sky, the extent of the damage from the 1999 blowdown was laid bare. Cooper had heard that Ogishkemuncie and Seagull lakes had gotten the worst of it, nearly every mature tree felled by the wind. The patches of flattened forest made Cooper fearful; the open, endless horizon seemed to her like death.

But, still, the route was so familiar, it was like walking around the block. This was their circuit, the Gosling circuit, their route, their road, the only place David was ever truly serene. The annual trip where, invariably, all was quiet, even his brain, an electrified reef teeming with strange thoughts. All around the canoe, the yellow grass in the channels waved in the breeze like flickering candles, bright against the black remains of the charred trees.

It had been Billie's idea to pull a permit and go back a month after the first attempt with Bill, when Cooper hadn't been able to navigate to Lake Gray, when David's ashes rode back to the launch point in a wet pack wedged in the center of the canoe. Billie had prepped everything herself, even spirited away the We-no-nah without Bill noticing. This time, Billie had the compass — not the antique compass that had failed Cooper, but a plastic one purchased at REI. On it, north was north.

Later, after they'd camped and eaten, and after Billie had climbed into the hammock, Cooper walked into the woods that fringed the campsite, the baggie in her hand. A few yards past the latrine, she fumbled in her jacket pocket for the empty travel-size vial of Tylenol that she'd hidden in her backpack before she and Billie had left Minneapolis. She opened the child-safety lid with her teeth and, using a birch leaf as a funnel, poured a teaspoon's worth of her brother's ashes into the vial. She wasn't asking for much, she told herself — just a fragment. Lake Gray could have the rest of him, but these motes, these particles. These were hers.

That night, she and Billie walked together

to the outcropping on Lake Gray and tossed David's ashes into the water without ceremony. Billie went back to the tent alone but Cooper sat at the fire, feeding it until the sky began to lighten with the dawn, occasionally touching the vial in her jacket pocket. Veils of mist hung above the water, as if waiting to reveal someone. And, indeed, Cooper saw a yellow We-no-nah gliding soundlessly through them. She went knee-deep into the lake, her eyes straining to catch another glimpse. In a moment, the canoe emerged from the fog, revealing a faceless man, and a Husky wearing a life-jacket. The man waved and continued on, and was once again enveloped by the mist.

Cooper climbed back up the sloping granite outcropping and looked down at her feet, at the bones of the continent. It seemed as if everything around her — the spiny arms of the pines bent over the water, the crackle of the fire she hadn't let die in the night, even the persimmon clouds of dawn — had receded completely. The silence was crystalline. Then, all at once, the sun emerged from the horizon, an undulating smear of orange. Cooper closed her eyes against the light.

When she opened them now, she was surrounded by snow.

■ ■ ■ ■

As Cooper approached their site, she heard a bright, resonant male voice singing "Famous Blue Raincoat." Pavano's voice quavered for a moment as it glided over the notes in the line *she was nobody's wife,* then fell silent. Cooper coughed loudly before unzipping the tent door.

Inside, Pavano was lying prone and tending a camp stove.

"How did it go?" he asked.

"It looks exactly like Pole," Cooper replied.

Pavano readjusted the Sterno canned heat with his mitten, and leaned back on his elbow. The expression on his wind-chapped face startled Cooper; peering out at her from the shadows, he looked almost macabre. His clear eyes took everything in, but betrayed nothing. Cooper felt something stir in her — possibly an idea. It was in Pavano's face; Cooper saw it in his strange eyes, in his angular features. As she gazed at him, committing each feature to memory, a noise issued from his mouth. It took Cooper a moment to recognize it as a laugh.

"What's so funny?"

"I was just thinking that it's been a long

time since I've had company," Pavano replied. "I'm a loner, if you haven't noticed. Not always by choice. I'm afraid I have forgotten how to make small talk."

"No small talk necessary," Cooper replied. "When do we get to work? Do we get to work?"

"In time. I'm waiting for a piece of equipment."

"I thought you were going to talk to the site manager."

"That won't be necessary."

"Well, let me know when I can help," Cooper said.

"I should mention that if the site manager refuses to budge on your approval status, any help you give me will likely land you in hot water."

Cooper shrugged. "I've already got a flag on my file. What's another one?"

She sat back against her canvas pack and pulled her sketchpad from the outer pocket. Across the camp stove, Pavano watched her remove her mittens in order to retrieve her pencil. She laid her sketchpad across her knees and rolled the pencil between her fingers as she considered Pavano. She could sense an artifice about him, but couldn't pinpoint it. Maybe it was the way his eccentricities could come and go:

Pavano couldn't meet her eyes in the galley but here on the Divide he could stare at her unblinking for whole minutes. At the station he skulked; here he lounged.

She turned back to her sketchpad. Started. Erased. The shape of his eyes was hard to reproduce — they were wide-set, but also deep in his face. She tried again, and, once more, erased the beginnings. On the bruised paper, she drew an outline of a penguin, but it looked morbidly obese, and she erased it, too. She tried a rendering of the Empire State Building with arms, but it looked like a Transformer.

"Problems?" Pavano asked.

"I've given up on you. You're hard to sketch."

"I'm flattered that you'd choose me as a subject. Who, would you say, might be easy to capture on the page?"

Cooper thought of the portrait she'd done of Tucker, how she'd sworn to herself that although it was turning out pretty well, it was a one-off, an exercise meant to get her across the bridge and into the land of polar art. After all the mittens she'd produced, she'd resigned herself to painting the standard skyscapes, cloudscapes, glacierscapes, and snowscapes that seemed to be the expected output for a visual artist at Pole.

But then she'd started that portrait of Bozer. And then, last week — after Cooper had noticed the two-inch scar above Pearl's right eyebrow — the one of Pearl.

"No one is easy to capture on the page," Cooper finally replied.

Pavano gestured toward the sketchpad. "Will this become part of your portfolio?"

Cooper shook her head. "No, I'm here to make grand statements, not portraits. That's what they want: statements. A face is not a statement."

"It's a statement of existence," Paveno replied.

Cooper set her notebook on the floor of the tent and inched toward Pavano on all fours until she was at his knees. He watched her as she reached up and took the bridge of his glasses between her fingers and pulled them from his face. His pellucid eyes regarded her impassively.

"You want to know if I exist," he said.

"Yes," Cooper said quietly. For a long moment, they gazed at each other, and the moment grew taut. The longer Cooper studied Pavano, the more familiar he seemed. He leaned in, drawing closer to her, and the world roared back to life. Cooper moved away, her heart thrumming. A blast of wind shook the tent, sending the Sterno canister

343

into a cartwheel. The time it took Pavano to set it right again gave Cooper a chance to collect herself.

"What did you gather," Pavano said, "from your peek into my soul?"

"I don't know anything about souls. They're a human construct, they're not real."

Pavano seemed discomposed, as if he were a translator who'd fallen hopelessly behind. "It's natural to say such things when you've been spending time with scientists," he finally said. "To them, everything is constructed."

"But you're a scientist."

Pavano hesitated. "I'm also a man of faith."

"You said you were an atheist."

"No, I didn't say that."

"You implied it."

His expression softened, and he sat back against his pack. "Yes, perhaps I did. I find implications give me just enough wiggle room to work in peace. May I have my glasses back?" Cooper hadn't realized that the glasses were still in her hand.

Pavano removed the teapot from the canned heat, and Cooper watched as he carefully selected two teabags from the outer pocket of one of his packs. "Sal says

344

you don't believe your own research," she said. "That you do this for the money because your career in academia tanked."

"Like most of Sal's theories, that's only about half accurate. As I'm sure he told you, I made some mistakes in my career that pushed me to the margins of academia. When you're in the margins, you're impossible to see. You find new frontiers, and you join forces with the people who live on them."

"Like Creationists."

"Theistic science," Pavano said.

"God."

"Methodological naturalism is religion."

Cooper rolled her eyes.

"What I'm trying to say," Pavano continued, "is that it's all religion at the end, whether it's me making the teleological argument at a conference or Sal trying to parse out the beginnings of the universe through his telescope."

"Sal's not religious."

Pavano handed Cooper a mug. "Sal Brennan is one of the most religious people I've ever known. For many years he worked on confirming the main model of the cosmos. His work was a kind of chase after his father's — my wife used to call them Odysseus and Telemachus. Anyway, Sal played a major role in building on Hawking and Penrose's model and making the inflationary model a widely accepted theory among the general public. Now he rejects it. He thinks he's found something better. Think about that for a moment, Cooper — here is a man who spent the better part of his career looking at what is essentially the same data he now has before him, coming to a conclusion that he believes is fact, and then changing his mind. And now he is a paragon of nonstandard cosmology, not to mention a cast-out son, and he's in danger of becoming as marginalized as the proponents of Intelligent Design he abhors. He's a believer, Cooper. His faith is immense."

"But he might actually be right," Cooper said. "There's no possibility that the earth is six thousand years old, that humans walked with dinosaurs."

"Forget Young Earthers and dinosaurs. Those are distractions. The compelling argument is that living things are too well designed to have come about by chance."

Cooper laughed. "The world is the least-well-engineered thing ever."

"You go too far."

No, Cooper thought. She hadn't gone far enough. "Explain suicide."

"The intelligence I'm talking about

doesn't deal in individual circumstances."

"It creates a machine only to have it self-destruct?"

"It is an engineer, and it engineered a creature that can intentionally end its life. Maybe in some people, when the wiring has gone wrong, suicide is instinctive. There are countless documented examples of this in nature — mostly birds, as it happens. Petrels that fly into campfires. Mergansers that seek out submerged roots and drown while clinging to them." He removed his glasses to wipe away condensation, and saw, with a start, that tears were leaking down Cooper's cheeks.

The welcome sound of an approaching snowmobile allowed Cooper to wipe her eyes while Pavano struggled to his feet and put his goggles on. After he walked out, Cooper leaned over his sleeping bag to peer through the tent door. Hitched to the snowmobile was a large pallet containing a small generator, several winches and cables, three long, skinny blue cylinders, and something that looked like an enormous tampon applicator. The man on the snowmobile looked nervous as Pavano handed him an envelope folded in half. As soon as he unhitched the pallet, he sped off back toward camp.

When Pavano returned to the tent, he was radiant.

"What's all that?" Cooper asked.

"It's an agile drill that can retrieve cores up to thirty meters," Pavano replied. "But since they integrated the new BID-Deep system, it can, theoretically, reach depths of up to two hundred meters." Cooper was startled to see how happy this made Pavano. "It has been signed out under another team's name and won't be missed for about twenty-four hours. Once I extract this core, it's mine. The lab will be obligated to store it, no matter how it was obtained, and then send it to Denver, where I will analyze it. It shouldn't take us too long to set up."

"You did a work-around," Cooper said.

"I did what I had to do."

"Let's get started, then."

"I'll only need you to help me erect the tripod and the double sheave. The rest I can handle. You go get dinner."

"Do you want me to bring you back anything?"

Pavano shook his head. "I've got a Cup o' Noodles."

The galley at the Divide was just a tent, and as she looked at the dinner offerings steaming away in the large aluminum warming trays, unrecognizable in various states of congealment, Cooper missed Pearl's cooking keenly. She held out her tray and a lump of something resembling meatloaf was dropped onto her plate. She picked a stale roll out of a plastic basket and scanned the room. Across from her, a man in a blond wig topped with a tiara sipped soup from a bowl. Next to him, Cooper noticed Sri and his team studying some printouts. Cooper tried to catch his eye, but he seemed to be ignoring her. She considered sitting at his table anyway, but decided instead to take a seat at an empty one.

As she was poking the meat product on her tray with her fork, Cooper felt someone staring at her. The ice-core tech Cooper sat next to on the flight in was scowling at her, a lock of purple hair obscuring her right eye.

"Why are you helping him?" she asked.

"Excuse me?"

"Frank Pavano. He's a pseudoscientist."

"I'm an artist," Cooper said, as if that explained everything.

"You his girlfriend or something?"

"Christ, no. I'm here for inspiration. A change of scenery."

The tech put her hand on her waist and

cocked her head. "Artists and Writers Fellow?"

"Yeah."

"But you're on the list as a tech. They put you on his manifest?"

"I know, weird."

"And what exactly are you painting?"

"I'm here to sketch and observe the field camp. And the surrounding ice sheet plateau, also." She cast about for something believable. "I'm calling it 'Transparent Truths.'"

"Transparent Truths?"

Cooper knew she had to get jargony now — jargon was the strongest shield for the professional with nothing to say. "I plan to create a suite of etchings and paintings on this source material, using color and implied texture, and focusing on a postmodern application of serial imagery."

The core tech relaxed a little. "Okay, sorry to grill you. It's just — having a guy who thinks global warming is a hoax at a climate research site is sort of big deal. My name's Fern."

"Cooper. And believe me, I get it."

A couple of other people sauntered over to Cooper's table. "It's just weird that you came on his manifest. That's not how this is usually done. I mean, you usually have your own flight order."

Cooper shrugged. "I don't even know what that means. I just do what I'm told."

"You know that he's on Big Oil's payroll, right?" Fern said. "This is basically like giving an NSF grant to Exxon." She paused. "What's he like?" The crowd around Cooper's table had grown bigger, but everyone remained silent, as if what Cooper had to say was extremely important.

"He seems normal."

"There's no way he's normal," someone from the edge of the group said. "Not even Pole-normal."

"The NSF is a craven, cowardly agency run by mealy-mouthed pieces of shit," another voice shouted from the back, this one belonging to the wig-wearing male beauty queen.

"Randy has that on his business card," Fern said, finally cracking a smile. "So you're here to help him extract a core? You know how to do it, right? Because it's actually really dangerous. They have people here whose only job is to do shit like that, and none of them are on his tech roster."

"I think he's going to do it himself. Seeing as no one will help him."

The room boomed with laughter. Cooper had no idea why.

Once she came to, Cooper's first thought was, why is Pavano puking? A few yards away, he was leaning over his knees, an entire Cup o' Noodles pouring out of his mouth and onto the ice in a steaming pile. Her second thought was that her hand was warm, even though she'd taken her mitten off to help Pavano with the corer, and last she remembered it was basically flash-frozen. She got to her feet, wondering why she'd been prostrate on the snow. Now Pavano was wiping his mouth with the back of his hand, and now he was shouting at her: *Don't look.* As if in slow motion, Cooper turned to see what he was going on about. Was that blood on the ice? Was that her finger, half attached — no, three-quarters detached — to her right hand? She felt consternation upon seeing the dangling finger, as if it were something stubborn, like a hangnail, and reached for it with her other hand and pulled it off. It came off easily, and she tossed it into the snow.

That gesture — the toss — seemed to trigger a sudden response, as if the cosmos had been waiting for this act, and now that it had been completed, the world splintered into shards. Each shard reflected the sun, like waves on a lake. Saganaga. The lake at the end of the Gunflint Trail. You stayed in the possession corridor because you didn't want to face the wind. Cooper was in the canoe, alone now, driving it straight for the shore.

Her mind was a museum. Only dusty relics remained: her hands guiding the elephantine drill onto the spot Pavano had marked on the ice. The sensation of her right mitten twisting into an infinite spiral as the generator roared; searing pain that quickly gave way to numbness. Pavano's noodles. His startled face. The blood on the ice and Cooper's mangled finger, which had been dug out of the snow by a compassionate research tech — Fern? — once the drill had stopped grinding and help began arriving. The finger had been placed in a snow-filled Coleman. Cooper remembered marveling at the Coleman, that such a thing could be found both at a suburban picnic and also on the West Antarctic Ice Sheet. There was the med tent and the disembodied face of the medic, displaying teeth in some facsimile of a smile. This was followed by a stretch of blackness, studded by occasional bursts of light and scored by a ceaseless shriek.

Someone had tried to peel open her eyes; she had fainted. Cooper had blinked against the assault and reluctantly focused her eyes until she realized she was looking at Doc Carla. That's when the pain arrived — decadent, laughably excessive. Cooper felt an intense desire to chop off her right arm.

Then there had been twenty-four hours in Hard Truth with Doc Carla — triage and treatment, including an awful irrigation of the "wound site." No one else had been allowed to speak with her. There had been one time when Sal — it was Sal, Cooper knew, because he'd touched her bare arm as she lay there, and she'd remembered the feel of his hand from that night in her room — sat next to the bed and read to her after Doc Carla had kindly slipped her a Vicodin when the expired Tylenol with codeine had failed. She couldn't remember what book it was now — it was the sound of his voice that had penetrated, not the words.

Doc Carla told her there had been an accident, that a finger on her right hand — the "pointer," the CEO of the hand — was gone, that they'd been unable to save it. Because Cooper couldn't visualize the injury, and because Doc Carla refused to let her see the wound until it had healed, it didn't seem real. None of it seemed real.

And because it didn't seem real, Cooper appeared to be taking it well.

Unfamiliar people showed up at Hard Truth. Men and women dressed in Pole gear who weren't Polies. They were from the National Science Foundation, they were from VIDS. Doc Carla sat in a folding chair while the admins interrogated Cooper — it was like a deranged version of *Inherit the Wind*. Again and again, Cooper went over every detail of her visit to the Divide. Her inability to be specific frustrated the admins, and when she mentioned Pavano's name, they became agitated. No one would tell her what had happened to him or where he was.

On their next visit to Hard Truth, the admin guys leveled with her. The media already knew what had happened, and this had opened the door to scrutiny. Pavano's congressional sponsors were claiming harassment and discrimination. There was talk that the two congressmen who had lobbied to get him on the ice wanted a federal investigation. This would mean subpoenaing every grantee who had had contact with Pavano — including Cooper, Sal, Sri, and entire climate research teams at the Divide. They would be expected to leave the ice to meet with investigators. The effect this could have on the ongoing experiments at Pole would be catastrophic. In an effort to stave this off, Alexandra Scaletta, head of the NSF, had invited the congressmen to Pole to assess the situation for themselves, as "a gesture of goodwill."

"So, am I being sent home?" Cooper asked the latest NSF admin to interrogate her, a stout, genial man named Warren.

"I know it seems like we've been asking you the same questions a hundred different ways, but we're just trying to figure out how this happened. Why you were there, why Dr. Pavano was working with equipment checked out under another team's grant number. Is there anything else you can tell us that will help us out here?"

"How is he?" Cooper replied.

"Dr. Pavano?"

"Is he still here or did they send him back?"

"I'm afraid we're not allowed to say," Warren said. His look turned pleading. "That's why we're asking you these questions. The sooner we can create a timeline of events, the sooner we can put this all to rest." Cooper smiled to herself. *Good luck with that.*

When she awoke in her own room, she

found her desk piled with homemade gifts wrapped in fax paper. There was even a bottle of Crown Royal in a purple sack with a note signed by Dwight. Pearl had left a basket filled with knitted items and various baked goods. Hanging from the coat hook on the back of the door was a small wooden birdhouse from Bozer, accompanied by a little sign that said *Glacier Sparrows Only.*

She glanced up at her tiny window, as if the constant sunlight could indicate the time. She peed in her pee can, holding herself steady by gripping the desk chair with one hand, so she could skip the bathroom — even though she couldn't remember the last time she'd brushed her teeth. She noticed now that Sal had left a note on the desk. *Radio when you get up and I'll come get you. Do not walk to the station alone. Sal.*

As she struggled into her balaclava, she saw Pavano's Scotch on her desk. She grabbed it by the neck and shoved it into the deepest pocket of her parka, along with her painkillers. Doc Carla had been careful: there were only three in the bottle, but at least they weren't expired.

Cooper was halfway to the Jamesway door when she turned around and went back to her room. Next to her compass was the vial containing David's ashes. She placed them both in her other pocket.

Outside the Jamesway, Floyd sat astride a snowmobile arguing with a fuel tech about glycol levels. When he saw Cooper walking toward the station, he cut the argument short and offered her a ride, which she accepted. As the snowmobile careened across the ice, Cooper tried to sort out exactly how she was supposed to feel about this finger thing. The whole experience so far had been like living inside Picasso's *Guernica*. She wasn't dead. She hadn't lost an arm. This wasn't cancer or a stroke. It was a finger. And yet Doc Carla had called it a catastrophic injury. Cooper felt as if she had been anesthetized. Where was her fear? Her outrage? Why did she feel nothing about this, besides the pain and the constant throbbing? She was disfigured — a painter, with hyperrealist tendencies, who'd lost a finger on her dominant hand. Was she an abstract painter by default now? Was she a painter at all? She didn't know. And right now, she hardly cared. All that mattered was that she get back to the station. Floyd drove the snowmobile up the entrance ramp and idled in front of Annex B.

"Please don't be nice because you feel bad for me," Cooper said as Floyd helped her off. "I don't want pity."

Floyd gave her a wry look. "You've been around long enough to know there's no such thing as pity here."

Inside her studio, Cooper found her easel where she'd left it and the blank canvas with the roughly outlined polar landscape. It seemed to have come from another era. She pulled the compass out of her pocket and set them on her desk. Then she shook off the mitten on her left hand — the bandage on her right was so thick it functioned as a mitten. After a couple of attempts, Cooper gave up on removing her parka. That would require help, and she didn't want any more help.

She slowly lowered herself to her knees and unfurled a measure of drawing paper from her roll. Doc Carla had cut away the top of the bandage so her thumb and remaining fingers were exposed, which would, theoretically, allow her to pick up her pencils and her brushes. Cooper seized a charcoal nib between her thumb, middle, and ring fingers, which, when squeezed together, functioned as a single digit. It felt awkward, and it hurt like hell, and when she set the nib to the paper, it moved as if following remote instructions from someone else, skittering all over the page and leaving a greasy black trail across the paper. After a few more tries, Cooper sat back on her haunches. There would be no more detailed studies of vending machine charms, no more hyperrealistic portraits of landscapes or roadside cafés. What about faces?

The door opened behind her, and there was Tucker, in sunglasses with a silk scarf tied around his neck and pulled up over half of his face. He was holding a solitary cupcake. "From Pearl," he said, his voice muffled. He set the cupcake down on the desk. Cooper glanced over at it. It was absurdly baroque, way out of proportion to its surroundings. The frosting had been colored pink with valuable food coloring, and a tiny purple violet had been piped upon it. A marzipan bumblebee, with two sliced almonds for wings, perched atop.

Tucker removed Cooper's paints and brushes from her stool and sat down.

"When do I rejoin the gen-pop?" Cooper asked. Tucker didn't immediately reply.

"Or am I being sent home?"

"I am not currently in the loop on that discussion," Tucker finally said.

"Does this mean my quarantine is over at least? Since you're talking to me. Even Floyd talked to me on the way here."

"You know that wasn't my decision. The NSF wants you ensconced here, hermit-like, so the media can't find you, so you can't get online and tell the world what happened. The place is leaking like any number of doomed ships in history."

She rolled up her drawing paper. "Tell the world what happened? *I* don't even know what happened."

"This whole business is my fault. I shouldn't have let you go to the Divide. I rarely make mistakes, but when I do —"

"This isn't your mistake."

Cooper walked over to the corner of the studio, where she kept the canvases: the beginnings, the orphans. "I want to show you something," she said. She found the portrait of Tucker. She pulled it out and shoved it at him without meeting his eyes.

"What's this?"

"You. That night. The Halloween party. Remember?"

Tucker looked at the painting — an eye regarding itself in a shard of mirror that was cupped in a brown-skinned hand. In the background of the reflection were the dirty tiles of a subway bathroom.

"I remember," he said quietly. He cleared his throat. "However, for true verisimilitude, I'm afraid you'll have to revise." He carefully removed his sunglasses and handed them to Cooper. Then he unwrapped the scarf, and Cooper saw that the left side of his face now seemed to hang slightly below the right. The left corner of his mouth fell slack and the corner of his left eye looked as if it were being pulled downward by an invisible thread. The unnatural smoothness of his chemically sanded face had given way to dark sprouts of wiry hair. He seemed half sad; and the look of half-sadness struck Cooper as far worse than a look of complete sorrow.

Cooper started to say something, but Tucker put his hand up.

"Self-pity is vain," Tucker said. "Don't encourage it, and don't engage in it." He stood up. "Eat the cupcake. Act normal. Act like you want to be here, like you're strong enough to be here. And start painting. As soon as possible. If you don't start immediately after the blow, you won't ever start again. I speak from experience." He cleared his throat and lightly stroked his cheek. "And now you have a whole new face to inspire you."

After Tucker left, Cooper felt a wave of despair wash over her. Her wound pulsed with heat as the dull ache gave way to scorching pain. She pulled out the pills Doc Carla had given her and tapped one out onto her palm. She took it dry, then sat down, trying to get a handle on the pain. She examined her bandaged hand. It didn't make sense to wait for Doc Carla in order to assess her disfigurement, to quantify what she'd lost. She had to see her hand now. But first she needed fortification. She pulled Pavano's Scotch from her pocket. It took two minutes, and the assistance of her teeth, but she was able to twist the top open. The first mouthful was medicinal. It burned, the way a wound burns the first time you run it under cold water. The second drink was smoother — still astringent, but warm. The warmth filled Cooper's chest, and it, along with the sublime cooling effect of the painkiller, took just enough of the edge off to give her the courage to assess her injury.

First, she released the insect-like jaws of the metal clamp biting the elastic bandage and began unwinding it. Her arm grew tired — the bandage seemed endless. Eventually, she reached the sterile gauze wrapping her hand in layers as thin as phyllo. After three circumnavigations, Cooper began to see the bloodstains and the thin slice of plywood that supported her hand.

She removed the final layer of gauze, tugging a bit to release it from the scabs, and there it was, a bloom of pith and dried blood. The other fingers, the thumb, the middle, the ring, the pinkie, were white and shriveled, glistening with moisture, and Cooper was overcome by revulsion. The pain came roaring back, crashing through the narcotic. It was as if the wound had sprung to life, as if it had a heartbeat of its own, and was determined to make itself known. Cooper wiped sweat off her forehead and tried to steady herself by taking another mouthful of Scotch. The pain didn't subside, and although somewhere in the far reaches of her brain she knew all she had to do was wait — just wait — she shook out the two remaining pills from the bottle. Cherry waited, and no one came. Cooper had waited, too, and David hadn't come. She was done waiting. She swallowed the pills with a double swallow of Scotch, and as the burn in her chest subsided, Cooper remembered that David's ashes were in her parka pocket. She jammed her uninjured hand into its depths and withdrew the vial. She sat down at the desk and set it next to the empty bottle of painkillers, and laid her head down next to them. As she stared at both bottles, they seemed to merge until it was impossible to distinguish one from the other.

Eventually, her thoughts returned to the igloo that Cherry, Wilson, and Birdie Bowers had made at Cape Crozier, the endpoint of the "Worst Journey in the World," just as they had in the weeks after David went missing. As the police searched, as Billie turned cold and Dasha and Bill turned on each other, Cooper thought endlessly of Cherry, Wilson, and Birdie huddled together in their igloo, waiting out a blizzard in complete darkness, save for the flickering glow of the camp stove. *For twenty-four hours we waited,* Cooper wrote. *Things were so bad now that we dared not unlash the door.*

They did, though. They had to in order to survive, and so had Cooper. In the spring, when they'd found the tire marks on the shore of West Lake Sylvia, out in Wright County, Cooper was the only one in the family who would go downtown to identify David's body. When she got to the morgue, they warned her. They told her they only needed confirmation. They told her they hadn't taken off his seatbelt. They told her about the book found wedged between the dashboard and the windshield. Cooper knew him only by his thick brown hair. It looked so much like her own.

She stood up so suddenly her chair fell backward onto the cement floor with an ear-splitting crash. The sound seemed to come from miles away. The opiates and the alcohol had met in her bloodstream by this time, and were finally mingling. Cooper tried to make a fist with her right hand, and though she could feel some dried blood crack, she felt no pain. When she looked into the fluorescent lights hanging from the ceiling, illuminated commas dove in and out of her line of vision. She may never paint again, but she would do this one thing. This was why she had come to this place, this frozen, dead place. And it was time. She picked up the vial of ashes and walked out of the studio, unaware that her parka was still hanging on the back of the door.

Cooper found the Dome silent, all the machines asleep while the Nailheads ate lunch, and as she walked down the entrance tunnel, she had to work to focus her eyes and steady her steps. She could see her breath, but felt warm. After what felt like days, she finally reached the bottom of the entrance tunnel, and looked out at the drifts surrounding the station. The cornices atop them loomed nearly twenty feet high. This was the moat of death, the deep, circular crevasse that formed around the Dome as winter progressed, but now it seemed bottomless. She glanced down and saw whales. Hallucinations, she thought, and congratulated herself for being able to tell. She blinked once and the whales obligingly disappeared. A hooded figure appeared at the top of the entrance tunnel, and then disappeared, too. Cooper's body was pulsing but her limbs felt stiff. She heard her name coming at her from all directions.

Across the plateau, she could see the caution flags that marked the sinking old station now buried beneath thirty feet of snow, its bones slowly being masticated by the polar ice. A hooded figure appeared again, this time running. Cooper gasped, and a mouthful of thirty-below-zero air scalded her lungs until she thought she'd collapse from the pain. At the same time, though, she felt uncomfortably hot. The person was still running toward her, and it struck Cooper that for some reason he knew what she was about. Perhaps he was coming to stop her. She couldn't let that happen.

She fell to her knees and began clawing at the snow with her left hand, holding the vial in the remaining fingers of her right.

Suddenly, her pursuer was next to her. He stopped and removed his parka. Before she could get a good look at him, the wind changed directions all at once. The snow was rising off the plateau, as if it were alive. A burst of wind knocked her off her knees, but she struggled to her feet. No, this wasn't the right place, this polar vehicle superhighway. No, she knew the right place for this. Beyond the Pole marker and the flags of all nations, at the place where Scott spoke from beyond the grave. That's where David belonged.

A high-pitched scream sounded in her ear. She could see boots just in front of her, and thought she could hear a voice. The boots moved away. Cooper dropped her chin to her chest and lay still once more.

Climb in the trench, kick out the roof, and go to sleep. Doesn't get any easier.

It was as if all of her muscles relaxed at once, like a building settling onto its foundation in a single movement. Cooper found she was standing alone in a clearing. Before her, a forest, pines and oaks twining together, meeting the edge of the snow. She walked toward it cautiously. All was silent. But life wasn't silent, Cooper knew — not even here, so this couldn't be life. Then, all at once, another clearing, and the sun trembling atop the ice like a gazing ball. Cooper closed her eyes against it. When she looked up again, the sun was gone, and in its place, a sparrow.

DEPARTMENT OF THE ARMY
U.S. TOTAL ARMY PERSONNEL
  COMMAND
ALEXANDRIA, VIRGINIA
  22332-0400

ORDER NO: 41-5
The President of the United States has reposed special trust and confidence in the patriotism, valor, fidelity, and abilities of CARROLL F. BOZER. In view of these qualities and his demonstrated potential for increased responsibility, he is therefore promoted in the Army of the United States from Staff Sergeant General to Sergeant First Class. Promotion is effective 1 May 1991 with date of rank 1 May 1991. The authority for this promotion is Section 601, Title 10, United States Code.
Format 307
BY ORDER OF THE SECRETARY OF THE ARMY:
                    MICHAEL K. VEASEY
            LIEUTENANT COLONEL, GS
        CHIEF, PROMOTIONS BRANCH
DISTRIBUTION:
EACH PSC (1)
EACH MAJOR COMMAND (1)

SFC BOZER (1)
ASSISTANT TO THE CHAIRMAN
 (OJCS)
WASHINGTON, DC 20310

MAN WITHOUT COUNTRY

I see her standing at the end of the tunnel. I let her go that far. I know the impulse, and I respect it. You don't survive here without putting your hands on it sometimes, but you have to know how to kill it before it kills you. This one doesn't know how to do that. That's why she got into this fix in the first place, why she came back from the Divide minus a fork.

She's not wearing a parka, and she's shaking like a hog on butchering day — but it's like she don't notice. She just keeps walking, and I see that I have to go after her. My radio crackles, and I consider calling Floyd, but Floyd's got a big mouth, so I figure this one's on me.

When I get there — and I run to get there — she's standing by the moat, her body seizing with the cold. She's looking into the ditch like she wants to jump in, and she's shaking so hard she might end up at the bottom even if she don't mean to. She sees me, and next thing I know she's on her knees, and not in a good way — she's digging, like she's set to bury something. When she sees me coming with my parka, she gets to her feet and takes off. It takes me a minute to catch her, and when I do, she fights me. I'm careful — she's ain't got her bandage on, goddamn it, but I end up catching her and wrapping her in my parka. I have to throw her over my shoulder, but it's done. We're going back inside. Christ, the cold, though. It's straight from hell.

Once we're inside, I take the bandanna off my head, snap it square, and wrap it around her hand. It's ugly because it's a fresh cut, but the fingerless don't scare me. In my line of work, they're a dime a dozen.

"What were you doing out there alone?" I say, once I've got her hand wrapped.

She says, "I'm not alone."

"Not anymore you ain't," I say, and when I put my arm around her shoulder, she sinks into it like it's a warm bed.

I steer her to El Dorm and try to get her to my room without running into any admins, but we run straight into Tucker. It's okay — Tucker understands how I work. I let him know with my eyes that I got this under control, but this girl's his favorite, so he watches me close as I walk her past.

Once we're in my room, I sit her down on my bed and look into her face. Her eyes are streaming tears from the negative fifty-degree wind, and her pupils look like pinpoints. I could take her to Hard Truth, but I ain't done that to anyone yet. The quickest way to get *NPQ* stamped on your dossier is a trip to Doc Carla. No one, not even the weak ones, wants that. But she looks only half here. Lucky for her, I'm all here. This is my quarter. I can bring them back. Done it a million times. Only sane one left on the mortuary team after we cleaned up the crash at Erebus in '79. Tourist flight from New Zealand — TE-901. They'd been running them over Antarctica for years — cocktails-and-cameras type of thing. The plane crashed in sector whiteout conditions. Two hundred fifty-seven on board, all dead on impact. They called us in from Fort Lee to help the Kiwis' recovery mission, the only army unit in a navy operation, and we spent a week camped in tents at the crash site. Body parts everywhere, no telling how the legs got separated, and sometimes even the feet, cut clean away. The human grease turned our parkas black. It soaked through wool gloves. I was eighteen, just enlisted, practically still a blue-head. First place they sent me was Antarctica. Figures. It was my first time on the ice. I didn't want to leave.

I can smell the alcohol on her breath. "You take any scratch with that booze?" I ask.

"I took all three pills, but don't take me to Doc Carla," she says. "She'll be mad. And I don't want to go home." Her wound is leaking — my bandanna is done for — so I pull out my supply kit. Pole docs get supplied like they was going on a Girl Scout trip, so I bring my own shit. I have hydrogen peroxide, two irrigation syringes, dental filling mixture, glucose paste, hydrocodone, antibiotic ointment, gauze, and four three-inch elastic bandages with hook and loop strips. I keep my own hospital, because someone's always getting scratched up at the site.

I crouch in front of her and unwrap my bandanna from her hand. She winces, but doesn't say anything. The wound's opened up. Looks like it's breathing. I see the finger's been cut off down to the proximal phalanx — a little beyond, because the joint's gone. There's lint and shit stuck to it, so I tell her I'm gonna wash the wound site, that it's gonna sting, and before she can say no, I pour the hydrogen peroxide over it in a good steady stream. It soaks my pants leg, but I don't mind. Cupcake, though, she's almost levitating. I tell her to stop moving. "Makes it worse." I want to tell her that after the deep frost of the burn will come a kind of clean feeling, but I don't know how to explain it right so I keep my mouth shut. As I work, I see she's looking at me, as if she's seeing me for the first time. Her eyes touch on every part of my face — mouth, nose, eyebrows.

I smear about a pound of ointment on the gauze, and wrap her back up. I ask her what she was doing out there. She doesn't say anything at first, so I ask her again, and she says, "You ever feel like pulling a Titus?"

"The fuck does that mean?"

"The guy in the Scott expedition. The one who walked out without his shoes on to save the others. Do you ever feel like walking out into a blizzard and never coming back?"

"Impossible," I tell her. "It don't snow at Pole." The snow here comes in on the wind from the coasts. To a Fingy it might look like a blizzard but it ain't. It's just snow on the wind.

Possible, she tells me. Been done.

"Not here it ain't." You can die a million ways here, but not by "pulling a Titus," the fuck that means. She looks at me like she wants a medal for not walking into a blizzard. She doesn't know about life. Example:

It would mean nothing to her to learn that a soldier could win a Bronze Star without stepping foot on the battlefield, that all you had to do was bring coffee to a four-star general sitting in a cool underground bunker in the desert, where the air is filtered and smells sweet as spring hay. You would not win shit for a search-and-rescue mission for an F-16 pilot who'd been hit by Iraqi gunfire and who put the plane nose-first into the sand at 130 knots. If you were honorably discharged because you were an old fuck like me, you would, however, get a job with the defense contractor responsible for cleaning up the shit left behind by the three thousand Abrams main battle tanks, the Bradley Fighting Vehicles, and whatever crackerjack bullshit Ali Baba used during Operation Desert Storm. That's what I did. I'm no good at serving coffee, but I am damn fine at cleaning up. Example: Kuwait City. The sky was dark at noon with smoke from the oil fires. The power grids were shot — Hussein had destroyed the transmission lines and distribution centers. Floyd, who'd been moved off a secret project laying DEW lines in Canada, was working at Shuwaikh, trying to get the grids back online. I'd met him at the Defense Reconstruction Assistance Office, where he'd been pitching a fit over a newbie Corps engineer assigned to his team. All his bluster told me was that he was tender as a newborn babe and had no business being in a war zone. He was a mess for the first few weeks, and the suits almost sent him home. I took him under my wing, and though he acts like he don't need me, he's followed me to every godforsaken outpost I've been assigned ever since.

One day, about a week after the U.S. military sent Hussein packing, I get the call to escort some Kuwaiti sheik from the Plaza Hotel to the airport so he could catch a flight to Ta'if, where all the other sheiks were running the country out of a Sheraton ballroom. I get to the eighteenth floor and see the door's open already. He's standing on the balcony, smoking. When he sees me, he tells me to come in. So I do, but he wants me on the balcony. As soon as I step next to him, the hair on the back of my neck is up. This guy ain't happy.

"Look at this," he says, pointing his cigarette at the city below us. It's sooty and dark. I see the same abandoned vehicles I saw on my way in, the same Iraqi tanks lying on their sides, the same sea of broken glass I'd walked across to get here, and the same Jawas standing guard at the door, except now there's a shavetail with them,

pointing at something beyond the smolder-
ing skyscraper across the street. In the
distance, the oil fires glow.

The sheik starts talking, and I'm only half-
listening, but I perk up when he tells me
he's the city's engineer. I don't know why it
hits me like it does, that even here, in this
backward-ass country where men hold
hands like schoolgirls and women dress like
ghosts, there's a man with the kind of brain
it takes to build bridges — to build entire
cities.

I'm still turning this over in my mind as
he tells me how the Emir single-handedly
turned a collection of mud huts into a city
of the world. "And see what they've done,"
he says, sweeping his hand in front of him.
The wind catches the sleeve of his dishdasha, fills it like a balloon. I can't tell if he's
talking about Saddam's army or ours. I
don't reply — I never do when these guys
jabber on — but he turns to look at me, his
eyes wide, brown, as pretty as a girl's.
"Look!" he shouts. Then he's grabbing me.
"I want you to look, soldier!" My standard
course of action when anyone lays hands on
me is to pull my gun, but I don't need a
genius to tell me this guy is just another lost
soul.

"The airport's done for, and your wells

are a mess," I tell him. "But the rest ain't too bad. Four years and you're back in business."

He hears this, but says nothing. He only drops the cigarette on the cement balcony and snuffs it out with one of his thousand-dollar shoes. He grinds it for too long, as if he thinks he can make it disappear. I find the oil fires again; I can't stop looking, the way you can't stop staring at a campfire. I'm still looking when, beside me, I feel the sheik walk to the other end of the balcony. I consider telling him that a river of money, courtesy of the United States taxpayers, is about to flood his city, that it'll get fixed up good, even better than what it was. But you can't talk to these guys. They're too sentimental.

I turn in time to see the edge of his dishdasha as it fills up with wind. I hear him land on the broken glass on the street below, and then I hear people shouting. What I notice is his cigarette flattened against the concrete of the balcony — a little bit of smoke still floats up from it. I walk to the edge and look over. The Jawas and the recruits are hovering over the body, and the shavetail is on his way back into the hotel to make a call. The engineer is dead, kissing the street. I curse him. I must shout it out loud, because the boys on the ground look up, trying to figure out where the sound came from so I have to step back. There will be questions and paperwork and then more questions. I won't be on the line for this. I ain't a suicide hotline, and this wasn't a mission fail. But the paperwork and the shrink — I'd rather pull my teeth out with pliers than deal with that shit again. I didn't need their help after Erebus, and I won't need it now.

I carefully set my supplies back in the tackle box and snap it shut. The girl's eyes are big — scared-big — and I ask her what's up. She says she left something out there, but she won't tell me what it is.

"Old Bozer'll get it for you," I say, like she's a baby. "Just say what I gotta look for." She shakes her head at me. Even though she still looks like someone killed her puppy, her eyes can focus on my face now. She's coming back. I see the shame is getting to her. She's too embarrassed to talk much. Good. What happened to her on the Divide ain't her fault, but this silly shit — going outside without ECW and playing in the snow — that is.

I got something to show her, so I take my old Palmer parka from the hook and help her into it. "Where are we going?" she asks while I pull her bandaged hand through the cuff.

"Just follow old Bozer."

It's colder in the Utilidors than it is under the Dome. No one comes to this door besides me. I drop my shoulder and lean it; it's ice-encrusted and gets harder and harder to open each year. I got the flashlight in my armpit, and once I break the door open, I have to crouch down and sort of shuffle through. She's not following me, though. She's watching me from the Utilidor tunnel, like she's scared of me. Denise wasn't scared. She walked in like a champ, no hesitation. She went right up to where me and Floyd had him laid out, went right up to him and told me to take the plastic off his face. But then it was me hesitating. My brains told me that the Man Without Country would look as pretty as he did the day he died — hell, this continent's got a whole baseball team of frozen explorers sleeping in the ice — but I wasn't keen on it. Denise was, though — she was real keen. And by this time, I woulda done just about anything for the woman, so I did it. I blew on the plastic to get it to loosen a little, and after that it was easy enough. Denise held his head while I unwound the sheeting like

I was taking off an Ace bandage. First to show was his beard. Next, his mouth, his white lips frosty. When I checked on Denise, making sure she wasn't too upset, I seen something that surprised me. A smile. First one I'd seen since she'd come down. Something was happening here. Didn't know what it was, but I wasn't gonna try to stop it. Not if it'd help her. And it did. It did help her.

I'd gotten the call right after Halloween 1999, from the U.S. Coast Guard, asking if I had any interest in visiting Newport, Rhode Island. A Boeing 767 had gone deep-sea diving shortly after takeoff from JFK, and the head of the recovery team — one of the boys from the Erebus crash site, Gluck, now a twenty-year navy veteran — had asked for me specifically.

I was a month into the season at Pole but VIDS put me on a plane the next day, and I was on board the USS *Grapple* within forty-eight hours. I hadn't done water rescue before, but I wasn't there to rescue. I was there to recover. Gluck told me the Atlantic Strike Team was young — half of them were raw. He wanted me there to show the youngsters how a man handles himself when the bodies begin to appear, how to lay out the remains on the deck, how to catalog limbs, how to see without seeing.

Some cracked, but most got it, and when the bodies started coming, we were a well-oiled machine. We didn't talk about what happened to this aircraft — not our concern — but it was hard to miss the people crowding the pier every evening when our shift ended. The families. Second day into the operation, I was walking to the hotel shuttle bus when someone shoved a photograph in my hands. Before I had a chance to look away, I saw it was a picture of a smiling man, all messy black hair and a mustache. "This is my husband." The voice was gentle — not accusing, like the others. It was almost as if she were introducing us at a party. I looked up and saw a short lady with frizzy brown hair and a pretty mouth. She wore a purple polka-dotted scarf 'round her neck. Her glasses made her big brown eyes look even bigger, and I noticed those eyes were dry. "Have you come across him yet?" she asked. I glanced down at the photo again before handing it back to her, and she told me his name. Didn't want to know his name, but now I knew it: Kevin. She told me he was on his way to Cairo, that he was a journalist. "For a very prestigious periodical," she told me, but I'd never heard of it. She seemed disappointed when I said this, but I told her not to worry, that I barely know how to read. That made her smile a little.

Gluck passed by with two of the divers and gave me a funny look. I knew I should leave, but I asked her name. I don't know why I did. I never ask. But I wanted to know her name, even if I didn't want to know her husband's. She told me, "Denise," and she asked mine. Before I knew what I was doing, I told her my Christian name, because suddenly Bozer didn't sound good enough. She told me mine is a nice name, but when I told her everybody calls me Bozer, she said that it was "more fitting." That's when the shuttle bus driver laid on the horn.

Next morning, Denise was there at the pier, with a cup of coffee for me. Gluck gave me another funny look when he saw us talking, but I ignored it. I knew what he was thinking, that I'm going soft, and later, on the ship, he told me just that. Said I was setting a bad example for the rest of the team, talking to the families during a recovery operation, making it personal. But when she was there that evening, too, I knew Gluck was wrong, because I was feeling strong as a bull ox.

I took her to one of the chowder houses on the wharf, and let her talk about her man. Guy sounded pretty regular to me but to her he was a king. So I listened. But then she noticed my tat — the one on my forearm, of Antarctica with a roofing nail shot through the middle — and asked me about it. So I told her about Pole, that I'd been there since Floyd and me cleaned up Kuwait City — six years and counting. I tell her I'm a lifer.

"If you're a lifer," she said, quick as a flash, "what are you doing here?"

"I'm here to find your man."

She needed time, and she had places to go. She told me what sociologists do and why they need to move around. At first, she wanted to go to Cairo, to see if she could understand why an Egyptian ex-military pilot would send a passenger plane into the Atlantic. "Perhaps he was traumatized by war," she told me six months later, when I called her from Comms to see how she was doing. By that time we were talking every week, and I could feel my heart winging around in my chest as it got closer to Monday, when I knew I'd hear her voice. "I learned that many members of his squadron were killed in the Yom Kippur War," she told me of the pilot who'd killed her husband. "I imagine there are many ex-military men grappling with the same awful memories." I

385

told her not to go to Cairo. I told her to come south. "If you want something to study, study us. Won't find a weirder bunch of people anywhere else on earth."

It took a season to convince her — she went to Brazil first to work with streetwalking trannies — but she came down, and when she came down, everything fit. I knew that was all she needed: a place where people don't fly planes into the ocean just because. Me, well, I just needed her.

When I showed her the Man Without Country that day, she looked at him for a good long time. It had been five years since that day Floyd and me found him a mile off the skiway. He hadn't changed a bit. For a minute, I worried I did the wrong thing. We never found her man — only a shoe, which she had to identify in an airplane hangar in Newport. True, no one knew who this man was, but at least he was whole. At least he was here.

When Denise got up from her knees, that beautiful smile was still on her face. I asked her what. She smiled wider. "He is everyone anyone has ever lost."

That's what I need to get Cooper to understand. We've all got our shit — me, Denise, the Man Without Country, who's got the worst shit of all 'cause he's stone-

dead and ain't nobody wants him. Everyone's got it, and it don't make you special.
Still, she won't walk in.

"You think I'm gonna go Dahmer on
you?" I say to her. "Get in here."

Now she's in and it's pitch dark, as it
always is. I wave the flashlight around the
room so she can see the four plywood walls,
get oriented. I take her arm, and we walk
toward the far wall, and she's not asking
questions — usually they're asking by now.
The flashlight ain't hit him yet, but when it
does, she stops short. I let her eyes get used
to him. The drop-kick lands, and she backs
up into me — her boots get tangled up with
mine, and I have to catch her arm so she
doesn't fall.

Now she's asking questions. "Bozer, what
is this?"

"Go ahead," I say, holding the flashlight
on him steady.

"Go ahead, what?"

"Go look. He's perfectly preserved." She
turns around and puts her face in my parka.
No one's done that before. I let her do this
for a minute, and then I peel her off and set
her on course again, and this time she walks
toward him. He's set on the berm we made
back when we found him, snow and ice we
scraped from the floor and walls. It was me

who thought to wrap him in sheeting from Logistics, and it's held up good.

"Who is he?" she asks.

"This here's the Man Without Country. He ain't got a home so we're leaving him here in the Tomb until we get word." She don't understand, so I explain. "We found him about a mile off the skiway. He was wearing a Vostok parka, but the Reds said he wasn't one of theirs. China, Chile, the Kiwis — nobody. The Program can't claim him because he's not a U.S. citizen. So here he lies." She walks closer to him now, looks at him. I can tell she notices that he wasn't wrapped hasty; it was done right. "You can see his beard," she says. She asks me why I'm showing her this, and I tell her the Man Without Country is here to tell her something. She looks at me with those sad dark eyes and asks me what he wants to tell her. "He says you don't come down here to commit suicide, honey. You come here so you don't."

I'm about to head to Skylab to look at the pool table next morning when I remember what the girl said about leaving something out there. There's already been a lot of drift overnight, and I probably won't find it. Hell, I don't even know what it is — she won't

388

tell me. But I'm on my knees at the entrance, sweeping snow away, looking for something that might not even be there. A couple of machinists walk by and make some smart comments; I only have time to flip them the bird before I spot it. A pill bottle. Size and shape of a Tylenol bottle, but the label's been taken off. I almost leave it where I found it, except the container's got that greasy look to it of having been searched for again and again in a pocket, or held tight like it was the only thing keeping a person alive. I pop the top with my thumb, expecting to find more scratch, but that's not what I find. I know as soon as I see it. Everything is clear as the new day.

When I get to Skylab, Floyd and a field engineer named Randy are looking at the pool table, beers in hand. "One drop on that felt and I cut off your balls," I say, and they step away from the table. There's already one here, in the game room, but it got brought down during Reagan's first term. Worse than that, the table ain't level. I been shipping materials down to build this one during my downtime — bundle it up with the three-quarter-inch plywood and snuggle it under a saddle truss or something. The delicate shit — the felt, the netting — used to come down with a cargo coordinator named Jose, but then Jose went Elvis one day on a toilet back home in Tulsa, and I had to start bringing it down myself. Anyway, this table is for the good old boys: no Beakers, no admins, just Nailheads.

I pull Floyd over to the table. "Get me a three-eighth-inch bolt and a Fender washer. You put the rails on crooked."

"They look all right to me."

"Just get me the bolts and the washer," I say. Floyd mutters something and leaves. If the Beakers see that anything about this table is off — and they will — they'll sneak into Skylab late at night with their laser levels, and we won't hear the end of it.

"I heard they're sending that girl back," Randy says to me. I take a piece of sandpaper from Floyd's toolbox and start working the edge of the rail.

"Which one?" I say, though I know.

"The finger girl. The *artiste.*"

"They ain't," I say.

"Why not?" Randy asks. I shrug. I don't know how the feds work down here. "Probably has something to do with the fact that Frank Pavano is the one who cut off her fork."

"Yeah, I hear we're getting a visit from Washington," Randy says. "They're all up in arms about the Beakers. They're saying

the Beakers bullied him. Fucking Beakers."
I brush the wood dust from my hands and
then blow it off the rails. Randy looks at the
table like he's gonna cum all over it. "She's
a beaut, Bozer. When will she be ready?"

"Soon. Sooner if that asshole will hurry
up with those bolts and washers."

I hear the sound of bunny boot on metal
staircase, and extend my hand behind me,
but someone, not Floyd, says, "I hear there's
a pool tournament at Equinox." I turn and
see it's a Beaker, that Indian one without
the accent. Sri.

"There might be," I say.

"Is this going to be a station-wide event?"

"Huh?"

"What I mean is — is this going to be
open to the entire station? Can anyone
enter?" I just look at Randy and smile. He's
new to all this. He needs to learn how to
make the Beakers squirm. That's how we
keep the equilibrium around here. Sri shifts
his weight onto his other leg. "Is there some
kind of entry fee? A case of beer?"

"I don't drink microbrews."

"I can get you more Schlitz," he says.

Although this does sweeten the pot, I
don't budge. "Look, you guys can keep buying me beer, but the tournament ain't open
to Beakers."

"But that's not fair."

"What's not fair about it?" I say. "This is my table. Use the one in the game room."

"You know that one's ruined," Sri says.

"Well, you Beakers shoulda been more careful with your Shirley Temples."

It's hard to get a Beaker upset. Sri keeps coming up with reasons why he should be allowed in the pool tournament, like logic has any bearing on my decision. Floyd finally shows up with the washer and bolts. He's out of breath, huffing like a steam engine going up a mountain pass. "Jesus, Floyd. You fat fuck."

"Karl Martin's here," he eventually coughs out. "He wants to talk to you." I don't care for Martin. He's fussy. He wasn't the one who hired me, either — that guy was an ex-military man who'd spent years in El Salvador doing shit that was neither sane nor legal. He was pushed out when VIDS decided to merge with a robotics manufacturer in '98, and that's when Martin, this former diplomatic pouch slinger, took his place. I will say that Martin mostly lets me do my thing. He's never come down and stuck his nose in between any steel girders. But still, I don't relish the opportunity to talk with him.

All-Call screeches on, and Tucker's voice

comes through the speakers: "Bozer, report to A3 ASAP. Bozer, report to A3 ASAP."

I find Martin waiting for me in the garage. He's trying to play it cool, even if he's made the fatal mistake of wearing the red parka of McMurdo. I can see the crew giggling at him, but he can't, and that's all that matters.

"Bozer, sir, good to see you," he says, slapping me on the shoulder with his mitten. "The new station looked great on the flight in."

"Just the bones, but we're set to put the last steel beam on B3 in ten minutes," I say.

Floyd pulls up on the snowmobile. Martin gets on like he's getting onto a stallion. This is a big moment. B3 will be the comms and admin pod for the new station.

We motor past the tourists cheesing for pictures in front of the Pole marker, and that's when I see the girl again, Cooper. She's standing alone, facing the opposite direction, her hands hanging at her sides. I pull up to where she's standing. She looks good — healthy, sober — and she smiles at me. I tell her we're putting the last steel beam on B3. "First of the new pods to get enclosed," I say. "History in the making."

"Where?" she says.

"Come on, I'll take you. All the bigwigs

wanna take pictures." I feel Martin lean in behind me to make room. She hesitates, but when I gun the engine, she allows Martin to pull her on. We're at the site in no time.

There's a small crowd by the Mantis crane. The sun glints off its steel body. All around me, I see cameras pointed in our direction, little ones, the kind that Polies brought down in their luggage. All of them snapping a photo that no one else will understand, a photo that will always have to be explained to people who weren't here: installation of the last steel beam on B3 — a state-of-the-art comms hub built at the world's baddest construction site.

Floyd moves away from the minder so that I can run the crane. The line is taut, and as I move that steel beast atop the structure, I feel as happy as a pig in shit.

Once I jump off the crane, Martin slaps me on the back, hard. He's giddy. He slaps me again, not so hard this time, and I can tell he wants to talk business. "How much faster can you move on this construction, sir?"

"We're moving as fast as we can," I say.

"No doubt," he says. The words come out as two separate clouds of frozen air. I wait for the rest. "We got a problem, Bozer. You been keeping on top of the news?"

"Two Fingys and a stolen ice-corer on the Antarctic Divide ain't never gonna end well," I say.

He leans in. I smell Pearlie's onion-fried hash browns on his breath. "They're gonna try to shut this show down, Bozer."

"I'm listening."

"Pavano's got two congressmen who are riding Scaletta hard. They can hold up the appropriations bill."

I shake my head. "Simple workplace injury, I've seen far worse."

"It's a shitshow, Bozer. It's politics. It's messy."

I don't need him to spell it out. I've been through budget cuts before, but there have always been ways around them. There's nothing a congressmen can throw at a Nailhead like me that I can't turn into a solid plan of action. I tell Martin this, but he shakes his head. Tells me this time they're going after the agency as a whole. They want to shut the whole place down in the middle of the research season, want to kill the experiments, kill the construction, put the station into caretaker mode until the Beakers and their bosses at the NSF cry uncle.

"You stop construction now, the entire thing's gonna be under snow in a month," I tell him. "They'll have to put up twice as many dimes to rebuild this bitch when they finally get their heads out of their asses."

"I know," Martin says. He looks like he wants to cry. "I'm calling a meeting tonight. Please be there."

Floyd pulls up and Martin climbs on the snowmobile. He waves as they pull away and head toward the station. It's lunchtime. I look around and see I'm the only one at B3 now. I take a long look at the site. Martin's right. This is a shitshow. But it's my shitshow.

NATIONAL SCIENCE
   FOUNDATION
4201 WILSON BOULEVARD
ARLINGTON, VIRGINIA 22230

Dear Ms. Gosling:
Please review and sign the attached ad-
dendum to your Release of Liability and
Indemnity Agreement and Covenant
Not to Sue contract, and return both to
your Station Manager at your earliest
convenience. Countersigned copies will
be placed in your personnel file. I wish
you the best for the upcoming winter.

Sincerely,
Alexandra Scaletta
Alexandra Scaletta
Agency Director, National Science
Foundation

A KNOWN ISSUE

2004 January 31
09:11
To:
  cherrywaswaiting@hotmail.com
From:
  Billie.Gosling@janusbooks.com
Subject: MIA

C.,
Saw on the news there was some
accident in Antarctica at a
place whose name I've already
forgotten but which isn't
Pole. I trust this is far from
your strip mall at the bottom
of the earth.

                           B.

2004 February 1
16:10
To:

cherrywaswaiting@hotmail.com
From:
   Billie.Gosling@janusbooks.com
Subject: MIA Redux

So . . . now they're saying
that the accident involved a
South Pole scientist and an
NSF grantee, which leaves me
wondering. I keep remembering
you saying that if you died
down there, we wouldn't know.
Dad has been calling NSF on
the hour every hour and is
getting nowhere. Something
about HIPAA and privacy. Mom
has resorted to burning sage
in the bathroom at work. Be a
pal and write back, or at
least have NSF send us your
death certificate so we can
collect your death benefits.

2004 February 3
21:02
To:
   Billie.Gosling@janusbooks.com
From:
   cherrywaswaiting@yahoo.com
Subject: RE: MIA Redux

B.,

Sorry. I'm alive. NSF said they contacted you guys. Right hand, index finger, down to the proximal phalanx, which basically means I lost the whole thing. I don't remember much, but I'm told that I was palming the ice in order to get a better look at Pavano's corehole, and god that looks bad when typed. Pavano lost control of this massive ice-corer and apparently my finger was in the way. At first they were going to send me home, but because of some political algorithm, it's better for everyone, self included, to keep me at Pole. I'm glad I'm staying. No offense. I like it down here. Anyway, it looks like this thing has set into motion some political crisis where Pavano is being framed as the exiled "minority-views" scientist using inferior tools because of the "culture wars," and now we are prepping for a visit from some Washington

dignitaries, who will land at
Pole in a week.

C.

p.s. It took me forty minutes
to write this e-mail. Tell Dad
I'm okay. Tell Mom the polar
bears say hey.

In the Smoke Bar, the vets were telling old station tales about the ones who went crazy: The guy who'd crammed a backpack full of graham crackers and beer and tried to walk to Zhongstan Station for hot-and-sour soup. The lady doing ice-core analysis last season who went on a vodka binge and tried to shave her underarms with a butter knife. The biophysicist who had torn the stuffing out of his pillow, because it "made too much noise in the night."

"You're *all* gonna be looney-tunes before this shit plays itself out," Bozer boomed from his seat at the bar, and it was Bozer who noticed Cooper first. "Welcome back, cupcake," he said. All eyes turned to her.

It had been two days since her trip outside, since Bozer had found her, fixed up her hand, and showed her a corpse. Seven pairs of eyes blinked at her, and Cooper couldn't summon any words. Finally, Doc Carla hauled herself out of her chair, walked over to Cooper, and led her to a table.

"Bozer told me nothing," she whispered. "But from here on out, you only get Advil."

Cooper smiled gratefully and sat down. Pearl brought her a beer, but no one spoke.

"So," Cooper said, taking a sip and looking around the room. "What happened while I was gone?"

Dwight and Sri glanced at each other, and then sped-walked to Cooper's table, each with a fistful of faxes. Based on communications Dwight had received from his counterparts at McMurdo and WAIS, as well as eavesdropping he'd done on the admin lines, he'd learned that Pavano had been triaged for shock at the Divide, and then put on the same flight as Cooper, which was supposed to continue on to McMurdo after a refuel. But once the plane landed at Pole, the trauma team — led by Pearl — decided to bring Cooper in to Hard Truth instead. Pavano had wandered out of the C-17 while Cooper was transported to the clinic, and commenced a "drunkvincible" walk toward the Dark Sector. Sal and Floyd had had to chase him down.

Cooper's ripped and bloodied mitten was currently in a Ziploc at McMurdo, along with the illegally procured corer. The tech who'd helped Pavano forge the sign-out had already been DQ'ed and put back on a plane to Missoula. That was the extent of the information they had about Pavano's whereabouts and his future plans.

Dwight shoved one of the faxes he'd been holding at Cooper. "The campaign has already started."

"Campaign?"

"Oh, you're famous, Cooper," Dwight said.

"As Jane Doe," Sri added. He shrugged. "HIPAA rules."

It was a small piece in the Associated Press daily digest, with the headline: "Injury reported at ice-coring camp in Antarctica." The reporter quoted a source as saying that Pavano had been denied use of the industrial corer to which all other climate scientists at WAIS had access. That same anonymous source indicated that Pavano's time at the ice-coring camp and at South Pole Station itself had been marked by open hostility, ostracism, and obstruction. In other words, climate scientists had made research impossible for him, so, out of desperation, he'd worked around them.

"And then these just came in tonight," Sri said, bouncing on the tops of his toes. He handed her additional news digests, the same ones that arrived every night, but Sri had highlighted the headlines, which included "Climate skeptic 'frozen' out at climate change camp," "Could Antarctica accident have been avoided?" and "Republican congressmen who pushed for climate skeptic say 'hostile working environment' to blame in Antarctic amputation."

" 'Antarctic amputation' sounds like a Lovecraft novel," Cooper said, but only Birdie laughed.

"It's not funny, Cooper," Sri said. "This is serious. They're coming to Pole."

"Who's coming?"

"The politicians, the suits, the directors, the congressional aides, the media."

"I think it was all a setup from day one," Dwight barked. "This shit was orchestrated."

"Dwight," Pearl said warningly.

Dwight looked over at Cooper guiltily. "I mean, I don't know if the finger thing was part of it, or . . ."

Cooper wondered if Dwight was right. What if it was all a setup? She recalled Pavano's preternatural calm in the line that first day at the Divide, when the "freeze-out" had begun. The way he'd come prepared with an envelope full of cash and the technical know-how to erect a twenty-foot-

404

high ice-core drill. It wasn't just that he expected the roadblocks; it was almost as if he'd welcomed them.

"So what exactly happened?" Sri asked as he paced under the dart board. "I mean, I know you're not really allowed to talk about it . . . but . . ."

"They didn't give him a tech. They didn't give him access to any drills, or give him any means of extracting a core. I wasn't approved either, as his research tech, even though Pavano forwarded me an e-mail the day before we left that said I was."

Sri scratched his head compulsively and muttered, "Oh shit oh shit oh shit."

"But he didn't seem too upset about it," Cooper replied.

"That's because he's incapable of showing emotion," Sri snapped.

"No, I just mean that he didn't seem surprised. He seemed — I don't know — prepared for it." Sri stopped pacing and stared at her for a minute. Then he slammed his beer on a nearby table and raced out of the bar. The beer was quickly claimed.

As the conversations picked up again, Cooper leaned over to Pearl, who had resumed her knitting under Birdie's adoring gaze. "Have you seen Sal?"

Pearl shook her head. "I haven't seen him

for days. I think he's sleeping in his lab. Alek comes and gets the team's meals. Must be important stuff happening."

The dystopian hum of the power plant rattled in Cooper's chest as she passed two arguing maintenance techs on her way to Hard Truth.

"What time is it?" one said.

"What *is* time?" the other replied.

"Shut up and tell me what time it is."

"But time is irrelevant here."

"I'm just asking if we're still on New Zealand time now or if we switched to Denver time yet."

"Where did the extra day go?"

"Smoke my meat, asshole."

As Cooper headed toward the entrance tunnel, she heard someone calling her name. It was Sal. She wasn't sure if she wanted to run to him or run away, but as he got closer to her, she felt her body grow lighter, as if she might float away. His gait bore no trace of that swagger that made him so easy to identify out on the ice, when everyone looked the same in their parkas and hoods. He walked as if he'd walk right through her, but when he reached her, he gathered in his arms and pulled her up against his body. She felt him take three deep, deliberate breaths.

"You didn't wait," he said. "You were supposed to wait. You were supposed to let me come get you before leaving your room. Fuck you for not waiting."

"I'm sorry, Sal," Cooper said, and meant it.

"Bozer told me what happened," he said into the top of her head. "Outside." His warm breath on her hair felt good. "He saved your life."

"I know."

"You should be on a flight home."

"I know," Cooper said. "Did Bozer tell everyone about what happened outside?"

"No, only me and Doc Carla."

"Why you?"

Sal pulled away and looked at her. "Because even he knows."

"Knows what?"

"Are you going to make me say it?" Sal said. She winced as Sal pulled her close again and her hand was caught under his arm.

"Christ, I'm sorry," he said. He glanced down at her bandaged hand. "How is it?"

"Doc Carla keeps telling me that it will start looking better, but right now it looks like bad sci-fi makeup."

"You shouldn't have been on the Divide
—"

"Sal —"

"No, let me finish. You shouldn't have
been there — but more important, like
vastly, vastly more important, Pavano should
never have been there." He let her go and
ran his hand down his beard as he paced. "I
don't know what to do. I mean, it's one
thing for oil executives to pressure Congress
to defund working groups on the human
impacts of climate change, but to send
someone like Pavano to the Divide, and
then to dangle him on stage like a puppet."
He stopped and looked at Cooper. "And
then your hand — your fucking hand, Cooper!"

As Cooper watched him pace, she found
she was becoming annoyed. "Why are you
doing this?"

"Doing what?"

"This. This 'I'm outraged' act. The last
time I saw you I was a mistake you'd made.
You were confused. You were sorry. Is this
you being angry at Pavano for hurting me
or you being angry that some politicians are
fucking with your sacred science shit?"

Sal looked at Cooper for a long minute. "I
deserve that. All of it."

Cooper hated him for saying this. It left

her nowhere else to take her anger.

Sal reached out a hand to her. "I have something to show you in the machine shed," he said. "Will you come?" Cooper looked at his mismatched mittens. One was black, a Gore-Tex, while the other — the one he was holding out to her now — was a fur-backed gauntlet with a large rip along the top. Cooper knew at once that the Gore-Tex mitten she'd found in skua, the one with the barbecue-encrusted tips — the one she'd painted months ago — was Sal's. For some reason, her anger dissipated.

She put her hand in his and allowed him to take her to the machinery arch.

When they got there, it looked like ground zero of a Scud missile attack. Cooper stepped over vehicle parts and long curling threads of metal and wood, toward the squeal of a lathe. A Polie in overalls and safety glasses stood hunched over the lathe, blue sparks flying from between her hands. Cooper recognized Marcy by her tangled blond hair. Sal walked around the machine so Marcy could see him, and she stopped working on the crankshaft she'd been repairing.

She pushed her safety glasses on top of her head and, using her sleeve, wiped the sweat from her forehead. "Jesus, you again?

Get off my back, man. It's done." She grinned at Cooper. "This asshole has been on me like tie-dye on a hippie about the new Pole marker. Hold on, I'll get it." When Marcy disappeared into a small supply shed on the other side of the arch, Cooper turned to Sal. "What's this about?"

"Marcy's in charge of making the new Pole marker."

"The one you designed," Cooper said.

Sal nodded. "I want you to see it before the ceremony."

"I thought the ceremony was supposed to happen on New Year's Day."

Sal grimaced. "Thanks to the war of bureaucratic attrition, the powers-that-be told us to reposition the marker closer to the end of the summer season, in mid-February."

"Why?"

Sal shrugged. "It's a directive from NSF. Some congressional committee wrote it into an appropriations bill. Arbitrary interference — just letting us know that they can control the operations down here. But if that's all the interference we get from Washington this year, I'll dirty-dance with Floyd in the galley."

Marcy emerged from the shed carrying something bound up in a rag. She gestured toward one of the worktables and they gathered around it. A coughing forklift pulled into the garage and shuddered off. Marcy leaned back to look, and, seeing it was Bozer, called him over. "I've outdone myself, boss," she said. "Come look."

As they waited for Bozer to lumber over, Cooper wondered what Sal's design would look like. She imagined it first as Viper, the coffee-filter telescope he had shown her. But that didn't touch the history of the continent, which was important. Something more generally cosmic, perhaps — a constellation, the Milky Way. Cooper remembered Sal's horrible drawing of the two branes colliding — the two pancakes — and stifled a laugh, imagining the sketch transformed into the Pole marker.

Bozer arrived and slapped his hands on the table expectantly. Marcy gathered the fabric between her fingers, then stopped and looked over at Sal. "I just want you to know that this was the hardest design I've ever worked from and that I've wished you dead pretty much constantly since you brought it to me. That being said, it's the best thing I've ever done."

Bozer told her to can it, and Marcy removed the rag.

The bright shop lights bounced off polished brass, creating white bursts in Cooper's vision. Slowly, the marker's shape became clear — the sinuous upslope of a bow, the sturdiness of two masts, and a web of rigging, like spun silk. Etched into its body were the words *Terra Nova*. Cooper realized she was trembling.

"That's good shit, Marce," Bozer growled, squeezing Marcy's shoulder. "That's very fine shit."

Marcy pulled a crumpled piece of paper from the bib of her overalls and spread it out on the table. "Well, I had a good design. A fussy-as-hell design, but still, a good design."

Cooper looked down at her sketch of the *Terra Nova*. Sal's precise mathematician's handwriting was all over it — numbers, and arrows, and measurements in centimeters and in millimeters. Instructions to Marcy, Cooper realized. Sal leaned over the marker, examining its intricacies, his face bright with happiness and admiration. When he turned to see what she thought, Cooper found she was unable to speak. She didn't notice Marcy and Bozer quietly walk away.

"Well," Sal laughed. "What do you think?"

Cooper could only shake her head and choke out, "Why?"

"This is me telling you that you belong

here, Cooper." He hesitated. "And this is me saying I think we should be together down here. I know I was a dick in your room that night, before you left for the Divide. It was just — when you were sitting on the edge of the bed like that, with your boots off, looking at me —" He looked away, frustrated. "Everything about that moment felt too important to be in my clumsy hands. I didn't realize how important it was until I was touching you." His brow furrowed. "This is hard to explain." He walked over to the forklift and back again. "Okay," he said, "I think I know how to say this to you. Math. It explains everything. There's a moment when every geek comes upon a mathematical equation that almost destroys him. For Alek it's the Mandelbrot set equation. For me it's the Riemann hypothesis. Whatever a great poem means to a poet, that's what understanding these things for the first time is to someone like me. I can't explain it to you. All I can tell you is that your face that night, that night in your room, it was like seeing the Mandelbrot for the first time, the Riemann. Like starting a single-variable equation and watching it turn into differential calculus before your eyes. It was scary. I was scared. I didn't know how to explain that to you,

413

and I didn't know what to do, either." Sal reached for Cooper and drew her close. "Then when you left with Pavano, I got angry, because I wanted you to be with me, not him. I was angry that he had that time with you, and that's when I realized: I can't even be away from you for a day without feeling like every minute is an hour."

These words created an incision in Cooper, which caused both pain and immense relief. She took his mitten in hers. "Come with me."

They walked across the plateau in silence. Once they were in Cooper's room in the Jamesway, she sat on her bed and lifted her feet toward him. Sal kneeled on the floor and took off her boots. He undressed her carefully, slowly easing the thick cuff of her parka over her injured hand. He eased her back onto the bed, and brushed the hair off her forehead. He peeled off his thermal sweatshirt, only taking his eyes off her as he pulled the shirt over his head. He slid one suspender off his shoulder, then the other, and once his base layer was off, Cooper saw his body was sinewy and muscular, and very pale. It seemed to Cooper at that moment the most beautiful, most desirable thing she'd ever seen, and her heartbeat pulsed in her ear. Her body wanted to disintegrate beneath his fingers.

He leaned over her and kissed her mouth, and he lay down on the bed next to her. Pulling her hair away from her face, he touched his dry lips to her throat, and told her to let go, so she did.

It was only later, long after Sal had reluctantly left her bed to return to the Dark Sector, that Cooper saw the vial on her desk. There was a note.

You don't do this kind of shit alone. Do it with us standing beside you. Bozer here.

When Cooper arrived at the studio the next morning, she saw that Denise had cleared their communal desk of textbooks and papers, and had tied a number of Blue Razberry Blow Pops into a bouquet with a note signed, *Good luck. Your friend, Margaret Mead.*

With one of the suckers in her mouth, Cooper walked over to the easel. She pulled off the dropcloth: Tucker's eye stared back at her. Without the Scotch and painkiller cocktail, she could better see that it was objectively decent. Despite what Tucker had told her that night, it needed no revision. In fact, it might even be done. Then there was the painting of Pearl. The brown eyes stippled with copper and the plain freckled face that burned with ambition.

Then there was the one of Bozer. She'd been outside, ready to start fresh in order to avoid becoming a tragic figure, observing the white wasteland to the west of the station. She'd tried to look at the landscape critically, the way she hadn't been able to do out on the Divide. It was an ocean, with wind-sculpted waves frozen in time. No — that was too generic. It was a desert — blowout dunes, sand seas. No, not that either. There was a reason, Cooper could admit now, that her desert series — "Richat Structure" — had not impressed nor sold at Caribou Coffee. ("This one makes me thirsty," she'd overheard someone say. "I refuse to be thirsty in my own home.") Then she'd blinked into the sun, and had been startled to see it was encircled by a purple and gold halo. It seemed impossible, as if her unchanging Minnesota sun had been replaced by a pulsating counterfeit. Deep black to the west, Cherry had written, shading into long lines of gray and lemon yellow round the sun, with a vertical shaft through them, and a bright orange horizon. His foot on the edge of the Antarctic Plateau, and Scott told him to turn back. Cherry had peered through his myopia waiting for them as he winked in the sun's faint gleam.

A metallic clatter of a load of beams falling to earth had made Cooper jump. She'd watched as the various construction vehicles circled the beams curiously. Marcy had gotten her bulldozer running again, and Bozer was on a snowmobile with an admin, gesticulating like a traffic cop. Cooper had thought about her sketches of Bozer, back in her studio. She'd managed a few broad outlines before losing steam and resorting to the hesitation wounds of a doomed painting — slashes of paint here, pointless halftones there. He saw her standing there, gaping at the gathering crowd in front of the B3 module; he motored over to her and told her to get on — something important was about to happen.

Whether it was important was almost beside the point — it had appeared to Cooper, once she was at the site with everyone else, that Bozer was simply placing a large steel beam on the very top of the new module. But then she'd seen his face, and she'd understood.

The canvas in front of her now was embryonic, but promising. A nose set in the middle of the canvas — the nostrils lined with flesh-pink and sprouting hairs, and burst blood vessels sketched in with pencil, unpainted, undecided. The overgrown,

Bobby Knight eyebrows with their searching insect antennas had yet to be considered. Ditto the stylized handlebar mustache
and the incongruous lumberjack beard, and
the glossy pate hidden beneath a series of
offensive bandannas. But she had figured
out the eyes, which was the only way into a
portrait. These eyes that told you, point-
blank, that manning a trawler crane at the
end of the earth was the only place her
subject belonged. She started to paint.

2004 February 3
11:57
To:
    cherrywaswaiting@hotmail.com
From:
    Billie.Gosling@janusbooks.com
Subject: RE: MIA Redux

I can't tell if your last
e-mail was an attempt at humor
or if you are really a new
member of the Nine Finger
Club. I'll assume it's the
former, and I'll bite: my
research indicates other members of the Nine Finger Club
include Buster Keaton, Jesse
James, Lee Van Cleef, Daryl

Hannah, and Galileo. Lee fucking Van Cleef, Cooper. But to be completely transparent, I should add that Galileo lost his finger post-mortem, when someone took the middle finger of his right hand straight from his corpse.

I don't know what to say. How are you going to paint?

B.

The station populace grumbled its way into the gym — Game Night had been cancelled and the half-finished games of Settlers of Catan from the week before would have to remain half finished. Once everyone had found a seat, Tucker walked onto the stage, where a crew of unfamiliar men, clearly not Polies, were leaning back in mismatched folding chairs, speaking to one another in low tones. Tucker, Cooper noted, was still wearing sunglasses.

"First, let me run through the week's Significant Activities." He consulted a notebook. "Two Twin Otters left to support the Chilean Antarctic Program — that was on Wednesday. In construction news, Bozer and friends have finished the siding trim on the upwind side of the new station and have installed SIP panels on the third section of the Logistics Facility."

"Footers for the second section were installed this morning," Bozer called out.

"Floyd, what's the status of the leak in the Emergency Power Plant right water tank?" Tucker said.

"Still exceeds," Floyd replied. "It's a known issue."

"Doc?"

Doc Carla stood up and recited from memory the week's sick calls. "One subungual hematoma, one thigh contusion, one mononeuropathy, one biceps tendonitis, one shoulder rotator cuff tendonitis, one thumb strain." She glanced sideways at Cooper, and added: "And therapeutics for one finger amputation." This was met with a rousing round of applause. Next, Pearl stood up with a file folder in hand.

"Here are the numbers from the Food Growth Chamber: nine pounds of green leaf lettuce; fourteen pounds of red leaf lettuce; and nothing else has sprouted yet. Water usage this week was nine gallons. And our dedicated produce maintenance volunteer is redeploying at the end of the month, so please come see me if you'd like to volunteer."

"Thanks, Pearl," Tucker said. "Finally, some of you asked me to update you on Changed Conditions Affecting Functional Operations. We've completed one hundred and ten LC-130 missions so far, but we remain seventeen missions behind schedule, which could affect our fuel supply." The room quieted down a little at this news. "We'll talk about this more at the operations meeting tomorrow night. Now, on to the matter at hand. As you probably know by now, we're going to be hosting some Distinguished Visitors shortly."

Someone in the back started a chant of "Tom Waits, Tom Waits, Tom Waits, Tom Waits." The rest of the room picked it up.

"It's not going to be Tom Waits, obviously, although if you want, I'll sing his catalog to anyone who's interested after the meeting." The men in the folding chairs behind Tucker laughed indulgently at this.

"Two esteemed members of Congress will be traveling to the ice next week, and because of the circumstances there will be new protocols. I'm going to introduce Karl Martin, our fearless VIDS president of Polar Operations, who will explain what's going to happen."

A man in a three-day scruff-beard, Kangol hat, and Carhartt work pants slapped the knee of the man next to him, stood up, and walked toward the microphone. His corporate mien was unmistakable, despite his clumsy attempts at native dress. Until this moment, Karl Martin had been nothing more than a reference point to most of the Polies — a corporate PR photo affixed to the dart board in the Smoke Bar.

"Maybe I should have worn my full ECW gear," Karl said into the microphone. "I mean, I see the black and green parkas, which is — heh heh — let's just put it out there: they make you the badasses. Nothing like those red parkas at McMurdo."

No one in the audience appreciated the pandering: the distant roar of the power plant was the only sound in the room.

Martin cleared his throat. "I get the feeling that I should get to the point, so folks, I'm going to speak frankly. The last week has been difficult for everyone. The blame game, rumors flying, tension between coworkers. These are all things that can complicate a working environment. Our goal at VIDS is, and always has been, a safer and more secure global community. Whether we're in Kabul, Tripoli, or right here at South Pole, it's our guiding principle. So when something like this happens

— the tragedy that unfolded at an NSF research camp — we're shaken. And even though the actors involved were not VIDS contractors, nor were they working at an official VIDS work site, we feel let down. And although no VIDS employees or VIDS-issued matériel were involved in this workplace incident — which, again, unfolded at a National Science Foundation research camp and involved NSF Fellows — we are reminded that safety is of the utmost importance. And our hearts go out to the NSF, which bears complete responsibility for this incident." People began murmuring, and Martin, sensing he was losing the room, reloaded.

"You know, this is tough, unprecedented stuff. I'm not going to stand here and pretend like I'm a great scientific mind, but I am a decent scholar of humanity — decades in various theaters of war will make you one. Now, I know we say that South Pole is the only apolitical place on the planet, a place where science trumps ideology. That's how we like it. That's why we're here. Nations collaborate, and have collaborated, here for many decades, overlooking policy differences to come together in order to advance science and human thought. I mention this because the individuals who will be visiting the station in the next week are, by any definition, political figures.

"As you know, our friends at the NSF typically restrict official visits to the station to dignitaries like presidents and ambassadors. However, due to circumstances, NSF has invited a couple of our national legislators to come see the station, have a look around."

"This wouldn't have anything to do with the fact that they're on the Congressional Budget Committee, would it?" Sal called from his seat next to Cooper.

"Mr. Brennan, right?" Martin said.

"Dr. Brennan."

"Sorry — *Dr.* Brennan, wouldn't want to neglect the honorific."

"It's not an honorific, it's an earned title."

The chuckles from the audience made Martin set his chin.

"Dr. Brennan, you'll need to take up your concerns with Alexandra Scaletta. The fortunes of the support staff who make your experiments feasible are tied directly to congressional appropriation. And that's my purview. In fact, let's talk about the support staff for a minute. I expect those of you down here on contract will represent VIDS in a positive manner. You are not to address the visitors unless directly addressed by them; and in that case, you do not express an opinion. You will restrict any comment to your everyday duties on the ice or your families back home. Any comments beyond that will not be allowed. If you choose to ignore this, your contracts will not be renewed. We decided to keep it simple."

"That's draconian," Floyd said from the front row. Martin looked down at him from the stage as if he were a pile of offal.

"I wonder if you know who Draco is?" Martin asked.

"A member of Devo?" Kit called between cupped hands.

But Floyd was seriously pissed. "I know what *draconian* means," he said. "I used the term intentionally. What you've just described is draconian." Onstage, Tucker remained inscrutable behind his sunglasses.

"I apologize," Martin said. "For a moment I doubted your grasp of the word's meaning because you said it like you think you're insulting me. In the places where VIDS operates, draconian systems are key to survival. Before Draco instituted his code of laws in Athens, daily life was governed by blood feuds. Draconian law gives members of a community clear expectations and consistent consequences. And if Lockheed

425

Martin wins the contract next year because the NSF budget is cut, you'll be praying to Draco that they hire you. Based on your demeanor, I wouldn't count on it."

From the back of the gym, a lone voice called out, "Tom Waits."

First came a procession of lower-level VIDS directors in from Denver. NSF reps arrived shortly thereafter, recognizable by their clumsy attempts to blend in. Together, they prowled the halls and tried to chat up the workers, drove out to the labs to "hang out" with the scientists, crashed 90 South asking for IPAs, and handed out swag from the agency's last grant conference. Meanwhile, the *Antarctic Sun* newspaper, published out of McMurdo, indicated that the congressional delegation would include an assortment of political aides, as well as the two Republican congressmen who had gotten Pavano on the ice — Rep. Sam Bayless of Kansas and Rep. Jack Calhoun of Tennessee.

The Distinguished Visitors, known at Pole as DVs, arrived around midnight, blinking at the sun as they stumbled across the skiway toward the station. Cooper and the other Polies who had gathered to witness their arrival made their way up to the

Smoke Bar immediately afterward to discuss.

The Polies were three drinks deep when Calhoun walked into the bar. His sudden appearance, and his shellacked coif, somehow unruffled by both his hood and the straight-line polar winds, caught everyone off guard. Even Bozer looked surprised.

Only Marcy spoke. "Congressman, you look like you need a drink."

"Make that plural, and we understand each other," Calhoun replied.

"One South Pole Highball," Marcy called to Alek, who was playing bartender.

"How'd you find us?" Doc Carla asked, carelessly winding a rubber band around her fingers.

"Nice Afro-American man told me I could get a stiff drink here."

Cooper and Sal exchanged an amused glance.

"So where's your security detail, Congressman?" Sal asked. "Your advance team know you're fraternizing with the enemy?"

"An honest man has no enemies," Calhoun replied, taking the seat next to Pearl, who was knitting another scarf for Birdie.

"Wrong," Alek barked from the bar, as he handed the drink to Marcy. "Honest man has more enemies than anyone."

Marcy brought Calhoun the glass and watched as he lifted it to the light. "What in the hell is in this?" he asked.

She clasped her hands in front of her and batted her eyelashes. "Try it, and we'll tell you," she said, pulling out an unexpected Betty Boop imitation that Cooper thought was damn good. Tickled, Calhoun took a huge gulp and immediately started hacking. He flushed red and grabbed at his throat. Cooper thought he was going to have a heart attack. He peered up at Marcy through watering eyes.

"Drain cleaner?" he coughed.

"Jet fuel," Marcy said. "Just a tablespoon's worth, but the best buzz on earth."

"Murdering a U.S. congressman is a capital crime, you know." But he took another, smaller sip. "It grows on the palate," he said. He held the glass in front of his face and swirled its contents around. "But if I were you, I'd conserve as much fuel as possible."

"What's that supposed to mean?" Sal asked.

Calhoun waved the remark away. "Nothing. I'm just saying you should conserve. I do. I'm green. Eco-friendly. I recycle. I compost. Well, shit, I don't compost, but I conserve. I'm a conservative."

Cooper could see that Sal was oddly charmed by Calhoun's deflection. "Conservative and incoherent," Sal said. "Amazing how often those two things go hand in hand." Calhoun raised his glass at Sal, and Sal grinned, despite himself.

"So you've got your eye on the JP-8," Bozer growled from the table next to Calhoun. Cooper noticed Denise quickly place her hand on Bozer's knee.

"JP-what?"

"The fuel. You plan on holding back supply until you get your way?"

Calhoun was surprised. He peered back at Bozer. "I plan on protecting the integrity of scientific inquiry."

"I don't know what that means," Bozer replied. "But I do know what it means when we don't got enough fuel to get through the winter. I've got a station half built out there and if anyone fucks with my fuel supply, it'll be buried under eight feet of drift-snow in a month."

Calhoun blinked back at Bozer, and Cooper felt a wave of compassion for the man. He had no business being at Pole. He was beefy Midwestern stock, about sixty. His dark eyes looked sad, even when he was laughing, and his second chin looked like another smile. The eyebrows were fuzzy, almost furry — black shot through with wiry white hairs. Cooper searched her pockets for her pen, found it, and painstakingly tried to sketch the congressman on a napkin. Sal saw what she was doing and smiled.

He turned to Calhoun. "What exactly do you guys want?" he said. "I mean, you come down here with your parade of imbeciles, squawking about scientific integrity, but in the meantime, no one knows what your point is. What's the plan? To hold the station hostage until you get reelected? To subpoena every climate scientist until there's no one left to do the research?"

Calhoun held Sal's steady gaze. "I have nothing to say on that subject. It is out of my hands."

"And whose able hands is it in now?"

"Scaletta's. We tried to compromise. She rejected it."

"What are you offering?"

"Basic fairness. Scientific integrity."

"Already built into the system."

Calhoun shook his head. "If it were, then Frank Pavano would have had freedom of movement while he was here, free access to equipment. He'd still be on the ice. The NSF ensures minority scientific views get a seat at the table. Equal access to taxpayer-funded research sites at the Poles."

A small, strangled scream caused everyone to turn. Sri stood in the doorway, his hood still on, holding a chess set with both hands.

"You want the NSF to fund research that tries to prove global warming is a hoax," Sri said, his knuckles whitening as he gripped the box. Calhoun finished off his South Pole Highball and set it on the table too hard.

"Young man, I'm not saying that's what I want. I'm saying that's the proposal on the table. Your bosses have said no. We will take advantage of the tools at our disposal."

"Including subpoenas? One of the WAIS researchers was subpoenaed yesterday by her state's attorney general. They're taking her off the ice because someone from your office called and —"

Calhoun rose from his chair unsteadily. "This shit's above your pay grade, and I've already talked too much. I was just looking for a nightcap and some conversation."

Sal stood up and took the congressman's arm. "I'll walk you to the DV barracks."

Calhoun yanked his arm out of Sal's grasp. "I can get there myself, son," he said, and, after putting on his jacket, haltingly made his way out of the bar.

After the congressman left, the room grew

loud and raucous with discussion about the unexpected visit, and predictions about the intensity of his hangover tomorrow after Alek confessed to putting a double shot of jet fuel in his drink.

Cooper turned to Sal. "I'm going to bed. Wanna join me?" He hooked his fingers into her belt loops and pulled her close, but then noticed Sri was lightly thumping his head against the wall. "I gotta console Sri," he said. "I'll come by later."

Instead of heading straight to the Jamesways, though, Cooper decided to drop by her studio, maybe fill out the sketch of Calhoun a little. She'd seen something in his face that she liked.

She had just opened the door to the trailer, when she heard someone mumbling from what sounded like the far end of the hall. Speak of the devil — there he was, in a crumpled heap, sitting with his back against the wall. He startled at the sound of her boots squeaking across the linoleum.

"Thank god," he said. "I wasn't out of there two minutes before the earth started spinning. I can't get in my room."

"That's because your room isn't in this trailer," she replied, as Calhoun struggled to his feet, using the wall for leverage. "It's in a much fancier one."

"Where am I?"

"This is the Artist and Writers' Annex." She gestured down the long hall. "Behind these doors all of us geniuses spend our days staring at blank walls, contemplating a career change." The cheap joke raised a laugh, and Calhoun asked her what kind of art she did. When she told him she was a painter, he laughed again.

"What's funny?"

"I'm just thinking about how many times I've said something like 'The federal endowments for the arts are wasteful and elitist, and steal much-needed funds from the hardworking folks of the middle class.' "

"Might be right about the wasteful part, at least in my case," Cooper said. "I painted nothing but mittens for the first three months I was here."

"Mittens?"

Cooper pulled her keys from her pocket and opened the door to her studio, careful to keep her right hand in her parka. "And one glove. Do you want to see them?"

Inside, Calhoun was taken by the mittens. He loved the mittens: he wanted to own them. After Cooper gave him the spiel — *It's a study of both the humility of the simple garment and the hubris of our belief that it protects us from this savage continent* — he offered to buy all four of them, including the triptych, on the spot. "I don't know much about art, but these — they speak to me." He wandered over to the canvas on the easel, the one covered by a dropcloth. "What else you got?" He pinched the fabric between his fingers. "May I?"

"Sure, but I warn you — that one's not a mitten," Cooper said. Calhoun pulled the cloth from the canvas, revealing her portrait of Bozer. Under the harsh fluorescent lights, his shining face seemed to take on a Wizard of Oz quality, hovering over them like a strange apparition. The bandanna was gone, revealing a long-ago-receded hairline and a broad, veiny forehead; a pair of untidy eyebrows held court over 7Up-clear eyes that looked beyond the viewer. The mustache and beard had been shorn clean, and left behind pink skin in their place. While the underlying structure of his face was built of clean, strong lines — having been painted before Cooper's injury — the rest of the portrait had a soft, almost tremulous feel to it.

"That looks like the fella from the bar," he said. "Except I believe he had a beard."

Cooper pulled her right hand from her parka pocket to drape the cloth back over the portrait. "It's not finished; I didn't have time to get to some of the details, and I —"

"So it's you," he said. Cooper realized he was staring at her bandaged hand. "You're the girl from the Divide." He looked from her face, to her hand, back to her face. "They told us you were a painter." He furrowed his brow. "Why the hell haven't you left this place? Don't you have people?"

"I have people. My people are here."

"You didn't want to go home?"

Calhoun's question took Cooper aback. "Home?"

"Home," Calhoun said. "The place where you live? Where you've got roots? You got people waiting on you, don't you?"

Cooper had not thought of home for weeks. Not of her father, her mother, not even, aside from their e-mails, of Billie. They belonged to another world now — a parallel universe, one of Sal's branes. And while at some point that world would collide with this one, the long rebound pulling them apart was welcome.

"I am home," Cooper said quietly.

Calhoun shook his head, and moved on to the nearly finished portrait of Pearl, which Cooper had set against the back wall — she had only to strengthen the background and shadow tones. Calhoun snuck another glance at Cooper's hand. "Did the accident affect your ability to, ah, to do this kind of work?"

"I lost a finger on my dominant hand," Cooper said. "So, yeah, it changed things. I'm not able to be as precise as I used to be." She surveyed Pearl. "But now I know that precision rarely tells the whole story."

"Aren't you angry? I'd be as mad as hell." When Cooper didn't respond, he added, "Proverbs says, 'Good sense makes one slow to anger, and it is his glory to overlook an offense.' "

"I know a better one."

"What is it?"

" 'If you are fearful, you may do much, for none but cowards have need to prove their bravery.' "

Calhoun seemed deeply moved. "Ecclesiastes?"

"Apsley Cherry-Garrard. Of the Scott party. He's sort of my spirit animal."

"Scott. They told us about him on the ride down here. Poor bastard. All that, just to come in second place. Never heard of this Cherry character, though. With that kind of name, he had to be a little — hey, you okay?"

To Cooper's surprise, the static of a developing sob was filling her chest; she tried, unsuccessfully, to cough it away.

"I'm sorry," Cooper said when she'd recovered. "It's just that talking about Cherry —" She glanced up at Calhoun and saw incomprehension on his face. "That talking about Scott makes me think of my twin brother. He was big into polar exploration. He died last year."

Calhoun's mouth quivered slightly. "I'm sorry."

There it was again — that thing in Calhoun's face that she had seen in the bar. Cooper had no idea what it was, only that she felt compelled to tell him about David, even if there was nothing that indicated Calhoun would even be interested. "We used to pretend we were members of the Scott party, back when we were kids. He was always Titus, I was always Cherry. Never made sense, because Cherry wasn't on the final slog — all he did was stand around waiting — but we never cared. Titus was the injured guy who walked into the blizzard in order to save the others — he was the hero."

"A true act of selflessness," Calhoun said. He clasped his hands in front of him and dropped his head, as if preparing to pray. "A true act of selflessness." Suddenly, he began fumbling with the zipper on his parka. He seemed to have no clue how it

437

worked. "I want to show you something," he said earnestly. When he saw Cooper's skeptical face, he guffawed. "Nothing like that." So Cooper reached over and helped him unzip his parka. He pointed to the lapel of his new North Face thermal. A glittering brooch in masculine red, white, and blue rhinestones had been pinned on the left breast. Cooper noted that it spelled out the words *Let's Roll.*

"Bayless makes me wear this damn pin wherever we go," he said.

"United Flight Ninety-three," Cooper murmured.

Calhoun nodded. "He says it buys political and social capital. I was nowhere near when it happened. I was in Scottsdale, for god's sake."

By simply listening to him, Cooper had unleashed something in Calhoun. It was as if no one had ever listened to him before. He told her he was a widower, that his wife's death from ovarian cancer had helped his last reelection campaign, even though it had destroyed him and his kids. His campaign manager had felt it necessary to use his bereavement to his benefit, and it had worked. Still, he told Cooper he was a failure as a legislator. His bills went nowhere, his committee assignments were unimportant. He despised his constituents, didn't even really believe in his politics anymore, didn't understand why they cared more about teaching evolution in the schools than the fact that they couldn't find good-paying jobs. But what else did he have? He was a sixty-three-year-old man with nothing — no job offers from lobbying firms, no universities eager to get him behind a lectern. Then one day, his campaign manager had called him at his home, saying a large donor was interested in making a substantial contribution to the campaign. "And he says 'when I say "substantial," I'm talking seven-figs substantial.' I get these guys on the phone — they don't tell me who they are right away — and I say, 'What's the catch?' They tell me they need help protecting the integrity of science. Why would I say no to that?"

When Cooper looked at the congressman, she realized he desperately wanted her to give him a reason to have said no. "Who was the donor?" she asked.

Calhoun smiled and walked over to examine another canvas, which was obscured behind Pearl's. "You know I can't tell you that," he said. Calhoun pulled the portrait away from the wall, and suddenly, his smile faded. He studied the gaunt, angular face, framed in a fur-fringed hood. The lucent eyes were gone, and in their place were two black caves.

Calhoun tore his gaze away from the portrait to look at Cooper. "I know this man," he said.

With an ear-shattering scratch, the All-Call system suddenly came to life, and Tucker's sleepy voice spewed out a host of acronyms and directives.

"That's for you. They'll turn this place inside out looking for you," Cooper said.

"Of course they will," he said as he walked to the door. "Their lapdog took a walk."

Cooper picked up the antique compass from her desk. She was ready to let it go; though it had failed her in so many ways, something told her it wouldn't fail Calhoun. "Wait, I have something to give you." She handed him the compass.

The wrinkles in the corners of his eyes deepened as he examined it. "You use this for inspiration?"

Cooper shook her head. "No. It was given to me. Sort of like your pin. Take it," she said. When he hesitated, she added: "Please."

Calhoun accepted it, gazing at it like it was the most beautiful thing he'd ever seen, his face radiant with happiness. For a moment, Cooper felt like she was looking at her father. *There's a whole generation of those kinds of fathers,* Birdie had told Cooper back at McMurdo.

Tucker's voice came over the loudspeaker again, talking about sectors and annexes.

"You better go," Cooper said.

Calhoun looked at Cooper, his eyes wet. "This means a lot to me, young lady. I take everything said in this room to heart."

Later, as she prepared for bed, Cooper got on her chair and gazed out the window at the endless expanse of snow surrounding the station. She reached for her ruler from the bedside table, and set it on the bottom of the window frame. The sun had sunk a half inch since last week. It looked like a burning ship, disappearing into the seam between earth and sky.

The next morning, on the same stage where Coq au Balls had performed on Halloween, Congressmen Sam Bayless and Jack Calhoun sat between the undersecretary for Democracy and Global Affairs and the NSF liaison for the House Appropriations Subcommittee on Commerce, Justice, Science, and Related Agencies. The Beakers considered Alexandra Scaletta's absence "conspicuous," but Tucker assured them that she

441

was back in Washington trying to negotiate with the more reasonable members of the House budget committee.

Bayless was a lean, whippet-faced man, with the kind of facial structure one typically only found in Manga. His hair, heavily gelled, gleamed under the fluorescents. Even seated, he exuded arrogance. But it was Calhoun whom Cooper studied. She'd expected him to look tired, perhaps even exhausted, after last night, but instead he looked wide-awake. He was even smiling.

As Bayless moved to the podium, Cooper remembered Sal telling her that these DV speeches were usually obsequious paeans to the brutality of polar life, full of admiration for the "unique" individuals who sacrificed all that was familiar to do important work under heinous conditions, and promises to safeguard the funding that made such work possible. All had gone as expected so far, except for that last point. And there had been no grand confrontation, aside from Sal's conversation with Calhoun in the Smoke Bar. The station population, which had been itching for a fight, had — save for cynical veterans who knew better — depended on the scientists to lead the charge. No matter how passionate the dishwashers and welders were about keeping politics out

442

of science, they were still just support staff, not climate researchers or theoretical physicists on government grants. The former could be dismissed as the partisan harridans and Libertarians they usually were while the latter were recipients of taxpayer funds that were currently under threat. The sense of unrest in the crowd was palpable.

"I'm told that you folks are not used to the kind of media attention you've been getting over the last few weeks," Bayless began. "I apologize for that, especially if Representative Calhoun and I have been the cause of any disruption to the important work being done down here. We are as surprised as any of you by the way the media has shown such robust interest in what's happening here. Dissent is the healthiest state of affairs in any democracy, of course. And while the South Pole is technically a continent without country, I do consider it a democracy." Cooper felt Sal stir next to her. "I think that democracy is under attack. That in a bastion of scientific thought, the covenant of free thought has been broken."

"There is no such thing as a scientific covenant," Sal burst out. "You're using religious language to describe science."

Two NSF admins approached Sal's row from either end. But the congressman put his hand up. "No, it's okay." He gripped the sides of the podium and leaned over it. "Without god, science doesn't exist." Half of the room laughed. "Oh, did I make a joke? I guess it must be funny to people who believe time, space, and matter came into existence unassisted. That planets and stars formed from space dust, not the hand of an intelligent force. That matter created life by itself and early life-forms learned to reproduce like Sea-Monkeys." At this, the room fell silent. "Look, guys — gals — we're on the same side. I believe in science. I also believe all findings of science will eventually be found to agree with Scripture."

"Amen," Calhoun said, dipping his head.

"But I know you don't care about my thoughts on science. You want to know about money. I know there's a great deal of speculation about the status of the NSF's budget. And it's true that discussions about NSF's operating budget, particularly for its polar operations, have been ongoing for the last few weeks — but so have the budgets of a number of federal agencies. This is not a deviation, it's not a conspiracy. It's part of the process. That being said, I would be remiss if I didn't tell you that the hostile working environment experienced by scientists working on alternative theories of so-called climate change has figured into the discussions as well."

Bayless gestured to one of his aides, and the young man sped-walked to the podium and handed him a sheet of paper. "There's still time to avert an unfortunate situation, so I want to talk about Frank Pavano for a moment. Dr. Pavano has been the victim of a systematic and sustained pattern of harassment based solely on his research." Bayless consulted the paper. "On November sixth, he was denied a username and password to access the West Antarctic Divide server. This was blamed on a 'majordomo error.' The next day, a research paper he posted in the common area was defaced, and then later removed. On November fourteenth, Dr. Pavano found a threatening cartoon taped to the door to his room, which featured a crude drawing of Christ, sitting atop an Earth-like planet engulfed in flames. On December eighteenth, Dr. Pavano was notified by the climate research chief — in writing and on NSF letterhead — that due to budget constraints, he would not be assigned a drill tech on his final research trip to the West Antarctic Divide. This was later found to be a false statement, and Representative Calhoun and I intervened on his behalf. In the days leading up to his final trip to the ice-coring camp, he was removed from the flight manifest — twice. Both instances were blamed on administrative error. Finally, upon arriving at the camp, he was denied use of taxpayer-funded equipment necessary to his research.

"All of this culminated, as you know, in a tragic accident involving a South Pole citizen. An accident that can be laid squarely at the feet of liberal scientists who will stop at nothing to muzzle anyone who dares to challenge them. And now she sits among you." Bayless peered into the audience. "Cooper Gosling, will you please stand up?"

Sal grasped Cooper's hand. Alek, in the seat on her other side, shifted in his chair, but did not turn to look at her. Cooper said nothing, but noticed the NSF reps glancing at one another.

Calhoun, having been summoned to the podium, now scanned the audience.

"Cooper, are you here?"

Climb in the trench.

No one in the auditorium turned to look at Cooper; their eyes fixed on Calhoun and Bayless, they betrayed nothing. At the side of the stage, Tucker remained unreadable behind his sunglasses. Simon, the VIDS admin, and Warren, the NSF admin, pretended not to see her.

Kick out the roof.

Calhoun's eyes finally found her, and for what felt like an age, he gazed at her.

Finally, he leaned over and whispered something to Bayless, and returned to his seat.

"Well, it looks like Cooper is not in the room," Bayless said. "Which is a shame, because I think it's important to underscore what needless collateral damage looks like. I understand this young woman is an artist. I imagine the kind of injury she suffered will have an impact on her future work. And it was completely preventable.

"I mention all this because there are factions in Washington calling for an agency-wide budget freeze because of this situation. Jack and I have smoothed a few ruffled feathers by proposing that some commonsense protocols be integrated into the NSF's grant-making processes. Rather than quashing scientific dissent, such protocols would ensure that those scientists with a minority view are given access to the same research sites and same taxpayer dollars as majority-view scientists. We've also proposed simple, straightforward guidelines aimed at preserving the integrity of the research station. Scientists hostile to open, honest discussions lose their federal funding. More

447

than one violation makes the program ineligible for federal grants for one year. An OSHA rep would be stationed here to ensure compliance. This approach protects the American taxpayer's investment in science. However, the head of the NSF does not share my commitment to scientific integrity."

"That's a lie," Sal said loudly.

"This is not a Q-and-A," Karl Martin shouted between cupped hands. He gestured to one of his VIDS minions and then pointed at Sal.

"This the same guy as before? No, let him talk, Karl," Bayless said. "This must be the alpha male scientist, I imagine."

"Yeah, yeah, I'm the alpha male," Sal said to Bayless. He dropped Cooper's hand and stood up. "Before even addressing the fact that your science is a failure, let's examine the reasons why you're even bothering to take up this subject, since I assume you are not a climatologist. I would probably further assume that your experiences with higher-level science are fairly limited."

"It is indisputable that I am not a scientist. I make this point with some frequency."

"So you vigorously oppose any policy — even any research — designed to halt climate change, while claiming that you do not know the science of climate change?"

"That's enough," Karl said, rising from his chair. Bayless put his hand up again, and Karl slowly sat down.

Sal continued, "Then you should be made aware of the fact that in the scientific community, there's virtually unanimous consensus that the earth is warming. It's not a matter of whether it's getting hotter, it's a matter of how hot it will get. I propose that instead of fearing this new knowledge, you accept it, and leave science to scientists. Please, Congressman, go home and let the grown-ups get some work done."

Bayless stood at the lectern, smiling. There was something to fear in his smile, Cooper knew, and when she looked back at Sal, she knew he'd seen it, too. But it was Calhoun she watched. He was smiling, too — but his lapel pin was gone.

As soon as the congressmen were wheels up and flying home, the NSF brought all of the scientists, including Sal, into a closed-door meeting, which Tucker said would likely have a passing resemblance to a Chinese reeducation camp. The funded agencies and institutions, including both Sri's and Sal's universities, had been spooked by Bayless's threats and the loud congressional support he'd received after the news stories started appearing. The universities ordered their grantees and fellows to shut their mouths, or else they would bring them back to do lab work and send other, more discreet scientists in their places. Funding was sacrosanct.

"Confidentiality agreements," Sal said, tossing the packet on Cooper's bed, before falling on top of it and landing face-first into her pillow. He turned his head to look at her. "It turns every scientific project and experiment on the ice into a classified operation. I'm considering adding an appendix to *The Crud.* I'll call it *A Scientist's Guide to Political Interference.*" He sighed. "And now there's no point for you to read *Skua Birds in Paradise,* since no one will be here this winter to benefit from it if there's a shutdown."

"Too late," Cooper said, scanning the papers Sal had given her. "Already read it. I'm really looking forward to that naked midwinter run from the sauna to the Pole marker."

She began to read aloud. " 'Details and results of NSF-backed experiments may only be released publicly after joint approval by the NSF and the scientist's home institution. Scientists and techs are prohibited

450

from speaking to the press in any capacity, even educational, without prior approval. All media requests must go through the NSF's media relations offices.' "

"And they told me I had to stop e-mailing with those kids in De Pere."

"What happens if you don't sign it?" Cooper asked.

Sal propped himself up on his elbow. "According to NSF, the scientists and techs who choose not to agree to these terms will be sent back on the next available flight, 'no questions asked.' "

"What about all the experiments?" Cooper said.

"Done."

Cooper and Sal stared sadly at the confidentiality agreement. She could only think of one thing to say to Sal. "Tom Waits."

He nodded. "Tom fucking Waits."

As the clock ticked down toward winter, more flights landed, carrying fuel but never enough. The pilots, who were typically gregarious and gossipy, worked close-mouthed, offering hardly more than grunts and monosyllabic answers to questions. Whenever Floyd mentioned the stingy supply of fuel, they'd shrug and get back into the cockpit as quickly as possible. It was clear the station's fuel was already being rationed.

Cooper tried to immerse herself in her work. She offered to paint portraits to help distract everyone from the looming crisis. Initially, only a couple of people came up to her during mealtimes, but once she set Pearl's portrait up in the galley, the requests came in steadily — especially since Pearl was extravagantly proud of being Cooper's first publicly displayed portrait. The work seemed to Cooper easy and meaningful, two qualities that had never coalesced over the course of her career.

One by one, more portraits appeared in the galley — Pearl hung them at evenly spaced intervals on the walls: Floyd, his hamster cheeks mitigated by shadows, the anger in his eyes replaced by the softness Cooper had seen there once or twice over the course of the season, usually when he was looking at Marcy. Kit in his Halloween gorilla suit, his mouth half opened. Dwight, sans cloak, his head dropped to his chest, his silky black hair obscuring his face. Doc Carla without her knit cap, her eyes an Edward Wilson blue. Tucker, still just the eye in the mirror shard. One by one the Polies had come to her studio or hadn't, and one by one, she'd come to know them a little better. None of the portraits had the photographic quality of her vending machine paintings; hyperrealism was simply no longer possible. However, the inability to be photographically precise had freed something in her.

Cooper was on her way to another artists' meeting in the gym, when she saw a group of women and two visibly distraught men crowded around a piece of paper taped to the outer wall of the trailer.

"What's going on?" Cooper asked.

"Dave's dance class," someone said. "He left for McMurdo."

"He promised to stay for the last class," another replied sadly. Cooper noticed one of the women was weeping quietly, while the others just stared at one another in disbelief. It seemed to Cooper a bad omen, and she hurried past them and into the meeting.

Propelled by their essential feelings of social impotence, and Denise's insistence in their last meeting that the artistic process is profoundly shaped by social settings, the artists and writers, save the historical novelist, had decided to make a statement that summarized their thoughts about political interference in science. They were certain their statement would show solidarity with the scientists ("who are just artists working in a different medium," the dancer said) and send a clear message to the politicians that they hadn't forgotten Helms and Mapplethorpe, and wouldn't let the NEA controversy be repeated in "science-y" fashion on the ice. If none of the newspapers bit, they'd publicize it via a blog.

"But I don't think horses make sense, in context," Birdie was saying when Cooper arrived at the meeting. "Although you could stretch the conceit and make as if the ponies Scott brought down here to their deaths are akin to the scientists. Scott being the government." He shuddered. "But that kind of parallel goes against every grain of my being."

"I don't even know if this is worth the effort," the literary novelist said. "Politicians don't get art."

"Well, as an agnostic Buddhist-and-pagan who is deeply vested in the principle of plurality, I find this conversation really complex," the dancer replied. "I'm committed to freedom of ideas, even the ones we dislike."

"The man has a right to do his research without being harassed," the historical novelist barked. "This whole thing is the worst kind of liberal arrogance. A coordinated campaign to discredit Frank Pavano's work." He laughed. "But look at it bite them in the ass."

"The man sliced off her finger," the literary novelist replied.

"It was an accident," Cooper said.

"Oh, no, sister," the historical novelist said, waggling his finger in her face. "This wasn't an old *whoopsie-daisy* kind of thing. That how they're spinning it to you? Nope. *Drudge Report* says the only reason he was coring without a tech was because the staff at the ice-coring camp wouldn't give him the tools he needed. If he'd been allowed to conduct his research without political interference, he wouldn't have had to use makeshift tools and you might still be a whole person."

"I still am a whole person," Cooper said.

"Fine. You're a whole person who is missing part of her hand. You're splitting hairs."

"I think the scientists' objection to Pavano and his research has to do with the idea that beliefs have no place in science," Birdie said, trying to regain control of the conversation.

"Beliefs have a place everywhere," the dancer said. "The world is built on them."

"You probably believe that the world is supported by a turtle," the literary novelist replied, his face darkening.

The dancer stiffened. "It's called the 'world-bearing turtle' and yes, I find truth in creation myths. Why do you care what I believe? How does it affect you?"

"You can't come down here to do research on Santa Claus."

"Forget Santa Claus," the historical novelist snapped. "Let's talk money for a minute. You guys want to get blacklisted?" He looked around the room. "These grants are my livelihood. What exactly are the chances of getting an NEA grant after this?"

"Zilch," the literary novelist said, sitting forward in his chair now. He tapped the dancer's knee three times with his finger. "But your chances of getting a Guggenheim or a MacArthur just increased exponentially." He sang the last word.

"It was a rhetorical question," the historical novelist growled.

"Let's reconvene tomorrow after we've all had some time to think this through," Birdie said. The artists murmured their assent and walked out of the gym. Cooper stayed behind.

"I don't do protest art," she said to Birdie, once everyone was gone.

"Me either. I haven't the faintest idea what to do. Perhaps I can find something in the life story of Birdie Bowers that echoes this current impasse, but the British government has always been very supportive of scientific endeavors."

"Don't rub it in."

The announcement came the next morning. Dwight laid the *New York Times* printout on the bar, and the Polies crowded around it. Bayless and Calhoun had finally put their money where their mouths were; the article detailed a House resolution they'd co-sponsored that would freeze the station's budget by suspending the National Science Foundation's polar regions department. Until the resolution got out of committee, additional funding requests would be in limbo. Because fuel was a fluid line item in the station's annual budget, each request was considered a request for new funding and would need to be approved, in triplicate. The fuel supply had essentially been halted. Even if the resolution got out of committee, the Program was facing a sequester: all Pole operations would cease — from the construction of the new station and the climate research taking place at the Divide, to the cosmological experiments in the Dark Sector, including the joint Stanford-Princeton experiment Sal was leading with Lisa Wu.

" 'The South Pole is touted as a bastion of scientific activity,' " Dwight read, quoting Bayless, " 'where minds converge to answer the most important questions of the universe. It is a place where open-minded discussion leads to breakthroughs. But that is changing; the time-honored tradition of intellectual debate is under grave threat from elements of the far left, and our ability as a nation to remain the leader in scientific achievement is now in doubt. Taxpayers are currently funding a number of scientists and scientific programs through the National Science Foundation, and I think they might be surprised to learn that their hard-earned dollars are going to support a liberal agenda rather than disinterested science.' "

Dwight looked up from the printout. Sri bent over his knees, his hands interlaced behind his head. His breathing grew rapid, and Sal placed a hand on his shoulder.

"I've got lawyers going through my research files back in Madison as we speak. My grants for next year are suspended pending further review," Sri said. "They've already forced Fern and her team off the ice. If they shut us down, I will lose three years of research. I can't have a gap in the data. I can't, Sal. I can't."

"What is he talking about?" Pearl asked.

"Sri just got subpoenaed," Sal said. "Bayless got the Wisconsin attorney general to initiate an investigation for violations of the Fraud Against Taxpayers Act. They're saying he manipulated his climate data to get federal grants. It's just an excuse to get Sri off the ice and interrupt his research."

"How is it possible that people like this have the power to shut down an entire research base?" Sri said to no one. "I mean, what about the medical science that makes it possible for them to go in for their triple bypasses and come out as fresh as a newly plucked daisy? Did a Jesus in scrubs float down on a cloud of ether and come up with the protocols for that shit? I hate humanity. And yet I'm down here because I want to save humanity from certain suffering and death once this planet bursts into fucking flames."

"You're a misanthrope with a heart," Pearl said cheerfully.

Cooper glanced over at Sal, who was still squeezing Sri's shoulder. "No," he said. "He's a scientist on a choke chain."

After breakfast the next morning, an announcement went out over All-Call directing the winter-over crew to meet in the

459

library — the individuals who had been approved to spend the winter at Amundsen-Scott. When Cooper arrived, she surveyed the winter population — the individuals who had freely chosen to spent months of perpetual night at the bottom of the earth. There were the Nailheads, including Bozer, Floyd, and Marcy; the Beakers, who would monitor their experiments through the season, Alek, Sal, and Lisa, and assorted research techs; Dwight, who would continue to run Comms and provide general research tech help; Pearl and Doc Carla; and two NSF "non-science" grantees: Denise and Cooper. Everyone else was contracted to move to McMurdo for the winter, like Birdie and Kit, or off the ice entirely. (Birdie had made his arrangements for a McMurdo transfer before meeting Pearl, and had spent the last two weeks trying in vain to get someone to approve him for a winter-over.) Cooper noticed Simon, the VIDS rep, and Warren, the NSF rep who had interrogated her in the days after her injury, were also in the room. Both looked as if they'd been invited to a slumber party at Guantanamo.

Cooper took a seat near Sal. He reached across the plastic chair between them and took her hand. His face was drawn and his eyes sunken; there was little remaining of the usual fire in them. He seemed, for the first time since she'd met him, almost beaten. On his other side, Lisa sat twisting a Kleenex in her hands. Cooper knew if the shutdown happened, hardly anyone in this room would be allowed to stay for the winter.

Before Tucker or either of the admins could begin speaking, Bozer stood up, his meaty arms folded across his chest.

"We don't have enough JP-8 to get through the winter."

"Calm down," Simon said dismissively. "We'll get to that later." Pearl looked over at Cooper, with raised eyebrows. *This* was going to be good.

"Actually, no, son, we'll get to that first," Bozer said. "I've winter-overed for nine seasons, but I'll be *fucked* if I stay past station closing knowing we don't have enough fuel to last us. My bags are packed. I have a seat on the last Herc out if that shit ain't here by next week."

"You realize this is your own fault, right?" Sri said to Bozer from across the room. Sal nudged him with his knee. "No, man, it needs to be said. If construction had stayed on schedule, and the planes didn't have to haul all your construction shit from Mc-Murdo, we could've made do with the fuel we already had, no matter what these politicians were trying to do." Cooper saw Floyd's entire body wince. "Oh, and your precious pool table? Everyone knows you've been illegally shipping materials for that since summer."

Bozer turned his gaze to Sri. "My dear swami friend, you are obviously a miserable worm in a lab coat, so I will keep this simple: fuck you. Here you are, jacking off into your beakers because I've been busting my balls down here for the last five years, building your lab. So go fuck another penguin, and I'll keep this station going in the meantime."

"This has nothing to do with construction, Sri, and you know it," Dwight said. "This is political. I mean, look at what you Beakers have unleashed! This whole thing is your fault! If you guys had been cool about Pavano instead of acting like eighth graders, none of this would be happening."

"What the F, Dwight?" Sri said. "You're the one who made him kiss your ring for satellite calls!"

"To be fair, Dwight does that to everyone," Pearl chimed in.

"Washington isn't worried about satellite phones, Sri!" Dwight shouted. "They're worried about — oh, what was it? Oh yeah

— threats and intimidation." He pointed at Sri angrily, his Livestrong bracelet trembling on his wrist. "Threats and intimidation, Sri!"

"What threats? What intimidation?" Sri cried. "These are fairy tales Pavano and his conservatard congressmen are spinning."

"Everyone knows it was you who took his name off the manifests to the Divide, Sri. Everyone knows your research techs deleted his username from the server. And the petitions? The multiple printouts, Sri, where you guys defaced stuff and made comments about Jesus. That debate, and the way Sal got up in Pavano's face while he was trying to give his talk?" Dwight looked over at Cooper. "And holy shit, her finger? Her fucking finger?"

"It's not their fault this happened," Cooper said quietly. Sal shook his head. He seemed to know something about Dwight that Cooper didn't, that this outburst was necessary and that Dwight should be allowed to go on, the way Floyd had been allowed to castigate Marcy that night at the bar when she'd returned from Cheech. And, in fact, letting that drama play out had worked — there Floyd and Marcy were, sitting perpendicular to each other, Marcy with her legs propped up on Floyd's lap.

Cooper looked around the room: Alek was sitting quietly, his demeanor as serene as if he were settling in for movie night. Pearl knit, while next to her, Doc Carla scratched her ankle. Tucker leaned against a bookshelf, carelessly flipping through a James Patterson paperback. Only the admin staff looked mortified.

"She says it's not their fault. Okay, that's good." Dwight nodded at Cooper. "King Beaker's ice-wife says it's not his fault, in her completely unbiased opinion. Look, Sal worked overtime being an asshole to Pavano and then he put on that show when Frick and Frack and the rest of the government suits came — don't you guys see? Don't you see what's gonna happen, what they're already doing?" Dwight was hysterical. "They're gonna shut us down! They're gonna stop payments, they're gonna close up shop. They're gonna send us home."

Tucker reshelved the Patterson novel and walked over to Dwight. He rubbed his shoulders, and to Cooper's surprise, Dwight let him. He turned to look up at Tucker. "I don't wanna go home."

Simon sighed, and hauled himself out of his chair. Cooper caught the eye roll he sent over to Warren, who appeared to have gone catatonic. "I'll address your question about the fuel supply," Simon said to Bozer, "despite your lack of manners. We expect the Hercs coming in over the next ten days will carry enough fuel to put us where we need to be."

"Negative," Floyd said. "Seeing as I'm actually the one who runs the power plant and observes the fuels, and reports back to you, I can say with, yeah, let's call it total certainty, that that's not what I reported to you last week."

"I didn't see that report," Simon said.

"According to my calculations, I believe that we would need twenty-seven air tankers ferrying nothing but JP-8 in order to survive the winter. All those 'delayed shipments' set us back."

"Send the Nailheads home," Sri said. "Stop construction and keep a small crew to keep the station and the labs going. We can live off the fuel we have. I need my data. Sal needs his data. I'm not leaving here without my data."

Floyd laughed. "You think you're gonna finish that shit?"

"I know I am."

Floyd shook his head, and muttered, "Moron."

Sri looked over at Sal. "What's he talking about, Sal?"

Everyone turned to look at Sal. Like Warren, he, too, had folded his arms over his chest and closed his eyes. Cooper realized both men were in possession of the same information, and that their demeanors matched because this information had impacted them similarly. "Sal?" Sri said.

"We have bigger problems," Sal finally said.

"Bigger problems than a fuel shortage heading into winter?"

"They have us — you, me, Lisa, everyone — going home in two days."

Sri paused for a moment. "Because we didn't sign the confidentiality agreement," he said, his voice dead. Lisa dropped her head in her hands.

"Just sign the goddamn thing, guys," Marcy said. "Everyone else did."

"They're research techs," Sal said. "Early-career scientists, some of them still post-docs. Most of them working on other people's projects. You expect me to sign away my life's work, my ideas? I can't." He looked over at Sri and Lisa. "We can't."

Cooper reached over and rubbed Lisa's back as she wept.

After leaving the winter-over meeting, Cooper stopped by the station post office to see if she'd received any mail. Along with the fuel shipments, postal delivery had slowed dramatically, further dampening everyone's spirits. The place was empty when she arrived, as were nearly all of the post office boxes. Halfheartedly, Cooper thrust her hand into her cubby and felt around. To her surprise, there was something there: a package, the size of a pack of cigarettes, lumpy and wrapped inexpertly in brown paper. There was no return address, and Cooper didn't recognize the handwriting on the mailing label.

She opened it and found something hastily wrapped in a page from a week-old *Washington Post.* With some difficulty, she was able to tear the paper away with her good hand. As she did so, something metallic fell to the floor. It sparkled under the fluorescent lights like a Fourth of July firework. When Cooper picked it up, she saw it was Calhoun's lapel pin. *Let's Roll.*

REGISTER NOW FOR THE 2000 DESIGN IN NATURE CONFERENCE HOSTED BY THE CENTER FOR COMPLEXITY AND DESIGN

Meet the most influential thinkers in the world of Intelligent Design and Climate Change while cruising through spectacular Alaskan landscapes at the height of summer. This weeklong conference will take place aboard one of Telkhine Cruises' most luxurious ships, the *Fantasy,* and will leave Seattle to cruise the Inside Passage. Our ship will call at Ketchikan, Wrangell, Hubbard Glacier, and other breathtaking ports and features, before returning via the Outside Passage. Spend time in the company of some of the world's foremost scholars, scientists, and design theorists and learn more about the most profound scientific questions facing us today: How did the universe begin? How did complex life develop? What does helioseismology tell us about fluctuating climate patterns? Is climate change real?

Featured speakers include Dr. Patton D. Rodale, *New York Times* best-selling author of *Alarmism and the Climate Change Hoax,* renowned Cambridge University mathematician and clergyman Dr. Jeffrey Osterholm, and Dr. Frank Pavano, a widely respected helioseismologist whose nascent research on the effect of global solar variations on climate fluctuations is attracting a great deal of attention. In addition to daily lectures and seminars, opportunities for more intimate conversations with our speakers will be available each night during formal meals and dancing.

Register today and experience the Intelligent Design of nature while basking in it yourself.

COMPLEXITY AND DESIGN

I see now that the cruise was a mistake, the *first cause,* if you'll allow the joke, of my current difficulties. But Annie had wanted so badly to go, and I felt this was something kind I could do for her after everything that had happened. It also appeared to be a career opportunity for me.

The cruise would leave from Seattle, dock at Juneau, sail through Glacier Bay, and then return — its only guests the individuals registered for the 2000 Design in Nature Conference, sponsored by the Center for Complexity and Design, an organization with which I had, until this point, been unfamiliar. I had been approached personally by the center's senior Fellow, who had received my name from a former colleague (I suspected it was Fred Zimmer, but the man on the phone would not confirm this). He showed particular interest in my most recent work, which had to do with solar acoustic pressure waves, and urged me to submit an abstract for the conference. But when I asked him to give me a sense of the conference's focus, he was evasive. He would say only that the expected audience would be comprised of academics, politicians, policymakers, Fellows of the Center for Complexity and Design, and regular citizens with an interest in the topic of science. He hinted that the organizers had detected in their audience a burgeoning interest in global warming, but offered no further guidance. It is telling to me now that I cannot recall the man's name.

It would not be inaccurate to say that, by this time, things had grown desperate for me. It had been three years since I'd been forced to resign from my position as the DuPont Professor of Physics at a small private college in the Midwest after the provost discovered I had plagiarized entire paragraphs in several of my research papers. In my area of study — helioseismology, or the study of solar wave oscillations — plagiarism was unheard of, and so when the University Research Integrity Committee began its investigation, there was great internal interest in the outcome. At its conclusion, I was given the option of resigning or being fired.

Annie was bewildered. I told her I'd been sloppy, that I'd been overextended, that I'd put too much on my graduate assistant's plate, and that he had cut and pasted from several sources directly into my master documents, intending, of course, to flag those sections so that I might rewrite the material. It had happened to several academics in the last few years, and even some journalists. Contrite, they'd all slunk into the farthest corners of their professions, but had slowly been able to piece their careers back together. Framed in this manner, Annie found it plausible that there had been no intent to deceive on my part, and this made it harder for her to accept that I had been treated so roughly by the university.

I had lost the support of all but one colleague — Fred Zimmer, the chair of the physics department and the man who had hired me. He was a theorist who had spent forty-five years studying quantum chaos, specifically entropy dynamics. He was warm and gregarious in a department known for its austerity, and he wanted to believe there had been a misunderstanding.

But the truth was that it went far beyond a couple of plagiarized paragraphs. It was systematic, a compulsion I could not keep in check for reasons I could not fathom. I began seeing a therapist. I told Annie the therapy was for generalized anxiety resulting from my resignation and the subsequent ostracism, but in reality, I was unspooling a career's worth of lies. My therapist accepted these lies; in fact she seemed to extract them, winding them back on a distaff from her chair across the room. And the question that hung over every session was *why?*

I had no answers to this, of course — the therapist had many, but she would pose her answers as yet more questions for me to consider. Could it be that, as a former "child prodigy," I had a pathological fear of failure that created a tension so unbearable that I had to affect the failure myself in order to relieve it? Could it be I had an inferiority complex because I was a first-generation college student, surrounded by individuals who had "suckled at the breast of the ivory tower"? (When I pointed out the somewhat mixed nature of her metaphor, she indicated this objection was a way of diverting the conversation, but this did not stop me from spending the rest of that session imagining an ivory tower with leaking breasts, sustaining an entire generation of infant-academics.) Could it be that I felt everyone's work was inherently better than mine, even when mine was yet unwritten, and so the compulsion to integrate the work of others into my own without risking a single change was a manifestation of both primary and secondary inferiority? Perhaps it goes without saying, but my therapist was a devotee of Adler. I found Adler's approach wanting in many areas, and as a result, I wasn't, in the words of my therapist, "doing the work." We terminated our relationship.

Annie encouraged me to mount an attempt to return to the halls of academia. The gap in my résumé would be hard to explain — a plagiarism charge is notoriously difficult to work around. Instead, I continued my work on the solar neutrino problem I'd been working on prior to my resignation, but this time only as a private citizen. Annie went back to work at Pricewaterhouse shortly after I left the university, in order to replace the steady paycheck and health insurance I had lost.

I wasn't aware that the man sitting next to me in the cruise terminal was addressing me until Annie nudged me with her elbow. Unlike the majority of the men milling about the waiting area, most of whom were dressed in khakis and polos, this man wore a business suit. He was clean-shaven and well groomed, and the symmetry of his face was pleasing. The gel in his hair gleamed under the harsh terminal lights, giving it a slightly plastic appearance.

"Scientists are prone to herd thinking," the man said, with the air of someone who was conspicuously repeating himself. Annie nudged me again. I was unsure of how to address his statement. He seemed to sense this, and, to my relief, he offered his hand. "Eric Falleri," he said.

"Frank Pavano," I replied, as we shook hands.

"Oh, I know who you are. You're the reason I'm taking this cruise." He grinned. "I'm very interested in your work."

Eric did not look like the sort who would typically take an interest in helioseismology — and besides that, I wasn't even speaking on solar acoustic pressure waves, the work for which I was known. I had proposed a series of talks on this topic, of course, but when the man from the Center for Complexity and Design called me after receiving my proposal, he'd asked if I'd be willing to speak instead about the impact of solar variations on global climate fluctuations. Although I was well versed in solar irradiance, I had very little background in climatology or knowledge of how spectral distribution could possibly affect climate patterns on Earth. However, when I mentioned this to him, he seemed unconcerned, and offered to pair me with another scientist who was preparing to submit a paper on the theory that total solar irradiance was a significant cause of climate change. "Though," he added, "as an organization we are skeptical that the climate is, in fact, changing."

I knew both positions ran against prevailing scientific opinion, and yet I was intrigued.

Eric and I spoke a bit about my lecture topic, and I confided that I felt far more comfortable speaking on subjects with which I was more familiar. He, however, seemed very enthusiastic. "Our conference participants are eager to learn more about the global warming hoax," he said. As I tried to process this, he added, *sotto voce,* "One of our most prominent sponsors asked us to reach out to you specifically, Dr. Pavano."

Annie was thrilled to find that we had been booked into a junior suite. There was a large fruit basket on the table, which she found deeply touching — any kindness shown to me during this time she appreciated with great fervor. She walked onto the small balcony overlooking the terminal building — we had not yet left the docks —

and remained there for some minutes, gazing at the Seattle skyline. When I gently reminded her that it was time to dress for dinner, she turned and smiled at me, her lovely brown eyes shining with happiness for the first time in months.

"If making small talk with people who believe the earth is six thousand years old is all it takes to cruise to Alaska in a stateroom, sign me up," she said. My stomach sank. The smile disappeared from her face. "Frank, you've got to start somewhere. You can shake these people off when the time is right." She walked over to where I was standing in my tuxedo, and put her hands on either side of my face. "Brilliance can't be contained for long," she said. Her face, as beautiful as the first time I saw it, looked angelic as she said this. And if it hadn't been for the tears standing in her eyes, I would have thought her beatific.

We saw Eric Falleri at dinner, dressed in a very fine tuxedo with gleaming monogrammed cuff links. Annie asked after his wife — she'd noticed his wedding ring back in the terminal — and he'd said she was "back home in D.C."

"What is it that you do, Mr. Falleri?" she asked. Something about Annie's question embarrassed me. Her curiosity, sharp as a blade, was sometimes mistaken as an attempt to injure, when it was merely a reflection of her deep interest in people. I, on the other hand, found people inscrutable, and relied heavily upon my wife's investigations to provide context for social situations. Eric seemed discomfited by her question, and it was obvious enough that even I noticed it. After taking a too-long sip of wine, he finally said, "I suppose you'd call me a consultant, Mrs. Pavano."

She asked him to call her Annie, and then asked him about the entities for whom he consulted.

"Various clients," Eric said, reaching for his wine again. "Mostly energy consortiums."

"Oh, you're a lobbyist," Annie said, and Eric's face darkened. I could tell Annie noticed this, too, but neither of us were sure of her transgression. (I've since come to understand that lobbyists do not like their intentions to be pointed out explicitly any more than does an Amway salesman.) Despite this, Eric's expression quickly regained its previous cheerfulness, and he said that he was on the cruise representing one of the conference sponsors, a private corporation that owned a few refineries, a handful of fertilizer plants, and other "industrial operations." He then turned to his neighbor, a schoolteacher from Oklahoma City, and Annie and I spent the rest of the evening making small talk with the other people at our table.

As the dinner was coming to a close and many of the conference participants and their spouses were heading to the dance floor, Annie excused herself to return to the stateroom so she could watch *Survivor,* a small vice of hers. As soon as she'd left, Eric moved around the perimeter of the table and took her seat. He pushed aside the remains of Annie's dessert and leaned toward me. "I've heard about your troubles, Professor."

As soon as he said this, I felt something in me break free, and I realized it was a tension that had been present since the moment the man from the Center for Design and Complexity had first called — I had been found out. It was the same strange feeling I'd experienced the day Fred Zimmer called me into his office to confront me with the plagiarism charges.

Eric placed a friendly hand on my shoulder. "Don't worry, Professor," he said. "I want to share an opportunity with you. I represent a client who is in a position to fund research into global temperature and climate patterns. This is a pressing issue that will likely dominate energy policy discussions in the years to come."

"Well, as I've explained to the organizers of the conference, my research focus is far afield from —"

"What you've done in the past is not important."

"I don't understand."

"Let me ask you a question: If I were to say that a free society requires open discussion of all sides of an issue, would you agree with that statement?"

"Naturally," I replied.

"Would you also agree that it has a chilling effect on science when those whose ideas go against the grain are demonized by fellow scientists?"

"Of course, though I suppose it depends on what you mean by —"

"My client is concerned about the fact that climate scientists are intentionally suppressing alternative findings regarding global climate fluctuations. He also believes the political response to climate issues should be based on sound science, not alarmism or emotions. As a scientist — even a disgraced one — you surely agree."

The barb stung, and gave the conversation a different tone. "Forgive me, Eric, but, again, I feel compelled to point out that while I find the discussion on global warming fascinating —"

"We prefer to use the term climate change. It provokes less emotion than *global warming*. Global warming is scary. We don't want to scare people."

It took me a moment to process this, and he took another long sip of his wine. Finally, I spoke. "While I am a curious bystander, my research interests are not aligned with this topic. Frankly, I'd be a bit out of my depth."

Eric opened his jacket and pulled the conference brochure from an inner pocket. He searched it for the description of my presentation. Once he found it, he tapped it with his finger.

"It says here you're speaking on the impact solar variations have on global climate fluctuations."

"My focus will be primarily on total solar irradiance," I said uneasily.

Eric slipped the brochure back into his pocket. "Perfect. This aligns with my client's interests."

"I can't imagine how."

"Dr. Pavano, my client is proposing an opportunity that would allow you to reenter academia, regain control of your career, and do meaningful research with the kind of financial support most scientists don't even dare to dream about."

Eric went on to tell me that his client was prepared to endow a professorship at a university to which he already had strong ties. This university would provide me with generous research grants for more study into the subjects about which we'd spoken. I quickly realized this would require a substantial shift in my current research interests.

As we spoke, I thought about Annie lying on the bed upstairs in our stateroom, watching *Survivor,* so grateful for the fruit basket that she hadn't taken off the yellow cellophane. The decision was not difficult.

My cruise ship lecture was so well received that within a week of returning home, I had six invitations to present the same talk at various conferences around the country. The fees offered were substantial. Until I'd embarked upon the cruise, I had had no idea that a parallel scientific world existed, one separated from mainstream science by a matter of degrees. It was a place where science was expertly mimicked and, at rare moments, even practiced. I was entering the fold. And I found the inhabitants of this world to be, without exception, kind, welcoming, in earnest, and thrilled to find a "real scientist" in their midst.

Eric Falleri kept in touch regularly, and by April 2002, although I was not affiliated with any accredited university, I was a fairly well established "climate change skeptic." In this parallel universe, "expertise" came quickly. Although some bloggers who had taken notice of my work referred to me as a "denialist," my reputation was bolstered by the fact that I did not entertain the conspiracy theories that had gripped some corners of this world — charges of scientific and criminal misconduct resulting in a general consensus that climate change existed and was caused by humans.

I made one misstep at this time, which was agreeing to counsel a young biblical archaeologist on a paper about the structural stability of Noah's ark. I considered it an interesting puzzle — how does one research the buoyancy and bilge radius of an imaginary seafaring vessel? To my dismay, the student added my name to the subsequent research paper. Although Eric was vexed, he felt that the journal in which it appeared was so obscure that it wouldn't pose any problems.

In late May, I was booked on a flight to

Washington for a meeting with the Client, whom by this point I had come to consider a proper noun. The meeting was held in the Royal Suite at the Washington, D.C., Four Seasons, at a long dining table and over an opulent meal. Falleri was there, but the easy insouciance that I had come to consider his trademark was nowhere to be found. Terse now, he asked for the confidentiality agreement he'd sent me the week before the meeting. Once I'd produced it, he grimly escorted me to a seat on the left side of the table.

Shortly after, a group of men emerged from an adjoining room. There was little to distinguish one from the other. They were of similar age — between fifty and sixty — and wore suits of a similar cut and of similar quality. Three were balding, two had full heads of silver hair. It would take a keener eye than mine to determine which one, upon a glance, was the Client. My only indications were the facts that he entered the room a full minute after everyone else and that he walked directly to the seat at the head of the table. His firm handshake lasted only the length of a breath, as if the ritual were inherently distasteful to him.

Throughout the first course, a Waldorf salad, the Client remained silent while the others spoke about trivial matters — golf scores, recent vacations, the Preakness. He finished his salad with astonishing celerity. One by one, the others at the table noticed and set their forks down, too.

In the break between the main course — Maine lobster thermidor — and coffee, the Client finally turned his eyes toward me. The table conversation dissipated at once.

"Dr. Pavano, we meet at a time of great change," the Client said. He looked at me steadily, waiting, as if I might contradict him. I decided to respond with "Indeed." This met with his approval, and he continued, "I trust Eric has given you an idea of where our interests lie." He gestured to the other men at the table without looking at them. "These men represent some of the largest energy companies in the world. We are here together tonight because we have agreed that the defining issue of the coming decades, not just in our industry, but also in federal and global policy, will be climate change. We are aware that the majority of the science emerging from this area of study indicates that the earth is warming, and that it's warming due to carbon dioxide emissions. The responsibility for this warming, and its attendant repercussions, will be laid at our feet." He paused here to take a drink from his ice water. "We would like to approach this issue proactively. One way we can do this is by directing our resources toward sound science that looks dispassionately at the data, which our own company scientists tell us do not support the idea of man-made climate change. Unfortunately, they are unable to place any research papers in reputable journals, so we are losing control of the messaging. This issue has become politically charged. And that's why you're here with us tonight."

To his right, one of the balding men gathered that the Client was finished for now and that he was expected to speak.

"Dr. Pavano," he said, "I represent Americans for Responsible Petroleum, a coalition of oil and energy companies. We are deeply concerned about the science coming out of the federal research programs, which is indicating, overwhelmingly, that climate change is verifiable fact and that its causes can be connected directly to our industries."

At this point, he pushed aside a vase of purple hydrangeas and laid out a map of Antarctica. Small red stars had been carefully affixed to various parts of the continent. "The majority of federal and university-funded climate change research takes place in Antarctica, specifically at

South Pole Station and the West Antarctic Divide. This work is overseen by the National Science Foundation, a taxpayer-funded federal agency. To date, there has not been a single climate researcher who doesn't go down there already convinced that climate change is caused mainly by fossil fuel emissions."

"Of course you know that a consensus exists among climate scientists that the fluctuations are, in fact, human-caused," I said.

The man smiled. "And you've played right into their hands, Dr. Pavano."

Chastened, I said, "I admit I know very little about the kind of research undertaken in the polar regions."

"Which is the other reason why you are here tonight," the Client broke in. "This coordinated alarmist campaign could have a devastating impact on the U.S. economy and lead to destructive government regulations. Think about the other alarmist campaigns that have been much ado about nothing. The population crisis. The so-called energy crisis. The hole in the ozone. We've sat on the sidelines long enough. To do so any longer would be irresponsible."

By the time the dessert plates were cleared away, I had recovered enough to begin asking questions, and they began to lay out the

Plan. It had five phases:

Phase One: Apply for a National Science Foundation–funded research position at Amundsen-Scott South Pole Station and the West Antarctic Ice Sheet (known as WAIS, or, colloquially, the Divide).

Phase Two: When, as anticipated, the application is rejected, identify at least two of the 135 known climate change skeptics currently serving in the U.S. Congress who might be willing to make National Science Foundation bias a platform issue.

Phase Three: Argue, in a coordinated media campaign, that the National Science Foundation, as a federal agency, is bound by law not to demonstrate bias (if bias is verifiable), or imply bias exists among National Science Foundation leadership (if no documented history of bias is available). If necessary, launch local and national campaigns to support the placement of a nonconformist climate scientist at the research base at South Pole.

Phase Four (assuming Phase Three is successful): Receive federal funding from the National Science Foundation, along with additional private monies from the companies represented at the dinner, via existing pass-through organizations, to explore the idea that climate change is caused by solar variations, not CO_2 emissions. (It had been previously concluded that countering the idea that the climate was warming at all was a "zero-sum game.")

Phase Five: Once funded and sited at WAIS, produce compelling data and, if the data do not support the Plan, manipulate it. Expect, and even welcome, obstruction from researchers and administrators. Document these actions but do not resist them. At the same time, disrupt the existing ecosystem in a manner that attracts the attention of the national media and solidifies the message of bias.

As I was mulling over the Plan (as with the Client, I gave it proper noun status), the discussion took the turn for which Eric had prepared me in the months leading up to this meeting: the Client asked if I was a "god-fearing man." Next to me, I could feel Eric shift in his seat, expectant but nervous. In our conversations, the lie to which we'd both agreed, and which I was about to tell the Client, had been difficult for Eric to accept. I knew he was raised Baptist, but was not "evangelical," as he put it. He knew I was an atheist, because Annie had mentioned it in passing to him at one point on the cruise. But when Eric told me what I would be expected to do — the spiritual mantle I'd have to wear if I were to be successful — I had no qualms. The burden of having failed to fulfill immense promise was substantial; I had thought many times over the years of what John Brennan said to me when I'd declined to join his department at Stanford: "No one is more unnecessary than a man who has failed to realize his gift." I had done many things since to escape the fact that I had failed to realize mine. Being something other than a profound disappointment seemed to me at that moment sublime, even if it required lying about something that, to me, was wholly unimportant. Faith was not so odious an idea that I wouldn't use it in the name of my own personal redemption.

At the time Eric first brought up the idea of turning me into a "god-fearing man," I sensed he was both relieved and repulsed by my easy acquiescence. "We'll have to build a narrative," he warned. "Otherwise, it will be too easy for the press to pick the story apart." This narrative-building required a crisis — an atheist scientist who has been thrown out of the halls of academia because of moral and ethical failings directly attributable to his lack of faith. A series of meetings had been arranged with a Pentecostal church in northern Virginia, which, Eric told me, had been chosen because it was fundamentalist in nature but modern in approach. I shared my manufactured narrative with the assistant general bishops, both of whom were deeply moved by the story of a scientist wrestling with his faith. I then met with the general bishop, who, toward the end of our meeting, grew animated and insisted I attend Sunday's service. "You are," he told me, "our Prodigal Son."

At the service, I was brought to the front of the church and surrounded by several individuals, including the general bishop, and experienced what I later learned was the "laying on of hands." I became a member in good standing of Olive Grove Christian Fellowship.

Annie had watched this unfold with growing unease. Being an atheist herself, she openly ridiculed my new membership at Olive Grove. She even spoke critically of the Client. Eric soon noticed that she was not, as he put it, "on board." This, he indicated, was a problem. In fact, things between Annie and me had grown strained since I'd undertaken the Plan. Annie had become distant — during the weeks I was in Washington and Virginia, she chose not to fly out on the weekends to join me. In the meantime, Eric wanted to know what could be done to influence her to become a more visible part of the narrative. I decided to ask her myself, and our conversation transformed into a fairly intense domestic squabble, in which Annie said things along the lines of "I don't know who you are anymore." Eric and I agreed to leave the Annie question alone for the time being, but I continued my active participation in Olive Grove, and even came to find the spiritual work invigorating, if not convincing. So by the time of the dinner in the Royal Suite at the Four Seasons, I was able to answer the Client's question with an assertion that I was an active member of Olive Grove Christian Fellowship. He then said that he understood I had been an atheist (specifically, he used the term *irreligionist*) and felt this was somewhat inconvenient, but acknowledged that it was difficult to find a reputable scientist who was a believer. Eric told the Client about my religious redemption, and how the story of an atheist scientist coming to Christ would be far more powerful than that of a churchgoing man experiencing an intensification of his faith.

"Luke fifteen," the Client said approvingly.

In the cab to the airport, Eric handed me an envelope containing a check. It was more than I'd made in the last five years combined.

When I submitted my proposal to the National Science Foundation, I chose Kibsairlin's ice cores as my research subject, with a secondary focus on methane levels in the Antarctic sedimentary basins. I suspected, or said I suspected — I wasn't yet sure what I wanted to suspect — that the levels were not as high as had been reported. I remained surprised at the speed with which I had become an expert in the world of climate change denial. In other disciplines, my lack of published and peer-reviewed articles would preclude me from such a rapid ascension. My reliance on meta-analysis rather than original research would be seen as a grave liability. In this collegial community of like-minded individuals, however, meta-analysis was the most effective tool for picking apart inconsistencies and sowing doubt.

"The idea," Eric told me, "is to make people think that there is controversy within the scientific community on whether climate change is human-caused. We won't be in trouble until the public thinks the conversation is closed." It was my job to keep the conversation going.

In early September 2002, the expected rejection letter from the NSF arrived, citing an overabundance of quality proposals. It was now time to move onto Phase Two of the Plan. In mid-November, I answered the door to find Fred Zimmer standing on my stoop. I managed to hide my shock, and invited him in. He asked after Annie, and I told him she was visiting her parents in Bismarck — going into the details about why she was no longer living in the house felt too complicated. I brewed a pot of coffee and we sat together at the kitchen table. I noticed how frail Fred was looking, how sunken his cheeks were, as if he'd been hollowed out from the inside and his skin had collapsed to fill the spaces. His thick glasses magnified his pale blue eyes so that they seemed to overtake his face, and his lips had curled inward, threatening to disappear completely.

"Colon cancer," he told me. "Metastatic.

But I didn't come here to talk about that." He scraped his chair forward so he could lean on the table with both elbows. "I got a call from the *New Scientist* yesterday, asking me about the circumstances of your resignation. What the hell's going on, Frank?"

When I feigned incomprehension, he hit the table with his fist. I mopped up the spilled coffee with a napkin, and noticed Fred's hands were shaking. I felt gripped by something — compassion, perhaps, or pity — and I gently laid my hands on his.

He kept them under mine for only a moment before snatching them away angrily. "What's happened to you, Frank, that you're running around with these tinfoil-hat-wearing reptiles?" Although I was used, after all these years, to Fred's candor, I winced at this and he noticed.

"*Cui bono,* Frank?" he said.

"Taxpayers want disinterested science, Fred, not political alarmism."

Zimmer's eyes widened and a look of inexpressible sadness crossed his old and gnarled face. He said nothing for some minutes. "The stealing, the plagiarism — did you do it?" For only an instant did I consider lying to my old mentor. I could tell that the question was merely a formality, even though Zimmer was not known to stand on such things. He already knew.

I looked down at the coffee spoons, which I had set on top of one another, the bowls and the stems in perfect alignment. I didn't raise my eyes again until I heard the front door slam shut.

The Plan steadily grew in scope. The Group (the consortium of energy companies with whom I'd met that night in the Royal Suite) had started meeting with the two conservative legislators who'd been chosen to take up the cause, in exchange for several generous campaign donations. I met the men once — a representative from Kansas named Sam Bayless and a representative from Tennessee named Jack Calhoun. Bayless was the younger, and more serious, of the two men — groomed, handsome, but not oleaginous. Calhoun was a husky man with crooked teeth, but a more sincere bearing. Bayless's participation was clearly an act of opportunism, while Calhoun's seemed like a last gasp. Both expected formidable challenges in the 2004 elections, and were eager to develop a major platform issue that would speak to their constituents.

Meanwhile, the promised endowed chair position was arranged for me with the kind of speed I'd thought impossible in academia

— perhaps because Freedom University of Northern Virginia wasn't exactly a principal player. In fact, I had never heard of it, despite its bloated enrollment logs. Nor did it have an established research track record, but the faculty and administration were remarkably enthusiastic about my work. I'd only been living part time at home since the Plan had been implemented, spending much of my time in a corporate apartment in Silver Spring, Maryland, but taking the Freedom University position would require a move from my sleepy Midwest college town. Annie and I agreed to put the house up for sale. She had no interest in moving to Virginia, so she rented an apartment a few miles away from our old home, while I drove the U-Haul truck to Fairfax alone. We formally separated a week after I arrived in Virginia.

I was put up in a spacious but sterile campus apartment, and began lecturing on my quickly evolving research. Along the way, I was introduced to the concept of irreducible complexity by a fellow professor at Freedom, an idea that proved useful in my ongoing work with Olive Grove. Twice a month, I delivered lectures via videoconferencing, which were always well attended (Olive Grove was an unusually science-minded congregation). I found my fellow congregants deeply excited by the science of Intelligent Design.

The Client had no objection to my delving into this area — he called it a "side gig" — so I began adding to my public appearances, speaking not only on solar irradiation and climate fluctuations, but also on topics of interest to adherents of Intelligent Design — who were also, I came to understand, very receptive to the idea that climate change was a hoax. I learned from Eric, and sometimes the Client, in our rare phone calls, that there were ways to frame the climate change issue that would appeal to the deepest fears and biases in human nature. I found this fascinating. We began to capitalize on the mistakes of the environmental movement, which seemed unable to effectively raise the alarm about the changing climate. We countered the science that indicated the arctic ice and permafrost were melting, and found more and more people rallying to our cause. Such ideas gave them hope that polar bears had a future. In fact, hope was our top commodity.

It would be going too far to say I began to believe in the research as a whole, but there were elements of the science that I found convincing enough. I spent more and more time with Representatives Bayless and Calhoun, and was eventually hired by both campaigns as a "senior science policy advisor." I was made to understand that the demographics in Bayless's district had been changing in ways that could be considered unfavorable to him — the population was younger, "browner," in the words of one of his aides. The only way to counter this was to "double-down" and "fire up the base."

My first ever television interview was with Fox News. According to the media consultant hired on behalf of the Group, I played well to my strengths. I had appeared awkward, she said, while also managing to underscore the talking points we had gone over prior to arriving at the studio: the scientific weaknesses of current climate research; the importance of airing a full range of scientific views; the lack of consensus among scientists regarding not just the cause of climate change, but its very existence (*consensus* was the term favored by climate scientists, a mistake upon which we capitalized — its inherent imprecision allowed us a thousand ways to move); and, most important, the obvious bias demonstrated by the National Science Foundation's refusal to fund any climate change research that did not take man-made causation as its starting point.

My blond interlocutor was outraged on my behalf. "I find it interesting," she said, tapping her pen on the desk separating us, "that the very same scientists who bemoan political interference in their own work are so blind to their own biases." No less than four minutes after the interview concluded, as Eric, the media consultant, and I were sitting in the green room, a CNN producer called.

Over the next week, I became so comfortable giving interviews that Eric warned I was losing my awkward demeanor. The *Washington Times* invited me to pen an op-ed about political interference in science. I wrote about the National Science Foundation's rejection of my grant application in detail.

The Client was pleased with our progress.

Soon after my initial media appearances, Representatives Bayless and Calhoun began joining me on camera. Eric warned me that as the story picked up speed, Democratic political operatives, along with enterprising journalists, would begin to dig into my past and reveal the plagiarism charges. This of course made me uncomfortable, but he assured me that it was part of the narrative, and that the mainstream media's refusal to allow me, a man of faith, to be "born again" would only increase the public's support. Again and again, the media underestimated the importance of the lost lamb to the churchgoing American.

I was not entirely surprised to receive Annie's e-mail asking for a divorce, but it marked one of only two times during my preparations for South Pole when I doubted the wisdom of this entire endeavor — the first being the hours after Fred Zimmer's unexpected visit. I found myself unable to focus on my papers. The research that had so engaged me now seemed uninteresting. Instead, I thought a great deal about Annie, and naturally dwelled upon our happier years. Again and again, an image of her walking out of the Electricity and Optics building at Stanford, talking to Sal Brennan, came to me. She was beautiful, with a gap between her two front teeth.

Later, I found Sal in his father's lab, and asked about the girl with whom he'd been talking after class. He told me her name was Annie and that she was a classics major who sometimes took science classes as electives. He said he'd introduce us — "I happen to know she has a weakness for idiot savants," he'd said. He added: "Too bad I'm not an idiot." I appreciated the offer very much, but I was wary. Sal and I had only known each other for a year, but we already had a fraught history. He was John Brennan's son, a beloved professor emeritus at Stanford, and was quite popular on campus himself because of his own extreme erudition, his good looks, and his easy manner. This was not a combination often found in the physics and applied physics departments. To complicate matters, the year prior we'd had a falling out, and although Sal was no longer ignoring me when he saw me on campus, he was uncharacteristically reserved when we spoke. At the time, Sal's father had spent a great deal of energy trying to convince me to join the astrophysics department. Although John Brennan was one of the world's foremost scientists, I'd demurred for many reasons, but the most salient had been the fact that Dr. Brennan was clearly suffering from early-onset dementia. I suspected Alzheimer's, and I had made the mistake of saying so to Sal.

Despite this, Sal, it must be said, was as good as his word about Annie. A week after I saw her laughing with him on campus, I was sitting across from her at the Student Union, talking about Ovid and Apuleius. She was smiling at me, as if she was glad to be there. Later, she told me I was staring stupidly at her the whole time. I imagine I must have been, because I don't remember a word she said, only the look on her shining, happy face. After we were married, I asked her why she'd agreed to a second date. Because, she told me, "you were brilliant, and unabashedly weird and yet completely oblivious to it."

. When he heard that Annie had filed for divorce, Eric visited me at my campus apartment. He tried to convince me that these domestic developments only deepened the theme of the misunderstood scientist. He suggested leaking to the media the fact that Annie was a professed atheist. At the look on my face, Eric fell silent. A few minutes later, he suggested another tack — the marriage could be framed as a casualty of a coordinated attack against my professional research interests. I admit that at this point I was beginning to fatigue of the falsity of the endeavor — what had initially appealed to those darker impulses that had pushed me toward plagiarism now seemed too costly. When I mentioned this to Eric, he told me he had the perfect solution: "Begin to believe in it. Stop acting. Buy in."

After he left, I sat on the edge of my twin bed for an hour considering his advice.

Faith had seemed anathema to every endeavor I had undertaken in my life; I found solace in fact, comfort in evidence. I was patient enough to wait for data. When personal tragedy touched me — as when my parents died within one month of each other when I was seventeen — I turned to probability density to parcel out the likelihood of such an event. That a likelihood could even exist brought me the kind of comfort that the well-meaning words of believers did not.

Still, I couldn't ignore the fact that I had summarily dismissed the very idea of faith; summary dismissal, I knew, was not something in which a true scientist engaged. I began to grapple with the idea proposed by some of the senior members of Olive Grove that scientific research and "sound reason" consistently supported the truth of a loving, transcendent god. I knew I would never accept the Bible as a work of literal history, and my church mentors accepted this, but the idea of a sovereign "creator" — for so long an idea that had nothing to do with me — became a great comfort.

For the first time in my life, I began to believe in something other than my love for my wife. I wasn't a true believer yet, but I was on the road to Damascus.

■ ■ ■ ■

On January 30, 2003, I received a call from Representatives Bayless and Calhoun. There were sounds of celebration in the background. "I have news, Dr. Pavano," Bayless said. "We just got out of a closed-door meeting with the head of the National Science Foundation." The line seemed to pause for a moment, creating a parenthesis in the celebrations, and I pulled the phone away from my ear, only to realize that Eric was calling me on the other line.

"Pavano, you there?" Bayless shouted.

"I'm here," I called back into the mouthpiece.

"Pack your bags, Doc, you're going to Antarctica."

It was only as I heard the hard *c* in Antarctica, which no one seems ever to notice, that I realized how badly I wanted to go.

The New York Times
March 21, 2004
South Pole Station: No End in Sight for "Occupation"

With the ambush of its personnel in Fallujah and an "illegal occupation" in Antarctica, the defense contractor Veritas Integrated Defense Systems is struggling to contain what could be a substantial blow to its operations. Citing the occupation of Amundsen-Scott South Pole Station, where Veritas provides support staff, as a "major and unnecessary distraction to global operations," CEO Daniel Atcheson Johnson has sent a team of lobbyists to Capitol Hill to help end the shutdown of the U.S. research station.

Last week, Republican Sam Bayless of Kansas and his colleague on the Congressional Budget Committee, Representative Jack Calhoun of Tennessee, delivered on a promise to freeze the station's budget if no agreement could be reached with the head of the National Science Foundation, Alexandra Scaletta, over proposed changes to the agency's guidelines that would make it easier for scientists skeptical of climate change to gain access to federally sponsored research sites.

At the heart of the shutdown is Frank Pavano, a heliophysicist who has voiced skepticism about global climate change. On a grant from the NSF, Pavano spent four months at Amundsen-Scott Station and the ice-coring camp at West Antarctic Ice Sheet before he was involved in an accident with another NSF grantee that Representative Bayless claims was a result of a consistent pattern of harassment.

It was in response to the alleged harassment, initially reported last fall, that Representative Bayless and Representative Calhoun demanded the NSF adopt formal protocols to ensure that "scientists with minority views" are provided with equal access to federal research sites and grant dollars. Ms. Scaletta, however, has refused to yield, and with the White House unwilling to enter the fray, the standoff has led to a temporary shutdown of operations at America's most remote research facility, which is currently being illegally occupied by ten individuals, a mix of NSF grantees and Veritas contractors.

The president has so far resisted calls to

send in the National Guard to forcibly remove the individuals who refused to board the last scheduled flight out of South Pole. Sources familiar with the situation indicate that, with operations in Iraq intensifying, the president wants to avoid distraction. Others, however, argue that this is precisely the reason why he may be open to intervention.

OPERATION DEEP FREEZE

The sky began changing in early February, as the sun began its month-long descent. Shadows were weirdly elongated, stretching toward a horizon that consumed the sun bite by bite. Once the sun had fallen out of sight, Cooper knew from the handbook, it would lighten the sky for two more weeks of "civil twilight," when Venus would be visible. Nautical twilight would follow, draining the sky of its pink blush. By the end of March, after the last flights had departed, all would be dark. This process was typically of great interest to the Polies, capped off, as it was, by the annual Equinox Feast, but anxiety over the possible shutdown had cast a pall over everything. Tucker decided to move the feast forward by five weeks in order to boost station morale — and, Cooper suspected, because he knew that in five weeks, there was a very good chance that no one would be here to celebrate the true equinox.

Preparations had been under way for a week when the letters from the NSF arrived in Tucker's in-box, with instructions to distribute to the grantees immediately. Cooper and Sal, who had been in Tucker's office when the letters had arrived, were the only other Polies who knew about them. All three agreed it made no sense to ruin the Equinox Feast with news that the station, and all the ongoing experiments, was going to be shut down.

On February 10, the galley transformed into Le Cirque. Pearl, Denise, and Doc Carla had hung strands of ice-blue Christmas lights across the ceiling that twinkled in the wineglasses set on the long table. The support beams were festooned with cheap silver tinsel, and battery-powered votive candles flickered in the corners of the room. The cloth napkins were removed from storage, and Kit had folded them into bishop's hats before placing them on the plates. Bonnie's absence — she'd flown to McMurdo the day after the bottle-throwing incident at Sal's lecture — was noted, and a place was set for her at the table, next to Dwight.

Everyone arrived in the one nice outfit they'd packed — Birdie wore his kilt, Dwight his formal cloak, and even Floyd had donned a polka-dotted tie. In the galley bathroom, Marcy lent Cooper her four-year-old purple metallic eye shadow. After pulling on the floral empire-waist dress she'd rolled into a ball and shoved in the deepest corner of her duffel back in Minneapolis, Cooper pulled her hair into a low, messy bun at the nape of her neck, and impaled it with bobby pins.

When she walked into the galley, the ceremonial equinox haircuts were already under way. Four Beakers sat in chairs, Sal among them, while their research techs lopped off their unruly locks with crafting scissors. Cooper grabbed a glass of Pearl's hot wassail and watched as Alek roughly shoved his hands into Sal's nest of tangled hair. He pulled on it mercilessly in order to straighten it for an even cut. Once Alek started cutting, Sal stared at the wall unblinkingly as his auburn hair fell to the floor in clumps.

Denise stepped next to Cooper, blowing on her wassail. She was wearing a rhinestone-encrusted headband, magenta lipstick, and a leather mini-skirt. Cooper nodded at her approvingly. "Ceremonies are so important," Denise said. "They are the social glue that keeps a community intact — especially one under duress." She gestured toward the crowd of Polies gathered around Bozer's portrait, which Pearl had hung the day before. "That's social glue, too." She looked over at Cooper. "I hope you don't underestimate how important you've become to the group."

"I'm important?"

Denise nodded. "There are two things you possess which are valuable to this particular group. One, you are a survivor. Two, at times of extreme anxiety, your paintings will remind the people here that they are not just cogs in the machine."

Cooper gestured toward the portrait of Bozer. "What did he think, by the way? Bozer, when he saw it."

Denise surprised Cooper by dissolving into giggles. "Oh, he executed the best Goffman-esque display of faux outrage I'd ever witnessed. You should have seen him — he was raging around like King Kong."

"Oh no," Cooper said, glancing around.

Denise put her hand on Cooper's arm. "No, you don't understand — his response was strictly impression management, basic maintenance of expressive control. He and I came back to the galley late last night, after he was sure everyone else was gone, and he just stood in front of it, staring."

"How did you know he didn't hate it?"

"He didn't put his fist through it."

A freshly shorn Sal stood up and placed a bowler hat over his head. He did a little dance for Alek as the other winter-overs gathered around him, but Cooper could see it was an effort for him. Denise left to take her seat next to Bozer, so Cooper wandered around the table until she found her place card. Sal sat down beside her and reached across to steal an extra wineglass. He set it next to his and looked at Cooper. "You look pretty tonight," he said.

Before Cooper could reply, Pearl leaned over her shoulder, bearing wine. "Red or white?" she said.

"Both," Sal said dully, tapping both of his glasses. "And leave the bottles here."

From across the table, Doc Carla — dressed in a peasant shift and long feathered earrings — lifted her wineglass to Sal. "Bottoms up to the bottom of the world, Doc," she said. Next to her, and dressed in a beautiful blue tuxedo, Alek raised a glass of samogon. "To our lady doctor," he said, "may you heal pain well." He turned to Cooper. "And to you, *artiste,* who completed lovely paintings with no penguins."

As soon as everyone was seated, bishop's hats unfurled on their laps, Tucker took his place at the front of the galley, flanked by

Pearl and Kit. "Working against the political odds, and a dire shortage of freshies due to the current difficulties, tonight's Equinox Feast is the work of two dedicated Pole civilian contractors who are so famous they need not be named." The room shook with applause and cheers. "We are here tonight, honoring Pole tradition, to mark the coming equinox, when we probably won't have the kinds of provisions we have here tonight."

"Or the fuel," Floyd grumbled.

"After dinner, we will go outside to move the flag and unveil the new Pole marker. There's a menu under your plates. All the artwork is courtesy of our fearless artist Fellow Cooper." The synchronous sound of plates being shifted arose from the table, followed by appreciative murmurs. Cooper watched as Sal looked over the menu card she'd designed — there was a sketch of the South Pole Telescope in the left-hand corner, the skyline of the Dark Sector in the right-hand corner, and an outline of the entire Antarctic continent in the middle. At the bottom were three images of men trekking through a blizzard — Wilson, Cherry, and Birdie. Sal smiled for the first time all night and pulled her in for a long kiss, which was met with applause completely devoid of sarcasm.

"Excuse me." Cooper looked down the long table and saw the interpretive dancer was on her feet, her Afghan tribal coin belt tinkling. "These momentous circumstances are so personally inspiring, that I'd like to perform a segment of the dance I've been working on since I've been here, a piece of nonverbal storytelling that encapsulates my experience at South Pole. I call it the 'Dance of the Anxious Penguin.' " Perhaps it was the wine, or the twinkling blue lights, but Cooper — and, to her surprise, everyone else — could not take her eyes off the interpretive dancer as she spun wordlessly around the room.

Once the performance, and dinner, ended, the Polies swapped their dining clothes for their ECW gear, and gathered around the geographic Pole for the ceremonial moving of the marker. With the sun hanging low in the sky, a pale compass rose, the Polies fell into line and one by one passed the American flag hand to hand from its former position to the new, drifted, but true South Pole. At the end of the human chain, Bozer removed the stake and installed the flag next to Sal's sheet-draped marker.

The Polies crowded around it, expectant, with cameras raised. Sal and Marcy each took a corner of the sheet and, at the count of three, pulled it off the tiny *Terra Nova*. Cooper remained on the fringes of the group, watching while everyone pushed and shoved to get a better look. Her heart was full. Above her, parhelions flanked the slowly sinking sun.

The next morning, everyone arrived at breakfast with their letter from NSF, which had been slipped under the doors in the Jamesways, Hypertats, and El Dorm overnight like hotel bills.

The exodus began almost at once. That evening, Cooper said goodbye to the literary novelist and the interpretive dancer, and even helped them bag-drag with her good hand. The historical novelist had been forced onto an earlier flight after an unfortunate incident with his manuscript. Cooper had heard the summons over All-Call that afternoon, and was halfway up the entrance tunnel when she saw the commotion. The historical novelist was wild-eyed — Rove in a rage — and pressed a huge manuscript to his chest. Polies began to appear from various parts of the station, and soon they had made a ring around him. Birdie approached Cooper and asked what had happened. She shrugged and the two watched as the historical novelist lifted the manuscript above his head.

"It's done," he shouted hoarsely.

Tucker took a step forward. "May I see it?" The novelist abruptly turned and began speed-walking down the tunnel, the pages peeling off the manuscript in his wake. Cooper and Birdie scrambled to catch them, but the wind blowing up the tunnel sent the pages skyward. As Floyd and Tucker tackled the historical novelist, Cooper managed to grab one of the pages before it flew away. It was blank. She snatched another one from the air as it gently fell, swaying side to side. It, too, was blank.

She looked over at Birdie — the pages in his hands were blank as well.

Lisa Wu told Sal her team was going to comply with Stanford's directive to follow the evacuation order and return stateside, and would have to abandon the joint experiment. Upon hearing this, he disappeared to the Dark Sector, kicking even Alek out. Cooper knew Sal had received the same directive from Princeton.

That evening, he burst into the Smoke Bar, where Tucker was comforting Alek and the rest of the remaining Polies. Sal locked the door behind him and looked at them.

"I'm staying. I won't abandon this project. I'm going to caretake the experiment for both teams." He looked over at Tucker. "Lisa knows."

Tucker tugged on one of the low-hanging strands of fairy lights, loosening it so that it swayed just above the table. "Does the NSF know? Scaletta?"

"No comment."

"I assume you understand the potential consequences of defying an evac order."

"I can always seek asylum at CERN."

Without thinking, Cooper said, "What if we all stayed? Like Alcatraz but in Antarctica."

Someone pulled at the door a couple of times. Tucker, who was leaning against it, reached behind him to unlock it. A new VIDS admin who'd been flown in the week before from Denver walked in, her brow furrowed.

"Why's the door locked?"

"Sorry," Tucker said. "Sometimes it sticks." Cooper noticed the woman's eyes were searching the room, as if she were looking for a fugitive. Distractedly, she handed Tucker a manila envelope and exited the bar.

Everyone watched as Tucker opened the

envelope and pulled out the caretaking roster — the names of those who would be allowed to stay at the station in order to keep basic operations running.

"Floyd. Bozer. Pearl. Doc. Marce. The rest are on the last flight out." Denise's child-like sobs shattered the silence, and Bozer pushed all of the darts into Karl Martin's face and went over to comfort her.

Tucker handed the roster to Sal. "Scaletta wants me in Washington. Let me know what you decide."

As soon as Sal had locked the door behind Tucker, Floyd said, "If we do this, none of you will get paid. They'll stop depositing your paychecks."

"I don't care," several people said at once.

"Can't they force you onto the planes?" Pearl asked.

"They're not going to walk us out at gunpoint," Dwight said. "They trust us to follow the rules. By the time they realize what we've done, it might be too late."

"What do you mean 'too late'?"

"Every hour we delay, the closer we get to the event horizon," Dwight replied. "Too cold to fly. No flights in, no flights out. If we can wait this out —"

"And create enough confusion and administrative chaos," Cooper added.

"— if we can do that, then there will be no chance of flights to haul us away. It will be too late."

Cooper noticed Sal watching her closely.

"What?" she asked.

"You sure you want to stay?"

Cooper rolled her eyes.

"No, this is serious, Cooper," he said. He looked around the room. "This has to be worth it to every single person here. If you violate this evac order, you probably won't work here again. You may even face federal trespassing charges."

"And what about you, Doc?" Bozer said to Sal. "You've got more to lose here than any of us."

Sal shook his head. "Me? It's this or nothing."

"When's the last flight?" Pearl asked.

"Monday," Dwight replied.

"That's Valentine's Day."

Dwight looked stricken for a moment. Then he shrugged. "So?"

"I'm just saying that locking ourselves into the station and occupying a federal research facility isn't exactly in the spirit of the holiday," Pearl said mildly. "It's like getting a Dear John letter."

"Nah, Pearlie," Floyd said. "You've gotta think of it more like a box of chocolates hand-delivered to the Congressional Budget Committee. Except instead of chocolates —"

"We get it, Floyd," Sal interrupted.

Bozer turned to Cooper. "You didn't answer your man's question. What about you?"

"What about me?"

"No finger, and no prospects after this is over. You good?"

Everyone in the room turned to see what she would say. She looked from face to face. Floyd's poorly groomed mutton chops and Doc Carla's slightly askew Yankees cap. Bozer's veiny nose and Alek's Fu Manchu 'stache. Pearl's white-blond eyebrows, Marcy's laugh lines, and Denise's frizzy curls. Sal's beautiful but tired eyes. Here were the faces that would surround her for the next six months, the brains with which she'd have to contend.

"Right before Halloween, I asked Sal why the station didn't just replace Frosty Boy instead of sending techs in every season to rebuild it," Cooper said. "He told me 'We grow attached to these temperamental pieces of crap.' Well, let's just say there are a number of temperamental pieces of crap in this room that I'm oddly attached to."

Everyone laughed at this, and this laughter

seemed to form an agreement. They'd do this thing, no matter the consequences. They agreed on a password to ensure secrecy: *Occupy or Die.*

Pearl went into a baking frenzy in preparation for the Valentine's Day Exodus. She didn't want the Polies who were being forced off the ice to go home empty-handed. She and Cooper stayed up all night baking trays of jam tarts, sheets of heart-shaped sugar cookies, raspberry linzers, a two-tier red velvet cake studded with fondant roses, and mini-cupcakes frosted in crimson and white. (Cooper had to talk her out of making pavlovas when she realized the effort would require almost all the eggs left on station.)

The Valentine's Day dessert buffet raised the morale of the departing Polies — the goodie bags filled with handmade pralines and Captain Morgan rum truffles almost made them smile. Birdie, who had been utterly broken since receiving notice that he was being ferried off the ice and who, thanks to Pearl's fear of the repercussions of a naturalized citizen getting involved in a federal crime, knew nothing about the plans to occupy, received extra goodies, including an extravagant peach melba that brought him to tears.

One other gesture of goodwill took place in the days before the evacuation commenced: Bozer had, according to Denise, "surrendered to the better angels of his nature" and challenged Sri to a game of pool before he left for Madison. Everyone crowded into Skylab, gorging on Pearl's homemade delicacies, and watched as Sri entered the room. He stood on one side of the pool table and gripped the polished top rails. His eyes were full of emotion. Finally, Bozer tossed a cue over the table toward Sri, who caught it smoothly. "Rack 'em up," he said.

For the next hour, Cooper and the other Polies watched as Sri and Bozer traded wins on the felt — to their delight, each man was an accomplished player — and for those sixty minutes, it almost seemed like nothing had changed. It was as if the entire polar winter lay before them, uninterrupted.

As Cooper finished off one of Pearl's chocolate cupcakes, Tucker pulled her aside. The sunglasses were gone, and so was the Bell's palsy. "You're better," she exclaimed.

"Doc Carla has been giving me prednisone. Sometimes it helps with Bell's palsy. Listen, I'm leaving tonight for Washington — Scaletta thinks I can help with the negotiations. Something about my cool gaze."

"I wish you didn't have to leave," Cooper said.

"You are in very capable hands down here." He took her bandaged hand. "Do you remember chasing me down the hall back in Denver to tell me why you wanted to come to South Pole?"

Cooper flushed at the memory and smiled weakly. "Yeah, and you bought it."

"No, you told me the truth. You told me you were afraid. That's when I knew you'd be okay here. For none but cowards need to prove their bravery, right?"

Tucker's radio crackled and Cooper could hear a tech sergeant barking orders, the sound of a plane's engine roaring in the background. "I might not see you before I leave."

"So this is goodbye, then."

"As Jimi Hendrix once said, 'The story of life is quicker than the wink of an eye, the story of love is hello and goodbye . . . until we meet again.' "

"As Tucker Bollinger once said, 'Quoting others suggests avoidance.' "

"A wise man."

The next morning, as the last LC-130 to

land at Pole, the one that was meant to take the rest of them off the ice, idled on the skiway, Cooper climbed down a ladder into the Utilidors with the other occupying Polies. With each step down, the scream of the plane's engines grew fainter. Above her, Floyd pulled the trapdoor closed and locked it. Below, the core group stood waiting, silent, their eyes wide above their balaclavas. Cooper reached the last rung and dropped down next to Sal. "Can't they just open the door and find us?" she asked.

Overhearing this, Bozer snapped, "Not where we're going. Now follow me." Silently, they made their way down the dark tunnel. It appeared endless, lined with corrugated metal and lighted by caged incandescents. All species of wire snaked across the ground, appearing to meld into a single cable in the far distance. Running along the walls of the Utilidor were the sewer, electrical, and data cables — Cooper imagined e-mails and fax messages coursing down this metal helix as she passed it.

She paused for Sal, and they allowed themselves to fall behind. He pinched the zipper of her parka between his fingers and pulled it up so it was completely closed, and took her face in his mittened hands — to his delight, Cooper had returned to him the dirty black Gore-Tex she'd found in skua, which she'd used to complete that triptych all those months ago. "I would like nothing more than to hole up with you for the next six months in a place where nobody can find us," he said. "That being said, I have to ask you one last time: Are you ready to do this?"

Cooper placed her hands on his. "This is like the Malibu Barbie Dreamhouse of unreachable civilizations," she said. "Maybe it's wrong to say, but I'm not upset this is happening."

Up ahead, the others were obscured by a veil of steam, which made them appear ghost-like as the pale light filtered through the vapor. For a moment, Cooper was startled; it was as if the image on David's copy of *Worst Journey,* of the three men in a backlit ice cavern, had sprung to life. "Everything okay?" Sal asked. Cooper nodded, and together they headed toward the phantom figures.

By the time they caught up, Bozer had already opened the metal door leading to the Tomb, where the Man Without Country lay hidden behind stacks of empty crates, wrapped in plastic sheeting. When they stepped inside, Bozer started to close the door, then stopped.

"Last chance for losers," he said. "You can still make the plane."

The group, huddled together in front of what Cooper knew was a frozen catafalque, blinked back at him.

"Occupy or die," Cooper said.

"Occupy or die," Marcy replied.

"I refuse to shout slogans, but I'm in," Doc Carla said wearily.

"Then I will: Occupy or fucking die!" Floyd shouted.

"Lower your voice, you dipshit," Bozer said. "Come on, let's go deal with the feds now. Marce, Pearlie, game-time. Dwight's waiting in Comms."

Cooper watched as the officially approved caretaking staff — Pearl, Marcy, Doc Carla, and Bozer — stepped out of the room, leaving the rest of them in the shadows thrown by an electric lantern. "Once we're sweet, I'll come get you." Bozer looked at Cooper, Sal, Denise, and Alek. "Last chance."

"Go," Alek growled. Bozer pulled the door closed. A moment later, they heard the key turn in the lock. Sal pulled Cooper close.

No one spoke for a while. The silence revealed the faraway roar of the idling plane. Eventually, Denise cleared her throat. "Because of the unusual circumstances, no one underwent the mid-season psych exam.

It'll be interesting to see how a control group wintering over without the psych assessment functions under stress."

Before anyone could reply, raised voices could be heard echoing through the Utildors. "Here they come," Sal murmured. Cooper tried to imagine the scene that would unfold if the tech sergeant and his minions found them in the Tomb, huddling behind a locked door, with a corpse for company.

The voices grew louder, followed by the sound of heavy boots hurrying through the tunnels. Next to Cooper, Denise fidgeted, her hands like birds that couldn't quite get settled. Cooper placed her hand on Denise's knee, but this only seemed to make things worse.

"Wintering-over exacts intense pressure on the individual psyche," she said, her voice strained. "We rely on social contracts more than we would in any other scenario you can conjure. One study shows that after a winter in Antarctica, at least five percent of people on station can be deemed clinically insane."

The footsteps were getting closer.

"Be quiet, woman," Alek said angrily.

But Denise seemed unable to stop. She stood up suddenly. "But of course that assumes a standard population, not self-selected potential felons."

"Sit down, Denise," Sal said soothingly. "Everything's going to be okay. Bozer will come get us once the plane is airborne. But right now you need to be quiet." Denise didn't seem to hear him. She approached the door.

"The point of sharing that is not to scare you guys, but to remind you of the stakes, and to encourage you to invest in sanity."

The footsteps slowed down and the sound of walkie-talkies became audible. When Denise began pulling on the door, Alek and Sal both leapt up, but Cooper was quicker. She gently took Denise's arm. "Just a little bit longer," Cooper whispered. Denise was trembling, but she allowed Cooper to lead her away from the door.

As Cooper tried desperately to think of something to distract Denise, her finger — or the place where her finger had once been — began to itch intensely. "Denise," she whispered. "I have a question for you. Lately I've been having this really strong feeling that my finger is back, like it's physically there. I can even 'move' it — I actually feel it bend. Do you know anything that can explain this?"

It worked. Denise seemed calm in an

instant. "Phantom limb syndrome," she replied quietly. "The perception of pain in an amputated limb or digit. Yes, this is real. One-armed men have been known to utilize their phantom limb to masturbate."

Sal brought his sleeve to his mouth, his shoulders shaking with laughter. Suddenly, the door began to rattle as someone pulled on the knob. Denise turned her eyes to Cooper — behind her glasses, they looked enormous, and they were full of fear. "I promise, it will be okay," Cooper whispered.

She knew the plane was idling, burning fuel, and that the temperature was dropping; she imagined the pilot was not exactly happy at the delay. Bozer had told them to expect this search of the station by VIDS and the NSF admins and higher-ups — they just had to wait it out. The door rattled again, more insistently this time. Muffled voices — including Marcy's — conferred on the other side.

"This is a WC," she told the others.

"A what?"

"Waste closet. Shit storage. Poo pantry. It's where we keep the leaky sewage drums. I can unlock it for you if you want to look around, but I warn you: it smells like a shithouse door on a tuna boat."

The search party hastily moved on. After

their footsteps had receded completely, Alek fell back in relief, muttering in Russian.

Seventy-two hours in, Pearl and Dwight were already nursing a beef that had started when Pearl whistled for an hour straight during dinner. Now, in the Smoke Bar, her whistling had become defiant.

"If I have to listen to your stupid whistling and stare at your Pollyanna face and your stupid greasy pigtails all winter I'm going to kill myself," Dwight said, gripping a nosegay of darts in his hand. "You will find me swinging from the rafters in a cold breeze."

"You know what, Dwight? I try to be smiley and nice to everyone, even if they're rude. I feel like people don't need grumps around all winter, especially under the circumstances."

"Don't pretend like you're some kind of angel, Pearl," Dwight said, sending a dart into the board. "The act gets old real quick." He turned to Sal. "Look me in the eye, Sal, and tell me that prolonged whistling isn't a form of torture."

"Can't you guys try bonding?" Doc Carla suggested.

"Over what?" Dwight demanded.

"Both of your ice-spouses are gone," she said. "What about the bond of broken hearts?"

Dwight scoffed, and drifted away to another part of the bar.

Cooper nursed a vodka tonic as she watched them bicker. She hoped Dwight's tantrum wasn't a harbinger of things to come. Whistling was a minor crime, and they had several more months of this, at best. Cooper hoped Dwight would just immerse himself in his comms duties, which included keeping track of the federal response to the occupation, via the Web, his ham radio, and satellite phone. It had taken the authorities two full days to understand what had happened at Pole. The U.S. Antarctic Program had operated with military precision for decades. That members of the Program would disobey orders came not only as a shock to VIDS and NSF administrators, it also paralyzed them. The prevailing attitude among those who were in charge was disbelief and utter confusion. Word had not leaked to the media yet, but Dwight was seeing some blogs mentioning rumors of an occupation at Pole.

Once the LC-130 with the tech sergeant, Tucker, and the last VIDS and NSF admins had gone wheels up, Bozer and Marcy cleared the snowdrifts from the perimeter of the Dome before shutting the outer doors. The temperature had dropped dramatically by now, nearing seventy below. Floyd assured everyone that no pilot would try to land at Pole at this point. Not even JP-8 fuel could remain liquid in these temperatures. The only unqualified positive aspect of the occupation so far, at least for Cooper, was that everyone now had a room in El Dorm — she'd taken over the room next to Sal's, which had previously belonged to a telescope maintenance tech. The convenience of not having to empty a pee can into a pee barrel was almost decadent.

Sal walked over to where Cooper was sketching Doc Carla awkwardly holding knitting needles. Now that Pearl had abandoned her whistling, she was trying to teach people how to knit. "I have to go back to the lab now," Sal said to Cooper. "Will you walk with me?"

They walked down the entrance tunnel in silence, past the fuel arches, which were now strangely quiet, running on caretaking mode. When they approached the entrance door, Sal performed an intricate routine with the lock, and together they pushed the door open. Then they were outside, in the half darkness of near-winter. Sal scanned the sky before taking Cooper's arm. "I keep thinking I'm going to hear a C-17 looping back to force us out by gunpoint," he said.

"Actually, it would be an LC-130," Cooper said. "A Herc."

"Oh my god, you're officially a Polie."

"What would you do if they did come back?"

"I've thought about that a million times," Sal said, his brow troubled. "I can't get any farther than suicide." He gripped her arm harder. "I'm sorry, Cooper, I shouldn't have said that."

Cooper said nothing, but noted that the word, even the offhand way it had been mentioned, hadn't pierced her in the way it used to. In fact, with all the commotion at the station, she hadn't even thought about David, or the vial, for days. She wondered if that jagged edge had finally broken off.

They were halfway down the road to the Dark Sector before Sal stopped. He pointed to the sky. The aurora australis, roiling ribbon-like sheaves of purple and pink light, filled the sky. They gaped at it in wonder. There was something else there, too, like a fingerprint on glass.

"The Milky Way," Sal said.

"Jesus, that's beautiful."

"It's cripplingly beautiful," he said.

Cooper looked over at him. "Even though it has a super-massive black hole in it?"

"Especially because it does."

As Cooper gazed into its frosty heart, she imagined the black hole, its density equivalent to a billion suns.

When the feds finally shook off their incredulity, directives began arriving via e-mail, fax, and satellite phone. It started with the NSF's assumption that this had all been a misunderstanding. In Comms, Cooper and the other Polies listened in silence as the South Pole NSF rep, Warren, back in Washington, D.C., now, played nice cop with Dwight.

"Perhaps we weren't clear," Warren said gently. "And I can own that, I can take the fall for that." He hesitated. "One might even argue that I've already taken the fall for that."

"There was no misunderstanding," Dwight replied. "This is intentional."

"Tell Karl Martin it's draconian," Floyd piped in.

Warren sighed. "Guys, I have no idea what you're talking about. All we're seeking is a peaceful resolution to the situation."

"What? We're not armed, dude," Floyd replied.

"Well, the FBI wants in on this."

Floyd cackled. "Yeah? Tell 'em to come

on down. They can fly Southwest."

There was a long silence on Warren's end of the line. Finally, he cleared his throat. "Just tell me how we can resolve this, guys."

Sal stepped past Floyd and leaned over the speakerphone. "The Wisconsin DA is tearing up Sri Niswathin's lab in Madison. Frank Pavano is doing more interviews than a starlet on a press junket. Bayless and Calhoun are preening in front of cameras and pretending to be the defenders of science —"

"Sal —"

"You're asking us how this will be resolved, and I'm telling you that this is resolved when Bayless and Calhoun let the budget bill go through committee. This is resolved when the sequester ends. It's not complicated."

"What the hell do you think we've been doing, Sal!" Warren shouted. "We've been working every angle here. I don't think you people understand — you are illegally occupying a federal facility. There's jail time associated with this kind of thing. Not to mention the fact that you've put your lives at —"

The call cut out without warning, reverting to static, and everyone turned to Dwight. "Satellite moved off-grid." He shrugged and looked at Sal. "Time to start contacting the media?"

"Permission granted," Sal replied grimly. Dwight shooed everyone out and got to work.

The next morning Cooper headed back over to Comms, where she was scheduled to relieve Dwight for a few hours. She found him sprawled on his ugly brown sofa, already asleep, so she spent her first ten minutes sorting the papers that had accumulated on the floor beneath the fax machine: there were separate piles for NSF communications, VIDS-related missives and threats, and the media requests, which had been pouring in since Dwight had started contacting reporters.

She'd brought along a mini-canvas and was priming it with gesso (Bozer had requested a small portrait of Denise) when the satellite phone began to ring. Its strange, insect-like buzzing woke Dwight immediately. Cooper brought the phone over to him.

The person on the other end of the line began speaking before Dwight could answer. His face contorted with effort as he tried to understand what he was hearing. Finally, he was able to break in: "Wait — wait, hold on. Hold on! No habla Russian." He put his hand over the mouthpiece and looked at Cooper. "Radio Dark Sector and get Alek in here."

Soon the office was crowded with the Polies. Alek had the enormous phone pressed against his right ear, his other hand covering his left. Sal, who had come over from the Dark Sector with him, threw himself on the couch and instantly fell asleep. The plosives of Russian spoken at high volume were making Cooper feel delirious, and she sat down on the couch next to Sal, lifting his legs with effort and sliding beneath them.

It seemed like ages before Alek got off the phone — enough time for Pearl to go back to the galley, make a batch of instant hot chocolate, and return to Comms with a tray of still-steaming mugs. After hanging up, Alek took a long sip of cocoa and carefully wiped his mouth with his fingers. "They want to come get me," he said darkly.

"Who wants to come get you?" Marcy asked.

"Rossiya," Alek replied. Marcy stared at him blankly. "Mother Russia. They want to come and get their citizen."

"And take you where, exactly?" Doc Carla growled from the other side of the room.

"Vostok."

"That's halfway across Antarctica," Cooper said.

"Twelve hundred kilometers, exact," Alek snapped.

"I thought it was too dangerous to fly into Pole at this time of year," Doc Carla said, growing irritated. "I thought that was the goddamn point of this whole game."

"In 1982, Vostok run out of fuel in the middle of winter. They make candle warmers out of asbestos fibers and diesel," he replied. "Russia doesn't give shit."

"Have they talked to the State Department?" Sal asked, awake again but groggy.

"No, they say not necessary."

"Actually, they're right; they don't need to," Dwight said, flipping through the papers on his desk. "But Russia is a signatory to the Antarctic Treaty, so they'll have to go through the secretariat."

Alek shook his head. "No, I don't want to go. I gave them better idea: airdrop."

Sal sat up suddenly. "You're a fucking genius, Alek."

"Not an evil monk?"

"No, you've achieved sainthood."

The airdrop, which Bozer had christened Operation Deep Freeze, had everyone giddy with anticipation. Airdrops were not unheard of at Pole — most winters, if the weather cooperated, a C-17 out of New Zealand would make a pass and drop supplies from its cargo hold. That was out of the question this winter: the sequester was still in effect, the station illegally occupied, and the resident population was accused of federal crimes. But Russia, sensing an opportunity to improve its standing in the international community at the expense of the Americans, was ready to help a comrade whose sense of duty to science had left him in dire straits.

Floyd began building the wooden wicks for the smudge pots, fires burning in fifty-five-gallon drums that would demarcate the drop zone now that the polar night — twenty-four-hour darkness — had fully descended. Bozer and Marcy spent nearly six hours grooming the zone, while Floyd split up the remaining Polies into teams. Marcy tuned up the forklift she'd use to locate the dropped crates and dig them out. Cooper was designated "project manager" since Doc Carla still didn't think she was ready to do any heavy lifting. Everyone who was working the drop zone pulled on the insulated refrigerator suits that had been hauled out of storage and awaited the transmission from the Russian pilots.

Finally an announcement came over All-Call. The Russians were ten minutes out. Sal, Marcy, and Bozer hopped on snowmobiles and headed out to ignite the smudge pots. Cooper glanced over at the temperature gauge. Sixty-three below zero. This was, as Floyd had mentioned many times, the kind of cold that could turn hydraulic fluid into pudding if the plane landed for more than two minutes.

Then came the call that the bird was two minutes out, and everyone rushed into the darkness, the team leaders gripping sets of night-vision goggles. Cooper could feel the rumble of the plane's engines in her chest as its under-wing lights appeared like bright stars on the horizon. Its roar grew louder and louder, until it seemed that Cooper's eardrums were going to burst, and that's when the parcels began drifting down from the inky sky. They floated softly on miniature parachutes illuminated by the teams' searchlights; Cooper thought they looked like jellyfish. The plane made a graceful turn on the far west side of the station, and passed back over them, waggling its wings.

In the distance, Cooper could see two Polies — probably Sal and Pearl — silhouetted by Marcy's headlights as she followed along behind them, waiting for cargo with her forklift. Cooper retreated deeper into the entrance tunnel, and her walkie-talkie started to crackle. Sal's voice broke through the static. "Are the doors open?"

"Yes!" Cooper shouted.

"The machines are loaded," Sal said. "We're on our way."

Floyd arrived on a snowmobile, pulling a pallet, with Pearl sitting behind him.

"They gave us oranges!" Pearl exclaimed, waving a bag of what looked like frozen suns. "Oranges! Can you believe it? Fresh fruit! Oh, I wish Birdie were here to see this."

Over the next fifteen minutes, the teams arrived with the rest of the cargo, which included a box of medical supplies for Doc Carla, DVDs of Russian soap operas, thirteen cases of vodka, and more oranges, which had been a gift from the flight crew. As everyone arrived, Cooper tried raising Sal on the radio again, but got nothing except static. She began asking the others if they'd seen him. Denise claimed he was loading cargo, but when Cooper tried to radio Sal again, she got no response. She mentally checked off every Polie who'd walked by her. Everyone was in, except for Sal.

"Give me a body count," Bozer said, suddenly standing next to her.

"Sal's missing," Cooper told him. The words made it real.

Bozer brought the radio to his mouth and called for Sal. Nothing. He tried again. Cooper was now gripped by panic. She'd been here before. She'd stood in one place, dumb and mute, and waited for someone who hadn't returned. She refused to wait this time. Cooper made a dash for the entrance tunnel, but Bozer caught up to her easily and roughly yanked her back inside. He pushed her away and jabbed a finger in her parka. "Calm down."

"Go get him, Bozer," Cooper cried. "Go get him."

Bozer pulled his mittens back on slowly. "Where is he on the grid?"

"He's supposed to be on the northwest quadrant." Bozer gestured to Marcy, who pulled her hood back over her head and walked toward the nearest snowmobile. Cooper started pacing.

Then a figure appeared down at the entrance end of the tunnel, red in the lights, hauling a pallet. Sal. It took a moment for Cooper to notice the two men skiing up the tunnel behind him. They were wearing ECW gear and carrying astoundingly large packs. Each was sporting a headlamp. It took her a minute, but Cooper realized with astonishment that they were the Swedes — the two men she had fed all those months ago. Halfway up the tunnel, they stopped, expertly plucked off their skis, and laid them against their shoulders before continuing.

Cooper watched as Sal and the Swedes reached the top of the tunnel. Sal's triumphant smile disappeared when he saw Cooper's face. "What's wrong?"

"I just — I thought you were lost," she replied, trying to sound calm, trying not to throw herself on him. "You didn't answer your radio. We called for you over and over. I was worried."

"Shit, I'm sorry," he said. "I lost my radio somewhere between the north and northwest quads. Then I found these guys. When I saw them coming in, I thought I was hallucinating."

By this time, a knot of people had gathered around to get a better look at the skiers as they loaded their gear onto Bozer's snowmobile. One of them had pulled out the familiar Swedish flag that Cooper had last seen draped atop a ski. She and Sal continued toward the galley, where the supplies were being carried for inspection. "Why are they here?" Cooper asked, though she hardly cared.

"They were camping at the Japanese base when they heard about the shutdown," Sal replied. "They felt it was their duty as international citizens to show support — they say they're loaded with goodies from Dome Fuji. I hope they brought mochi."

But Cooper barely heard what Sal was saying. She couldn't stop looking at him. It was as if he had been raised from the dead, as if she had spotted a lone figure waving at her from across the Beardsmore.

Inside the galley, chaos reigned. The Polies ripped open the crates with crowbars and the handles of metal soup ladles. There were thirty-pound bags of yellow onions, tins of instant coffee, canned cheese, and an entire pallet of gold foil–covered military rations, each containing a half-pound of beef, dried biscuits, and dehydrated potatoes. Doc Carla picked through the medical supplies, while Dwight sifted through the various DVDs and produced an old cassette tape of the Red Army Choir's greatest hits.

Nothing had been packed especially well, and a box of powdered tomato soup in cups had exploded, covering its crate with a fine red dust. But in the last box, lovingly packed within three layers of bubble wrap and placed in a bed of straw, Alek discovered sixteen bottles of ice-cold Russian vodka —

Green Mark. His joy was equaled only by his teary-eyed nostalgia at hearing the strains of the Red Army Choir's "Song of the Volga Boatmen" trudging out of the speakers.

It took twelve hours for news of the Russian airdrop, and the unexpected Swedish delegation, to hit the news cycle. The Kremlin was quick to trumpet its act of philanthropy, while the Swedish station on Dronning Maud Land sent out a press release praising its countrymen for their hardiness. Soon, offers of help were coming in from the Kiwis at Scott Base, the Uruguayans on King George Island, the Indian scientists at Bharati Station on the Antarctic Peninsula, and the French Polies working through the winter at Dumont d'Urville. The Brits at Halley Research Station were more circumspect, seeing that they were literally floating on an ice shelf in the Weddell Sea.

The Polies gathered in Comms, save for Sal and Alek, who remained bunkered in the Dark Sector, as Dwight read the statement from the Chinese Ministry of Foreign Affairs, which had come in over the wire.

" 'The world watches as a two-party government stalemate holds international science hostage. The People's Republic of

China offers the scientists currently abandoned at the American research base in Antarctica full logistic and scientific support for its threatened experiments, many of which have global importance.' "

As everyone exited Comms, murmuring excitedly, Dwight pulled Cooper aside. "An e-mail came in for you," he said. Dwight's regular corpse-like pallor had gone ghostlier, and Cooper's stomach lurched.

"Is somebody dead?"

"No," Dwight replied. "But someone's charade might be." He handed her a folded printout.

```
To:
   Amundsen_Scott_Comms@nsf.gov
From: fpavano@freedom.edu
Subject: Attn: Cooper Gosling

Dear Cooper,
I've clung to the root for too
long. I refuse to drown. I've
ceased my activity on behalf
of Bayless and Calhoun. I know
it's too late, but I hope it
helps.
                    Sincerely,
                    Frank Pavano
```

*De Pere Students' Correspondence with
 South Pole Scientist Comes to Abrupt End*

Did you know that Antarctica is the largest desert in the world? Did you know that in winter, no planes can fly in or out of South Pole? Do you know how to build a snow trench?

Every year, the fourth grade students at Marshall Elementary School study Antarctica during their unit on the earth's polar regions. But this year, their studies had been enhanced with personal correspondence with a scientist living and working at the South Pole.

Dr. Sal Brennan, a thirty-six-year-old astrophysicist from Princeton, had been communicating with the students via e-mail since September. He sent pictures and answered questions about his life on the cold, desolate continent. However, the students found their Polar unit merging into their U.S. Government and Civics unit when Dr. Brennan told them that, as a federally funded scientist, his experiment would be shut down as a result of the current standoff between Congress and the National Science Foundation.

"The students were thrilled by Dr. Brennan's e-mails," noted their teacher, Carlotta Beardsley. "They were constantly thinking up questions for him, and they'd enjoyed sending him e-mails about what they've been learning."

When the students learned of the decision made by several scientists, including Dr. Brennan, to remain at South Pole Station in violation of the government's evacuation order, and federal law, a lively debate ensued in the classroom, Beardsley said. "We are all heartbroken that politics have affected his ability to conduct research, but at the same time, it's a teachable moment for the students. We debated whether Dr. Brennan had done the right thing by staying and about what would be lost to the global scientific community if he'd left."

According to student Griffin Wakefield, Dr. Brennan was putting himself and others in danger. "I just thought, you have to do what the government says. What if he runs out of fuel or food?" Fellow student Diani Soltau, however, thought Dr. Brennan was doing the right thing: "You can't just restart an experiment. I think I would do the same thing if I'd spent so many years working on something."

THE RIEMANN HYPOTHESIS

Sal hadn't been sleeping much. It was Sri, back in Madison, tussling with lawyers and subpoenas. It was Lisa and her team, who'd reluctantly left the joint experiment in his hands. It was his stake in the experiment — cyclic universe or bust — now in its final year, the third. *Three.* Pythagoras' "noblest" number — the only number to equal the sum of all the terms below it.

Both experiments rushed forward now, in their waning stages, like binary stars mid-collapse. The e-mails poured into Sal's in-box, an engorged river of inquiries. From Kavli at Stanford, from Lebedev in Moscow, from Princeton — even from CERN. From the journalist-geeks, from the bloggers, from *New Scientist* and *Scientific American*. And then the e-mails from the Russians at Vostok volunteering to provide telescope techs, even to travel overland to do it. Or the Chinese, who offered to send their own team of physicists from Zhongshan via sleds. Sal assumed the U.S. government would see these particular offers as posturing, but he knew better. This went beyond secretariats and embassies and politics — this was science. Everyone who mattered knew what was at stake.

Now Alek was sitting on a folding chair, his hands between his knees, tears trickling down his face. Sal looked around the lab. The fluorescents sounded like cicadas; one bulb flickered, trying to die. The hard drives hummed ceaselessly. And above him, the telescope clicked as it rotated on its plate on the roof, searching the sky, looking for the curls in the polarized cosmic background radiation that the inflationary theorists had been so desperate to find, and which he had, it seemed, found for them.

Sal and Alek had been up for forty-two hours straight. They had not eaten anything besides stale Chex Mix and Mountain Dew, and had ignored all faxes and e-mails, except one. Sal had just hung up after a four-hour phone call with Peter Sokoloff, his boss and mentor at Princeton, going over data Lisa and her team hadn't yet seen, because they were back in Palo Alto, waiting to hear from Sal. He knew the rumors had been flying for months already —

particle physicists, cosmologists, and astronomers all over the world seemed to sense something big was going to happen at the Dark Sector. That the research station was officially shut down — in "caretaking mode" while simultaneously being "occupied" — only made the anticipation more intense.

Dwight had set up the call to Sokoloff, and had kept the satellite clear for the four hours it had taken for Sal to painstakingly read out the data, line by line, to his mentor. When he was done, there had been an excruciatingly long pause.

"It's five-sigma, Peter."

There was another long pause. "Does Lisa know yet?"

"No."

Sokoloff sighed. Sal imagined the sigh leaving Sokoloff's lips, then bouncing off the pockmarked MARISAT-F2 satellite two hundred miles above the Earth's atmosphere, before diving into the GOES satellite's terminal just outside the Dark Sector. "This could just be synchrotron radiation or light scattering from galactic dust," Sokoloff had finally said. "It's too early to hand out Nobels."

But Sal had heard the change in Sokoloff's voice. Uncertainty. Not of the scientific variety — hell, that was their native language.

No, this was uncertainty of the personal kind. Before they got off the phone, Sokoloff had added, "Tell your father before anyone else. Let him be the first to know."

"You know he won't understand," Sal replied.

"No, Sal," came Sokoloff's voice from the satellite. "That is the one thing he will understand. I'll call Lisa and hold her off until this sequester business is resolved. Do this in person."

"There is a theory, which states that if ever anyone discovers exactly what the Universe is for and why it is here, it will instantly disappear and be replaced by something even more bizarre and inexplicable. There is another theory which states that this has already happened."

Sal tossed the Douglas Adams book onto his dorm bed. The man was creative, Sal remembered thinking as he swilled down the dregs of a warm Budweiser, but a scientific illiterate. It was only years later, when Sal had learned to take the long view, that he understood Adams's genius. And it wasn't until this season at South Pole Station that Sal realized how prescient Adams's words were, how they seemed to speak specifically to this experiment, to this shutdown, to the appearance of Frank Pavano. After all, it was Adams who had heralded Pavano's arrival into Sal's life, because the moment Sal had tossed *The Hitchhiker's Guide to the Galaxy* onto his bed had also been the precise moment his new roommate had walked into their dorm room at Stanford's Roble Hall. Gangly and skinny, with eyes wide and penetrating as an owl's, the kid had stood there, frozen, unsure of what to say. By this time, Sal was familiar with the common anxieties of the nerd, so he reached between his legs and drew another beer from the six-pack. "They're warm, but who cares, right?" he said, holding it out.

Down the hall, someone turned his boom box to maximum volume and indistinguishable heavy metal filled the hallways. This seemed to shake the kid out of his catatonia, and he stepped into the room and shut the door behind him.

"No, thanks," he said, his voice as raspy as a two-string violin.

Sal shrugged and put the beer back. He wiped his hand on the leg of his jeans and stuck out his hand. "Sal Brennan."

The boy set his duffel down gingerly, as if it contained a hundred Fabergé eggs, and cautiously shook Sal's hand. "I've heard of you." His gaze was unexpectedly direct, and it lasted too long.

"Everyone has," Sal replied. "I've basically lived here since I was a toddler."

"You're Brennan's son," Pavano said.

"That's me. You are?"

"Francis Pavano. You can call me Frank if you want."

So this was the prodigy from Indiana whom his father had been stalking for the past four years. He had expected a dark-haired Italian kid, not this cut-glass automaton. So this, Sal thought, was what Midwestern genius looked like.

He slapped the bottom bunk he was sitting on. "I took this one. You okay with the top?"

Pavano nodded silently and picked his duffel up again. "Don't you live in Palo Alto?"

"Born and bred."

"Why are you living in the dorms?"

"I spend twenty out of twenty-four hours with my father. I need to be able to escape for the other four."

Pavano nodded again and approached the bunk. Sal watched as he gripped the ladder and shook it, assessing its stability. Convinced it was structurally sound, Pavano set his bag on the desk under the window. He turned and gazed at Sal for a long, awkward minute. Finally, Sal took the hint. "I can come back."

Pavano seemed greatly relieved by the offer. "Thanks, I'll only be a minute."

Sal took longer than necessary to leave. There was something about the kid that held him there. He wasn't a thief. He wasn't a pervert. He was a ninety-nine-point-ninety-niner. Behind heavy-rimmed glasses, his round, girlish eyes regarded Sal as if he were a bibelot catching the light. He was a Jehovah's Witness without Jehovah, only the unsettling gaze of a witness.

Sal spent the afternoon at the physics building on Lomita Mall, where his father and the post-docs were feverishly trying to finish the last draft of a proposal for an independent lab, which had been in the works for a decade — it was going to be called Kavli Institute for Particle Astrophysics and Cosmology, after the major donor, and was tentatively sited in Santa Barbara on a cliff overlooking the Pacific. Professor Brennan waved Sal into his office, where the other favored undergrads were going over data from an ongoing joint experiment at South Pole that would, it was hoped, eventually confirm that dark energy had driven the universe apart at accelerating speeds. Sal worked on the outputs for a while, but his mind kept returning to his strange new roommate.

"You're distracted," his father said without looking up from his computer, "and now you're proving a distraction. What is it?" The other physics students looked up at Sal. He hated them — hated the way they quieted down whenever his father walked into the room, the way they guarded their words, the way they answered him with an upswing in their voice, as if they were unwilling, or afraid, to say anything with finality in his presence.

"Nothing," Sal replied. Simultaneously, the undergrads turned to look at Professor Brennan. The professor kept his eyes on his computer screen. "Speak or leave," he said. "I cannot have distractions."

"Met my roommate today."

At this, the senior Brennan looked over at his son. "Ah, so he's arrived."

"You know him?"

"Of course — I arranged it all with the bursar. Francis Pavano. We're trying to coax him into particle physics. He's a gifted science mind, Sal. We just need to convince him that inflation is far more interesting than plasma physics."

"He wants to do heliophysics?" Sal asked,

incredulous. "Matthews is a crank."

"Your influence would be much appreciated."

Sal groaned. "I have enough eccentrics in my life."

"Please try to remember that in this world, you're the outlier."

Sal got back to work, but found, after a few minutes, that he still couldn't concentrate. He looked over at his father, who was perusing the latest WMAP results. "Fine, I'll talk to him, see if I can coax him away from Matthews."

His father turned slowly from his computer and said, "Who?"

None of the students dared to look up from their work. "Pavano," Sal said.

After a moment — no more than a second, but a second too long — his father nodded. "Yes, please do talk to him. Tell him more about Kavli. I imagine for someone of his caliber, it would be quite an inducement."

When Sal returned to the dorm, the halls were quiet — it was dinnertime, and everyone had left for the cafeteria. When he unlocked the door and walked in, he saw that Pavano was standing at the window in front of a desktop easel, shirtless, his glasses atop his head. Pavano seemed unsurprised to see him.

"You okay, man?" Sal asked.

"I'm painting," Pavano said, gesturing toward the canvas on his easel. "I hope that's okay."

Sal dropped his backpack under his bunk. "You paint?"

"Occasionally," Pavano said. "It's just a hobby."

Sal walked over to where Pavano was working and looked at the painting. The canvas was daubed in bright, almost blinding white oil paint. A tidy black line split the painting neatly in half. Sal took a step closer and squinted. The left half of the canvas was blank. The right half of the canvas was filled with tiny equations and mathematical formulas. Sal recognized Euler's equation, standard-model Lagrangian, an attempt to render infinite pi — the typical doodlings of a mathematics nerd in love with the most elevated equations in the discipline. He was about to walk away from the canvas when he spotted it: unmistakable in its beauty and impenetrability.

$$\zeta(s) = 1 + \frac{1}{2^s} + \frac{1}{3^s} + \frac{1}{4^s} + \frac{1}{5^s} + \ldots = \sum_{n=1}^{\infty} \frac{1}{n^s}$$

The hairs on the back of his neck stood

up. The Riemann hypothesis, which extended Euler's zeta function to the entire complex plane. Sal had lost interest in the distribution of the primes when he was in junior high, but it remained one of the great unproved theorems — any mathematician recognized it the way others would recognize a stop sign at an intersection. Still, it struck Sal as overly fussy that Pavano had included it in whatever was sitting on the easel. No, it was more than that. It seemed a desecration.

"What do you think?" Pavano asked.

"What do I think? I think it's the work of a beginner," Sal said. "A beginner painter and a beginner mathematician."

Pavano gazed back at Sal, his face a pale lake. Sal sat down at his bunk. The painting haunted the room like a squatter, whose presence was impossible to ignore. He knew he was being a dick, and he wasn't sure why, but seeing the Riemann on Pavano's canvas disturbed him. It was like seeing a classmate doing a nude life study of his mother.

"Put on a fucking shirt, man," Sal said. Pavano complied immediately, retrieving his shirt from the back of his chair. "I hear you want to go into heliophysics."

"I'm considering it."

"You know, heliophysics is like one step

up from cybernetics," Sal said, glancing over at the painting again. "And Matthews is a fringe-riding lunatic who is only here because he's a fossil." Pavano remained impassive. "My father says you turned him down. Why?"

"I have my reasons."

Sal scoffed. "You think choosing Matthews over my father is the best course of action?"

Pavano paused uncertainly. "I do."

"Why?"

Again, Pavano hesitated. "I don't think Professor Brennan can meet my needs as a scholar."

Sal laughed. "My father will win the Nobel prize when they find b-modes, and they will."

"It's not that. It's that . . ." Pavano looked at Sal for a moment before turning away.

"What is it?"

"It's just that — I've spent a great deal of time with your father now, and I believe he's suffering from some form of dementia. Early stages, of course, but it's there. I saw it most vividly last spring when I spent that weekend with the department."

Sal gripped the edge of his bunk. Something deep in his brain told him to run, to leave the room as quickly as possible and pretend he hadn't heard what Pavano had just said. But he was immobilized. "My father is the top theoretical physicist in the world, you idiot."

"Yes, of course," Pavano said quietly. "But Matthews agrees with me. As do other members of the faculty."

Sal realized he was now standing. His body ached with rage. He wanted to wrap his hands around Pavano's skinny throat, crush the protuberant Adam's apple, hear vertebrae crackle beneath his fingers. Pavano took a step back. When he saw Sal stalking toward him, he retreated even farther until he was up against the cool cinder-block wall.

Sal's eyes fell on Pavano's Riemann hypothesis again, and, without thinking, he grabbed the canvas off the easel and put his foot through it, throwing the ruined painting at Pavano. It landed with a thud. Pavano's eyes — freakish and clear as glass — merely gazed back at him.

Sal returned to the physics building that night. It was deserted, but the lab was, as always, open. He spent two hours going over the day's data coming in from the South Pole Telescope, but found it hard, once again, to concentrate. He hated Frank Pavano with every cell in his body — hated his unnaturally smooth face, his hollow cheeks, his cavernous, simian eyes. He hated how his father had pursued him with a cupidity that was embarrassing, and which stimulated in Sal persistent envy.

Mostly, he hated that Pavano was right.

Somewhere, melted snow dripped down an exterior wall; Sal could hear the quiet growl of Bozer's snow mover digging out the construction site. The roar of machines had diminished to occasional animal-like noises as Bozer, Marcy, and Floyd struggled to keep both the station and the site from being buried. Sal missed the din. Hearing the discordant sounds of construction had been a comfort to him over the last seven months. Here, in the lab, the sounds of progress were less straightforward — in fact, they were damn near inaudible. The only proof you were getting closer to the truth, it seemed, was the chatter of an overworked desktop computer with a stuck spindle.

His laptop pinged, and Sal scooted his chair past Alek to look at his e-mail. It was another message from the NSF. It was, like all of the missives since the occupation had begun, marked URGENT. Sal forwarded it to Dwight without reading it, same as all of the other e-mails he'd received from government agencies. He would deal with the fallout later. Right now, he had to take care of this.

Alek had fallen asleep sitting up. Sal stepped past him again and lay down on the floor. *The inflationary paradigm is fundamentally untestable. Hence, it's scientifically meaningless.* Sokoloff had said this so many times that Sal had told him it was going to be his next tattoo. As he stared at the ceiling, he tried to convince himself that his mentor was right, that they could play the uncertainty card and keep the cyclic theory on life support. But wasn't that exactly what Pavano and his ilk were doing? Promoting doubt in the face of uncertainty? Five-sigma, they'd found. Less than one chance in 3.5 million that those b-modes — those curls — were a random occurrence. Less than one chance in 3.5 million that the universe hadn't unfolded exactly the way the inflationists said.

God, the fucking inflationists. They hated the name — it was an insult — and although he used it with abandon, Sal knew this was childish. For some reason, he always thought of the inflationists as balloonists — foppish men in top hats gazing down at the rabble as they ascended, their bony hands gripping the side of the basket. Of course, that was ridiculous — most of the men and women who felt the standard model was as close to truth as science could get were just like him. The most passionate among them were his father's acolytes. And maybe that's why he hated them — the balloonists — the ones who were able to float away on the winds of a scientifically problematic theory.

He would stay here, rooted to the ice, and do whatever he could to dismantle it. The inflationary theory was unwieldy, made up of disparate parts, and covered with ugly surgical scars. One of the very first things Sal's father had taught him was that truth was elegant because it was simple. The universe itself was simple — fundamental physics was simple — and the theory could not be more complex than the universe it described. But the inflationists had fine-tuned their theory until it was a Frankenstein's monster. It was this half-dead thing that his father had expected him and the other bright young minds in cosmology to elevate to natural law.

Sokoloff had taught Sal that the truth does not need fine-tuning. This theory — the Big Bang — was not simple, and so Sal knew it was not true, no matter if they'd found "proof" of the b-modes. His model — the cyclic universe model — was so stunning, so elegant, that when Sal heard Sokoloff and Turner speak about it at the monthly Joint Theoretical Seminar at Princeton, he'd felt woozy. But when he looked around the room at the other physicists, he saw nothing but rolled eyes and open skepticism.

After the seminar, Sal had rushed down to the podium and grabbed Sokoloff by the sleeve. "Doc, it's a fucking phoenix." Sokoloff was amused. He even laughed.

"I've never heard it put that way," he'd said, "but you're absolutely right. Can we sell it like that?"

What Sokoloff and Turner were saying, and what no one in the room besides Sal was willing to at least consider, was that the universe built its own funeral pyre and stepped into the flames, destroying itself only to be reborn. It was engaged in an endless cycle with endless variations, of which this one — this moment, this life — was nothing more than chance, the result of a hip check with the universe on the other side of a minuscule gap.

At dinner that night, Sokoloff reminded Sal of the weaknesses of the inflationary theory — weaknesses Sal's father had brushed aside as trivial. The standard model could tell us what had happened between the Big Bang and the universe as we currently know it, but it could not tell us what would happen next. Perhaps more important, it could not explain, and in fact even disdained, the very idea of exploring what had happened before. Sokoloff and Turner's model could. Sal's father had, somewhat famously, no patience for questions like this. "Let's leave that to the preschoolers and the Baptists and focus on finding b-modes," he'd said when Sal returned from Princeton that summer. "Don't get seduced by contrarians. They exist in every discipline of science." But Sokoloff wasn't a contrarian. He'd actually been an architect of the inflationary theory himself. Sal's father was right about one thing, though — Sal had been seduced.

By this time, Sal was heir apparent at the Kavli Institute for Particle Physics and Cosmology, which his father had spent the last ten years trying to build. What Frank Pavano had seen five years earlier was now an open secret: the mind of the eminent physicist had slowly been spackled with plaques. Alzheimer's. Pavano, having chosen another university for his doctorate when Matthews retired, was now publishing on wave oscillations in the Midwest.

Sal opposed his mother's desire to hide the truth from his father's colleagues and devoted students, though he also understood the impulse. He allowed her to believe he was in agreement, but he knew better. He had to tell — otherwise the changes his father had undergone would become part of his biography rather than seen as the pathologies they were. Especially because it was no longer heterotic string theory that spoke to his father; it was strange pop culture conspiracy theories that sometimes seemed to share the same DNA. They had the resonance of fairy tales, and the deeper they resonated, the more plausible they became.

This was true: at South Pole an enormous telescopic mouth gaped at the heavens, swallowing invisible particles that tiny scientists then examined in the machine's underground gut. The particles carried information from a place 13 billion years away. They told, or would tell, of a universe sprung from a singularity, where equations break down and energy is infinite.

This was not true: a system of caves and caverns traversed the earth's mantle beneath the ice of Antarctica — polar voids where an anti-civilization thrived, where, if our civilization were to encounter it, the two would annihilate each other, like matter and anti-matter. Hitler was a believer of the Hollow Earth theory. In fact, some believe he is there now, having been escorted via U-boat by a German sailor, who located the narrow underwater passageway (wormhole?) on an expedition to South Pole.

Both were fabulist tales. Only one was true. Knowing which was which, Sal realized, was the difference between lucidity and dementia, and his father was now on the wrong side. After the now-infamous evening physics lecture, in which Professor Brennan had deviated from a talk on the Calabi-Yau manifold to consider the role that the Argentine naval base at Mar del Plata had played in Hitler's escape to the German Antarctic city-base buried deep beneath the ice, the provost had asked Sal to come up with a "plan of action." The "plan of action" was meant to allow Professor Brennan to retire "with some degree of dignity."

A year later, on the day of the phone call Sal had received from the MacArthur Foundation notifying him that his work at Kavli had earned him a "genius grant," Sal found his mother bent over the kitchen counter, trying to glue a plate back together. Her hands were shaking. Sal quietly picked up the remaining shards piece by piece and dropped them into the trash, leaving only the one, which his mother still had between her fingers and could not seem to let go.

Upstairs, Sal found his father ensconced in his study, a sun-filled room on the top floor of their California Mission–style home. He was standing at the large window that overlooked the pool, an unintentional infinity symbol filled with sparkling blue water.

"Your mother tells me you have good news," Professor Brennan said suddenly.

"MacArthur likes the new model for radiatively induced symmetry breaking I introduced last year." The words were bitter in Sal's mouth. He tried again. "The model plays," he said, hoping a joke would remove the taste, but his father didn't respond. Sal wondered if he could slip away unnoticed. Outside, a car honked, and Professor Brennan leaned into the glass, straining toward the sound. Sal noticed for the first time that the room smelled like old man. He looked around at the bursting bookcases, the crystal awards, the framed degrees; the photo of Sal as a boy in a baseball uniform, his hair a mass of red-blond curls, his smile a series of gaps.

Sal saw, then, that his father had turned from the window and was looking at him. His eyes were clear. They were fixed on Sal's face. Sal gazed back at the strong jaw, the broad, deeply lined forehead, the prominent but structurally perfect nose. He wanted nothing more at that moment than for his father to embrace him. Then the horn honked again, and the interstice dissolved.

Sal went down to South Pole for Kavli that fall, the fall of 1999, to work on Viper, the telescope run by the guys at the University of Chicago. Sal knew then that this would be the last time he'd look for proof that the standard model of the universe was correct. Later, when the first installment of the MacArthur money was deposited into his account, he wrote a check for the entire amount, made out to the Kavli Foundation. Now he was free.

Two days after writing that check, four months after returning from his first research season at Pole, eight months after Professor Brennan had quietly retired, and sixteen months after talking to Sokoloff that night in Princeton, Sal left Stanford. When his mother asked him where he was going, he told her he was following the phoenix.

Sal didn't hear Cooper come into the lab. He must have fallen asleep, because she was squatting down next to him, her fur-lined hood framing her beautiful face. "They've been trying to get you over All-Call for the

last fifteen minutes. Something's happened." She looked over at Alek, who had
awakened and resumed his silent weeping.
"What's going on? Why's Alek crying?"

Sal rolled over on his side and from his
back pocket pulled the folded paper Alek
had given him ten hours earlier. He handed
it to Cooper and watched her scan it, her
dark eyes moving from word to word. He
knew it would mean nothing to her, and he
was envious of her ignorance — Alek's tears
would do more than anything to tell her
what was on this piece of paper.

Cooper sat down next to Sal and looked
at him questioningly. He pointed to the
symbol that Alek had circled three times in
brown marker, the color of each ring growing deeper as his fury strengthened his grip.
Together, they looked at it.

5
Σ

Sal looked again and again and, as before,
he couldn't stop. It was the most beautiful
thing he'd ever seen in his life, and it was
also the most disappointing. "This is why
Alek's crying and you're on the floor,"
Cooper said.

"Short of finding life on other planets or

directly detecting dark matter, it's the most important discovery in astronomy. It supports a lifetime of theoretical work. And it eliminates my model."

As she absorbed this, Sal thought of her question that day she came to his lab, the one he'd dismissed because it was inconvenient: *No, I mean how it started before it started.* He thought, too, of her paintings, which she'd begun photographing for her NSF portfolio before handing them over to everyone: the one of Pearl, how her golden hair — always hidden under that filthy pink bandanna — coiled around her neck; how her eyes laughed, but how they also clearly belonged to a woman with insatiable ambitions. Doc Carla, startling without her Yankees cap, her eyes fixed on a point in the distance, her entire life, somehow, in those eyes. Bozer, stripped to pith. Denise's unmistakable sadness. Everyone else, even Alek, even Floyd and Dwight. Everyone else but him.

But he didn't wonder why his likeness was not among the portraits; it was obvious that he had not allowed Cooper to truly look at him. He had never minded if the others looked — they couldn't see like she could. Post-docs, research assistants, waitresses, lawyers. Some understood the work, or pretended to. Some didn't, and some didn't even feign interest. It was fine. It was all fine. He took what he needed without being a dick about it, and they got whatever they wanted in return. This history made Sal notorious at Kavli for what was regarded as his "charm" — though in the world of cosmology and particle physics, the bar for charm was admittedly low.

It helped that he'd taken after his father, with his strong features and tall build, and that from his mother he had inherited the sort of face that women considered attractive (though one girlfriend had assured him that "beauty is neutral"). But what set Sal apart from other cosmologists, particle physicists, astronomers, and all the others who so desperately wanted the world to understand the implications of their work, was that he was bold. He said nothing until he could say it with authority. He hated hedging — framing ideas with conditionals that annihilated them. Margins of error as wide as crevasses, and therefore too dangerous to attempt a crossing. These were the inviolable commandments of science, but they were also the reason that the public paid science so little attention. Scientists were lame messengers, often handing off their findings to their weakest practitioners to share with the world, celebrity scientists who performed a kind of homeopathy that distilled them to nothing, or nearly nothing. He refused to be like them.

Then Cooper pushed his stupid petition away that day in the cafeteria. Disdainful. Solitary. Like a particle that was also a wave, Sal's heart was both closed and open. He tried to ignore it, but then she was everywhere. She was in the lab, she was in the equations that Sal still did by hand, she was at the telescope, blotting out the cosmic microwaves. She was outside, walking alone, looking at the sky. Looking. Each day that passed changed something about her, made her more beautiful. A glance in the cafeteria. A very slight smile. A smudge of paint on her cheek. A smart remark. Nothing rational. None of it precise.

First, he laid her out for Alek, like she was a cadaver in a nineteenth-century medical theater, to prod and insult in every way imaginable. Alek soon tired of this; he felt Cooper was ordinary and therefore inoffensive. Still Sal's heart thundered for her. *You're distracted,* he heard his father saying to him, *and now you're proving a distraction.* He could not afford a distraction. Not this season.

When the feelings persisted, Sal eventually declared that his intense attraction to Cooper must be evolutionary biology at work. There could be no other explanation. Alek felt strongly that Sal's vow of chastity for the season was to blame. No, Sal insisted, it had to be biology — millennia ago, he and Cooper must have been part of the same tribe. They would simply have to fuck so he could get back to work. Masturbation would cure this reptilian-brain desire, he thought. But it didn't.

Time passed. In the evenings, he drank, and he broke his vow of chastity with that Frosty Boy tech from McMurdo. These encounters typically meant nothing; now they had the sharp taste of betrayal. Although there was no one to betray, the feeling was unshakable. He couldn't stop thinking of Cooper.

Then one day, out at the telescopes, as he raved about his cyclic model like a meth-fueled evangelist, she asked why he was the only one who believed it. The question had enraged him, and it was only later — much later, in fact — that he understood why, and then he was even angrier. He was an apostate. So was Sokoloff. And at conferences where he'd seen his old Stanford colleagues, he'd loudly congratulated himself for being one. After all, the fact that a scientist changes his mind is proof that the scientific method works — that they can overcome their affinities for their cherished ideas and thereby protect the integrity of the whole endeavor.

But when Cooper had asked him why he was the only one who seemed to "believe" in the cyclic model, he grew angry, because instead of thinking of the great apostates of science — Darwin changing his mind on pangenesis, Marcelo Gleiser repudiating his hopes of a unified theory, crusty Fred Hoyle and his steady-state universe foolishness, Peter Sokoloff — Sal thought of Frank Pavano. Pavano, who was unworthy of even speaking Sokoloff's name. No, Pavano was not an apostate; he was a fraud. He was paid for his conclusions. Worse, Sal was convinced that Pavano didn't even buy into the pseudoscience he was peddling.

But still, a thought began eating away at him. It filled him with shame first, and then with dread. Wasn't it right, he began to wonder — unquestionably right — that Pavano was on the ice alongside him?

It was a week after the accident out on the Divide, after Cooper's injury and after the media had picked up the story and after Bayless and Calhoun had scheduled their flight down, that Sal approached Sri with his thought about Pavano. Tucker had come out to the Dark Sector the day before to tell Sal that Scaletta had met with the congressmen and had been told that unless NSF formalized a process to grant "minority scientific views" a place at federal research facilities, they would hold up the agency's polar regions budget in committee, which would quickly prompt a station shutdown. Scaletta had refused, and asked Tucker to begin preparing the scientists for the possibility of a station shutdown.

So Sal went to the climatology lab and put his idea to Sri: let the skeptics come. There weren't many of them — it was a 90/10 split among climate scientists already — and their research wouldn't yield anything dangerous. He tried to sound confident — dismissive, even. Let the children have dessert at the adult table — the meal's almost over, anyway, right?

It didn't go well. Sri paced the eight-by-eight room over and over again, muttering incoherently (Sal caught words like *betrayal* and *end of science*). But it seemed the easiest way to make the threat disappear — and, in some tenuous way, it adhered to the principle of scientific freedom. But Sri felt Sal's plan was morally reprehensible, that his motives were suspect — "selfish" — and Sal wondered if his friend was right. He let the idea go, and tried to ignore the growing sense of doom in the labs. But, like his constant thoughts of Cooper, he found his mind returning to the question again and again.

"What do you think about my idea?" he asked Alek one day after the congressmen had returned to Washington. Alek only shrugged. "You have no opinion whatsoever on capitulating to the demands of two science-illiterate congressmen? Sri says funding a climate skeptic would be like funding Bigfoot research. Or an archaeological dig for Noah's ark. He says I'll do anything to keep my experiment going."

Alek sighed. "I tell story. In Leningrad, 1987, I am seventeen years old. St. Isaac's Square is full of people, because the authorities just demolished Angleterre hotel. This place is sacred. The great poet Yesenin end his life here. Understand, for us, this is like destroying Shroud of Turin. So we must protest. But this time, there are no arrests. No one can believe this — *glasnost* was slow to come to Leningrad. So the protests continue for weeks. I visit and help distribute *samizdat*. One day someone comes running to tell us dissidents are giving speeches in Mikhailovky Gardens. This is new — such things did not happen. But when we get there, a military band is playing and no one can hear the speakers. We are told the authorities have sent the band to play so the dissidents cannot be heard. The speeches stop and an old man puts half a lemon in my hand. 'Suck,' he tells me, and points to the band. 'Make sure they see you.' Before I can say, I see everywhere people sucking on lemons. At the front, I see the crazy old dissident Ekaterina Poldotseva handing them out from a basket. When the old man sees I am not sucking on lemon, he slaps my hand, he tells me, 'Poldotseva says the band will stop playing once when they see everyone sucking on lemons.' Empathetic saliva, he tells me. 'They will not be able to play their instruments.' Ten minutes later, the band packed up and left. They never return."

Alek turned back to his computer.

As Sal stared at the back of his friend's head, he wondered if Alek was, in fact, insane.

When the subpoena from the Wisconsin attorney general arrived for Sri, Sal had watched his friend's research techs bag-drag to one of the LC-130s that were evacuating nonessential staff in advance of the shutdown. It was like watching someone toss Darwin's dead finches off the side of the *Beagle.*

Once the letters from NSF began circulating, Sal began spending hours away from his own lab in order to get up to speed on the Kavli team's work — aside from her outburst at the winter-over meeting, Lisa Wu had remained stoic, but as they went over the data together, Sal noticed her fingernails had been chewed to the quick.

As each scientist shut down his or her experiment — from the experiments in the Atmospheric Research Observatory to the seismology labs — Alek's words began to take hold of Sal. To his consternation, the story about the lemon wedges was beginning to make sense. A week into the shutdown, he already knew what had to be done. He started sending e-mails. He started with the National Academy of Sciences listserv, followed by one to the Intergovernmental Panel on Climate Change, proposing the idea he'd pitched to Sri: Let them come. There would be a provision for practical requirements that would seem reasonable, even to backwater congressmen — like a track record of peer-reviewed science — but which would be difficult for a denialist to acquire.

"Science is a mirror that reflects nature," Sal wrote to Alexandra Scaletta at NSF. "Experiments are attempts to polish that mirror. Not all of them rub off the streaks, but these don't hinder the experiments that do." Sal wasn't sure he believed this last part — he wasn't sure of a lot of things now — but he sent the e-mail anyway.

The initial response from his fellow scientists ranged from disbelief to actual horror. He heard nothing from Scaletta. He waited. He wanted to give the Pole-based scientists, whose experiments had been ruined, enough time to reflect on the idea.

Then came the phone calls, all of them asking for Sal. He was spending twenty hours a day in his lab, analyzing the readouts from his own experiment, so Dwight fielded things as they came and took messages. He brought these scraps of paper to the Smoke Bar each night, so Sal could go through them.

"What are they calling about?" Cooper asked.

"The shutdown. How to end it."

Alek scoffed at this. "No, he is buying lemons."

"Lemons?"

"Alek," Sal said, his voice hoarse.

"This is how shutdown will end," Alek

said.

Floyd made his way over to where Sal was sitting. "And how are you going to go about doing that?"

Sal pinched the bridge of his nose. "I think NSF should agree to fund a climate skeptic on the Divide once a season."

"Wasn't that the opposite of what you were railing on about earlier in the season?" Pearl said. "I don't mean to sound like a jerk, but it sounds like you're just changing your mind because you don't want your experiment to be affected."

"You're right. But I think we should give Pavano the opportunity to fail. I think we should let all of them fail. That's all they want — the opportunity to be totally, unmistakably wrong. If we don't give them that opportunity, they'll just keep stirring up this idea about uncertainty — 'we're not sure, there's no consensus, let us show you the science.' I say, let them try. And in the meantime, we can get back to the real work of science." This earned him a blank look, so he sat forward in his seat and cleared his throat. "Let me tell you a story about lemons."

That night, he'd awakened in Cooper's room to find her out of bed, standing at her desk. The room was dark and she remained frozen in the strange shadows cast by the seam of light under the door. Although her naked back was facing toward him, Sal could see she was looking at something, studying it intently. It took him a minute to see the pile of bandages and gauze on the desk.

"Cooper," he said softly. "Come here." He could see her stiffen, and she shook her head without turning around. Sal threw the blankets off and got out of bed. As he approached, she curled into herself, cocooning her injured hand. She shook her head again, as if, for the first time since he'd known her, she was unable to find her voice. When he wrapped his arms around her, she heaved a great sob.

"Let me see," Sal replied, pulling her closer. She had tucked the injured hand between her rib cage and her left bicep, as if keeping it warm. He gently pulled at her wrist until her hand came free, and in the fading luminescence of the twilit sky that stole through the tiny window, he saw, for the first time, how her right hand looked pale and wrinkled with moisture, and how the place where her finger had been was knobby and scabbed. It struck him as so uncommonly beautiful, so like a tesseract, that he felt tears spring to his eyes. But he could tell from the way Cooper hung her head, and the way her body tried to become small as he cradled her hand, that she considered it ugly, and for once, he knew the kind of incomprehension everyone else experienced when looking at the Riemann hypothesis. They couldn't see why its uncertainty made it beautiful. He couldn't understand their blindness. Maybe there was something ugly in Cooper's disfigurement, but he couldn't see it, no matter how hard he tried.

In his lab now, where his phoenix had incinerated itself, Sal looked into Cooper's face as she kneeled over him, her eyes wide and happy. Before he had a chance to speak, the sound of All-Call filled the room. Sal propped himself up on one elbow — there was cheering in the background.

He stood up, and he, Cooper, and Alek crowded around the speaker. The chants grew louder.

"What are they saying?" Sal asked.

Cooper turned to him, her eyes wide. "That's why I came out here to find you. It's over." She kissed his dry lips. "Listen," she whispered.

Sal, Sal, Sal, went the chant.

The lemon wedges had worked. Sal looked at Cooper and realized that while there was nothing left of his experiment but a pile of ashes, in the cinders the phoenix already stirred.

NATIONAL SCIENCE FOUNDA-
 TION
4201 WILSON BOULEVARD
ARLINGTON, VIRGINIA 22230
Cooper Gosling
PO Box 423
Minneapolis, MN 55410

Dear Ms. Gosling:
At the close of every grant period the
Antarctic Artists & Writers Program as-
sesses the output of each grantee following his or her return from Antarctica.
We have now had a chance to review the
portfolio you sent. What follows reflects
the comments from our distinguished
panel of artists and arts administrators.

While we by no means consider ourselves the arbiter of "good art," the
panelists were confused by the complete
lack of landscape in the collection. In
fact, its absence suggested, as one panelist put it, "an act of will." As you know,
the United States Antarctic Program is a
science-based research program, which
takes as its sole directive the interaction
with and better understanding of Nature. The Artists & Writers Program was
designed specifically to convey this

587

directive to the general public through different media. The panelists felt that your collection of portraits, while quite fine technically, could have been painted, in the words of one panelist, "in any local bar."

There was one exception. We were particularly moved by the portrait you titled "David." That the subject's face was represented only by a smear of white seemed an appropriate homage to the courage and selflessness of the great polar explorers. The mitten cleverly embedded in the background added depth. We hope you build on this strength in your future work so you can provide, for yourself and others, a greater understanding of the heritage of human exploration in Antarctica. We also encourage you to consider applying for another Artists & Writers grant. Enclosed is an application for the upcoming research season, along with a preliminary psychological questionnaire.

Regards,
National Science Foundation Antarctic
Artists & Writers Program

ONE TON DEPOT

2004 July 10
20:46
To:
    Billie.Gosling@janusbooks.com
From:
    cherrywaswaiting@hotmail.com
Subject: Prodigal daughter's
    return

B.,
Thanks for all your e-mails.
Tell Mom and Dad we're all
okay. I'm sorry I haven't been
able to respond sooner. Once
the station shut down, Dwight
forbid all personal e-mail,
since it took up bandwidth
during the satellite fly-bys.
Whatever that means. Anyway,
looks like this shitshow is
coming to an end. We got word

last week that Jack Calhoun decided to commit political hari-kari and break with Bayless to end the impasse on the budget committee. I guess once Pavano did that interview with *60 Minutes* about the oil consortium, he had to cut his losses. I suppose it helped that NSF says it's willing to talk about formalizing a process to ensure grant money for "non-traditional scientists." They're going to insist on a robust body of "peer-reviewed science" from each applicant, and Sal tells me there is no such thing as "peer-review" in climate denial — but don't tell the deniers that! So we're free! (well, free until September when the first plane can fly in.) We're basically eating nothing but Ry-Krisps and canned tuna now, but we still have a shit-ton of Russian vodka.

C.

By mid-August, nearly everyone knew

enough Russian to sing all three refrains of "The Song of the Volga Boatmen." Cooper had learned how to use the rodwell to melt Antarctic ice for the station's water supply, learning, too, that the water swishing around in the station toilets might be made from snow that had fallen in the fifteenth century (if you dug down far enough). She had finished nearly everyone's portrait, except Sal, whom she found she didn't dare commit to canvas since his countenance burned so brightly and so beautifully in her mind. But it was time, she knew, to do the last portrait — the one of David. The one, she now understood, that she'd come down here to paint. And to do that she had to do something else first.

Cooper found Bozer and the others in the bar the night after the announcement of the sequester's end. When Bozer glanced up at her and saw the vial she displayed to him in her hand, he nodded and stood up. The ragged crew around him immediately understood. Sal gripped Cooper's left hand and squeezed.

The entrance tunnel was bathed in red, but outside the sky was black as ink, the cold winds rolling off the East Antarctic Plateau and the southern lights streaming across the sky in refracting sheets of color.

When they reached the Pole marker, the crew gathered around its silver globe expectantly, and their reflections swelled and shrank. For an instant, Cooper saw herself just as she'd been that first day when she'd looked into Alek's mirrored aviators.

"Not here," Cooper said. She pointed toward the *Terra Nova,* the geographical marker. "There."

Bozer looked at her for a moment. "You know if you bury him here, he won't be here next year. He'll drift."

Cooper held his gaze. "I'm counting on it."

Bozer tucked the ice augur under his arm and they began walking toward the *Terra Nova,* their flashlights casting milky beams into the darkness. When they reached the marker, Cooper pointed at a spot of ice at its foot, and Pearl and Doc Carla trained their flashlights on it.

Bozer leaned on the ice augur. "We're all here because of some shit. Everyone's got it, but you ain't got to be alone in it." He grunted. "That's all I've got to say."

He looked over at Cooper, his balaclava obscuring all but his clear eyes, and she nodded. He drove the blade into the mark. The group watched the auger rotate in silence; to Cooper, the spiraled blade seemed a vision of infinity. It was only when Sal gently nudged her that she realized Bozer had finished coring.

She stepped to the edge of the hole and dropped to her knees. Sal helped pull off the mitten on her right hand. Carefully, he opened the vial and emptied the ashes onto the flat of her mitten. For the first time since that night on the edge of the lake, she looked at the gunmetal gray of her brother's remains. Her hand trembled. She couldn't move.

Then the others were kneeling beside her: Dwight, Denise, Floyd, Doc Carla, Pearl, Marcy, Alek, Sal — even the Swedes. Only Bozer stood apart, leaning on the auger. She closed her eyes and released David's ashes into the deep cut in the continent.

The sun was warm. The sound of birds had not yet become familiar again, and Cooper was thinking wistfully of the silent song of Bozer's glacier sparrow. Sal drove the rental like a kid on a learner's permit, hands at ten and two, his body taut, eyes fixed on the road ahead. As they drove through Palo Alto, the lush lawns — freshly watered and glittering under the sun like sheets of emerald — struck Cooper as about as probable as a McDonald's on the Divide. The piebald hills seemed ostentatious. The tidy parks were exquisite. The palms fronting the university looked as flamboyant as showgirls, and the occasional appearance of children seemed deeply strange. Cooper and Sal drove through the streets in silence.

They hadn't even stopped in Christchurch. The others had back-channeled hostel bookings and begun making plans online as soon as the end of the sequester had been announced. Floyd and Bozer sketched out an appeal to the New Zealand government to give the Man Without Country a proper burial; Denise went looking for a thrift-store wedding gown, having agreed, finally, to marry Bozer when they got off the ice. Pearl found Birdie waiting for her at the airport with a bouquet of daisies and a finished manuscript, and Dwight haunted Internet cafés until he found Bonnie in a cosplay chat room. Tucker was still in Washington, helping Alexandra Scaletta and Daniel Atcheson Johnson pick up the pieces, and lobbying for a dismissal of possible federal charges against the occupiers. The support staff arranged to meet in Denver to plead their cases to VIDS. One thing everyone had agreed upon was that they would all be back.

But Sal had to tell Professor Brennan *five-*

sigma. The sixth milestone had been reached. Slithering toward the telescope like an army of infinitesimal Slinkys, the gravitational waves had confirmed what the inflationists had claimed all along: that space was a wild, chaotic place marked by violence, and that humanity occupied a remote pocket universe carried along by eternal inflation. There were no branes, no hidden dimensions, no hints of elegant cosmic evolution — there was only the vacuum, and a planet adrift in a multiverse. And he wanted Cooper with him when he did it.

The rumors continued unabated, of course, and by the time Sal had flown out, even *Science* was speculating. Sal told Cooper that he'd talked to Sokoloff one last time before leaving Pole, and that he'd told Sal that Lisa Wu had petitioned Kavli to wait on the announcement until Sal had returned stateside, so he could be the one to tell his father that the inflationary theory had been confirmed.

Now they were here, pulled up against the curb, and Sal was staring at the steering wheel.

Cooper put her hand on his shoulder. "Do you know what you're going to say?"

"All I have to say is 'five-sigma at point two.' He'll understand." He paused for a moment, thinking. "I hope he will." Sal looked over at Cooper. She saw fear in his eyes. She leaned over the shift and ran her hand over his now-lush auburn beard.

Sal tapped the steering wheel. "Sokoloff says it might be dust or synchrotron radiation from electrons in the galactic magnetic fields. He thinks Kavli shouldn't announce until they can rule that out." Cooper chose not to remind Sal that he'd mentioned this to her several times on each leg of the flight from New Zealand. She knew he wasn't really talking to her anyway. He chewed on his lip for a moment. "But I won't say that to him. No, not now. I'll just tell him." He looked over at Cooper again. "He was right, you know."

"Your father?"

"Pavano."

"Right about what?"

"That I believed. I knew it was wrong to believe, but I did anyway. From the first moment I heard Sokoloff speak, I wanted to believe this was true — I wanted what was beautiful to be true, rather than the other way around. That's why this hurts so much."

Sal looked over her shoulder, through the passenger-side window, and up at the house. Cooper turned and saw a figure looking out at the car, moving between panes, made faceless by the reflection of the sun on the front windows of the house. As they watched, the figure disappeared momentarily, and the front door opened. Backlit by the setting sun, the door looked like a portal, the figure like a ghost.

"Let's go," Sal said.

Cooper shook her head. "No, you go. I'll wait here."

She watched as Sal ascended the steps. When he reached the top, the figure in the doorway held out his arms. Sal fell into them like a little boy.

Yes, Cooper thought, *of course.* This was what Cherry had strained to see for six months, waiting for the Scott party to return. You waited at One Ton Depot, just you and the dogs, certain the men were just over the rise. You overcame your myopia and you navigated using the faint gleam of the sun. You blamed yourself, wondering if you had only laid better depots, if they would have made it.

And then someone appeared, pulling a sledge.

ACKNOWLEDGMENTS

This book is set at the "old" South Pole Station, which was officially decommissioned in 2008. Although set at what once was a real place, this novel takes liberties with the station's layout. I also switched up the timeline of when certain telescopes in the Dark Sector were installed. There's probably other stuff here that will drive veteran Polies crazy. Sorry about that.

The late Nicholas Johnson wrote the first funny book about Antarctica, the brilliant *Big Dead Place.* Set largely at McMurdo, it captures the absurdity of life on the seventh continent, and will never be equaled. Dr. Jerri Nielsen's memoir, *Ice Bound,* gave me a peek into the world of polar medicine. My copy of *The Worst Journey in the World* by Apsley Cherry-Garrard spontaneously combusted the day I finished my last draft of this novel. The canon of Antarctic literature is immense. If you're interested in learning more, I suggest you contact my father.

Stories derived from this novel appeared in *Third Coast, Southeast Review, 32 Magazine, Lascaux Review,* and the *Los Angeles Review.*

I owe thanks to many people for their support and encouragement. I'm deeply grateful to Tony and Caroline Grant of the Sustainable Arts Foundation. Thank you, too, to these talented Minnesota writers: Maggie Ryan Sanford, Sara Aase, Frank Bures, Douglas Mack, Dennis Cass, John Jodizo, Lars Ostrom, and Jason Albert, who introduced me to Breakout: Normandy. I'll also never forget the incredible generosity shown to me by Yona Zeldis McDonough, Elizabeth McKenzie, Julie Schumacher, and Robin Sloan.

I'm immensely grateful to the formidable and funny (or formidably funny) Lisa Bankoff, who immediately loved my hygiene-challenged Polies, believed in the story, and who makes me laugh every time I talk to her. She's the best in the business. My editor, the preternaturally gifted Elizabeth Bruce, is Maxwell Perkins with a penchant for temporary tattoos, an encyclopedic knowledge of college basketball, and a brain the size of Antarctica. I could not be more grateful for all she did to make this book better. The crew at Picador/Macmillan have been a joy to work with. Thanks to Declan Taintor, Kolt Beringer, Darin Keesler, Henry Sene Yee, Karen Richardson, Emily Walters, and, of course, Stephen Morrison, without whom this book would be in a drawer somewhere.

Per usual when it comes to all things explorer, it was my dad who introduced me to Cherry-Garrard. Mom wanted to know why there wasn't more sex in the book. I'm so grateful for their love and support. Delta Larkey read a draft of this book when she had much more important things to do, and her support means so much. Lacy Shelby is one of only a handful of women in history who have winter-overed at South Pole Station. She shared just enough of her own experience there to inspire this book while staying true to the Pole axiom that "what happens on the ice stays on the ice." This book would not have been written without her. Jeff and Scott Meredith gifted me with two great lines and would both be royalty at South Pole. I will always be grateful to my best friend, Starr Sage. *Vaya con CL.*

Finally, this whole thing is for my patient and understanding husband, Emmanuel Benites, and my funny, loving, straight-up amazing children, Hudson and Josephine.

They sledged right along with me, and, when I faltered, they never considered leaving me behind. Guys — we're done. Let's get a pizza.

ABOUT THE AUTHOR

Ashley Shelby is a prizewinning writer and journalist. She received her MFA from Columbia University and is the author of *Red River Rising: The Anatomy of a Flood and the Survival of an American City,* a narrative nonfiction account of the record-breaking flood that, in 1997, devastated Grand Forks, North Dakota. The short story that became the basis for *South Pole Station* is a winner of the Third Coast Fiction Prize. She lives in the Twin Cities with her family.

AshleyShelby.com